Hellified

A Novel

Tracy Grant

Visão Press

Published by Visão Press, Inc.
P.O. Box 20596
New York, NY 10025-1514

Cover Photos: Derrick Jones/Uproar, Inc., Oggi Ogburn/Oggi's Kitchen

This is a work of fiction. Names, characters, places and incidents either are the product of the author's imagination or are used fictitiously, and any resemblance to actual persons, living or dead, events, or locales is entirely coincidental.

ISBN 0-9672836-0-4

Printed in the United States of America

In Loving Memory

Bernice Estwick Grant

Still sometimes I cry myself to sleep. I miss you terribly.

Prologue

Gina smiled from ear to ear as Will led her to his side of the room. Troy took Roach by the hand and led her over to his bed, which was adjacent to the door. Their room wasn't as big as the rooms in Harbin Hall, the dorm they would live in as freshmen, but with the boys' makeshift counter/headboard partition, they had the privacy of two bedrooms.

"We've got some Bartles & Jaymes in the fridge," Will remembered. "You ladies want some?"

"Only if you do," Roach answered.

Will got up to get the wine coolers. He tossed two over to Troy and Roach. He had thought it would be a good idea to keep refreshments around for the girls, and he had been right. As long as Tad and Arnelle, his resident assistants, never saw the bottles, there was no risk. The girls cracked open their bottles and sipped. Will and Troy, playing hosts, drank as well, although neither of them drank wine coolers regularly.

Troy and Will had been listening to Ready For The World. The ladies bopped their heads to the music. Will's customized tape had the uptempo songs on one side, and the ballads on the other. The auto reverse on Will's boom box flipped on the ballads, just in time. Gina was lively, and Troy and Roach could hear her laughing at Will's jokes. Roach was quieter, exchanging pleasantries with Troy while she waited to see what he would do. Troy didn't mind; the more time she spent waiting, the better his chances would be.

Soon the conversation on both sides of the room died down. Ready For The World was singing "Love You Down." Will was the first to make a move.

"Hold it, wait!" Gina yelped.

Troy thought Gina would be leaving soon, but he was wrong.

"This is how it's done, Will. Who taught you to kiss like that?"

Roach and Troy had to fight to contain their laughter, but Troy knew he would face the same test soon. He had been stroking Roach's leg for forty minutes. When he made his way up her sundress, he was met with no resistance, only smiles. A loud knock startled him and Will out of their beds and onto the floor. The girls broke out in hysterics.

"Who the hell is it?" Will yelled.

"Bedcheck! You guys in there?" It was the resident assistant, Tad, making his rounds.

"We're in there all right!"

Tad had to have heard the girls, who were laughing wildly. Troy put on a new tape of Luther Vandross songs. With the music and the wine coolers, the roommates were shooting to release the inhibitions of their guests. Almost getting caught made the whole episode even more exciting.

Roach was right where Troy had left her, waiting with open arms. She took his tongue whole into her mouth. Her body was a palace, gradually welcoming Troy as he unbuttoned the sundress from the back. It wouldn't be long now, and Troy was more than ready. The lights were all out except for Troy's nightlight. Will and Gina were giggling away on the other side of the room. Roach was nibbling on Troy's earlobe when another knock erupted from the door.

"Willard! Troy! Are you in there?"

Troy couldn't believe it. It was Latanya and Michelyn, two upperclassmen who were also spending the summer on campus. He must have jumped three feet across the room to the closet. Will again jumped out of bed, amid shrieks of laughter from Roach and Gina.

"Hold on! Hold on!" the boys yelled in unison.

Will zoomed across the room, looking like a black comet. Both he and Troy were almost naked.

"Are you guys busy in there?" Michelyn chuckled.

"Just hold on!" Will shouted. "We'll be right there!"

"What's your girl doing here now?" Troy whispered to Will, referring to Latanya.

"Hell if I know, but Michelyn looks good, so don't fuck around."

Latanya and Will had grown up together in Philadelphia. She was like a sister to him. Michelyn Gibson, Latanya's friend, was the finest girl around that summer, and probably one of the finest in D.C. Whatever the circumstances, her visits were not to be refused.

Seconds later Troy and Will stood outside their door with their other visitors. All Troy had managed to grab was his Yankee jacket, which with his Fruit-of-the-Looms made a ridiculous ensemble. Will wore only his boxer shorts.

"Actually, we were sort of doing something," Will told them. "What brings you two here now? You know we have a curfew."

"Michelyn wanted to visit."

A couple of girls from the summer program came out of their rooms and spotted Troy and Will in their underwear. They immediately commenced to laugh hysterically at the sight. Troy couldn't stand there for much longer.

"Michelyn, can we come by tomorrow? I mean, if we knew you were coming..."

"Yeah," Will agreed. "You just popped up."

"We're not the only thing that just popped up," Latanya retorted, looking down at Will. "But we'll let you get back to your guests. Come on Michelyn. If we're lucky, we'll see these two hoes tomorrow."

Michelyn tried her best not to laugh, but she couldn't help it.

"See you two," she snickered, turning the corner with Latanya.

Thankfully, the second visit was over. Will slammed the door from the inside, and breathed a long sigh of relief. Roach and Gina were laughing just as much as the girls in the hallway. Troy and Will were relieved that they were still in a good mood, so the boys acted as if the last few minutes never took place. Gina was fine with it, but Roach wasn't quite as comfortable.

"We should go somewhere else," she told Troy between kisses.

"Come on, girl. Keep it right there," he told her, mimicking Luther Vandross.

"Baby, let's go. I'm ready."

"Where? Your dorm? Don't you have a roommate?"

"She's in here with yours, silly."

"Oh yeah. Well come on, then."

Troy wasted no time getting dressed. At first he was certain that Latanya and Michelyn had ruined his chances with Roach, but apparently not. Will and Gina were unaffected. From the sound coming from Will's bed, Troy deduced the commotion had worked in his favor.

As they were leaving, Will's head came up from his side of the partition.

"Uh, could you get that light, champ?"

*   *   *   *

As he packed his bags to leave for college, Troy chuckled to himself, fondly remembering his days as a Georgetown City Scholar. The City Scholars Program was designed to help prepare minority students for the rigorous academic challenges of life at Georgetown. During those five activity-filled weeks, Troy had made up his mind that college was for him; the carefree lifestyle, the freedom of it, was what he'd been craving for years. His mother wouldn't be there to tell him what to do and there were always girls around. Although students took a course and lived in the dormitory, to Troy and many others, it had been one big party.

Troy had seen and done more in those five weeks than he could have ever imagined, sneaking girls in and out of his room; getting drunk with Will, then walking on the edge of the rooftop; partying with the fraternity members. He could hardly remember classes, except for having to read Plato. During the summer Troy had broken curfew and gone to a party in Baltimore while even bolder students broke curfew and stayed out until Monday. He saw Tad, a senior resident assistant, get body slammed and beat up by a freshman, and a girl no less, who had consumed an entire bottle of Wild Turkey. One weekend the mischief got out of hand when a bunch of guys had gotten together and put acid in a student's curl activator. The student, Sharon, was bald shortly afterwards. When she saw a group of guys laughing in the hallway, Troy included, she went berserk and threatened to cut the first one of them she caught, chasing the boys with a steak knife. Troy and his friend Will told a professor to her face that they were late to class because they overslept, and he remembered the feeling of glee when the professor sent them back to their dorm room.

Troy's laughter faded when he recalled that Travis Gordon, Director of the Office of Minority Affairs, had flirted with Troy's mother when he first arrived in July. After a couple of run-ins with him during the summer, Troy hoped that Travis would disappear, but he knew better; he was going to have to deal with him whether he liked it or not. Still, he couldn't have been happier to be finally starting college. He didn't know what lay ahead, but if the first semester was anything like the summer program had been, Troy was in for plenty of escapades.

First Semester

One

The late August afternoon brought heat so hostile that no one stayed in the open sun for long. The campus' narrow streets were jammed with slow-moving cars full of anxious students and their belongings. Harbin Hall stood at the back of the parking lot entrance, its façade unchanged since Troy's summer stay on campus. The brown brick walls and rectangular windows were reminiscent of New York project buildings, and he could see why it was commonly referred to as "Harlem Hall." The bottom of the staircase that led from the parking lot to the front of the building was a blitz of move-in activity. Cars, kids and parents were everywhere — whizzing by, unloading, and checking their carefully written instructions.

Troy's mother parked the Nissan Sentra near the staircase by Harbin Hall, and together they began to unload his paraphernalia. One of the orientation crew members immediately came to their aid and helped to carry Troy's luggage and records, but Troy knew where his room was, so he headed directly upstairs. He had been assigned to Room 228, and he hoped that Randy, his roommate, would already be there. Troy met Randy during a recruiting trip that spring and after being the only black students on the trip, they had agreed to be roommates in the fall. After meeting Will and a host of other black students over the summer, Troy wasn't sure if his decision had been premature, but he'd soon see. Troy was looking forward to Randy bringing some music with him from New York, his lifelong home until he and his mother moved to Maryland nearly three years ago. Although Troy was a DJ and tracked rap music like a private eye, his current home in Landover, Maryland didn't keep him updated with the new music that came in hot off the presses over New York radio. *If he's anything like me*, Troy thought, *he'll have some tapes.* Randy was already in the room unpacking when he got there. They'd kept in touch since meeting in April, but their first meeting as roommates was as though they'd never spoken to one another. Looking at him, Troy sensed no hostility, only a mutual curiosity.

"What's up?" Troy asked, surveying the room.

"What up brother? Come on in!"

Troy, followed by his mother and an upperclassman loaded down with milk crates full of records, entered the room. Troy introduced Randy to his mother, and she and the helper returned to the car, leaving Troy to his unpacking. Randy looked at him like he wanted to laugh and Troy sensed it was because of the blue and white Adidas jogging suit he wore, which was far too much for a summer day in D.C. Troy didn't care; he was comfortable in it. Randy wore a pink short-sleeved oxford, blue slacks and penny loafers. Troy would have normally attributed this style of dress to being square, easily taken, soft. However, since Randy was a New Yorker, Troy mentally forgave the corny style of dress, reasoning that his roommate couldn't be all bad. He was noticeably short and muscular, light-skinned and wore a beard. The facial hair stirred up pangs of envy in Troy; he was certain that the look would drive the girls crazy and he couldn't grow hair on his face to save his life.

"How'd you get here?" he asked.

"Drove down with moms."

"I hear that. I had to take the bus down. Wasn't fun."

"I bet. How did you get all your stuff on the bus?"

Randy laughed. "We shipped most of my stuff. It all got here, too. And I didn't really bring that much, not compared to you. Oh, that's right, you're a DJ."

"Most definitely," Troy said proudly. "And I be rockin' shit, too."

Troy could see Randy roll his eyes, unimpressed. Where he lived, everyone and his brother claimed to be a DJ.

"You scratch and stuff?"

"I do all that shit. I wasn't going to bring the set here, but some brothers I talked to over the summer when I was here said I should. I may not have much spare time, but I'll see what happens." The truth was that Troy was prepared make time to DJ at any cost. Randy may not have related to his passion for spinning records, so he figured he'd play it safe during the conversation.

"Speaking of that, did you bring any tapes from up the way?"

Randy shrugged. "Nothing much, just some stuff from KISS-FM, some Rakim, you know."

"You got some KRS-One though, right?"

"Of course! I saw him at the Quarter this summer. Motherfucker didn't come on stage until three. He was rockin' though." The Latin Quarter was New York's legendary hip-hop club where every well-known rapper performed. Having gone to school in Maryland for the last two years, Troy had never been to the club, which was the epitome of rap music authenticity.

"Damn, I wish I'd been there! KRS at the Quarter? I know that was dope!"

"Yeah, but the smell of crack kind of gets to you after a while. New York is just ill now."

"I hear you." Troy was sure they'd get along.

Troy's mother and the upperclassman returned with more of Troy's things. "Boy, you better come downstairs and get the rest of these bags. What do you think this is?"

Troy tried to shake his humiliation as he went down the steps, but he couldn't.

"Don't sweat it," Randy said, patting him on the back. "Mothers are like that."

"I don't know any like mine," Troy replied, almost whining.

"You're an only child, right?"

"Yeah. How'd you know?"

"'Cause I am, too. My mama cried so much when I left, I almost missed the bus."

"Word?"

"Yeah, brother. It was hard for her. It's hard for any mother to let go of their only child."

The upperclassman moved on to help other students when he saw that Randy was helping Troy. On the way back to the car, Troy and Randy noticed a few brothers surrounding a girl on a bench. The guys all wore red and white.

"You know them?" Randy asked.

"Yeah, from the summer. They're Kappas."

"You know that girl?"

"Who? Oh shit, that's Michelyn!" Troy waved, hoping to catch her eye, but she was too preoccupied with the frat guys to notice. Some of the Kappas saw him wave, but ignored him.

"Go talk to her," Randy suggested.

"Nah, I'll see her later."

"She's bad!"

"The baddest."

The roommates continued down the staircase into the parking lot. Troy found a man talking to his mother, who sat in the seat of her car. She was smiling and laughing. Troy could only see his back. What was so funny?

"Travis, stop it," Troy's mother urged. "You're killing me."

"No, really, I'm serious."

"Excuse me," Troy interrupted. "I have more bags."

"Oh! Mister Harris," Travis answered. "This must be Randy," he said, extending his hand to him.

"Very nice to meet you brother," Randy replied.

"How are you?" Travis asked.

How are you my ass, Troy thought. "Shouldn't you be somewhere else Travis? You know, helping somebody?"

"We were just talking about that. We're all going to need some help adjusting to your first year in school."

"What?"

"Troy, you have some records in the trunk," his mother advised.

"Mom, I need you upstairs."

"Okay."

"Now, Mom."

"I'll be there when I'm ready," she said. "Don't make me act the fool."

Troy glared at Travis Gordon and was fuming. Travis waved at him as he and Randy went back upstairs with his records. The Kappas were still at the bench, but this time they watched the freshmen as they returned inside.

"Motherfucker!" Troy shouted as he returned to the room. Randy turned around, perplexed. "Not you, Travis Gordon."

"Isn't he in Minority Affairs?"

"Yeah. Bastard's trying to get up on my mom, too."

"What?"

"You heard me."

"Oh, shit! That's not good, brother."

"No, it's not. Look, I don't want to talk about it."

"Sure, no problem."

The room began to take shape as the boys got settled. Troy had his records and stereo equipment to consider. He wanted to put the turntables on his desk, but he might need that space to study. The only space left was at the bench under their window on the left side of the room. He hoped Randy wouldn't mind. Randy carefully laid a small rug across his desk.

"That's a nice piece of carpet you got there," Troy observed.

"It's a prayer rug."

"You mean for praying?"

"Yeah, brother. It's Islamic."

"So you're a Muslim?"

"Uh-huh."

"You wear bowties and all that?"

Randy laughed. "Sometimes. But I'm not in the Nation."

"Why not?"

"I'm still studying. Look, why don't we go back outside?"

"All right." Troy followed his roommate out the door. Randy was shaking his head and laughing as they walked out.

"Something funny?" Troy asked.

"I just wasn't ready for the question about bowties."

"Oh." Troy decided to change the subject. "If Travis is still downstairs, I might have to cuss him out."

"Take it easy," Randy told him as they headed outside. "Is that your car over there?"

"Yeah. He's gone."

Troy and his roommate descended the steps leading into the parking lot. Troy's mother offered to take the boys for a bite to eat.

"Just let me go park."

Troy nodded. His mother sensed his attitude, but ignored it.

Troy's mother left him and Randy to wait in the courtyard. They stood outside the front door to observe the other new students. It was still hot and humid outside, but a slight breeze was picking up, making the day more bearable.

"Troy! Yo, Troy!" someone shouted from behind. Troy turned around to find his partner from the summer.

"There's my homey!" Will shouted.

They both laughed and exchanged street handshakes, fists clutching then twisting into a double finger snap. Will was clearly as excited to be there as Troy. They both kept looking at one another and laughing. Troy was thrilled to see Will again, and now that the semester was starting, he could tell how much fun they were going to have. Will knew it too, and so they continued the greeting ritual, laughing with familiar anticipation.

"Oh, my fault, my fault," he apologized. "Randy, this is my man Will. Will, this is Randy, my roommate." The two of them slapped hands and nodded at each other.

"Hey, moms is going to take us to get something to eat. You want to come?"

"No thanks, man, I still have to unpack. I'll check you guys later, though."

"Definitely." He slapped hands with Will before heading back to the parking lot. Will pointed to Randy.

"Later, Randy."

"Peace out."

Crossing the courtyard, Troy, Randy and Troy's mother headed up a set of stairs to a path taking them to the school's front gates. The trio walked through the gates, past the campus apartments and reached the building where Troy's summer class had taken place. At Westmiller's, a popular campus café, Troy's mother bought sandwiches for the three of them and they ate while sitting at the shaded tables on the sidewalk. After a walk around the campus, they made their way back to Harbin Hall, which had quieted down considerably. By then, the evening was approaching and Troy knew it was almost time for his mother to leave. He was overcome with a sudden anxiety, the same nervousness he swore he wouldn't allow inside when it was time to say goodbye. The more he tried to fight it, however, the stronger it grew. By the time he and Randy walked his mother to her car, sadness was all over his face. Unlike her son, Troy's mother didn't try to conceal her emotion.

"Call me tomorrow, okay?" A tear was forming in the corner of her eye.

"Sure, Mom." Troy wasn't expecting her to cry, and her tears made it harder for him to keep it together.

"I love you."

"Love you, too."

They hugged and kissed, then Troy's mother got in the Sentra and drove off. Troy and Randy waved as she drove away. Troy could only think of calling her up, of being sure to talk to her on the phone as much as possible. The upperclassmen said the dorm phone lines wouldn't be on until October, so calling would be inconvenient. The only phones that were available were the pay phones in the downstairs lobby and there were already long lines to use them. Such was life. Now that his mother was gone, he and Randy were left to peruse the other dorms. He also wanted to find Will.

More black students were collecting downstairs in front of the dorm. Troy and Randy blended in, introducing themselves and each other. Troy could see that some were particularly comfortable talking and people watching, just as he had done back home. *Got some city folks up in here*, he thought. *Cool.* Someone said there was going to be a party the next evening, but that left nothing on the agenda for that night. After a couple of hours of socializing outside of Harbin, Troy decided to turn in. Randy remained downstairs, talking late into the night with other freshmen.

Troy was blinded by brightness when he pulled the curtains back the next morning. Troy was thankful for the quiet hum of the air conditioning under the window. He figured Randy had turned it on during the night. His roommate's bed was empty, but it had been slept in.

Troy pulled out a schedule from his orientation folder. He noticed that a campus-wide party was scheduled for that night featuring a reggae band. There was nothing academic to do until Monday, when the freshmen would have diagnostic tests to determine their placement in certain classes. Each school had a different test, depending on the high school record of the student. Troy would be tested to determine whether he could place out of Pre-Calculus. Everyone in the Business School was required to take Calculus, and if one didn't pass the diagnostic test, Pre-Calculus was also a prerequisite. Troy had resolved not to take any more math than he had to, test or no test. He was totally unconcerned, otherwise he might have made some attempt to prepare. The academic component of college was still secondary in his mind. He was there to have a good time. Randy came in, dripping wet and holding a towel around his waist.

"What up, man?"

Oh goodness, Troy thought, *a morning person.*

"You tell me! What was up with your girl last night?"

"Oh, we were just talking. She's from Wyoming."

"Wyoming?"

"I'm for real. Wyoming."

"There are black people in Wyoming?"

"Apparently so, man. I didn't know either. When she told me, I thought we'd be talking about corn husking and life on the plain." Troy laughed. He knew New Yorkers tend to see very little of the world outside of their own.

"What's her name?"

"Phyllis. From Rawlins, Wyoming."

"That's a real city, right?"

"Yeah, there are cities out there. She said she'd be at the reggae jam tonight with her friend from North Dakota. I think there are brothers out there, too."

"Niggas in North Dakota? Really?" This was news to Troy. He couldn't wait to talk to these black people from beyond.

After the roommates finished straightening up, Troy turned on his stereo. He was anxious for Randy to listen to him mix, but Randy promised him he'd listen later and instead opted for a morning run. Troy grabbed the first two records he could reach and began mixing. The window of Room 228 faced the courtyard, where Troy saw a gorgeous caramel-colored girl leaning over the side wall by the staircase. She wore a white T-shirt and a white denim mini-skirt, revealing a magnificent pair of legs. Her position placed her ample behind in full view. Troy forgot all about the music, tracing the slopes of her backside and legs with his eyes. Unable to believe what he was seeing, he put his face into his hand. Hands down she was the most beautiful girl, the most beautiful *thing*, he'd ever seen. *My God*, he thought. Honey brown complexion. Fabulous legs, beautiful ass. It was insane. How would he ever get any work done with girls like her around? He suppressed the urge to run downstairs and talk to her. There would be time for that. He closed his eyes and turned up the volume.

Troy's discipline evaporated in seconds. He continued to mix with the records, but he couldn't stop himself from looking out the window. She was incredible. A faint thump came from behind him. It was Randy, returning from his run.

"What's up brother?" he asked.

"Come here."

"What?"

"Just come here."

Randy hurried over. Troy pointed out the window at the girl in white.

"Do you see that?"

"Daaam...I was just out there and I didn't see that! Who is she?"

"I don't know, but I'm damn sure going to find out."

The girl turned away from the wall and walked into the dorm. At that moment Troy and Randy developed a true appreciation for the view from their window. No longer able to admire the girl's physique, the roommates turned away. Troy put a tape in the tape deck, unable to continue mixing.

Like most freshmen, Troy and Randy were on the meal plan. The plan, however, didn't begin until the following Tuesday. Until then, they were on their own. Just as they were ready to leave, there was a knock at the door. Randy opened it to find Will, looking ready to take on the world.

"What up, Will?"

"What up, homey?"

"Where you been, dude?"

"Nowhere, just around."

"Yeah, right. Trying to come get some food with us?"

"Hell, yeah!"

While eating at Burger King on M Street, Troy and Will told Randy about their summer, the antics in the hallway, Troy's frustrations with Travis Gordon, the adventures with Roach and Gina. Randy cracked up after hearing about the two of them in their drawers, in front of Latanya and Michelyn. Troy realized with Randy around, now there would be three skirt-chasing, hip-hopping financial aid recipients instead of two.

"So what's been up, man?" Troy asked.

"Nothing, really," Will said. "What you guys do last night?"

"I crashed," Troy lamented, "but Randy may tell you otherwise."

"No big deal," Randy offered. "People just stayed up talking in the lounge."

"You should have seen the girl outside the window, Will." Troy told him.

"Fine?"

"Blessed," Randy added. "Fat as shit."

"She as bad as Michelyn?"

"Yeah," Troy answered. "Maybe badder."

"No way."

"Michelyn is that girl who was with those frat guys, right?" Randy asked.

"Yeah," Will said. "That's our big sister. You seen her?"

"Yes indeed," Randy replied. "She's fine, too."

"Yeah, well, we haven't got a shot. Take it from my friend from home, Latanya. Her and Michelyn are tight."

"That's all right," Randy said. "There's plenty more around here. Right, Troy?"

"You ain't bullshitting," Troy answered, still thinking of the girl in white.

Later that afternoon the boys were back in Harbin and Will came to hang out in Troy and Randy's room until it was time to check out the reggae party. Before the party, there was a floor meeting in the dorm, an official introduction and information session. Troy and Will knew the routine since they'd experienced it over the summer. Students gathered in the hallway by the elevator and sat on the floor. The Resident Assistant, Andrea, introduced herself and discussed the basic rules of the dorm.

"Here we go again," Troy whispered. Andrea made everyone introduce themselves.

"Okay, let's just go around the hall, starting over here."

Troy wondered how many more times he'd have to do this. Some people were happy for the chance to say where they were from, but Troy, fortified by his new friendships, was indifferent. Still, it gave him a chance to notice the other residents on the floor. During the introductions, Troy began to match faces with the names on the doors. Counting Randy and Will, there were only seven other black students on the second floor, most of whom were girls.

The floor meeting soon broke into small conversations in the hallway. Students roamed from room to room, visiting and getting acquainted. He saw people looking over the posted weekend schedule, and a couple of them were talking to Andrea about registration, an activity that had yet to enter his mind. Deep down he knew that his attitude would get serious once classes started. Maybe the kids talking to Andrea already had their goals in mind.

When Troy and Randy returned to their room to get ready for the party, Troy sniffled.

"What's with you?" Randy asked.

"I don't know, something in my nose."

"Here." With one swift motion, Randy reached into his desk drawer, pulled out a pack of Kleenex and threw it at him.

"I doubt I'll need these, but thanks."

"No sweat."

"Will is going to meet us outside, right?"

"Yeah, he was talking to this girl Yvonne. She was here over the summer with you guys, right?"

"She was here, but nothing happened. We just hung out."

"That's okay!" Randy laughed. "They can't all get boned."

Speak for yourself, Troy thought.

Two

A rich Caribbean rhythm wafted from the parking lot. Troy was pleasantly surprised by the groove of steel drums and an electric bass; he hadn't expected a band. There was a huge tent set up at the end of the lot where the gym was, and people were drifting in from all directions. The reggae musicians were stationed towards the back of the tent. Troy's expectations quickly rose. This was going to be cool, even if Randy and Will had dates. He, Randy and Zelena, whom Randy had met last night, finally reached the tent and strolled in to meet a sea of people. Many were already drunk and still trying to dance. Troy and Randy looked at each other and shook their heads.

"Caucs," Randy sighed.

"What?"

"Caucs. Caucasians. They're hilarious!" Troy agreed. Still, he couldn't help but wonder if two white guys were there somewhere saying, "Nigs."

The band was jamming. It could have been his mood, but Troy's musical ears knew a quality performance when they heard one. He had just gotten into reggae and that had been another reason why he'd looked forward to the party. Troy was hoping to see that gorgeous girl in white, but he couldn't find her. He did see Latanya and she quickly pulled him into the crowd so they could dance.

"Where's Michelyn?" he asked.

"She's around. What's the matter, I'm not good enough?"

"Oh, of course you are, of course you are," Troy responded, smiling. Latanya was attractive, but she wasn't nearly as fine as Michelyn.

A couple of hours later, the freshmen met up outside the tent by the gym. Troy spotted Will with Yvonne, another freshman, and waved them over.

"About time!" Troy shouted. "Had motherfuckers waiting for you."

"My fault, my fault. What's wrong with your voice?"

"Nothing," he sniffled. "What's with yours?"

"I'm drunk. I have an excuse."

Troy hoped for a snappy comeback to pop into his brain, but one did not. Zelena recognized one of the other girls and turned away from

Randy. Troy felt moisture form on the tip of his nose, waiting to drip down. And the insides of his nostrils were thickening. *It's 85 degrees out,* he thought. *What the fuck is going on?*

"Phyllis! Over here. This is Randy, and his roommate Troy." Zelena shot her a look that said 'this was the one I was talking about.' Troy knew the look wasn't for him and he hated it.

"Hi, Randy, hi Troy." Troy saw an attractive black girl, but heard the squeaky voice of a child.

Randy stepped forward, shielding the girls from Troy, who was on the verge of laughter.

"Nice to meet you, sister."

She looked at Randy incredulously. He looked at Troy and now they were both smiling. Phyllis was the black girl from Wyoming. Troy still couldn't believe it. Since he wasn't able to brace himself for the Laura Ingalls dialect, he kept his eyes on his sneakers. He was tempted to ask her to do an "Alvin and the Chipmunks" impression, but thought better of it. Troy envied Will, who stood oblivious to the conversation. Troy tried to do the same, but only felt his head growing heavier by the minute. *May as well face it,* he thought. *I've got a head cold. In the summertime.* He was able to keep pace with the serious discussion Randy and Phyllis were having about the present state of blacks in America. Why they felt the need to have it there at the dance was beyond Troy, but this was a far cry from the boredom of the night before, so he didn't mind listening. Troy looked up in shock when he heard the basis of Phyllis' argument:

"America would be a better place without black people."

Everyone around her stood still. Troy was sure he had misunderstood her.

"What did you just say?" Randy asked.

"No, I mean it. Everyone talks about us like we're such a problem, we're at the bottom of everything, none of us are happy. America would be better off."

Ain't this a bitch, Troy thought. *Here I am at a party, where people of all races are dancing to reggae music, being told by a sister from East Bumblefuck that America would be better off without us.* Troy figured life in Wyoming must have been good.

Troy thought he'd hear an immediate response from Randy, but even he was too stunned to speak. Yvonne was surprised as well, and Zelena had to be restrained to keep from hitting Phyllis. But Phyllis didn't care, she just kept right on talking, fueled by the surprised expressions on everyone's faces. Randy eventually came back to earth and tried to finish the debate, but all he could say was "Are you out of your mind? I mean, are you out of your fucking mind?"

After a while only Troy, Randy, Phyllis and Zelena remained outside the tent. Troy felt his cold gathering strength. He found that the longer he walked around, the stronger his cold became, until the cold eventually took over. Within minutes he was chilled, tired, and to make matters worse, his nose began to drip like a faucet.

Troy still didn't want to leave, but he forced himself to start walking back to Harbin Hall. It felt like the longest walk he'd ever taken in his life. He could still hear the music, and he knew he'd run into someone if he stayed, but his body just would not allow it. The air turned freezing cold as his nose dripped relentlessly. Randy's tissues were almost gone. Why hadn't he gotten there yet? As if in response to Troy's prayers, the side staircase leading from the parking lot to Harbin Hall finally appeared. He still had his ID from the summer, but he didn't pull it out until the student guard at the front desk asked for it. After another long search through his pockets, he finally found the key. Just then, the door swung open.

"Brother," Randy asked, "could you do me a favor?"

As disoriented as he felt, Troy knew what the favor would be. Randy had taken Zelena back to Harbin; he had done it quickly to beat Troy to the room. Troy's head was in a complete fog, and he yearned for his own bed, but he wasn't going to prevent his roommate from getting some action. Randy knew this and had every intention of taking advantage of this understanding among men.

"Can I get the crib tonight, brother?" he asked, oblivious to Troy's runny nose.

"Huh? Oh, yeah, yeah. No problem."

He was happy for Randy, but where could he sleep? As Randy explained about Zelena, he just stood there sniffling. All he wanted was a bed. The girl to go with it could come later. Troy sneezed.

While Troy was in the bathroom wearing out toilet tissue with his nose, Randy went through the side exit to find Will, who agreed to put Troy up for the night. Randy left, and Will went off to get a mattress for Troy to sleep on. Hardly able to stand, Troy collapsed against the door of the john right outside of Will's room. He knew that he was within his right to refuse Randy's request, but it seemed a little late to change his mind. Besides, Randy would have to return the favor one day. Just as Troy started drifting off, Will and his roommate Carl came around the corner, dragging a mattress they found in the basement. Troy wasn't sure how he'd gotten into Will and Carl's room, but he didn't have enough energy to figure it out.

Troy's new landlords finished dressing the mattress. He'd never seen a bed look so inviting. Without removing his jacket or sneakers, he collapsed onto the mattress. When he landed on it, a cloud of dust rose from the floor, which was more than enough to trigger a hearty sneeze.

*   *   *   *

Troy felt refreshed the next day, but his nose was still congested. He stood up to go to the bathroom for a new supply of toilet tissue. Slowly, the previous night's events came back to him. It was time for him to get back into his room, no matter who was in there. It would be a shame to have to throw Zelena out. His mind made up, Troy pulled out his key and opened the door. Blessedly, the room was empty, and there was no sign of either of them. Then he noticed the clock on the end table; it was 5:30 in the afternoon. No wonder there was no one around. At least now he'd be able to regroup a little. Randy, Will and Carl came in just then, interrupting his thoughts, laughing loudly.

"He's alive!" Carl yelled.

"There he is! What up, man?" Will added. "And I thought I was fucked up!" Apparently there had been guffaws galore over last night.

"Wasn't too cold on that floor, was it homey?" Will was enjoying himself.

"Nah. It was fine."

"Yo, I'm sorry about that man," Randy said. "Now I feel bad. Will told me you were sick, I didn't know!"

Right, Troy thought. As if he wouldn't have done it had he known. It bewildered him how people in the wrong had so much remorse after the fact.

"S'alright, just let me know next time."

Randy proposed that whenever one of them expected a female guest, the other man would have to have enough notice to find other sleeping arrangements. If a situation came up unexpectedly, an Opus magnet (of

"Bloom County" fame) would be left on the message board by the occupant. Using this system, the roommates would never prevent each other from having a girl in the room alone, or "cock block," as they liked to say. If Will or Carl needed similar accommodations, they'd look out for them as well.

Later that night, Troy spotted the girl in the white mini-skirt outside Harbin Hall. He was again stunned by her beauty. She wore a peach blouse and a tight fitting pair of jeans. Troy could see that she was well-developed. He promised himself he'd talk to her this time and rushed downstairs.

"Hey," he called to her, practically running over to the wall where she stood.

"Hi."

Troy pushed himself through his nervousness.

"Hello. I'm Troy. And you are?"

"Angel."

"I can see why." She smiled at the compliment. Troy couldn't believe what had just come out, but it worked.

"Let me guess. You're a senior."

"No, I'm a freshman," she said, still smiling. She looked like she could be Mexican or Puerto Rican, but she spoke without an accent.

"You can't be a freshman. I'm a freshman!"

Angel laughed. "Then I guess we have something in common. Do you live here?"

"Sure do, Harlem Hall."

She laughed. "I've never heard that. That's hilarious!"

"I'm sure you know why they call it that. Look at the building. Doesn't it look like the projects?"

She looked up, only to begin laughing again.

"My God, you're a trip! I never even thought about it like that. I don't know if I want to live here now."

"Wait a minute. You live here?"

"Mm-hm, on the second floor."

"The second floor? How come you weren't at the hall meeting?"

"I heard about it, but I had dinner with my family that day."

"Oh. Well, I live on the second floor! Room 228!"

"Okay! Room 202!"

"I'll remember that. I saw you out the window the other day. I was going to come say hi, but you looked a little distracted."

"You should have come down. I was just looking at the sky."

She looked him right in the eye, and he couldn't help but crack a smile.

"Listen Angel, if you're not doing anything later on, you're welcome to stop by. You know, so we can talk."

"Okay, maybe I'll do that."

"All right. Bye." He was ecstatic. He couldn't have asked for a better chance meeting. She really was an angel.

The next day, Troy found out that they had a great deal more in common. Angel Davis was from Maryland, of all places, and she graduated from a high school not far from his. She loved rap music, and she was fascinated by Troy's stories about how much he missed his old block in New York, where he lived before moving to Maryland. He didn't want her to return to her room, but when she insisted, he relented, not wanting to appear pushy. It was far too early to try anything.

"She's dope, man. She's dope," Troy told Randy over and over.

"Yeah, brother. You better jump on it." The other Georgetown girls were now insignificant, and Mimi, his girlfriend of two years, no longer existed in his mind. If Angel saw in him a fraction of what he saw in her, he reasoned that life would be perfect.

Several hours (and pizza boxes) later, the second floor of Harbin settled into quiet. The next morning Troy, Randy and Will planned to do some shopping and put the finishing touches on their rooms. Troy and Will had their respective diagnostic tests, but besides that formality, the day would be free. On Monday night there would be a special reception for minority freshmen hosted by Travis Gordon and the Office of Minority Affairs. Troy envisioned another introductory meeting, except on a larger scale. The freshmen would meet their Program Assistants, or PAs, black upperclassmen assigned by Travis to mentor black and Hispanic City Scholars. PAs were assigned according to what school the freshmen registered with, so they would be able to answer questions concerning coursework, prerequisites, professors and anything else school-related. The fact that there would be a resource of older black students available was a great relief in Troy's mind. As it turned out, Troy's PA was Latanya. Latanya was also in the Business School and majoring in finance.

Employment was another issue the freshmen needed to consider. Troy, Randy and Will were in the work-study program common to most colleges. The minimum wage on campus was $4.50 an hour. It was less than what Troy had made at his last job, but his concern was securing a job where Angel worked. He still had some savings, and he was sure that his father would send him something each month, although this year he had been pretty slack with the child support. At the same time, he hated asking his parents for money and wanted to make as much of his own as possible. Troy's aid package was light on grants, heavy on loans, and counted work-study income from a job he had yet to acquire. Troy figured that whatever else he got was extra. If he got on a roll deejaying at parties, he wouldn't have to worry about money at all.

$*$ $*$ $*$ $*$

That afternoon, Randy came in to find Troy in his own musical dimension, bopping his head to the music from his headphones.

"Sounds good," Randy told him. Troy was oblivious.

"Hey!" Still nothing. Randy came over and turned the volume down, startling Troy.

"Oh, what up, man!"

"You're in here getting busy."

"Most definitely. I may not have as much free time later on."

"True. How was the test?"

"I'll let you know when the scores come back. Where you been?"

"Just walking around, checking out the library."

"Uh-huh."

"I seen Will, he said something about trying to find your big sisters from the summer."

"Yeah, that would be Latanya and Michelyn." Troy turned off the music and sat at his desk. "You down to roll by the bookstore? I still have to pick up a few things."

"We can do that, but fair warning. It was crowded two hours ago."

Troy wanted to call his mother and let her know he was okay, but he didn't feel like standing in the long lines for the pay phones. Instead, he and Randy headed for Healy Basement to buy snacks from Hoya Vittles, a student-run grocery store that carried items cheaper than in off-campus stores; a can of soda, for example, was only thirty cents. Directly across the hall was Sundries for Saxas, the drugstore with a similar, student-run theme. There were rugs being sold from a truck parked in front of the campus and the roommates bought a beige one for the room.

The roommates saw a few more black people that they hadn't seen previously and socialized outside before returning to their dorm. Troy wondered if all of the black freshmen lived in Harbin. So far, it really did look like "Harlem Hall," with a few white freshmen as window dressing.

Both Troy and Randy were excited to see Will once they got back to the second floor. Yvonne was also there.

"You guys watching the new Michael Jackson video tonight?" she asked.

"Oh, that's right," Troy nodded. "The video for 'Bad.' We can watch it in the lounge, there's a TV in there."

"What time does it come on?" Randy asked.

"Eight," Yvonne said.

Will approached them from behind, wrapping his arms around Yvonne's waist. Troy and Randy smiled.

"There's that black freshman meeting tonight," Randy reminded them.

"Oh, that's right," Will replied. "You don't want to be late when Travis Gordon calls a meeting."

"Word up," Troy affirmed. "But he always goes off anyway. I still might watch some of the video. A few minutes won't be so bad."

"I'm down if y'all are," Randy added. "If I get in trouble I'll just tell them I was with you guys."

Half an hour later, Troy, Randy, Yvonne and the others debated on how to get into the meeting unnoticed. Troy hadn't counted on 'The Making of the Video' and all the preview material. The closer they got to the building, the more Troy had a feeling that Michael Jackson could have waited. Coplin Hall had entrances on both ends of the building, and the meeting was in the formal lounge on the East End. The large picture windows revealed what looked like hundreds of people in an audience being addressed by someone, probably Travis.

"There's nothing we can do about it now," Will decided aloud, "so we might as well just walk in."

Troy shook his head, suddenly overcome with pity for the other students. The clock on Healy Tower said quarter to nine. It was the last thing he needed, another reason for Travis Gordon to notice him. At least he, Will and Yvonne had some idea what they were in for, but the others didn't have a clue. They'd be better off trying to take on Mike Tyson. They walked through the entrance on the right and turned the corner. A couple of black students were standing in the hall. The doors to the lounge were open and Travis' voice addressed the room over a microphone.

"You're going to have to learn a very important word while you're here, and that word is 'No.' That's right, 'No!' You're really going to need it around mid-October, when you get what we call 'freshman burnout'..."

Travis spoke as if the entire country was listening, and even hearing the middle of it, the speech had the impact of a presidential address. It occurred to Troy that if they needed all this information, the white freshmen needed it just as much. Despite what their City Scholars records had indicated or what the admissions officers had determined, they were in now. And the City Scholars had already suffered through five weeks of class! He didn't understand why all of the formality was necessary.

If they could just sneak in, Troy thought they would be okay. But his hope was shattered as they proceeded down the long ramp by the staircase. The ramp was a reed-thin wooden board so every step was a stomp, as if they all wore steel-toe boots. Troy and the others followed along while Randy lead the way. Shaking his head, Troy tried awkwardly to lose himself in the small crowd with whom he'd entered the room. *God help us*, he thought. *We're fucked.*

The sound of the slow stampede filled the room, which had clear acoustics. In mid-sentence, Travis Gordon stopped and glared across the room at them, consternation all over his face. The entire room turned around to see the source of the noise, causing the four freshmen to stop. Two hundred black people followed with their eyes, staring at Troy, Randy, Will and Yvonne as if they were aliens. Troy gave Randy a nudge to keep walking, and they continued their march down the ramp. Troy felt like he was on death row. People were laughing and girls looked at them with amusement and pity. Adding to his embarrassment, Troy saw Angel looking and laughing.

Yvonne dragged Will away from his friends, and now it was just Troy and Randy. The whole audience was still viewing them like they were on stage. Troy didn't want everyone to think they were ignorant, so he tried to act as if nothing out of the ordinary had happened, drawing confidence from his roommate. There were no empty seats up front but they found a spot along the aisles on the side of the room, by a piano bench a good thirty yards from Travis' podium.

It wasn't over. People were still looking and pointing. The laughing had grown from a few chuckles to roars from all over the room. To look relaxed, the roommates sat with their arms crossed, and looked at each other to reassure themselves. Travis was exasperated by now and continued his address. As Troy predicted, he threw in his infamous lecture on punctuality. There were more familiar tidbits, like the importance of calling home, so their parents wouldn't think he'd done something to him.

"The motherfucker's ego is huge," Troy muttered.

Finally the introductions began. Troy fantasized about Travis overlooking them, but there was no chance of that. Just as they had earlier, the entire audience turned to face them, with laughs again accompanying the attention.

"Randy Lambert." The commotion quieted to suppressed laughter. Randy turned to his roommate.

"Troy Harris." Everyone looked as if Troy had something else to say.

"Troy Harris!"

Shrieks of laughter came from the other students.

"Where are you from?" Travis asked.

"What?"

"Where are you two from?"

"New York!" cried the two of them in unison. The audience exploded with laughter and applause.

After Travis concluded, he directed the students to the tables that were set up to provide information about registration, which was the next day. Neither Troy nor Randy could get their registration materials until they got past Travis, who stopped them in their tracks.

"I don't know what you clowns are trying to prove, but you better watch it. You'll be out of here before you see one credit."

"Who you calling a clown?" Troy shot back.

"Don't interrupt me. You think I'm playing? You want to try me, Harris?"

"We just came a little late, sir." Randy interjected.

"I'm only going to say this once," Travis said, leaning forward. "It's obvious that you're going to be a problem and that's your business. But everyone will see you pay a price for acting the fool in here. Everyone."

He turned to Randy. "You better watch how you pick your friends, son. This one likes to make an ass out of himself. Your mother would be heartbroken if we had to send you home, too." Randy nodded in silence as Travis turned to walk away.

"Fuck you," Troy whispered under his breath.

Travis came rushing back. "Excuse me? What was that?"

"Nothing."

He glared at them, then left to greet some of the other students. Randy let out a nervous laugh after he left. Troy was quiet, realizing that what he'd just said wasn't too smart. He knew Travis had heard him, but if the guy had it out for him, it was going to come to a head sooner or later.

"You had to stomp in here like Gigantor, didn't you?"

"You were the one who wanted to watch Mike," Randy retorted. He had enjoyed the scene almost as much as everyone else. Troy sucked his teeth. He hated to lose an argument.

"Fuck Michael Jackson."

Troy and Randy met their PAs at the registration tables. Latanya went over the basics of registration with Troy, reminding him of the time he would save during the process, since City Scholars were already pre-registered. She obviously enjoyed being a mentor. Randy was over at the table for the School of Foreign Service students. Troy noticed that Will was at Michelyn's table, and to his chagrin, so was Angel. He should be so lucky!

"Don't worry," Latanya told him, seeing where he was looking. "We're both taking our kids out for ice cream after this. You'll get to see her."

"Actually, she has a student that I'm, um, talking to."

"Oh? You don't waste time, do you, loverboy?"

Troy made a face. "It's not all about her. Will's there, too."

"Yeah, well don't forget what I told you. Classes start soon."

"Right, right. Look, I'll wait for you outside, okay?"

"Sure."

Randy was at the door, also preparing to leave. Troy hurried to meet him but before they could escape they were met by upperclassmen, members of the all-black Kappa Alpha Psi fraternity, whom Troy recognized. One of them smiled and folded his arms as soon as he saw Troy.

"Yo, man! I'm from Nu Yawk. Bet' not fuck with me. Word!" The short upperclassman had his friends in hysterics. His buddy joined in.

"Hey Bizzy, is it true that in New York high schools you have to scratch the beat before you graduate?"

Screams of laughter erupted from behind them. The hurt in Troy's face incensed Randy.

"You gonna let us through or not?" he barked. "What the fuck's up?" His fists were clenched.

"What you want, nigga? Come make us move!" Bizzy challenged. Randy advanced with his fists up, but another Kappa jumped in between him and his frat brother.

"Easy now, no need for that. We're just fuckin' with y'all. Hey, I'm from New York, too." He extended his hand to Randy. The freshman took it, calming down. Troy did not move until he knew the way to the door was clear. As he walked out behind Randy, Wendell patted him on the back. "That's all right, troop. Get yours."

"Fuck you!" Troy snapped.

Wendell and his friends laughed as the roommates walked out. "Them some hellified fools right there."

"You ain't lying," Bizzy agreed. "Did you see the way they came in? They've gotta be out of their minds."

"That's freshmen for you. Ain't got a credit to their name, but you can't tell them shit."

Will was outside with Michelyn, Latanya and their group of students. Troy's anger faded when he saw Angel with the rest of them.

"What was with those fools at the door?" Will asked.

"Nothing," Troy spat.

"You know we can go back and smash them niggas," Will suggested. "I got you."

"Nah, that's all right. Latanya, thanks for waiting."

"Oh, anytime," she replied, suppressing a laugh. "Randy, would you like to join us?"

"No, thanks, I'm going back to the room."

"All right."

"Hey Latanya, y'all go ahead," Troy advised. "We'll catch up to you."

"Okay. Let's go, y'all."

The group left the three boys outside Coplin.

"Hey," Randy asked. "Did you hear what they said about us?"

"Who, those Kappa fools?"

"Yeah."

"What?" Will asked.

"They called us hellified."

"That's what we are," Will insisted. "Hellified homeboys."

"Word," Troy added. "The Hellified Homeboys of Harbin Hall."

Randy nodded. "The 4-H Crew, hm?"

"There it is," Will affirmed.

"All right fellas," Randy said as he slapped hands with his two friends. "Catch you later."

The junior girls took their charges to Thomas Sweet in Georgetown, a well-known ice cream shop. Troy and Will were the only guys to come along, but it was fine with them. The freshmen girls all mentioned Troy and Will's dramatic entrance to the meeting. It didn't bother them; Will was happy to be with Michelyn and his girl Yvonne, and Troy patiently waited on the opportune time to approach Angel.

Troy sat next to her after ordering his ice cream. He had been extra fast to make sure he got to the seat next to hers before someone else did.

"So how are you doing?"

"Fine." Angel could hardly keep from laughing.

"Ha ha, I know. We came in like a bunch of idiots."

"No you didn't. Well, maybe you did. But it was cute."

"I'm glad you thought so." While he ate his ice cream, Troy looked into her eyes, desperate for the right thing to say. She was even more beautiful than before, wearing diamond earrings and a thick herringbone chain.

"Troy, I saw you with those guys when you were coming out. Is everything okay?"

"Oh yeah, nothing to worry about. I know those fools."

"They're Kappas, right?"

"Yes," Troy sighed. "They're Kappas."

"Hmm. Well, I bet none of them can DJ."

Troy couldn't help but smile. "You know you're a cutie, don't you?"

"You're not so bad yourself."

He reached for her hand, but Michelyn appeared out of nowhere.

"All right, you two, break it up. We're heading back."

"Already?"

"Yes. Angel, watch out for this one. I could tell you a funny story about him and Will, but I'll let him."

"Oh, really?" Angel inquired.

"Some other time," Troy muttered as he got up to join Will outside the ice cream shop, leaving the girls to talk among themselves on the way back.

"How'd you get Michelyn as your big sister?" Troy asked.

"Arts and Sciences, my man," he replied. "Lucky for you Angel has her for a PA. Maybe she'll put a good word in for you."

"Maybe. But hopefully I won't need it."

*   *   *   *

Registration the next day forced Troy to consider why he was supposed to be in college in the first place. What was it that Latanya said to do? He couldn't get around the endless lines or the red tape that came with them. The upperclassmen were busy with activities of their own, today was just for freshmen and sophomores. Troy was on his own and at the mercy of Georgetown's bureaucracy. He spent the entire day in the Cultural Center lobby, standing in lines and getting directions to even longer lines. Randy and Will appeared at random, engaged in their own torture. When the nightmare finally ended, Troy had classes, a schedule and no other free days besides weekends. The relaxed attitude of the past few days was gone, replaced by the rigidity of a schedule that dictated when he had to wake up, where he had to be, and how much less free time he had. While none of it was a pleasant thought, there was one consolation: in his heart Troy knew that none of the others, black or otherwise, were any smarter than he was. He had no fear of the academic challenge, especially since he'd done well as a City Scholar, but it was tough to accept that playtime was over.

Troy, Randy and Will turned in early that night. While he lay in bed, Troy reviewed the major developments of his life during the last few years. He had finally made it to college. He'd heard all sorts of stories about it, read about it, and had seen more movies about it than he could count. Already what he had witnessed was better than anything he could have read about college. His two friends were as crazy and fun-loving as he thought he was. They were cool like him — real brothers, not like those oreos or preppie suckers he had made fun of in high school. Like him, they were happy to be away from their mothers' households. Troy and his crew had arrived and there was no turning back.

Three

The interior brick walls and high ceilings were new to Troy; he had never been in a Healy building classroom. The rest of the Accounting class was filled with other students, almost all of whom were attentive-looking white kids. Because the professor had not yet arrived, Troy couldn't understand why his classmates were so perky. *Surely there won't be any work given out today*, he thought. *Why can't these people relax?* Troy had come early himself, afraid he might miss something if he hadn't. Despite his contempt for the administrator, Travis' speeches were influencing him.

The professor finally arrived. He put his name on the board for the class to see: Professor Newcomb. He was a relatively young guy who created a friendly atmosphere by talking about himself and his career goals.

"This is my first year at Georgetown, and I hope to be here for a while," he said. "Whatever I can do to help, just let me know."

Give me a fucking 'A,' Troy thought. Sighing, he knew he'd have to earn it if he wanted it. Professor Newcomb gave an overview of how the class would run, the material to be covered, and his suggestions for studying and test preparation. There was no telling the class outright what they needed to do to get good grades, no laying it on the line, only friendly suggestions. He did manage to communicate some interest in his students' success. And it was obvious that he loved his job. Troy didn't think it was possible to love something as boring as accounting, but he was growing accustomed to learning something new every day. Professor Newcomb handed out a syllabus. As they were forwarded to each row of students, Troy wondered what would be on the stapled sheets of paper. From the one he had used in July, he thought it would be an outline listing material to be covered in the course. This one had exam dates and chapters to be discussed for just about each day the class met. Because there had been no exams in the English-based City Scholars program, this caught Troy by surprise. He didn't mind too much though, because in high school he never knew when an exam was coming until shortly before. Now he would know exactly when he needed to study and when he could slack off. He tried not to think that way, but he couldn't help it.

After his speech and dispatch of the syllabus, Professor Newcomb had concluded his introduction. By then, it was only 9:25. Troy knew he had a few more days before any real work began, but he didn't want to get used to the false sense of freedom. Maybe he'd get an assignment in his next class. He could have gone to the bookstore that morning to get the accounting book, but it made more sense to get the syllabi for his other classes first. That way, he'd get all his books in one trip.

Troy headed back to Harbin Hall for a nap. The bustle that met him as he came back to his dorm was different. A sense of quiet apprehension had overcome Harbin Hall. During the past weekend, everyone had been excited, but now the concepts of obligation, deadlines and preparation were omnipresent. Freshmen entering and exiting the building were getting head starts in what would be a long race against time and responsibility. When Troy woke up that morning he hadn't felt his normal urge to stay in bed, but suddenly he felt like he hadn't slept in days. He set the alarm clock to make sure he didn't oversleep, then he hit the bed like dead weight.

In the 1:15 slot, Troy's schedule read "Novel/Short Story." It wasn't hard to find since he'd been in the building all day before registering. Troy smiled, recalling Will's tart explanation to Professor Perez that they had overslept last summer. There could be no more of that, he had to get off on the right foot. He strolled into the classroom, which was tiny and quiet. Moments later, a 20th Century elf walked in, sat at the desk in front and said "Hi." Judging from where he sat, Troy guessed that he was Professor Larson. He had silver hair and a pointy nose as if he'd walked out of a storybook. The whispered conversations in the room ended; Larson was the new center of attention. He took turns making small talk with each student. His squeaky, nasal voice matched his elf-like appearance and he wore the typical college professor fashion. Apparently, anything brown was acceptable. The nasal effect coupled with the silver hair made him appear quite a character. All he needed was a pair of pointy shoes.

When it looked like all the students had arrived, the elf began.

"Our class will be pretty straightforward; lots of reading and discussion, a few papers, no exams."

Troy liked him immediately.

"You'll be allowed to skip class up to three times."

All right, Troy thought. The professor's three added up to about six or seven in his book.

"If you miss any more, you will automatically fail."

So much for six or seven. But Troy still liked him for coming to terms with the fact that students skip class on occasion. He gave out a syllabus, somewhat different than the one from Newcomb. This one had a book list and an outline of the class discussion format. Based on those discussions, Larson would determine when the next book or paper had to be finished. The class was small, and as Larson noted, "the participation of everyone is important." In other words, the kid who sits there and doesn't say anything will look like an idiot and get an inferior grade.

Later that day, Troy and Randy exchanged stories about their first classes. Troy's roommate was less fortunate than he, having to wake up for Intro to French at 8:15. Randy then went to Political Theory and Western Civilization, the School of Foreign Service's equivalent to Troy's European Civilization course. They agreed that the College of Arts and Sciences, of which Will was a member, wasn't the place to be.

"What are they thinking?" Troy asked.

"God only knows, brother."

"I mean, do you know what they have to take? Math and science, or both? Senior theses? Shit!"

"Except for English majors, they don't write theses."

"Yeah, but look what they have to take! Shakespeare? Milton? I can't fuck with it. We have some wack classes too, but all I have to do is graduate. Even you have a proficiency exam in French. Better you than me."

Will came in as if he'd just been running. "What up dudes?"

"We were just talking about you." Troy told him. "You went to class or what?"

"Come on man, of course."

"Have a seat," Randy offered. "All excited, look at you. How'd it go?"

"Troy's lucky he placed out of Expository, it sucks. Good thing I'm taking German."

Troy and Randy looked at each other, then back at him. "Shit, my roommate's taking it. If he can do it, so can I."

"This brother's ill," Randy laughed.

Troy had thought the same thing when he met him. "Ill Will," he said to no one in particular.

Ill Will laughed. "You guys are clowns."

City Scholars had a jump on some things at the start of the semester, but eating in the dining hall that night would be as new to Troy and Will as it was to the rest of the freshman class. Troy and Randy had eaten there in the morning, but they were both too preoccupied with classes to notice their surroundings. Eating in the dining hall that night would be a totally different story. All the freshmen Troy knew were on the meal plan, and he was looking forward to seeing them as well as others he hadn't met yet, especially the young ladies. Upperclassmen had said the cafeteria food was risky. When Troy asked what the big deal was, he only got a "You'll see" as a response. Troy saw Bizzy at the table and looked over at Randy. His roommate gave him a look that said it was okay.

"New York's in the house!" Bizzy announced. "What's up, New York?"

Troy said nothing and began to eat. Talk at the table died down and Troy felt people's eyes on him. He was flushed with shame, knowing everyone remembered the other night at the meeting.

"Hey, Mr. DJ. I'm talking to you! Trying to ignore me?"

Troy looked up. "Don't start it."

"Oh shit!" one of the girls said. "Did you hear that?'"

Bizzy saw his frat brothers laughing.

"Yeah, yeah, all right," Bizzy laughed along. Troy felt himself relax.

"Why do they call you Bizzy, anyway?" Troy asked. The other Kappas around the table howled.

"Because, fool, I be getting busy," he answered, slapping hands with his friends. "You hear me? B-I-Z-Z-Y. But if you want to send me a check, my name is Brian."

Troy rolled his eyes. Bizzy, or Brian, was a clown if he'd ever seen one. There was another voice at the table that wasn't as familiar.

"So Darnell, what's up for this year?" one of the upperclassmen asked.

"Same old thing, y'all know what time it is. But you know, we'll have some meetings."

"That party last summer, though!" said Bizzy. "My goodness!"

"Yeah," Darnell laughed. "Big man would shit if he knew." By now the conversation had piqued Troy's curiosity. Randy was also listening intently.

"Nah, for real though," Darnell added, noticing the freshmen around him. "We're going to do some things this year."

"What's that about, fellas?" Randy asked.

"No big thing," Darnell answered. "You guys keep getting situated. If you need anything, let a brother know."

Randy turned to Troy, who shrugged his shoulders. Whatever they were talking about, the whole story wasn't being told.

The volume on the TV was turned up to the max in Room 202. Troy wasn't sure if Angel would hear him knocking. After another loud barrage on the door, Angel answered.

"Hi, Troy!"

"Hey. You busy?"

"Not at all. Come in."

The room was a hodgepodge of posters, photos and trinkets. One bed was neatly made, immediately facing the door. To the right was Angel's bed, cluttered with a zoo of stuffed animals, books and clothes. The scent of microwave popcorn filled the room. At the foot of her bed was a 12-inch color television, the source of all the noise. How could anyone study with all of the visual goings-on in the room? Angel sat up on the bed.

"Here, have a seat," she offered.

"Thank you." Troy felt his heartbeat quicken when he sat next to her on the bed. Her cream-colored silk pajamas slid along her hips. Her top was partially unbuttoned. Troy felt a hard-on forming in his pants.

"I didn't see you at dinner."

"Most of the time I eat at St. Martin's on the north side. Besides, I'm on a diet."

"A diet? What the hell for?"

"I just need to drop a few pounds."

"I don't get it. You look fantastic."

"Thank you, but you wouldn't understand. You're a man."

Just then, the door swung open to reveal a tall, white, blue-eyed brunette. Her jeans and T-shirt were ordinary, but she was shapely. Troy had seen her on the second floor before.

"Hey," she said.

"Hi. Cyndi, this is Troy. Troy, this is my roommate Cyndi."

Troy stood up to shake her hand.

"Nice to meet you, Cyndi."

"You too, Troy."

"Were you at the hall meeting?"

"I was there, you just don't remember."

"You must have had something else on."

"Yes, but I did say my name like everyone else. Angel, is this the one you were telling me about?"

"If you must know, yes." Angel smiled. Troy was thrilled on the inside, but he remained cool. Angel had talked about him!

"Don't worry, I didn't say anything bad."

"She didn't," Cyndi confirmed. "Look, I just came to get my books, I'll be out of here in a minute."

"That's okay, you don't have to go," Troy insisted, though he hoped she would leave.

"No really, I have to. Angel, thanks for loaning me your cellular phone before."

"Sure," she replied. Angel lowered her eyes, embarrassed.

"You've got a mobile phone? Damn, people here are rich!"

"I have a friend who sells them. My mother worries about me, so she likes the phone."

"Must be nice."

"It's no big deal."

"Yeah. Um, listen. I was thinking maybe we could hook up over the weekend. There's this party."

"Over at Howard, right?"

"Yeah! You wanna go?"

"I'm afraid I can't. I have to go home this weekend."

"Oh. I see."

"Hey, it's not the end of the world. We'll hook up."

"That's cool. You know, I don't want to pressure you."

"You're not. That's why I like you."

Troy was at a loss for words. He had to strain to keep his eyes on her face and off her pajamas. Angel began to rub her hands over her knees, as if she knew she was being watched.

"Hey," Troy said, attempting to gather himself. "We'll talk later this week, right?"

"I hope so," Angel replied. I'll see you around."

"Yeah." Troy stood up. "Cyndi, it was a pleasure."

"Nice meeting you, Troy."

"You, too. Bye, Angel."

"Bye." Troy shut the door gently behind him. As he passed down the hall, he heard Angel and her roommate break into laughter.

Four

Troy and his friends settled into their respective routines, standing on line at the bookstore, gagging at how much their books cost, buying laundry tickets as they needed them while others bought enough to last them for weeks. Finally it dawned on Troy that he was attending school with rich kids. It was commonplace for them to spend hundreds of dollars on books, groceries, and whatever else they needed. Then they'd buy parking stickers and have their cars conveniently on campus, their tanks filled with premium gas. Troy was secretly disturbed to have his father's MasterCard. Although it was only for emergencies, to him it was a perverse violation of who he was. He never told Randy or Ill Will about it, afraid to be thought of differently. It wasn't that he didn't appreciate the card, which was the fruit of his father's hard work. His mother worked just as hard, but this was the type of luxury she couldn't provide. Troy now understood her impending return to New York for a better job; she had talked about it during the summer, but Troy's mind was consumed with getting out and starting school at that time. She always had trouble with any extra expense, including her son's college application fees. When Troy's gigantic school bills did come, he wouldn't be as concerned as his two buddies, but he could still relate. He had vivid memories of his mother's struggle to make ends meet, even when he was a small child. He was always somewhat detached from his father, who was a stranger in his and his mother's home. Conversations with his dad were strained, no more than mazes of polite inquiries that occasionally lead to mutual understanding. Despite his different problems with his mother, Troy considered himself her child.

After the first week of class, Troy retreated to his turntables in Room 228. Angel, home in Maryland for the weekend, was constantly on his mind. When he found out that Angel worked at Copy Services, he applied for a work-study job there. His boss, Adelaide Barnes, had said there weren't any shifts available, but Troy had returned each day and begged until she gave in. Ill Will would also be working there, having secured a slot weeks earlier. Adelaide Barnes was a sweet black woman who worked at Georgetown so her children could be educated for free. She could appreciate young brothers like Troy and Ill Will who, like her own sons, had to work to supplement their financial aid packages. Early the following week, Troy found himself helping Angel with the copy machines.

"There," he advised. "You just pull the paper out slowly when it jams."

"Thank you. You're pretty good at this."

"Yeah, well, Adelaide beat it into me." Angel laughed.

"Hey," Troy continued. "I looked for you last night. Didn't you come back to the dorm?"

"No, I just came back in the morning."

"Your family didn't want you to leave, huh?"

"It wasn't that. I wasn't ready to come back yet. I was just thinking about the semester and what it would be like, you know, if I'd make friends, stuff like that."

If she could make friends? *Jesus Christ*, Troy thought.

"You won't have any problem making friends. I'll be your..." Troy caught himself. He couldn't indicate he wanted to be anything but her lover.

"You're sweet. Look, my shift is over. You've been wonderful. See you later?"

"All right. See you later."

Troy could still smell her scent after she left. It was ridiculous to him that a girl who had everything to offer was so shy and unsure of herself. He couldn't have been the only guy who noticed her. He realized, with dread, that she probably had a boyfriend. Whoever he was, the bastard didn't deserve her.

*   *   *   *

Troy found time to meet with his mentor Latanya during the week. She was constantly extolling the value of Travis and the Office of Minority Affairs.

"I hear you, but I just can't fuck with Travis," Troy told his program assistant.

"Why not?"

"You wouldn't understand."

"Troy, listen. Lots of brothers have had run-ins with Travis. But in the end, he has their backs."

"I know what you're saying, but I'm just not there."

"All right," she told him. "But you're going to need Minority Affairs sooner or later."

"Yeah, well hopefully it'll be later."

When Friday rolled around, Troy and Randy returned from classes, eager to greet the weekend and pump up the volume. Ill Will headed for Westmiller's for malt liquor. When he and Troy prepared to pay for the beer, two uniformed police officers asked to see his identification. Ill Will thought quickly. He protested, saying that he always came there to buy alcohol.

"Is that right?" asked the policeman.

"Yep." Ill Will eyed the clerk, daring him to deny the accusation.

"Officer, it's okay," the clerk interrupted. "Really, it's all right. I know him."

Ill Will handed his Pennsylvania driver's license to the officer. Troy knew it was fake and looked away to keep from laughing. The policeman looked at it, then at Ill Will, then at the license again before finally giving it back.

*   *   *   *

By October, the phones were on in the dorms. Troy and Randy stayed on the line with their mothers and their friends from high school, inviting them to Georgetown. Troy couldn't wait for his friends from high school to visit, and he even looked forward to seeing Mimi at Georgetown, although he had no idea how to explain Angel. Ill Will ran around trying to speak German while Randy studied his political theory. Troy hung on to his balance sheets as best as he could, but breezed through English almost effortlessly. Different campus groups had begun to aggressively solicit membership. The Student Activities Commission (SAC) had hosted a fair in front of the Cultural Center a few weeks before. At the fair, new students were exposed to the different student clubs, which all had display tables, literature, and sign-up sheets. Randy got Troy interested in the Black Student Union and the NAACP, despite his early reservations. In high school he had been a member of the Ebony Awareness Club, which operated primarily as a social club, it's biggest achievement being a homecoming float. Would a black club at college be any different?

Sitting at the table was Darnell Washington, president of the Black Student Union.

"So, Darnell, what's on the agenda for this year?" Randy asked.

"We've got quite a few things lined up. We're having a party next weekend to raise money, for one thing. Each admission will be good for a membership. Are you guys coming?"

"Hell yeah!" Troy's antennae went up at the very mention of a party. "Who's the DJ?"

"DJ Breeze. He does all our parties."

Troy's excitement quickly evaporated. "Oh."

"Don't worry though. You'll get your chance."

"You should put him on, the boy is nice," Randy added. "But let's get back to the BSU. What else are you guys doing? I mean, why should we join up? What are you doing for our community here at Georgetown?"

Darnell became defensive. "What are you trying to say? Are you saying we don't do anything?"

"No, just that you may not be doing enough."

"It's only October, Randy. I don't know what you want when people don't even know us yet."

"It's all right brother," Randy assured him. "I'm not trying to give you a hard time. I'm sure you're doing a fine job. I'll talk to you about it at the next meeting."

"Sure."

They moved on to other tables at the fair. Troy had never been more impressed with his roommate, not even when he was about to fight Bizzy. His focus never swayed from black empowerment. What was he doing at Georgetown?

Michelyn and Latanya were seated at another table, where a huge banner marked "Black Expressions Dance Group" was hanging from the front. Troy was always happy to see Michelyn, regardless of why she was there.

"Hi, Michelyn!" Troy shouted, practically running over.

"Hey, Troy! Hi, Randy!"

"Good afternoon, sisters," Randy said, his eyes glued to Michelyn. As usual, her perfect smile and smooth, dark complexion captivated men.

"Good afternoon Randy," Latanya answered, sneering at Troy. He had been oblivious to her until that moment.

"So, uh, Latanya, you all dance?" Troy asked.

"Latanya does, but I may try out this year," Michelyn announced.

"Michelyn, I'm sure you'd do very well," Troy imagined her in tights and leotards.

"You're too kind."

"We could always use some men," Latanya told them.

"No thanks, we'll just come and see you."

"Don't worry," Latanya said. "We put on a really nice show. Chances are you'll be there, for the girls if nothing else."

"Latanya! Come on," Troy pleaded. "We'll be there for the culture!"

"Oh! Hi sweetie!" Michelyn called.

Troy turned to see who she was talking to. He couldn't believe who it was. He and Randy watched, dumbfounded, as Brian 'Bizzy' Hendricks came over and gave Michelyn a passionate kiss. Latanya was indifferent.

"Happens all the time," Latanya said. "Oh, I'm sorry. I guess y'all didn't know. Troy, pick your mouth up off the floor, it's not the end of the world."

The kiss finally ended. "So we're hooking up tonight, right baby?" Bizzy asked.

"Of course," Michelyn answered.

"Good." Bizzy turned and looked right at Troy.

"See you fools later."

*   *   *   *

Angel pierced the furthest corners of Troy's mind, and he knew he'd have to express himself soon. He was seeing less and less of her at the dorm, settling instead for fantasies in which they screwed ferociously against his door.

Troy set out to forget about Angel on the night of the first BSU party. Many students hadn't had a chance to unwind in weeks and this weekend to them was like a holiday. For party animals like Troy, Randy and Ill Will, it was the same old story. They made their way to the site of the party, Village C Lounge. They didn't expect the party to really start until midnight, but this way they'd see what kind of girls were there and size up the overall potential of the evening. Both Troy and Randy remembered their agreement about use of the room. The first weekend was permanently embedded in Troy's memory. He could have invited one of his girls from Howard, but there was no point. There were already enough girls to dance with, and he didn't feel like hearing the "why don't you come pick me up" speech.

"Too bad you're not doing the party," Randy told Troy.

"Don't worry," Troy told him. "I will be. Besides, this DJ Breeze kid is supposed to be good."

"One thing's for sure," Ill Will added, "there's plenty of women out here."

"So?" Randy huffed. "You and Yvonne are practically married."

"Maybe, but I can look."

A mob surrounded the doors to the lounge. The music was blasting and people tried to look in before biting the bullet and paying. Taking the initiative, the trio paid their admission and went inside. In seconds their money was gone, their names went on a list, and they stood in a large room with half the other freshmen who also weren't patient enough to wait.

"Maybe we should have waited," Randy lamented.

"Fuck it, it's still early," Ill Will said.

DJ Breeze was doing a good job with the music, blending the latest rap and R&B songs. Nonetheless, Troy was far from impressed. He and Randy noticed every female that walked by, as they did whenever they hit a party together. For the most part, the ladies were dressed to kill, flaunting stockings, pumps and matching accessories. But for others, a snug pair of jeans was all it took to get the brothers' heads turning. Before long, sisters from Georgetown, Howard and all over D.C. were piling in. A few upperclassmen made their way in, the majority of whom were also female. The women received a heartfelt "Goddamn!" from the lips of one drunk student as they walked in.

By 11:30, DJ Breeze was only playing rap music and the dance floor was full of partygoers. Randy and Ill Will were on the floor with two girls and Troy began his search for a dance partner. There was a truckload of girls he knew, but they were his classmates and there was no challenge in getting them to dance. He wanted someone he'd never met before. After a few minutes, he found her, smiling brightly enough to blind someone. Troy returned her smile with one of his own. She wore a tight-fitting pair of designer jeans, showing off a firm, round butt. Troy wanted to ask which building she'd jumped from to get into the jeans, but he didn't want to offend her. Even in the dimly lit room he could see she had beautiful skin and took excellent care of herself. He couldn't wait any longer to approach her because "Rebel Without A Pause" from Public Enemy was on. Troy walked up, presented his right hand, and off they went. It was no surprise to him that she was a natural on the dance floor; she'd been moving her head to the beat from the moment he saw her. Before he could think of what to say, she began the conversation.

"You go to Georgetown?"

"Yeah, but don't hold it against me."

"Now why would I hold it against you?"

"I know how you Howard women are."

"And how do you know I go to Howard?"

"What school do you go to?"

"Howard, but that's not the point."

There was the blinding grin again. *Oh boy*, Troy thought, *we got a live one here.*

They danced for over an hour. In between songs Troy learned her name, Ronnie, and that she was a freshman like him. He was getting hot and tired of dancing, but he didn't want Ronnie to think he was leaving or trying to get rid of her, so he kept going. The room got more crowded and stuffy. His pride gave way to the heat.

"Do you mind if I go to my room and change my shirt?"

"No, I could use a little fresh air myself."

"Cool."

Without another word, Troy headed for the door with Ronnie's hand in his. Noticing the girl, someone let out an emphatic "Oh shit!" then let out a loud yell.

"TRRROY! TRRROY!"

Troy and Ronnie made it out the door before the heckler could draw much more attention to them. Ronnie looked up at the stars and at the buildings on campus. They both remarked at how nice it was to be outside breathing fresh air. Troy kept the conversation going until they reached the front doors of Harbin Hall.

"What's that sign on the door?" Ronnie asked, pointing to the notepad.

"Oh, 4-H," Troy answered. "That's our little crew."

"I see. There are four of you?"

"No, just three. 4-H is for 'Hellified Homeboys of Harbin Hall,'" he announced proudly.

Troy fumbled with the key for about ten seconds. Opus wasn't on the notepad, so Troy figured he had the room to himself and he did. The plants and the prayer rug were on display, and the fridge even had some juice in it. Ronnie took in an eyeful, from the message board on the door to the needles on the twin turntables.

"Who's the DJ?"

"Me."

"You have to make me a tape." *Yeah, whatever,* Troy thought.

Troy waited for his guest to finish surveying the room. Now he had a much better view of the girl, who had the vivacious build that Troy suspected she had. He offered her some juice and while she drank, he pretended to look for a shirt, thinking that by the time he came up with the shirt, she'd be too comfortable to go anywhere.

No sooner did he head for his drawer than Ronnie requested that he put some music on. With all the records he had, she left him with a decision that he didn't want to make. On top of that, there was no sense in taking a chance on a selection she didn't like.

"I'll tell you what. Pick out a record and I'll put it on."

"What do you want to hear?"

"Look. I live here. You're the guest. It's not about what I want to hear."

"Yeah, but you have so many records, I...fine, I'll go and pick one."

Ronnie got back up and walked over to the crates to pick out some music. She bent over at a 90-degree angle to look at the album titles, her plump, heart-shaped behind directly in front of him. Troy was in awe of the view before him; he quickly pulled on his jogging pants to keep his erection from sticking out. Ronnie put on a Luther Vandross album, *The Night I Fell In Love.* Sauntering to "If Only For One Night," she slowly made her way back to the bed.

Stick a fork in her, Troy thought, *'cause she's done.*

Ronnie looked right at him and he returned the stare. By now there was only one light on, and it was on Randy's side of the room. Two or three inches separated their faces and she was in his arms. The idea was to look at her and communicate without saying a word. Maybe she'd read his mind. Apparently picking up Troy's telepathy, she began singing along with Luther. *"I won't tell a soul,"* she whispered, nibbling on Troy's earlobe. *"No-ooo one has to know..."*

She tried to finish, but his tongue was in her mouth midway through the second verse.

Now this was the way to start a weekend.

Troy laid Ronnie down on the bed, then got up to start the record at the beginning and turned off the light. In the dark, he resumed his position over her. He began undressing her, meeting no resistance. Her top came off easily, but her jeans took some extra effort. He could see why when he finally got them off. Lord, was this going to be fun.

BOOM BOOM BOOM! Troy looked toward the door. *Must be Randy,* Troy thought, *making sure nobody was in here.* No problem, he'd just tell him that he'd forgotten to use their signal and he had a guest.

"Troy? Troy are you in there?"

It was a girl's voice.

BOOM BOOM BOOM BOOM BOOM!

"Troy! Open the door!"

Troy froze when he recognized the voice.

"Who is it?" he squeaked.

"Angel and Cyndi!"

Damn it! he thought. Ronnie's jeans were almost off.

"Stay still," he whispered to her. Ronnie shook with suppressed laughter.

"Uhhh, what's the matter?" he yelled.

"Nothing! I just want to talk!"

"Look, I'm sleep! Why don't you come by in the morning?" He couldn't hide the panic in his voice. The record was still on, so he yelled to drown out Luther's crooning.

"C'mon, honey! I've seen you in your underwear before!" *But not in Ronnie's,* Troy thought. He could hear Cyndi snickering outside.

"Nah, not like this!" Now he had to cup Ronnie's mouth to keep her from laughing out loud.

"Look, I'm sleep. I'll talk to you later, okay?" Cyndi's snickering got louder.

"Oh, okay. I'll talk to you later."

"You bought that?" Troy heard Cyndi say as they left. "Sleeping? Give me a break, on a Friday night? You idiot, he's got someone in there!"

"No. Not Troy. If he says he's sleeping, he's sleeping."

Troy could hear the two of them arguing the point on their way down the hall. For a moment, he took comfort in Angel's defense of him. He could feel Ronnie under him, but he was too frazzled to respond and felt a sudden urge to urinate, as if he hadn't gone to the bathroom in days.

Angel's surprise visit was more than enough to destroy the mood Troy had worked so hard to create. Although Ronnie was not at all angry, she wasn't half-naked on the bed anymore either. They both got dressed to the sound of the needle skipping at the end of the Luther Vandross record. Ronnie smiled, looking at her host and shaking her head.

"Sorry," he sighed.

"That's okay. I had a wonderful time."

"Listen, um, I can go back to Howard with you if you want. You know, maybe we can get something to eat on the way. The night's still young."

Ronnie smiled to keep from laughing.

"I don't think so. Why don't you work on getting me a cab, okay?"

Troy offered to walk Ronnie to the front gates, but she declined, opting for the taxi to come directly to Harbin. In the few minutes before the cab came, Troy tried desperately to persuade Ronnie to stay, but the magic was gone. She left him with a warm hug, a long, full-bodied kiss, and a raging erection. After she walked off, Troy sat still on the bench just outside the front door. Finally, he dragged his dejected body back to his room. With the lights off and the turntable still on, he fell asleep on his back with the needle making a light popping noise over "The Night I Fell In Love."

*   *   *   *

The news of Troy's evening had Randy and Ill Will laughing for hours on Saturday.

"Now see, if you had let somebody know," Randy advised, "we could have run interference for you."

"Yeah," Ill Will added. "4-H is supposed to stick together."

"There wasn't time," Troy insisted. "It just happened."

"Wait a minute brother," Randy said. "Tell me again. Angel was at the door…"

"I had the girl's panties halfway down when she started knocking."

Randy and Ill Will tried to respond, but their speech decomposed into laughter. Troy could only wince at his own memories of Friday night.

There was no more time to waste with Angel. Everyone else knew how he felt; Cyndi and his boys insisted that she liked him, but none of them could explain her flaky behavior. Still, in his mind Angel was the girl for him, so he'd put it to her and that would be it. At least then he could move on.

Five

"Mmm," Troy said as he chewed. "Mrs. Davis, this is incredible."

"*Gracias,*" Angel's mother replied. "You've never had *arroz con pollo,* eh?"

"I have, but not like this." Angel beamed at the compliment. After much insistence from Troy, she had agreed to let him come home with her. Her mother, who was Dominican, had invited him to stay for dinner.

"C'mon, Ma, everyone's had chicken and rice before."

"Sure, Angel. You know everyone, hm?"

"No, Ma. Not everyone. Troy, let's go in the living room."

They had traveled for over an hour on the train and the bus to get there. Because Angel was always so well-dressed, Troy hadn't been prepared for the modest apartment where Angel's family lived. The complex reminded Troy of his old block in Harlem, except the buildings were smaller and more widespread, separated by lawns with small trees. Angel's two younger sisters stayed there along with her mother. Her father, who was black, was out.

"Don't forget to thank your mother for the food," Troy told her.

"I won't. She was glad to have someone else to cook for." There was a 12-inch TV on in the living room, providing the only light. He could hear Angel's mother and sisters washing dishes in the kitchen, speaking Spanish. Angel moved closer to Troy on the couch.

"So, *papi.*"

"So." Troy prayed his nervousness wouldn't show.

"Not everything you expected, is it?"

"What? Your place is cool."

"Maybe, but it's small. Maria and Lindsay are getting big. They want their own rooms and clothes."

"Where's your dad?"

"He's at work. He's always working. He does maintenance. Cleans offices during the day, cleans offices at night."

"Hmm. Well that explains how he keeps you looking good," he observed, touching her gold earrings.

"No, dear, that's all me."

"Yeah, right. I know where you work, you know."

"Yes, but I worked at Nordstrom's all through high school. My friends still give me discounts."

"I see," Troy replied. He thought she might be lying, but she looked so good that he couldn't disapprove. "Your family must be very proud of you."

"I don't know why."

"Come on. You're doing just fine, taking care of your own. Besides, you got into Georgetown, didn't you?"

"Yeah, but staying in. That's the problem."

"It's nothing you can't handle."

Angel smiled. Troy was getting used to seeing that smile. "You say the sweetest things, Troy."

"That's not hard to do when you're around. Angel, do you, do you have a…"

"Boyfriend?"

Troy held his breath.

"I'm flattered, but I don't think you should worry about that now."

"Angel, what does that mean?"

"Nothing. Only that I need a little time."

Troy turned away. He had not been prepared for such a letdown. Angel took his hand.

"Look at it this way. If anything, you're here with me. You think I let anyone in here? Hm?" She took his hand.

"No. No, I guess not."

"That's right. Now you've got to get back to campus. I know you've got studying to do."

"Yeah, and so do you."

"I know. Come on, I'll walk you to the bus stop."

Troy said goodbye to Angel's family and let Angel lead him back to the bus stop. It was dark, but little children were everywhere, riding bikes and playing in the grass. He wanted to continue the conversation, but a bus appeared as soon as they arrived at the stop.

"Call me when you get back, okay?" Angel asked.

"What, on your cell phone?"

"Don't be a smart ass."

"Bye."

"Bye, sweetie." He reached for a kiss, but Angel touched his lips with her index finger. The bus driver gave a loud honk.

"Honey, the bus is waiting."

Reluctantly, Troy got on the bus back to Washington D.C. *Goddamn Metro*, he thought. He bet if he had come to her house in a car, she would have kissed him. He tried to study his Accounting on the way back, but he could only think of the past few hours. Angel had opened herself up to him, to some extent, but he still didn't know where he stood. What was all that 'don't worry' stuff? Troy knew bullshit when he heard it. Some other guy was probably the real source of all those clothes and the mobile phone. She probably just worked to keep her parents happy. Still, just as she said, he had been in her home, and he couldn't offer her such high-priced gifts. He hoped his love would suffice. He thought of consulting Randy and Ill Will for some perspective, but he was too embarrassed. Besides, they probably thought Angel was just another girl.

*　　　*　　　*　　　*

A couple of days later Troy stood in the lobby of the library, waiting on his new tutor. When Wendell approached him, Troy thought he was just saying hello.

"I'm just chillin', waiting on my Accounting tutor."

"I know. You ready?"

"For what?"

"To get started."

"You're my tutor?"

"Mmm-hm. Accounting major."

Troy was accustomed to seeing Wendell clowning around with his frat brothers, and mostly in social settings on campus. He was surprised to find that Wendell was disciplined, and in this instance, consistent with the academic setting of college. They dived straight into the material and the senior did his best to salvage what was left of Troy's time in the class. It became clear to Troy that he may not have studied hard enough in general during the past weeks. Now he had to give more effort to Accounting just to keep up, let alone do well. As for Euro Civ, he had no excuse, but it was simply a boring class to Troy. If only all of his classes were like Novel/Short Story. This course presented no problems because it required little besides reading and speaking up in class. Troy considered his contributions to class discussions sincere and thoughtful. Professor Larson tended to agree with him most of the time, so Troy concluded he must be a skilled talker. That skill couldn't transfer to other courses, but given a chance, it just might transfer to Angel.

Troy longed for the comfort of his room, but he knew he was doing the right thing. *What the hell,* he thought. Except for Randy and Ill Will, the academic success of other students never concerned Troy. Ill Will was doing badly in German, but he was determined to improve. Randy had maybe one "C" in Microeconomics, but he said that for his class, that was good. All three of them had put the constant party-hopping on hold.

"Troy!"

"Huh? Oh, what's up, Wendell?"

"Look, I'm not getting paid that much to do this. The only reason I took the job is because you're my boy. Now this is serious, it's almost time for finals. You fuck around and you won't even pass. You can't afford to be sitting up here daydreaming."

"My fault, my fault."

"S'alright. Let's go over this again, and pay attention this time."

Later that day, Troy sat at the desk alone, trying to decide how best to overcome the seemingly endless work that lay ahead of him. With only a few weeks left before finals, nobody wanted to get caught unawares the way midterm exams had caught many Georgetown freshmen. Troy remembered Travis Gordon's speech about the burnout phenomenon that showed up in mid-October, when freshmen became homesick and tired of school. Troy wasn't burned out, but he did wish he was somewhere else, a place where all this work didn't exist. Still, there was a price for everything. Besides, it wouldn't have been cool to be expelled for academic shortcomings. Hard as it was, now was the time to remember the real reason he was supposed to be there. He and the rest of the 4-H Crew resigned themselves to actually doing something productive on Saturdays: studying. A transformation in all of them had gradually occurred.

Troy's free moments were few and far between, but during those times he could be found mixing in his room. The black freshmen talked about buying tapes from him, but no one was committed enough to buy any. Admittedly, people were studying and there wasn't much time to sit around listening to rap music. Troy didn't mind; in fact he was glad that word was getting around about his mixing. Ill Will was just as enterprising; making and selling fake IDs to freshmen who wanted to buy liquor or get into nightclubs; that is, when he wasn't at Copy Services or trying to speak German. Randy had no side operations, but he was always involved in some political debate. Study sessions with him and his classmates often became passionate discussions about the state of democracy, religion, race. Members of the student government knew Randy, not just the black student groups. His voice on campus quickly moved beyond Harbin Hall and the freshman class.

The following Friday afternoon Angel was scheduled to work at Copy Services. Troy came in to find a note with his name on it. Recognizing her handwriting, he tore open the envelope. It was a slow day, so he began to read her letter. Adelaide was oblivious, wrapped up in a newspaper. Troy sat there with his letter, happy as a kid finding money on the sidewalk. Before actually reading it, he closely inspected the letter itself. It was typewritten on blue paper, the kind of paper available only at Copy Services. Troy settled down to read his newly acquired, prized possession.

Dear Troy,

I can't tell you how happy I am to have met you. When I first got here, I wasn't sure if I'd fit in at all, much less meet a wonderful guy like you. If you weren't here, I'm not sure if I could stay. I'm really glad you've become a part of my life, you don't even know what that means to me. Nobody makes me feel the way you do, nobody. I know we have some things to talk about, and I know I have some explaining to do. You want to know how I feel and I don't blame you.

Basically, I love you to death. You are one of the nicest, sweetest, funniest guys I've ever met. The problem is I'm sort of involved with a guy from Howard who I've been talking to for a little while. This thing with you just happened, and I wasn't sure what to do. I kept asking myself, where were you three weeks ago? This is just a case of bad timing. If Kenneth hadn't come along when he did, I'd be yours, that is if that's what you wanted. But now he's kind of in the picture and right now I'm not prepared to deal with the both of you. I don't know what else to tell you except that I don't want to lose you. Please try to understand, it's just one of those things. You'll always be my special friend, and maybe more. But for now, I have to see this through. I hope you know I'll still be here for you! Let me know if you want to talk, I'll be in my room. Love, Angel.

Her words froze him in his place; what he suspected was now confirmed fact. The facts stared at him from the paper like anxious executioners. She had a boyfriend, and it wasn't him. Troy had treated her like royalty, and she wanted to be with someone else. He made her laugh constantly, and she wanted to be with someone else. He made her feel good about herself, and she wanted to be with someone else. When Troy heard that nice guys finish last, he didn't believe it at first; now he knew that the phrase included him. He was nauseous and quickly headed for the men's room.   In front of the sink he took deep breaths, attempting to calm his stomach. He just needed some cold water — if he splashed his face with water, he'd be fine. Then he could return to read the letter again. Maybe there was something he missed.

By the sixteenth read, Troy was deep in analysis. 'Where were you three weeks ago?' What did she mean, where was he? He was probably out trying to find her! Then again, three weeks ago was right around the time of the party when Ronnie was in his room. Was that why she couldn't face him? Maybe she knew after all. Every possible explanation for Angel's behavior went through his mind, taking him away from what the letter said. She had a man. According to her, Troy was nice, sweet, funny and she really enjoyed spending time with him, but she had someone else and that was it. Love, Angel.

All those weekend runaway trips, all that time away from Harbin, away from him, and she was with some other kid. It figured, too. Here he was thinking he'd found the one, placing no one, really nothing, above her, and now this. He knew Angel would have made any sane man happy, but she had to have had some idea of how he felt — at least by now she did. When they did see each other, they talked extensively and she never mentioned this guy. She never talked about him and Cyndi never said anything. And then she said she hadn't been with him for that long! What could this guy possibly have that he didn't?

"Something wrong with you, boy?" Adelaide asked.

"Huh? Oh, no ma'am."

"Can't you see you have a customer?" Adelaide pointed at the counter. Troy looked up to find Darnell Washington, who rang the bell.

"Dude! Come on man, I don't have all day."

"Sorry, Darnell. What do you need?"

"You should like this. Flyers for the next BSU meeting."

Troy faked a smile. "This too?" he asked, pointing at a form.

"Nah, that's a purchase order. I got that. Can you get these done in an hour?"

"Sure, no problem."

"Cool. Oh, and bill it to Minority Affairs. You'll find the number in Adelaide's file. Oh, Hi Mrs. Barnes."

"Hello, Darnell. How is everything?"

"Great. You take care, all right?"

"You, too. Troy, make sure Darnell gets what he needs."

"Yes ma'am," Troy mumbled.

Darnell's visit did nothing for Troy's mood. *How does he know about Adelaide's file?* he thought. *Guess he used to work here.* Troy had been sitting like a lump at his desk, paralyzed with dejection while Adelaide extracted crumpled pages from inside the Xerox machine. He reread the letter ten or twelve more times, determined to find meaning but always came up with the same unsatisfying result. A guy from Howard, she said. A guy who couldn't have much to offer, because she made it clear that if not for Kenneth, she'd be his. The only thing Kenneth had over Troy apparently was timing, and if timing was that important, there was surely more to Angel than she had let on.

"Boy, go on home," his boss advised. "It sure don't look like you're doing any work."

"No, no, Mrs. Barnes, really. I can finish my shift."

"You've obviously got something on your mind. What's going on?"

"Everything is fine."

Adelaide smiled. "Mm-hm, sure. I can see you don't feel like talking. But listen to me."

Troy turned around. He had never seen this side of Adelaide.

"Boy, this is not an easy thing you're going through, not at any school. You've got to find what's working for you, and whatever's not."

"Yes, ma'am."

"Listen, Troy," she continued. "The things that work for you don't always feel good. And the things that feel good ain't always right. Now whatever's troubling you is something you got to get through, like it or not." The woman chuckled. "Probably ain't nearly as bad as you think."

Troy hated to admit it, but he actually felt better.

"Trying to tell you what I know," she added.

"Thanks, Mrs. Barnes."

"Anytime. Now go'on."

Troy thought of Adelaide's words while in his room, but he still hadn't figured anything out. He knew nothing about this Kenneth except that he was a Howard student, and so he really couldn't have had a lot that Troy didn't, except maybe a ride and a lot of cash. Troy was proud of the fact that he didn't need status to attract girls, particularly now that he was in college. He wasn't a basketball star and he certainly wasn't built like an athlete, but he felt that whatever shortcomings he had, he more than made up for in personality. Girls always seemed to have fun around him, so he never had reason to think he lacked anything until now. Usually Troy could think quickly on his feet and knew the right thing to say and when to say it, or so he thought. None of his previous encounters with Angel had prepared him for this. While he was heartbroken, Troy couldn't shake one thought: if she chose someone over him after being with him, either something was wrong with her or he wasn't getting the whole truth. He wasn't rich and he didn't have a car, but so what? He didn't attend Howard, but he went to the same school as she did! Maybe Georgetown boys weren't cool enough for her.

"Who's cooler than me?" he wondered aloud. It was impossible.

Randy entered the room.

"S'up, brother?"

"S'up."

"What's wrong?"

"Nothing."

"Angel's fucking up, huh?"

"That's about the size of it."

"Don't worry about it."

To Troy's relief, Randy began studying at his desk — he really didn't want to discuss the matter further. At his own desk, Troy exchanged Angel's letter for his Euro Civ book. Angel's letter would go inside the cover of his Pre-Calculus book from high school, right next to Ronnie's note of weeks ago. On that fateful night, along with her phone number, Ronnie left a note saying "Remember – It's Real..."

What the fuck, he thought. He didn't know which way was up, let alone what was real. He still needed to study, regardless of what was or wasn't going on in his love life. Randy and Ill Will didn't seem to have trouble disciplining themselves, or at least Randy didn't. Then again, neither of them had found an Angel. Troy sat at his desk with his book and his highlighter, determined to be productive. He finally began and was soon deep into 13th century European history. When he was satisfied that he had a handle on the chapter, he got up to take a walk around the floor.

The second floor now had a normal mid-week quiet time, a sure sign its occupants were trying to study. Troy wanted to see what Ill Will was up to, but neither he nor Carl was in their room. With his rounds completed, he was still restless. He was willing to do anything to forget about Angel. When he returned to his room, he quickly grabbed the telephone to make some calls. It was about time he checked on Ronnie anyway.

"Hello?"

"Hello, Ronnie?"

"Who is this?"

"It's Troy. From Georgetown."

"Oh, hi! How are you?"

Troy could hear her giggling, probably remembering the events during the night of the party. He didn't mind; it was good to hear her voice.

"Chillin'. Thinking about you."

"Really. Then what took you so long to call?"

Troy chuckled. "Hey, don't be like that."

"No, I know, you've been busy."

"What are you doing?"

"Studying. In fact, I was about to ask if I could call you back."

"Oh, no problem, no problem. Call me tomorrow, all right?"

"All right. I'll talk to you soon."

"Bye."

The more Troy went through his phone book, the more he realized how little attention he'd paid to the other girls he'd met. In his heart, he had been sure he'd be with Angel, so he hadn't gotten to know the girls he had met at parties. After a couple of weeks, they hadn't seemed worth the trouble. That cavalier attitude came back to haunt him now. He could have called a number of his boys from high school or his mother, but he wanted a girl on the line. After more fruitless attempts, he sat in bed with the receiver in his hand. Troy watched his roommate study and listened to the silence in their room. As if he was reading Troy's mind, Randy closed his books.

"Couldn't get anybody on the phone?"

"Nah."

"Yeah, me neither. That's why I started studying!"

Troy laughed.   After a few minutes, he was able to forget his disappointment.   Since they'd all been hitting the books, the 4-H Crew hadn't really talked lately.   Troy barely even saw Ill Will at work because their class schedules differed.   Troy told Randy about Angel's letter, and he recounted to Troy his recent troubles getting girls into their room. They all talked about coming to visit Randy and left messages for him on their notepad, but lately Randy hadn't been that lucky.   Before long, they were reminiscing about girls from high school, and Troy considered inviting Mimi for a visit.

"She won't front," Troy told his friend.

"I hear you," Randy replied.   "When in doubt, call an old girlie."

The boys laughed at their own pathetic state of mind, and thinking it appropriate, Randy put on a Billie Holiday record, to echo their own sense of unrequited lover's lament.

Six

Classes ended earlier in the week leaving nothing much to do but show up for work and prepare for finals. Troy, Randy and Ill Will decided to take a study break. Since it was too cold to go anywhere, the three of them and Yvonne planned to stay in and play cards. Ill Will was drinking, but by then they were all oblivious to it. The four of them were arranged in a circle on the floor of Room 228.

"All right you clowns. Me and my woman against you two."

"Yeah, yeah, you know you gonna get waxed. Just deal."

"Randy, you talk a whole lotta shit for somebody with no skills."

"Boy, you crazy! I was playing spades when you were still in the womb!"

"Please. I'm older than you!"

"Dear, would you just deal the cards?" asked Yvonne.

Admiration was all over Yvonne's face as she watched her boyfriend deal. Ill Will, with a mouthful of tobacco, spat in his cup constantly. Randy put on the "Criminal Minded," album from Boogie Down Productions. Each hand was a hilarious adventure; everyone adding a little drama to his or her bidding and dealing. Ill Will kept drinking, and before long, Yvonne was helping him finish the corner of vodka that was left in the bottle. As the hours passed, Ill Will became less rambunctious and vocal and his eyelids began to droop. For the first time since Troy had known him, he thought Ill Will may have had too much to drink. His plastic cup was nearly full of an absolutely gross mixture of tobacco and spit. While reaching to take the last tip from the half-gallon bottle of vodka, he knocked the cup over, spilling the brown goo in front of him onto the beige rug.

"Aw dammit man, will you look at that?" Randy shouted.

"I told you about that damned tobacco in here!" Troy barked. "Randy, get my rag from off the bookshelf."

"Oh, pipe down." Ill Will muttered as he sat still, head bowed, his eyes half closed.

"Pipe down my ass!" Randy said. "Look at the rug, fool! Yvonne, hand me that dish detergent, please?" The carpet was ruined, but its owners, in denial, were determined to save it. Randy darted into the bathroom to wet a rag. Totally focused on the giant tobacco spit stain, Troy squeezed *Palmolive* onto the middle of the rug.

"I think you might have overdone it this time, know what I'm saying?"

Silence.

"Motherfucker, listen to me when I'm talking to you!"

A silent Ill Will was so strange to Troy that he turned from his rug cleaning to face him. Ill Will hadn't moved or spoken since the cup spilled, he only kneeled on the floor. He usually indulged heavily on weekends, but never with this kind of result.

"Honey, are you all right?" Yvonne asked.

"Shut up."

An abrupt swing of Ill Will's right arm caught Yvonne square in the face, which sent her reeling across the room. The foot of Randy's bed broke her fall. Troy tackled him and they both landed onto the slippery stain.

"Did you see what you just did? Did you see that?"

Troy was screaming at the top of his lungs, hoping to bring Ill Will back down to earth. He remained silent. Yvonne let out a thunderous scream. *Shit*, Troy thought. *If not for the damned soap and spit on the rug, I'd have some leverage.* Ill Will was breaking his hold on him. Randy returned to find Ill Will struggling to break free of Troy's grip.

"Get him!" Troy yelled. Randy was immobilized by shock. Ill Will wiggled out one arm and grabbed the vodka bottle. Troy grabbed his wrist, but he still couldn't stop him from flinging the bottle into the air. The bottle hit the ceiling, raining vodka and broken glass all over the room. Randy ran over to shield Yvonne from the fallout.

"Why are they fighting?" Yvonne sat trembling, in tears. A huge welt had formed on her face.

"He's fucked up!" Troy shouted. "He just smacked the shit out of her! We've got to knock him out!"

"No!" Yvonne cried.

People were gathering at the front door. Randy jumped in and the three of them rolled around in the slick brown pool that the carpet had become. Troy was having the damnedest time containing Ill Will alone, and he seemed to get stronger with Randy on him. They bumped into Troy's dresser hard and the impact knocked open his cabinet, causing his *Drakkar Noir* to fall out. When the cologne hit Troy's desk, more pieces of glass burst onto the floor. Randy was on the right side of Ill Will, with

Troy on his left. But Troy was being thrown to the ground, then back against the dresser, with Ill Will's one free arm! Troy now knew what was meant by the phrase 'the devil's in him.' Satan had indeed made his home in a vodka bottle that night. Ill Will never said a word, he never even blinked. With all of his weight on it, Troy pinned Ill Will's arm behind his back. Just when he thought the roommates thought they had restrained their friend, he slipped out from their grasp. Randy was losing his grip, too.

"Grab his legs!" he yelled.

"I got him!"

But in reality, Ill Will's legs were stronger than Troy's arms. It took everything Troy had to control his kicking. Troy could feel the sting of broken glass in his arm, and a warm liquid covering his back. Randy had one arm, but he was slipping and sliding on his knees. When Randy slipped, Ill Will shoved him into the bench where Troy's stereo equipment sat. Ill Will rolled over, taking Troy with him on top of the tobacco stain. Randy quickly recovered, but was met with a chair hurtling towards him like a baseball.

"Holy shit, did you see that?" asked a student in the doorway.

"Somebody call campus security, for Christ's sake!" another student shouted. "He's gonna kill someone!"

"Who started it?" asked another student.

"I don't know, but it's pretty bad. Their room is like, wrecked."

"Goddammit, call security! That's it, I'm calling. Where's Andrea?"

"Nooo!" Yvonne cried. "He'll get expelled! Nooo!"

"Yvonne, shut the fuck up!" Troy shouted. Randy was floored once again, this time with a chair on top of him. With his arms free, Ill Will was pulling out Randy's dresser drawers and flinging them away as if they were weightless. Troy and Randy were witnessing superhuman strength. Room 228 was a shambles. In her delirium, Yvonne ran over and grabbed Ill Will's arm. Her lower lip was bleeding badly. An incensed Randy stood over the three of them.

"Yvonne, get back!"

"No! Nooo! Don't—"

"Shut the fuck up and get back!" Troy yelled. "You wanna get hit again?"

Yvonne refused to let go of her boyfriend. Randy tried fruitlessly to peel Yvonne off of him while Troy held Ill Will's legs with all his might.

Her screaming only encouraged Troy and Randy to scream at her more. Meanwhile, Ill Will punched Yvonne in the mouth again with frightening force. Since Randy was behind her trying to pull her away, she was vulnerable. She let out another loud wail from her bleeding mouth.

"That's it. I got his legs. Randy, get him up top and I'll come around."

"Nooo!" Yvonne wailed. "Willard!"

"If you don't shut up, I'll knock both of you out!" Randy shouted. "Yvonne, get out the way!"

Yvonne, too, had newfound strength. She was glued to Ill Will, punches and all, and Randy couldn't seem to move her. Because Yvonne threw herself at Ill Will, Randy couldn't get a good shot at him. Neither of them wanted him hurt, but in their minds there was no other way to subdue him. Randy finally got a hold of Ill Will's free arm, and now the four of them were squirming on the rug, on which Troy could see Yvonne's blood.

"Yvonne, get back!" Randy insisted. "You're not helping!"

"Get the fuck back!" Troy added.

"Fuck it, I'm knocking 'em both out!"

Randy attempted to hold Ill Will with one arm and swing with the other. Yvonne stayed in front, guarding him relentlessly. The murmur of the small crowd by the door escalated to screaming and shouting. The newest screamer burst forth.

"Oh my God!" The familiar voice of Carl clouded the room. "What happened?"

"Vodka, what do you think?" Troy shouted.

"Carl, help me get Yvonne off him!" Randy instructed. "Then the three of us can hold him!"

"Okay, but watch out! There's broken glass on the floor!"

"Just shut the fuck up and help him please!" As far as Troy was concerned, the sooner Yvonne was out of the room the better.

Randy and Carl began to tug away at Yvonne again while Carl politely asked her to come with him to his room. Her lower lip was hideously swollen now, as if it had met with the force of a baseball bat. Their neighbors were cheering them on, hoping for Yvonne's sake that she'd get out of the fray. She continued to perform like a woman possessed, screaming as loudly as she could. Troy was left with the task of containing Ill Will in some way. They had been sliding back and forth in the muddy mixture on the rug and both of them had cuts from the broken bottles. Troy loosened his grip to move up to Ill Will's waist and he was now trying to drive him into a corner. Ill Will was still too much for him, responding with books, sneakers or whatever else he could launch into Troy's face. They were silent, but the room was as noisy as a crowded playground.

Randy quickly jumped back into the melee after helping to get Yvonne to safety.

"Where's Carl?" Troy asked.

"He ran off as soon as Yvonne was out of here," Randy shouted.

"Punk ass."

Randy reached under Will's armpits, applying a full Nelson. Troy moved back down to his legs, at least then he could keep him from rumbling all over the floor. The carpet reeked with the outrageous stench of tobacco and sweat. Ill Will's flexing muscles shook both of his opponents, but Troy and Randy held on. He didn't appear tired at all.

"Whenever either one of us gets a shot," Randy called.

"I got it," Troy said. "Only to the head."

Troy pounded Will's knees and calves, but since he was also holding him, there wasn't enough wind behind the blows. The faint buzz of static by the door grew louder and more insistent. Briefly distracted from the bullfight with his drunk friend, Troy recognized the sound as walkie-talkie commands. Someone had called campus security after all.

"Okay fellas, just hold on to him." The officers slowly entered the room, stopping short of the mixture of broken glass and stains.

"It's not that easy," Troy told them.

"Yeah, why don't you come help?" Randy asked.

"No need to get smart. If you need some help, that's all you had to say."

One officer was white, the other black. Two other white officers were by the door, interviewing the witnesses. The silent Ill Will still wasn't the least bit subdued even while Randy had a vise-like grip on his upper body, around his neck and under his left arm. Troy held his thighs on the floor, keeping him off balance.

The black officer came forward and bent over, putting his weight on Ill Will's feet. He was at least six-three and probably weighed 225 pounds.

"Okay, just keep holding him down."

"Watch the glass," Troy warned. The cop's weight brought another quick surge of 'Incredible Hulk'-like energy from Ill Will, and all three of them were forced to move with him and hold their grip. Then the second officer came forward.

"Jesus Christ, pretty strong dude we got here." He was shorter and stockier, but still very fit. He appeared to be a slightly younger than the black officer, and his long dark hair fell over his face when he moved forward.

"Now let's just see if—" The white cop was interrupted by a wild swing of Ill Will's right arm. His last free limb reached for the officer's neck.

"Whoa, hey, now take it easy, pal." The white officer grabbed Ill Will's arm with both hands and swiftly pinned his arm down. With Randy, two campus security officers and Troy holding on, Ill Will could not move. Troy could feel his friend's uncanny strength under his arms, but he was finally immobilized.

"This should do it," quipped the good-humored white cop.

"Hey Tommy, are the GERMS guys here yet?" The black officer called to another officer at the door.

"Yeah, they're out in the hallway." GERMS, Georgetown Emergency Response Medical Service, was the school's student-operated ambulance service.

"Let's get them in here with the stretcher." The burly black officer seemed to be in charge. Campus Security had come in and taken control of the situation. Nonetheless, for all of their crisis management skill, it had taken the two of them, Randy and Troy just to hold Ill Will, and he was still kicking! The crowd by the door parted for the GERMS team. The two students came in with a slim white cot, covered with thick orange straps. They would have to hold the stretcher above the broken glass while the campus cops, Troy and Randy loaded Ill Will. Other students watched with mixed horror and fascination as the GERMS strapped Ill Will onto the stretcher.

A half-hour later, Troy and Randy were being treated in the emergency room. Ill Will was in an adjoining section down the hall. Troy's lower back and sides were smarting with bruises and cuts from the shards of glass. Blood and tobacco spit was splattered all over his formerly gray sweatshirt. The sweatshirt seemed to weigh fifty pounds as the doctor lifted it off. Randy didn't look as bad, but it was obvious that he, too, was taxed.

"You all right?" he asked, half grinning.

"Yeah, now that some of this vodka bottle is out of my fucking arm."

"Did you ever see Ill like that?"

"Nah, and we drank all summer. But he drank most of that vodka himself. Brother shouldn't have even been conscious."

"True," Randy agreed. "He always drinks a lot, though. I mean usually it's no big deal, but when he punched Yvonne, that's when I knew we were in for something serious."

"Yeah. Well, Phyllis and them are looking after her so she'll be all right. Did you see Andrea?"

"Nope." The second floor resident assistant wasn't around for any of the melee. In fact, Troy couldn't remember when he'd seen her last.

"That's good though, because people on our floor be fucking up."

"Yeah, but she's supposed to be on duty or something. Or let us know if she's not and give an emergency number. I bet she would have showed up if a white student was getting drunk and going off like that. Don't you think?"

"Yeah, could be."

Troy wasn't up to having a confrontational dialogue right then and there. No matter what was going on, wherever they were, it was always a black thing to Randy.

"This is a real fucked up situation, brother."

"You think I don't know that? Look, it could have been any of us. Could have been you."

"I don't get drunk, brother."

"Yeah well, we're in it now, or he's in it."

A commotion down the hall steadily grew louder. Troy saw an old security guard fly by, doing the backstroke in mid-air. Next were two or three young doctors and a nurse, all dashing down the hall as though they were in a track meet. They were preceded by a young dark-skinned man dressed only in a white tank top, white briefs and bright orange straps on each arm. Troy and Randy looked at each other and sighed.

"Brother, did you see that?" Randy asked.

"You know I did."

"You don't suppose—"

"Don't even ask. You know that was him."

"Hey, we're not finished here," the doctor told them.

"Sorry," Troy told her. "Excuse us."

Once their brief shock passed, they bolted from their chairs and joined the chase. Ill Will was on the loose in the hospital and Troy and Randy were sprinting behind the emergency room staff, leaving their bandages only half-done. Ill Will swiftly climbed two staircases to reach another floor, knocking on doors and throwing trays, medical supplies — everything in his path — to the ground. Troy, Randy and the hospital staff continued to give chase until Ill Will was finally cornered at the end of the hall;. he was attempting to jump out of a window when Troy, Randy and a doctor finally grabbed hold of him.

"He's sedated!" one of the doctors yelled from behind.

Randy laughed. "If that's what your sedative does, I'd hate to see your anesthesia!"

Ill Will was silent and gave no resistance as he was held at the end of the hall. Everyone in the medical unit seemed to be busy — calming disturbed patients, cleaning up shattered bottles and instruments, recovering papers that had been swept off the counter. A phalanx of campus security and medical staff filled the hospital floor. The older doctor who had helped to catch Ill Will was now diagnosing him.

"The student is inebriated," an orderly told him.

"What the hell happened?"

"He ran out," the orderly told him, pointing to the broken straps on Ill Will's arm. "He was sedated."

"Sedated? You just told me he's drunk!"

"The EMS guys had no choice. It was the only thing that would contain him and even that didn't work."

Troy and Randy looked at each other while the medical staff continued to analyze Ill's condition. Ill Will was in trouble, and there was little else they could do. Troy was overcome with helplessness.

$$*\qquad*\qquad*\qquad*$$

The next morning, Room 228 still looked like a hand grenade had exploded inside its four walls. When Troy looked around, he didn't know where to begin reassembling the room. The ruins of books, papers, pens, photos, toothpaste, cologne, cassette tapes, candles, overturned plants and clothes extended from Troy's side of the room to Randy's. The tobacco-spit stain on the carpet was about three feet in diameter, and smaller brown specks peppered the rug. Troy's blood also stained the rug and shards of the shattered cologne and vodka bottle were everywhere. The rank odor of the carpet permeated the room and Troy's nostrils. Randy rose quietly, opened the window, put on a Billie Holiday tape, and began picking up pieces of glass. Troy followed, emptying all the glass he could find into a big trash bag from the men's room. The late blues singer's lyrics couldn't have been more fitting. Eventually, Ill Will showed up.

"Hey."

Troy and Randy looked up, but said nothing.

"I came by to say I'm sorry. I don't know what happened, but they told me it was pretty bad."

"Take a look," Troy said.

"I know. I saw Yvonne, too. Look, I...I don't know — "

"Forget it," Randy interrupted. "It's over."

Ill Will nodded, then left.

By Saturday afternoon, everyone in the dorm was talking about Friday night's incident. Ill Will was on his way to becoming a Georgetown legend. Of course, the excitement of the previous night led to exaggeration about what took place. One account said that Ill Will's superhuman strength had come from PCP. Another version said the campus police had to pull Troy and Randy off of Ill Will for hurting Yvonne. A third version told how the whole thing started over a card game, and that all three of them would be expelled. A couple of students even came by the room to say goodbye! For many black students in Harbin, Ill Will's misfortune was the first exposure they'd had to the problems students face as a result of drinking, much less illegally. Even in high school, Troy had never heard anything like this about a black student. The fact that they too could be guilty made Troy uncomfortable, but the truth was black kids drank too much and had their own DUI charges. He and Randy were concerned for Ill Will, but they held fast to their "freshman principle":

No screw up couldn't be fixed so long as you were a freshman and it was your first offense. All you had to do was act innocent; as a freshman, you weren't supposed to know any better, you were supposed to make mistakes. Ill Will had fulfilled this principle enough for the entire freshman class.

Ill Will's adjudication hearing was swift; everyone on the board reviewed the file detailing his blood/alcohol level and his rampage in the hospital. There was some talk of suspension and even expulsion, but precedence for freshmen prevailed; worse infractions by freshmen in the past were treated only with warnings and notations by the disciplinary board to keep an eye on the guilty parties. Ill Will received the same treatment, but his infractions were officially added to the records of Student Affairs, Protective Services, and Minority Affairs. It was rumored that even Father Donaly had heard what happened. From the top of Georgetown's administration down, the name Willard Dorsey became synonymous with trouble.

Seven

As the fall semester drew to a close, Troy and Randy continued to monitor the Black Student Union and the NAACP. Neither group had done anything since the party, except for Darnell's 20-minute meetings at the Black Student House. Aside from Troy and Randy, hardly anyone ever showed, thus prompting Darnell to adjourn the meeting and kick everyone out of the house. The NAACP President, Layla, was hardly ever on campus. Latanya explained to Troy that upperclassmen often lost interest in the BSU; juniors and seniors opted to focus on their majors, or simply pursued other interests. The BSU was primarily about parties. Darnell Washington had spoken eloquently on behalf of the BSU at the beginning of the year, but recently he had been quiet. The original event schedule was a bone-dry listing of a couple of meetings and a party. Randy held Darnell personally responsible.

"It's his fault. I've seen him around here creeping. He knows this is a freshman dorm! He hasn't been here visiting the brothers!"

"I've seen him at work, too. He's got some kind of scam going, I just haven't figured it out yet. But he's not wrong for checking the honeys. What, BSU officers can't get pussy?"

"That's not what I'm saying," Randy argued. "But if the brother doesn't want the job, he shouldn't have run."

"Yeah Randy, but anything could be going on. He could be having a tough semester."

"No tougher than ours."

"He's a sophomore!"

"So? He knew what he was getting into. Darnell is supposed to be one of our leaders. Universities are really a microcosm of the larger society. We as a people should have the same attitude about all our leaders, from college up to the federal government. If we held our leadership more accountable, they wouldn't be able to get away with some of their actions, or the lack of them."

Troy nodded, still analyzing his roommate's reasoning. Talking to Randy made him want to read and learn even more about black Americans and their quest for empowerment in society, although he considered himself knowledgeable in this area. His mother had always ensured that he had a solid background in black history. Books by W.E.B. DuBois, Carter G. Woodson, Marcus Garvey, Martin Luther King and Malcolm X covered her bookshelf at home. Troy's mother also collected the writings of Eldridge Cleaver and the work of Maya Angelou, Ralph Ellison, James Baldwin and Sterling Brown among others. For as long as Troy could remember, his mother had the music of her generation playing on the stereo. Styles didn't matter; on many occasions, Marvin Gaye, Aretha Franklin, Al Jarreau, and Rashaan Roland Kirk would all help Troy through a Saturday afternoon of housework. Because of his mother's love for him and for their people, his psyche was firmly embedded in black culture, and had been so all of his life. Because of these experiences and environments, no one could tell him he didn't know who he was.

Yet when Randy started talking, Troy felt like a cultural inferior. His friend had already read and done so much, and all Troy wanted to do was play records and get with Angel. Randy shared his involvement in the Muslim faith, and how older brothers in the projects had led him to Islam as a child. He spoke of the Five Percent Nation, and Islamic summer camps where he and a buddy would do hundreds of push-ups per day just to be able to hang with the other brothers. Randy had been president of the student body at his high school and during his senior year, he had organized students socially as well as politically. For Randy, spirituality and politics went hand in hand. Troy noticed that he didn't drink or use the phrase "nigga," even in passing. He also spoke as if he had once been a member of the Nation of Islam, but he couldn't have been; Troy knew that Nation followers had to be celibate. Troy made mental notes as his roommate continued.

"Brother, the black undergraduate population at Georgetown is about seven percent, or roughly four hundred students. They'll say 'twenty percent minorities,' but that also includes Asians, Hispanics and Native Americans. Ain't but a handful of us."

"I know troop, but that's for many reasons."

"Don't fool yourself, I'm sure many more of us applied."

"Not everyone can afford to come here!" Troy argued. "Nineteen thousand a year? My peeps ain't got that and neither do yours."

"True," Randy agreed, "but we're here, right? If they wanted more of us here, we would be. It's not like they don't have the money.

"See, this whole thing is bigger than us. A lot of brothers and sisters who get recruited to come to Georgetown are middle and upper class, content with their status as second-class, so-called American citizens. They don't understand that a struggle is still going on. Their parents have protected them. Some of them have no idea that black folks are still at the bottom, economically and politically."

"So what, they're not black 'cause they got dough? Come on."

"Listen to me," Randy told him. "These blacks are less threatening, less likely to agitate and call for change."

"Yeah, but aren't you generalizing a bit? You don't know which brothers and sisters are gonna do what, just because their families have money."

"Look at what the BSU has done all year," Randy continued. "Look at the NAACP on campus."

"What does that have to do with the brothers who are here now?"

"Let me put it this way. Do you think it would be this way if there were more brothers like us?"

"No."

"That's what I'm saying. There's nothing wrong with us having money, or coming from money. But usually those black families who want the best for their kids protect them from the struggle, until their kids don't even know anything's wrong. They don't realize what it took just for us to be able to come here, money or otherwise."

"Hold up, black," Troy interrupted. "We're in college, this ain't the Congressional Black Caucus. What can we really do?"

Randy kept on, though he could see Troy's patience was at an end.

"You agree that blacks aren't thriving economically in this country."

"Hell yeah!"

"If we're in such bad shape in America, the only way out is through doors that our parents opened for us. We can only advance through education, leading to opportunity and inevitable empowerment. Therefore, brother, it's critical that black people everywhere have bold, uncompromising leadership wherever they are. Not just in government, but in church, in school or wherever. Darnell and Layla are not providing leadership. We have to be the ones to work for change — our generation! Our parents are worn out and the President doesn't give a fuck about us. Nor should we expect him to, we're not his kids!"

Randy believed that by organizing, by unifying at school, the wheels of change would begin to turn. He thought that young blacks only asked what they could do because they didn't know what Africans had done in antiquity. That was why it was so important to "Know Thyself," as Randy was fond of saying. If black students at Georgetown had a better grasp of African thought and their true history as well as a real grip on the sad condition that they were really in in America, then they could rise together and advance in society. This was the crux of his roommate's argument and Randy was as firm in his beliefs as anyone Troy had ever met. Although he had much to discover within himself, Troy knew that he believed in what Randy said and thought everyone needed to hear it. With these thoughts in mind, in early November, the roommates decided to run for the Black Student Union office. Randy would run for President, and Troy would be his running mate, opting for the seat of Vice-President.

Troy was now curious about how other black students felt about their situation at Georgetown and in America in general. Instead of being caught up in his own world as usual, he looked more closely at his peers. He knew there was nobody in their class like Randy, so he figured he would check with the upperclassmen. They all agreed that in the past, both black student groups had been lethargic in the achievement of most of their goals and seldom had any goals at all. Students who ran for office like Darnell Washington did enjoy the privileges of running a student organization; having an activities budget, and in Darnell and Layla's case, using the free housing in the Black Student House, courtesy of Travis and Minority Student Affairs. When he and Randy got in, Troy was confident that they would get much more done. And as Vice-President, he would get to DJ all the parties!

Troy's mother was supportive of his new interest.

"That's wonderful, Troy. Good luck."

"Thanks. How's everything going in New York?"

"Fine. Apartment's the same, the block is too. Thank God you're not here, your little friends are getting arrested left and right. Trying to sell drugs."

Troy paused. Hearing about his old friends forced him to consider why his mother had been so adamant about moving to Maryland. Uprooting the both of them had been for his sake. Soon after Troy had been accepted into Georgetown, his mother prepared to return to New York for a better job opportunity. He knew his mother had loved Landover and he vowed to never again be a burden to her, so that she could return to Maryland in a couple of years.

"How's Grandma?"

"Oh, she asks about you all the time. You need to call her."

"I will."

"Call her, Troy." Troy's mother would not be put off over the phone. "You'll be here on Thanksgiving, right?"

"Sure, I'll be there."

"Okay, I'll see you then."

"Bye, Mom."

Troy could hardly wait to see his mother. His father, on the other hand, was another matter.

"You shouldn't join any clubs for at least a year."

"But Dad, it's not until next semester! We wouldn't take office until February."

"It's too early. Wait until next year."

"Then I'd have to wait a year and a half. Look, I just wanted you to know what I was doing."

"It's not a good idea. Troy, I'm telling you, your only activity should be studying."

"Okay, Dad. I'll think about it."

"What's to think about? Just don't do it!"

With silence hanging between them, Troy slammed the receiver down. He understood his father's fear of him overextending himself, but no activities at all? That was ridiculous. After all, his father was the one who wanted him to have the college experience, and even he knew that college was more than just classes. When he told his father he'd think about it, a vicious defiance rose in him. Now he was going to run no matter what happened, if for no other reason than to prove his father wrong. David Harris was the only human being on the face of the earth who could frighten him. He didn't think this was how it should be, and sulked in his room after talking to him. Just then, Ill Will came in.

"*Hallo!* What up, homey?"

"Nothing." The phone rang.

"Aren't you going to get it?"

"Nah. It's my pops."

"Mmmm, I hear that. What, you were just talking?"

"Yeah, something like that."

Ill Will smiled, then his smiled faded into reflection. "Really, you should be glad you can shoot the shit with your dad."

Ill Will's father was a Vietnam veteran who had left shortly before his son was born. His whereabouts, whether he was even alive, were unknown.

"Yo, there's a new message on the pad for you."

"Yeah, from who?"

"Your girl."

"Who?"

"Angel, who else?"

"Really."

"Don't front motherfucker, you know you excited!" Ill Will broke into laugher. Caught red-handed, Troy could only laugh along with him.

Troy found Angel's handwriting on the door's giant notepad, already filled with visitor's greetings and comic strip sketches, created by him, Randy and Ill Will. Her note read simply, "Need 2 C U ASAP. XXXOOO Angel." Troy grew annoyed after analyzing the situation. They hadn't spoken since Troy had received her gentle rejection letter. Angel always had something to say after she had time to think about it. She probably wrote on the door just so that she could say she'd been by. *Give me a break*, he thought. He strutted past Ill Will, who was cheering him on like a ball player in a playoff game, then hastily he made his way over to Room 202, home to Angel and Cyndi, his personal house of pain. He gave a sharp knock on the door, which brought a nervousness to his insides that had been absent minutes before.

"Come in!"

Angel lay in the bed under the covers, looking at a notebook. Troy shook his head. Why was he doing this to himself? Hadn't he had enough punishment? Troy was inside the room, but Angel was still oblivious, or acting oblivious, to his presence. Already exasperated but trying to look patient, Troy peeled back her notebook and waved.

"Hi," she said, smiling.

"Hello."

"How are you? I haven't seen you in so long! Where have you been? You never come talk to me anymore."

You know where the fuck I've been, he thought. "I'm here now, so what's up?"

"What's up with what?"

"I got your note on the door."

"Si, *papi*."

"Oh, now it's *papi* again, huh?"

"I just wanted to say hi, you know, see how you were doing."

Troy felt his heart plummet into his sneakers. The note on the door had been for nothing. He had been quick to respond to her message, only to be toyed with as if he were Pinocchio. With his mind drifting into a daze, he stood and stared at her while trying to make some sense of the simultaneous radio and TV noise.

"Actually Troy, there was something I kind of wanted to talk to you about..."

Within seconds his attention returned. She really did have a reason to leave that message? Was this a dream?

The perplexed look on Troy's face caused her to smile once again. What was she so giddy about? Didn't she know what she'd done to him? It was bad enough that he never stood a chance with her in the first place, but to be played with after the fact was a crushing blow to his ego. Only a bothersome curiosity kept him from getting sick on her carpet.

"I've been talking to...you know, Kenneth...and, well, you know, I mean you know who Kenneth is, don't you?"

"Why don't you tell me anyway."

"Kenneth is from Howard, and, well, he's kind of the person I was dealing with."

"I see."

"I'm...I'm not so sure if it's a good idea that I still see him."

A new shock came over Troy. Was she actually coming around? Troy fought to keep from grinning. Damn it, this was good news, but he couldn't break down like a kid in front of her. His heart and his ego went to war. When they both reached a stalemate he didn't know what to say, but he knew he should say something.

"Is that right?"

Angel's look of glee slowly turned to scorn as Troy watched. He knew from the look on her face that he'd said the wrong thing.

"Is that right? Is that right? I'm telling you that I stopped seeing someone for you and all you can say is 'Is that right?'"

"But Angel, I—"

"Don't 'but' me, you bastard! Get the fuck out!"

Troy ran for the door, hoping to escape before a book came flying at his head. Behind him he heard Angel screaming.

"God, you can be such an asshole sometimes!"

Before he could respond, she slammed the door in his face.

Me, Troy thought. *I can be an asshole.*

Troy strolled back to his room in disbelief. He kept thinking of her choice of the word "asshole." He, who cared for her seemingly more than she did for herself. He, who had put up with her nonsense and continued to come back for more. What could have prompted such a performance? One minute she was coy and sexy as usual, the next minute she was up for Bitch of the Month. Had his response been that indifferent? Troy tended to be sarcastic most of the time, but this time he hadn't meant to be. Besides, she had some nerve getting mad at him, as if he didn't take her announcement seriously. How could she think that? Didn't she know he thought about her every day? Maybe she didn't, but how would she ever know if he always had to fight for her attention?

Troy was glad Ill Will and Randy were gone. He laid on the bed to contemplate. Angel hadn't even said what it meant now that Kenneth was out of the picture, she'd only hinted at it. She had yet to tell Troy how she really felt about him face-to-face. According to Cyndi, he was even more dear to her than she was to him. When he tried to confront her he only got, "Oh Troy, you're so sweet" and "Troy, you know I love you to death." That, of course, was the problem. Everybody loved him to death, but who would be there while he was alive?

Then again, maybe she had left the Howard kid for him. Maybe she was right to be mad because he hadn't shed tears of joy, but she hadn't given him a chance to react! A man's got to have some pride, and she still hadn't made her intentions clear. She liked him, but did she *like* him like him or did she just like him? He had told her he wanted to be with her, which was what prompted the letter. Now she wasn't going to see Kenneth anymore. That *had* to have something to do with Troy, or else she wouldn't have mentioned it. So she probably was coming around, finally. But Troy wanted her to acknowledge it. He had put his heart on the line, why couldn't she? She'd severed a relationship for him; he had left some kind of impression on her after all. He reached for the phone, but it rang before he could pick it up.

"Hello?"

"Troy, I'm sorry! I don't know what came over me."

"It's okay, honey, I'm sorry, too." Damn! Why was he apologizing? He had done nothing wrong. "Talk to you later?"

"Okay, honey."

"All right, bye."

"Bye, honey."

Troy ended the conversation to keep from spouting more apologetic gibberish. Angel's voice, her smile, her perfume, all of these traits made him lose his sense of reason. Her hugs and her touch were almost more than he could stand. He realized that he had it bad when weeks passed by without him making a move on her. He hadn't been alone with her often, but still, aside from an occasional kiss on the cheek, he was hesitant during those moments. Of course he wanted to do more, she was the sexiest girl alive to him. But the risk was too much; if he went too fast, she'd think like everyone else that this was all he wanted. Since that wasn't the case, he would bide his time and wait for the right moment, even though it was driving him crazy.

When Randy turned up later, Troy informed Randy of his visit to Angel's room. He got a laugh out of it.

"That's good. It's about time y'all get together!"

"It'll happen soon," Troy assured him. "Somebody needs to get some in here."

"Word. But that's okay, Judy's coming over on Friday."

"Judy from the track team? Big legs, fat ass?"

"That's the one." Randy came over for a high-five from Troy.

Troy was in such a good mood that he got up to mix. By using his headphones, he was able to keep the volume down so Randy could study.

Over the next couple of days, the boys tried to stay focused on their work. Troy met with Wendell for Accounting tutoring, and he caught up on more reading. Randy was never around, except to meet with other guys on the floor who had Econ with Professor Chaudhi. Ill Will was never in his room either; he was somewhere choking on his German or creating fake IDs.

*   *   *   *

Since the temperature was quickly dropping, students tended to do their shopping earlier to avoid the cold; Vittles and Sundries for Saxas were packed when Troy came in that afternoon. He grabbed his normal groceries, among them Pop Tarts, chocolate milk and Oodles of Noodles, and stood on line. Darnell and Layla were on line in front of him. He hoped they wouldn't say anything, but Layla noticed him.

"Look who it is, the DJ! How are you?"

"What's up, Layla."

"What up, dude?" Darnell asked.

"S'up, Darnell."

"I hear there may be some new blood in the BSU this year," Layla said.

"Where'd you hear that?" Troy hadn't mentioned it. Had Randy said anything?

"I just heard. Darnell, you'd better stay on your P's and Q's. Him and that other one are serious."

"Indeed," Darnell nodded. "They had better watch themselves, too. They both have a lot to learn."

"Don't be talking like I'm not here, all right? I'm not the one, I don't give a fuck who you are."

"Relax, cowboy. I was talking to the lady. It's cool though, I hear you. Just don't say I didn't tell you."

"Tell me what?"

"Troy," Layla interrupted, "I think you and your boy will really go far if you run for office."

"Layla, what is he talking about?"

"That's just him. Come on, Darnell."

Darnell could hardly keep from laughing. "Later, dude."

The upperclassman offered his hand to Troy who refused it.

"Oh, it's like that? No problem. Hey Layla, drop me off by the Metro station."

Troy would rather have washed his hands of the whole incident, but he knew if he really believed in what he and Randy had been discussing, they would both be seeing Darnell Washington soon.

As they drove past Dupont Circle on their way downtown, Layla asked Darnell, "Why are you messing with those freshmen?"

"I don't have no problem with either of them," he replied. "Truth is, I like him. Randy, too. But they're trying to come in too fast, especially Randy. I can tell he thinks he's Malcolm X or somebody. They want to make some noise, that's fine. But I got a system. And I worked too hard to set it up for some freshmen to come in and fuck it up, let alone benefit from it."

"You're just a sophomore yourself."

"But I got a lot of experience, don't I?"

Layla cracked a smile.

"Mmm-hm," Darnell told her. "You know what time it is."

Eight

Troy cranked on the stereo and began a mix session, playing LL Cool J's hit, "I'm Bad." Randy came in bopping his head to the music.

"What up?" Troy asked, feigning a pleasant mood.

"What up black man?"

"You tell me. What's up with Judy?"

"We'll see. She'll be here later."

"Just let me know, and I'll be out of here." Troy continued mixing.

Randy put away some items he'd purchased from the bookstore. Troy kept mixing, *Make you say 'go LL' and do the wop... make you say 'go LL' and do the wop... make you say 'go LL'...make you say 'go LL'...make you say...make you say...make you say...*

"You're getting nice!" Randy said, acknowledging his roommate's dexterity with the turntables.

"Yep."

While Randy tidied up his desk and Troy lit "Strawberry Delight" incense, they both recited LL Cool J lyrics. A loud bang on the door interrupted them both in mid-chorus.

"Who is it?" Randy shouted.

"Judy!"

He and Randy looked at each other. If Troy stayed, he would be 'cock-blocking,' but if he left now, it would appear obvious that Randy wanted to be alone with her and may hurt his chances of getting in Judy's panties. He could stay and then leave, but then Judy would have the convenient excuse of not knowing when he'd return. There was only one thing to do. He shrugged his shoulders as Randy pointed to the closet.

"Just a minute!"

Troy jumped into Randy's closet and shut the double doors behind him. Through the crack in between the doors, he could see Randy's bed and some of the left side of the room. If he put his eye up to the crack, the view became wider, as if he were watching a movie on a small screen. Randy answered the door, and Troy could see him hang Judy's jacket up in his closet. She would have no idea that there were three of them in the room. Troy watched her move past the crack of the doorway to his roommate's desk. They made small talk and Randy began the grand tour of the room. "Strawberry Delight" seeped in from under the door. In seconds, Judy became a child in a toy store, totally enthralled by the prayer rug, the plants, the incense, and even his stereo equipment.

"Oh, this is nice, Randy! Did you and Troy do all of this yourselves?"

"Yeah, we put together everything ourselves."

Judy carried on as if they had consulted an interior decorator for the room. Randy went into the standard explanation of how he and Troy met, and how the different items in the room reflected each of them. When Randy lost his patience with all of Judy's questions, he began his own friendly interrogation. Judy had no problem conversing with his roomie, a sure sign that she liked him. The freshman track star was petite, muscular and good physical match for Randy, who was noticeably short. Randy had put music on; a selection by saxophonist Najee, which in Troy's opinion was a bad choice. Then again, Randy was the one with the girl, and he was the one watching like an idiot. *Must be the "Do you like jazz?" thing*, he thought.

The only lighting in the room was from his lamp on the end table. Combined with the smoke from the incense, it created a dim haze over the room and cloaked it in a shadowy, golden shade. Soon Judy was on Randy's bed receiving one of his patented, sure-to-please back rubs. Randy had no problem letting the ladies know of his prowess as a masseuse. Judy lay face down on his bed, letting out occasional moans of satisfaction. Troy regretted having agreed to this charade. He knew what was coming next and had no desire to witness it. He couldn't move around without making noise, so his only option was to keep his eyes closed, hoping Randy would turn off the light, but his roommate remembered that he was in the closet, and intended to put on a show. Troy kept his head turned.

"Aaaah!" Judy moaned.

Biting his lip to keep from laughing, Troy opened his eyes. Judy was now sitting up on the bed, naked, clutching Randy's head to her chest. The back of Randy's head was all of Troy's view from that vantage point. He waved to the closet, behind his back. Troy feared that he'd go into hysterics any second. Judy was getting louder.

"Aaaah, shit!"

Apparently she was enjoying herself. Troy giggled as quietly as he could, confident that neither Randy nor Judy seemed to hear him. He bowed his head and tried to pretend he was somewhere else. After hearing the record crackle and trying to ignore the other noises, eventually Troy heard something else. Judy was now speaking to Randy in a different, less amorous tone. Troy couldn't quite pick up on everything she was saying, but she was clearly bothered about something. She mentioned something about being sorry and how this had not been her intention. Troy smiled now at how she was as naked as a Butterball turkey before she realized what her intentions were. Randy looked upset. He went over to his desk, sat in his chair and listened. After he felt he'd heard enough, he spoke.

"Don't let me keep you."

"What do you mean?"

Randy pointed to the door. Blood now trickled down Troy's chin from biting his lip so hard. He would have given anything to laugh out loud just then. He watched with impatience as Judy quickly got dressed.

"Bye," she mumbled as she walked out.

"See ya," his roommate said sarcastically.

Randy didn't bother to see her to the door. Troy jumped out and ran for his pillow to stifle his fit of hysterical laughing. Randy joined in. After a couple of minutes they calmed down and Troy put some Vaseline on his lip.

"4-H baby," Randy called out, slapping Troy's hand.

"4-H."

In the coming week, Troy would score no better. Angel claimed to be ready to get together with him, but he could never get her alone long enough to get anything started. None of the other girls in Troy's phone book were willing to come over. Troy was even willing to travel to their dorms or pay for a cab for one of them. He needed some affection soon, and he needed someone who would never refuse him.

When Mimi came to his mind he was ashamed. Although they had little contact since breaking up in August, she meant far more to him than just a good time; after two years with Mimi in high school, Troy felt the need to be free, but his feelings for Mimi hadn't totally diminished. In this instance, though, he viewed her as if she were any other girl, any other prize. It didn't help that she was attractive; within seconds he was remembering her behind in his hands, her body pressed against his, and soon he had an erection. It was a good thing Troy had stayed in touch with her; he couldn't invite Mimi to Georgetown with the guilt of neglect hanging over him. It was also a plus that he had broken up with her before coming to school; she wouldn't expect anything from him. In fact, his gracious invitation might improve his standing in her eyes. Regardless of his slump, there was a part of him that genuinely wanted to see her, but he would not have been driven to such lengths if Angel, or anyone else, had been treating him better.

Mimi had written him recently, but he hadn't written back. A week after his stint in the closet, he pulled the letter out to recall what it said. Mimi made it a point to let him know she missed him, but she didn't hide the fact that she was enjoying her first semester at Cornell. Troy didn't want her to know how much fun he was having, despite his recent drought with the girls; he wanted her to be sympathetic when she came to see him. Had she known about his and Randy's antics, especially recently, she would not have been pleased. Putting his uncertainty aside, he gave her a call.

"Hello?"

"Hi!"

"Troy!"

"Is this a bad time?"

"I always have time for you, Troy."

Troy smiled, recalling Mimi's expertise at telephone flirting.

"That's sweet of you. I didn't want anything, it was just so nice talking to you last time, and, well, I just thought about you today."

"Troy! You're still a sweetheart, you know that, don't you?"

Troy had her right where he wanted her.

"If you say so. You know, when I called before, I wasn't sure what it would be like."

"Me neither, but I'm glad you did. Did you get my letter?"

"Yes, I just got it."

"Just got it? I sent it a long time ago."

"They screw up the mail around here a lot. In fact, I started to write you back, but then I decided to call."

"How nice."

"No I'm not. Listen. I know Cornell is treating you well, but there's something we didn't talk about before."

"What's that?"

"You know it's been a while since we've seen each other. And I know you've got some new friends."

"Darling, what's your point?"

Troy felt the conversation turn to Mimi's favor. Now he was against the ropes.

"I just want to know how the guys are treating you. I mean, you know."

"What do you mean?" Again with the sarcasm.

"You know what I mean. I know I'm not your daddy, I was just curious."

"Troy, I'm flattered." Her smile came right through the phone. "But I'm not going to tell you."

"Why not?"

"I have my reasons."

"What if I guess?"

"Guess all you want dear, you'll never know."

She was no longer the innocent girl Troy knew in high school. He realized, then, that maybe she never had been. Maybe he had been the child all along.

"I'm sure those Georgetown girls are taking care of you."

"Maybe, but there are none like you."

Troy sensed her smiling again. Despite his recent mishaps, in his mind he still 'had it' when it came to his game with the ladies.

"I don't know how you're going to take this," he began, "so I'm just going to say it. What do you think about coming down to see me for a few days?"

"I would love to." Mimi replied with a sexy voice.

"Really?"

"Really."

They made plans for Mimi to visit a few days before Thanksgiving break. As long as her parents didn't find out, it would work. She originally planned to come home the Tuesday before Thanksgiving, but now she would leave a couple of days early, missing a day of classes to see Troy. After talking to Mimi, his thoughts eventually returned to Angel. He burned for Angel, but the two of them were still tentative at best. Mimi was probably the best thing for Troy. Attempting to fool himself, Troy deduced that if he still had strong feelings for Angel after Mimi left, then he'd know for sure that Angel was for him. If he didn't, he would know he had merely wanted some of the greener grass on the other side.

A knock on the door interrupted Troy's musing.

"Come in."

"Hi!"

Angel came in, wearing a black silk top with matching skirt, stockings and pumps. *Lord,* Troy thought. *Why did she have to look so good?*

"Hey! I was just thinking about you."

"I was thinking about you, too."

"You look fantastic."

"Thank you!"

"No, thank you. What, are you going somewhere? Why aren't you home with your folks?"

"I don't know, I just didn't feel like going home. Cyndi and I are going shopping today."

"And that's your shopping outfit, huh? You guys aren't going to the game?"

"You mean the basketball game?"

Troy was baffled at how Angel always seemed to be out of the loop. "Yes dear, the basketball game."

"I don't know, maybe."

"Come on, you two should come with Randy and me. You can't miss the first game."

"We can always take Cyndi's car to the Capital Centre if we have to."

"Oh, excuse me, that's right. Well, we don't have it like that, but this game is at the gym on campus."

"Come on Troy, that's not what I meant. We'll see, maybe we will go. Hey, did you know Anita Baker's coming to town?"

"No, I didn't know that." Troy still preferred rap concerts.

"She is," Angel repeated. "Just thought I'd let you know. Anyway, I gotta go, Cyndi's waiting."

"Hold up, you just got here." Troy whined.

"Don't worry sweetie, I'll be back."

She quickly turned to leave. Troy chased her to the door. When Angel turned to say goodbye, Troy kissed her. She tried to deflect the kiss with her cheek, but he caught her on the lips. She stood still, holding the kiss for a few moments. Angel didn't speak, but she left smiling.

Troy's heart was racing after the kiss. His hope swelled. Maybe the two of them would be together after all. As he fell back on the bed in a state of bliss, he heard a ripping noise from under him as he landed. He turned to find Mimi's letter; he'd forgotten all about her already. What would he do when she got there? Now that Angel was coming around, the scenario could get a bit hairy. Still, if he could get through those couple of days with Mimi, he'd be okay. Troy hoped that his plan would be enough.

Nine

When Randy returned to the room from lunch, Troy was still mesmerized by Angel's kiss.

"Morning brother, or should I say good afternoon."

"S'up, black."

"I just saw Angel and Cyndi outside. Angel's looking good!"

"Yes indeed, she just left."

"You hit it? Teeee!"

"Nah, nah. I'm in there, though."

"Yeah, okay." Randy punctuated his response with a sarcastic 'A-Okay' sign.

Troy laughed. "Check it. You remember Mimi, the one I told you about?"

"Your girl from high school?"

"Yeah. I just invited her to come down."

"Guess I'll be in Ill's room. When is she coming?"

"The Sunday before Thanksgiving. She'll be here for a couple days."

"Word? Then you're gonna have fun, huh."

"Oh, believe that shit."

Troy slapped hands with his roommate. Having Mimi at Georgetown would definitely be risky, but he would handle it with Randy and Ill Will's help.

*   *   *   *

Harbin residents were relieved to be leaving for Thanksgiving. Almost everyone Troy knew in his class would be departing, as most freshmen did for the November break. A few of the white students on their floor discussed lavish ski trips to Vail, Colorado and Seven Springs, Pennsylvania. Troy envied their ability to take such large-scale trips in a couple of days, going first-class all the way. *Damn, are they paid*, he thought. *Must be nice.* He and his boys were just happy to be going home, and Troy was doubly excited because Mimi was coming the Sunday before everyone left. The rest of the 4-H Crew agreed with him that she could have no contact with Angel. On the day before Mimi's arrival, the trio held a brainstorming session.

"You might could swing it," Ill Will told Troy.

"That's what I told him," Randy piped in. "Just keep Angel out of here."

"*Genau*," Ill Will said.

"What?" Troy asked.

"Exactly. That's German. Anyway, if you have to fuck with her, do it in her room. We'll keep your girl occupied in the meantime."

"Just keep the room straight," Randy added. "As long as Angel don't know both of you are staying in here, you'll be all right."

"Hopefully they won't meet at all."

"That ain't gonna happen Tee," Randy insisted. "Half the floor's already gone, and Angel lives here, so she'll be around."

"What makes you so sure? She's gone most of the time anyway."

"Still, it'll be just your luck to have her show up. She's on the nuts now."

"Nigga must be doing something right!" Ill Will and Randy broke into wild laughter.

"Wait, but bust this," Randy said. "He got Anita Baker tickets."

"What, for Angel?" Ill Will's eyes lit up.

"Nah, for the other one. How you like them apples?"

Ill Will looked over at Troy with wide eyes. "If Angel finds out, you're done."

"That's why she isn't going to find out," Troy declared. "You clowns look out like you're supposed to and everything'll be straight."

"Oh, we'll look out," Randy retorted. "You just do what you supposed to."

"Let me tell y'all something," Troy assured them, "It ain't no thing but a chicken wing."

Angel was away for the weekend as usual, so Troy had ample time to prepare for Mimi. He and Randy gave Room 228 a cleaning suitable for a military inspection. They even spruced up the plants with a pruning and new soil. Troy had picked up a green thumb years before by taking care of his mother's plants while she was away at work. Whenever one of the plants died, he got yelled at, so he had learned the hard way.

In the middle of their cleaning detail, Cyndi came in.

"Hey guys!"

"Hey Cyndi!" Randy called her. "Come here sweetie."

Cyndi embraced him for her usual hug. Troy smiled at Randy's comfort around Cyndi; although he was as pro-black as they came, the fact that Cyndi was white meant nothing to him. Troy was sure that her hips and legs also had a lot to do with it.

"Wow, looks great in here! What's the occasion?"

Troy shot Randy a look. He quickly shrugged his shoulders.

"Uh, someone's coming from out of town."

He wasn't sure if he could trust Cyndi with the news. As close as she had become to he and Randy, she was still Angel's roommate and best friend.

"Oh, a buddy of yours from high school?"

"Yeah."

The uncertainty in Troy's voice gave him away.

"Oh, I get it. That's why you're cleaning up so nicely! My goodness, what will Angel say when she hears about this?"

"Cyndi, please, come on now. It's just an old friend."

"Uh-huh, an old girlfriend I'm sure. What am I, an idiot?"

"Cyndi, it's not like that!"

"Relax Troy, I won't say anything. But only because you didn't try to lie to me."

Troy let out a loud sigh. "Thanks."

"Anytime. It's going to be hard though, she talks about you all the time now. 'Troy, Troy, Troy,' that's all I hear about. Sounds like she got laid."

"I wish."

"Don't worry, your day will come. Won't be for a while at this rate, ha ha!"

"You just keep her under wraps. When she gets back, tell her I'll see her later."

"When's your friend coming?"

"Tomorrow night."

"Oh, then you're okay. Angel won't be back until Monday."

Troy let out a sigh. "Copa."

"Copa? You're going to the Copa? Isn't that in New York?"

"No, no," Randy mediated. "He means 'copacetic.'"

"Oh. Well, I just came to say hi, I'll see you guys later."

"Wait a minute young lady," Randy teased. "Where you going, mama?"

"I have a date tonight for your information. That is, if you don't mind, sir."

"Just be in by ten," Randy joked.

"I'll be in all night."

"Oh that's right, Angel's gone!" Randy remembered.

"Don't do anything I wouldn't do," Troy chimed in.

"Give me a break. Bye, guys."

Troy was smiling after she left. Maybe Cyndi really wanted things to work out between him and her roommate. He made a mental note to talk to her more often.

After dinner, the boys hit the books then caught a late movie off campus with Yvonne and Zelena. Troy was anxious to get away for a couple of hours, to temporarily take his mind off Mimi's arrival. He hadn't counted on being so distracted.

"Hey, Bizzy!" Darnell called. "There go your boys!"

The freshmen turned to find Darnell and Bizzy behind them on the ticket line, separated by a few people. Michelyn was with them, along with a girl they didn't recognize. Darnell, Bizzy and their dates caught up with the freshmen inside the theater lobby.

"What up, Darnell? What up, Brian?" Randy asked, slapping hands with the both of them.

"What's going on, baby?" Darnell replied. "The three musketeers. What up, Will? Or is it Ill Will?"

"My name is Willard."

Ill Will slapped hands with the upperclassmen, but his eyes were fixed on Michelyn. Troy and Randy collected their standard hugs from her, but Ill Will didn't dare in front of Yvonne. Troy saw the envy on Ill Will's face as he hugged Michelyn tightly.

"What's up, girl?"

"Hello." She was unusually curt, as if Troy were a stranger.

"New York in the house!" Bizzy called. "DJ Troy, what's up, man?"

"You, man," Troy answered, while looking at Michelyn.

"You the man, nigga! All of y'all! Randy and Ill got their little mamas with them and everything. Oh, I'm so sorry. My name is Brian. These fools call me Biz." Bizzy offered his hand to Yvonne, who took it and smiled.

"I'm Yvonne."

"Nice to meet you, Yvonne." He also shook hands with Zelena, who grinned politely.

"Y'all going to see 'Eddie Murphy Raw'?'" Michelyn asked.

"Yep," Troy answered, trying to move the conversation along.

"Hold on, chill." Darnell said. "You all never come out during the week."

"Just taking a break," Randy replied. "We'll be busier next semester when we're in the BSU."

"Is that right?"

"Yeah. That's right."

"I hear you, big boy."

"Hey," Ill Will interrupted, "we have a movie to catch."

"Will, calm down," Yvonne ordered. "I want some popcorn."

Troy and Ill Will reluctantly followed the rest of the group to the concession stand. Troy noticed Michelyn's arms wrapped around Bizzy's waist. And although Yvonne looked average next to the gorgeous Michelyn, she was there for Ill Will. Darnell's girl, whoever she was, wasn't bad looking either, while Randy had Zelena with him. Troy was just there, the fifth wheel. Darnell caught Troy staring at his date.

"Where's your girl at, man?"

"I don't know. Maybe she's with Layla. You know Layla, don't you?"

Darnell chuckled self-consciously, knowing that to answer would emphasize Layla's obvious absence. "Funny, that's real funny. Listen, if y'all want a ride back to campus, let us know."

"That's all right," Randy replied. "We'll get back."

The five freshmen saw the upperclassmen as they left the theater, but made it a point to go in the opposite direction. They noticed Darnell driving a red Audi as they crossed the parking lot.

"Whose car is that?" Yvonne asked.

"Don't matter, he's driving." Ill Will offered. Randy pretended not to see, while Troy just shook his head in disbelief.

"The boy's doing something," Randy observed, "whatever it is. It's something." Troy agreed, though he remained silent.

Troy soon forgot about Darnell and Bizzy after settling in that evening. But anticipation kept him up half the night, his mind imagining Mimi's visit from the moment she arrived. He knew how he wanted it to go; their conversation, everything. He replayed the scenes in his head until a brief sleep overcame him. In his dreams, Mimi was already there, sharing his covers.

Troy woke to find Randy and Ill Will moving Randy's mattress into Ill Will's room. Randy noticed the childish enthusiasm smeared over Troy's face.

"Look at you. You're going to have fun, aren't you?"

"You know that."

"Shit, he's due, isn't he? You had him all ass out the first weekend we was here!"

Randy suppressed a chuckle.

"You know it's true! Anyway Troy, you better get your act together. She'll be here soon."

"What are you talking about? She's not coming until tonight."

"No, brother," Randy told him. "If you hadn't slept all day, you'd know she called. She's on her way."

"What time is it now?"

"Four-thirty."

"Why didn't you motherfuckers wake me up?"

"Because fool, we knew you wasn't getting no sleep tonight!" Ill Will doubled over, howling with laughter. Randy, too, laughed out loud.

Troy jumped up to take a shower. The second floor was virtually empty and so were the showers. It did feel like the middle of the afternoon. *Damn!* He hadn't meant to sleep so long. The movie scenes of Mimi's visit began their run in his head again. Troy had to concentrate on the present moment; Mimi was coming soon, he had to focus. Was the room clean enough? Randy and Ill Will had taken care of the bed. What was left? He quickly showered and headed back to Room 228 to get dressed. The phone rang as he looked at himself in the cabinet mirror.

"Hello?"

"Troy Harris?"

"Yeah?"

"You have a guest downstairs."

Troy checked himself in the mirror again before going to the lobby. He glanced back and noticed the photos of some Howard girls still taped to the mirror.

Too late now, he thought. *That's her.* His first love was downstairs.

Troy tiptoed down the staircase as slowly as he could. He thought he heard Angel's voice in the lobby and paused for a second. No, not until Monday, Cyndi told him. It was time for Mimi now. He emerged from the stairwell to find Mimi standing by the security desk. She wore new burgundy schoolgirl glasses and a broad smile.

"Hi!"

"Hey!"

Troy stepped up quickly to give Mimi a hug. She appeared to be the same pretty and petite girl with whom he had spent his high school years.

"Mmm," She was as soft as ever, even through her coat.

"Would you like to sign her in?" The student guard interrupted.

"Yeah. What, you got somewhere to go?" Troy snapped.

Troy hated the student guards in Harbin. Students had to show their IDs whenever they entered a dorm, but these guards knew who Troy and his friends were. Troy didn't like the fact that they continued to make them flash their IDs, even if they were doing their job. What could they do if somebody came in with a gun?

Troy signed Mimi in and took her suitcases to the elevator. She kept her eyes planted on him, smiling the whole time. It was a quick elevator ride, but not quick enough for Troy. Mimi was working her charms on him with her seductive stare and he was losing his composure.

"How've you been?"

"No dear, the question is how have *you* been?" She knew Troy was glad to see her.

Mimi found a welcoming committee in Troy's room. Randy, Ill Will and Yvonne were smiling as much as she was.

"Hi, you must be Mimi! Nice to meet you sister, I'm Randy."

"Nice to meet you, Randy."

"Nice to meet you, too. We've heard about you, haven't we Ill?"

"Oh yeah. I'm sorry, my name is Willard and this is my girlfriend Yvonne."

"Hello." Mimi smiled at Yvonne. "I take it these guys are close."

"They're inseparable," Yvonne told her. "They've been running buddies since day one."

"Now Eevie, don't bore the girl with our stories," Randy said.

"What did you call her?" Mimi held her laugh to be polite.

"Eevie," Yvonne explained. "They have nicknames for everybody. They call Willard 'Ill Will.'"

"Ill Will!" Mimi giggled. "I guess he's ill!"

Mimi tossed the slang around as if she'd heard it all her life. "I already know Troy is 'DJ Troy.' He forced it down our throats in high school."

"Don't even try it," Troy argued. "That name was given to me."

"Yeah, by you. What's your nickname, Randy?"

"The R," he answered, beaming.

"Yeah," Ill Will said, "for 'running his mouth all the time!'" The comment left everyone giggling. Troy was the first to calm down.

"So, did you get in okay?"

"Mm-hm. My sister dropped me off here from the train station. My parents don't know I'm here."

"So you live in Washington?" Yvonne asked.

"No, Landover. It's in Maryland."

"Oh," Yvonne said. "That's where Angel lives."

"Who? Do you know someone who lives there?"

Troy grimaced. Randy and Ill Will looked at each other. Ill Will tugged Yvonne's arm.

"Come on, we've got to go. Nice meeting you Mimi, we'll be seeing you."

"Okay, nice meeting you. Bye, Yvonne."

Yvonne barely got out a "Bye!" as Ill Will pushed her out the door.

"They're going out," Randy explained.

"Oh."

"I'd better be going, too. I figured you might want to be alone, so I'll be next door."

"Thank you Randy," she said, eyeing Troy.

"Sure. We'll see you in the morning." Troy rubbed the back of his neck. Randy could have saved his comments.

"Okay."

Mimi watched as Randy collected some toiletries, slapped hands with Troy and left. For the first time since last summer, Troy and Mimi were alone. Troy approached her to remove her coat.

"Now let me get a look at you."

She stood still as Troy walked around her compact, voluptuous frame. Her cream-colored sweater and faded blue jeans were far from glamorous, but they accentuated her figure nicely. Mimi had curves that could make almost any outfit a sexy one.

"Do I look different?"

"No, but you still look good." Troy paused. Was it that obvious that he was gaping at her? "You got a new haircut."

"It's not new anymore, but I guess it is for you. Let me look at you!"

Troy stood still for her to give him the 'once over.' Now he felt stupid and self-conscious. He hoped he hadn't made her feel as awkward.

"That's my Troy." Troy couldn't contain his smile. He liked the sound of "her Troy."

"Here, have a seat."

Troy sat her down on the foot of the bed, just as he usually did with Angel.

"You sure this is going to be okay? I don't want you to get into any trouble."

"If I couldn't handle it, I wouldn't be here."

"Just making sure."

Troy stood up to play some music. He had made a new tape of slow songs for the occasion.

"Your friends seem very nice."

"Yeah, those are my boys."

"You kicked your roommate out for me, didn't you?"

"No! He volunteered!"

"And you didn't mind that a bit, did you? You devil."

Troy didn't mind Mimi calling him a devil. Nice guys finished last. He took a peek in the mini-fridge.

"Would you like something to drink?"

"No, thank you. Maybe later."

*   *   *   *

The couple passed the hours catching up over Domino's pizza. By nightfall, after exchanging stories about their colleges and recalling high school friends, the informal conversation was drying up. While eating, Troy had been sitting at his desk, but now he joined Mimi on the bed. She was sitting up with her legs stretched out.

Troy had no idea what to say. As long as Angel doesn't come through, this weekend could be hassle free.

"Troy, why are you staring at the door? Are you expecting someone?"

"No, no. Just thinking."

"About what?"

"I just can't believe you're here."

"I missed you, too."

She turned his head to hers and kissed him full on the mouth. Earth, Wind and Fire were singing "Reasons" on Troy's slow jam soundtrack. When the moment he'd waited for finally arrived, the tiny specks of guilt that had clouded his mind about Mimi's visit quickly faded, replaced by a strong erection. He recalled all the times they'd been together as he unbuttoned her sweater. The outfit and the underwear were new, but Mimi's smooth skin was familiar, as were her warm thighs, which filled her pantyhose. She still liked to kiss for a long time, but Troy had to move down past her neck to revel in her newly exposed breasts. He felt her nipples expand and harden in his mouth and sucked relentlessly, with his fingers swirling inside her, until she writhed and reached for his crotch. Once he was fully inside her, she moved easily with him and guided him, arching herself for him to hold her behind the way he liked. When Troy's rhythm picked up speed, he stopped himself and turned Mimi around on her stomach.

"That's right," she whispered. She soon got on her knees and lowered her face down to the pillow. Before long Troy was leaning on top of her, holding the headboard with one hand and Mimi's behind with the other, giving her long, hearty strokes from the back. Mimi returned by rotating and pressing her ass back each time, causing Troy to go faster. They shared a thunderous shout and Mimi gently kissed his neck and massaged his head. Within minutes they were making love again, though this time more slowly and gently.

Mimi snuggled in Troy's arms like a kitten the next morning. Sunshine crept through the opened curtains onto the wall, turning the room bright gold. He caressed Mimi's back for a few minutes. They had been up almost all night making love. Troy wanted to go take a shower and get dressed before Randy came back, but Mimi wasn't ready for him to move.

"Where are you going?" she mumbled.

"It's time to get up, honey. I have class."

He kissed her and left for the men's room. When he returned, she was in her pajamas. Troy directed her around the corner and headed for Ill Will's room. So far, so good, no sign of Angel. He knocked on the door to find Randy and Carl already awake.

"There he is!" Randy shouted. "Casanova!"

"I heard you were bumping boots!" Carl chimed in.

"That's 'knocking boots,' you imbecile," Troy muttered.

"Oh, bumping, knocking, same thing."

Troy was already exasperated. Why was it such a big deal that he had sex last night?

"Come on, Randy. Where's Ill?"

"Upstairs with Yvonne."

"Yeah," Carl said. "She kicked her roommate out, too!"

"Thank you." Troy answered. "Later."

"I was just kidding! Her roommate left for break! See you later!"

It occurred to Troy that by staying with Carl, Randy was making a big sacrifice for him. He had only endured one night with Ill Will's roommate, and his head was so stuffy that night he was asleep and oblivious to his presence.

"Thanks, black."

"No problem, brother. You'd do the same for me."

Randy got some towels and headed for the showers. On the way out, he bumped into Mimi, who exchanged "Good Mornings" with him.

"So what's your first class?"

"Accounting. I won't be back until lunch. Will you be okay until then?"

"Sure, I'll just read a book."

"There's a TV in the lounge by the elevator. And some yogurt and stuff is in the fridge. I'll be back soon and we can go to lunch together."

"That would be wonderful."

Troy grabbed his books and headed out.

"Troy?"

"Yeah?"

She motioned for Troy to come back into the doorway, where he was met with another kiss. Mimi then gave him a tissue to wipe off the traces of her newly applied lipstick.

"Have a good class."

There was almost no point in Troy being in his Accounting class. He tried to keep up with what Professor Newcomb was covering, but thoughts of Mimi and Angel kept invading his mind. Had he known the semester would go the way it had with Angel, he probably wouldn't have broken up with Mimi. They were apart anyway, but with Mimi attending

Cornell, it wasn't like they'd really broken up; last night was proof of that. He still loved her, or at least he thought he did. How could he be in love with two girls at once? He couldn't. His shame returned with the realization that he loved the security of Mimi. She would always soothe him and love him when he needed it. Maybe he and Angel simply needed more time. Students began closing their books and packing their bags to Troy's surprise. Before he even learned what the topic was for that day, Professor Newcomb was finishing his lecture.

"Remember, this unit will definitely be on the exam. It's a tough unit, so be sure to get as much help as you can if you're having trouble. Have a happy Thanksgiving."

Troy had no idea what Newcomb had been discussing. Having a love life had its downside. He went to Euro Civ fully intending to go to sleep. Since receiving a "C" on the midterm, he had been making more of an effort in this class, but Shebel's lectures were still too boring for him. Listening to Shebel was like taking NyQuil. Today Troy would have no choice but to put his head down. When he awoke, another group of students was in the room. None of his classmates had bothered to wake him up. Troy suspected that they'd resented the fact that he had slept while they took notes.

$$*\qquad*\qquad*\qquad*$$

Mimi was laughing and conversing with Randy and Ill Will, who was doubled over in his chair.

"Hah ha ha hah! You're kidding!"

"No, it's true. Hi honey!"

"What's true?"

"You used to dance like Michael Jackson? Hee hee!" Randy was having a ball.

"Get the fuck out of here," Ill Will said.

Troy turned to Mimi. "When did you ever see me dance like Michael Jackson?"

"At the sophomore dance. It was our first date. Don't you remember?"

His friends were laughing deliriously. Troy didn't like looking foolish.

"Please. I only did that because you asked me to."

"Oh, right. You ready to go to lunch?"

"Yeah, we can hit Wisconsin Avenue."

"Sounds good to me."

"Whoa, excuse me!" Ill Will shouted. "You never take me there for lunch."

Ill Will and Randy could not stifle their enjoyment.

"Let's go, Mimi." Troy snorted. "You can talk to these fools later. Peace, you two."

"Later Mike!" Randy shouted.

Au Pied du Cochon, a French bistro on Wisconsin Avenue, was packed with professionals on their lunch hour and there was a long wait for a table. Troy and Mimi didn't mind; they passed the time with more reminiscing about how they first met, their first kiss, the senior prom. While they ate, Mimi told Troy about her job at Cornell's student café. She liked it because it was a simple job. He told her about his classes and his concern about his grades.

"You'll do fine."

This was easy for her to say. Mimi had been a brilliant student in high school, and her arsenal of advanced placement credits exempted her from many freshman prerequisites. She was, therefore, free to take more of the courses that interested her.

They walked back to campus holding hands. Troy was oblivious to the few students he knew who saw them together. Most of them didn't know Angel, and the ones who did never spoke to her. She was going to pop up sooner or later, but as long as he saw her first, he would handle the situation. He had one more class to attend before he and Mimi could spend the rest of the day together.

"I'll show you around, let you see some sights."

"As long as I'm with you, it doesn't matter."

Troy was determined to outcharm her. "I've got a surprise for you."

"Give me a hint."

"You'll see tonight."

"Oooh, I love surprises!"

Mimi's smile was enough to make Troy want to skip class, but he couldn't afford to do it. Novel/Short Story was the only class where he still had a chance to get an "A." He dropped her off at his room and kissed her goodbye.

Fortunately Troy's last class moved along rapidly. He was anxious to get outside again, to make sure he spotted Angel before she had a chance to see him. He couldn't understand why he hadn't seen her yet. Playing it safe, he went by Copy Services to see if she was there. Ill Will was inside working.

"She was here earlier, but she left," Ill Will told him.

"Where's she at now?"

"Nigga, I don't know! She was looking for you."

"Aw shit."

"Yeah. You'd better find her before she finds you."

Troy left Copy Services and the library, having had enough of Ill Will's pessimism. He walked back to Harbin Hall with his eyes peeled, hoping to see Angel or Cyndi. Apparently she wasn't outside. He wasn't going to her room, and if she was in his, he would have to face the music right then and there. He took it slow coming onto the second floor. Looking both ways in the hallway, he tiptoed into his section like a secret agent. There were some voices coming from the lounge, but none belonged to Angel. Saints be praised! Troy unlocked the door and entered to find Mimi alone, her nose in a romance novel. She looked up when she heard the door open.

"Hi!"

"Long time, no see!" Troy joked.

"Very funny."

"Where's Randy?"

"He was here a while ago, he just came in and out."

"I don't know why, he always studies in here, except for Econ."

"He's probably just trying to leave us alone."

"Yeah, but he doesn't have to leave us — never mind. You ready to have a look around?"

"Sure, just let me put something else on."

"What's wrong with what you're wearing now?" Troy asked. He didn't want her in the ladies' room where she might run into Angel.

"Honey, I'll only be a minute. Just sit tight."

Mimi pulled some clothes from her suitcase, and was off to the ladies room. He knew he could stand a look at his books, especially to get some idea of what had been covered in Accounting, but by the time he got started, Mimi would be ready. This was his rationale for turning on the stereo equipment to mix. As usual, the turntables were a welcome distraction; he hadn't thought about mixing for some time. There was a new rap group, EPMD, whose music had been winning him over. He put one of their records on and imagined himself playing in a nightclub.

A few minutes later, Troy turned around to find Mimi watching and listening to him mix. Randy had also come in.

"Why didn't you say you were back?"

"I tried. You were too wrapped up in the beats."

"I was going to tap on your shoulder," Randy told him, "but Mimi said to let you go."

"I should have been looking at my notes anyway. You ready?"

"Let's go."

"Have a good time kids."

"We'll see you later."

"Bye Randy!"

"Bye-Bye Mimi, take care."

With winter fast approaching, the sky was already growing dark, but the November cold had not yet arrived in Washington D.C. Troy and Mimi found a taxi at the front gates. They were headed for an Italian restaurant downtown, not far from the campus. The plan was then to walk around near the capitol, and eventually back to Georgetown.

Troy had heard about the Spaghetti Den from Arnelle, his RA from the summer session. He and his boys all liked Italian food, and in D.C. they preferred the Den because the restaurant served generous portions. The Den was a mid-sized restaurant, in full Italian décor with red and white checkered tablecloths and paintings of Sicily on the walls. The owners and waitstaff all spoke fluent Italian, which impressed Mimi.

"Where'd you find this place?"

"Me and Randy heard about it from a friend."

"You must have lots of friends."

"What's that supposed to mean?"

"Oh Troy, really. I mean, how dumb do you think I am? You just happened to get me here while everybody's home already. I know you have some girls around Georgetown somewhere."

Troy wasn't prepared for Mimi's observation. He knew his boys hadn't told her about Angel, and when Mimi wasn't with him she was in his room, practically locked up. How did she know? He could not reconcile the fact that Mimi was so confident about the situation.

"Wait a minute. You don't know anything."

"Dear, please. Give me some credit. I know you."

"It's not like that, Mimi."

"Oh, it's all right, Troy. Just don't think you're pulling one over on me."

"I'm not trying to," he said righteously. "All these girls you're talking about can't all be home. Where have they been all this time?"

"I've only been here one night."

Silence.

"Besides," she continued, "you were the one who wanted to be free, remember?"

Troy had no reply. Mimi's words disquieted him. The garlic bread they had ordered as an appetizer arrived just in time to keep him from having to respond. Troy helped himself.

"This garlic bread is dope. Wait 'till the manicotti gets here."

Mimi nodded, chewing her garlic bread. Her intent stare told Troy that the food didn't distract her from the conversation. He would have to deal with the matter at hand.

He began, "I didn't know what was going to happen when I got here. I was just trying to be real. It doesn't mean I wanted something to happen. Look how far away you are."

"Troy, you don't have to explain anything to me. It's okay. I wouldn't be here otherwise."

Troy couldn't stand that Mimi was so at ease, but at the same time he loved her for being so understanding. He couldn't help but wonder how Angel fit into the scheme. It was just another bridge he would have to cross when he came to it.

"I'm glad you're here. No matter what happens, there's no replacing you. That's why I have a surprise for you."

"And the surprise is?"

"Anita Baker tickets."

"No! Troy, you got Anita Baker tickets?"

"Yep."

"Oh Troy! Tomorrow's concert?"

"Tomorrow night. I know you were leaving tomorrow, but I was kind of hoping you'd stay."

"Of course I'll stay! Anita Baker! Oh Troy, Anita Baker!"

Anita Baker was literally Troy's ticket out of guilt city. These were the same tickets that would have won Angel's heart for sure, but he felt much more comfortable taking Mimi. Besides, Angel would never know.

Soon the manicotti arrived and the couple enjoyed their meal with no more talk. Mimi was all smiles, as seemingly smitten with Troy as she had been when they had first met.   Yet, he sensed that whatever their relationship was at this time, it would never be the same after Mimi's visit; she probably knew it, too.   By the time they made their way back to campus, Troy's mind turned from analysis to relaxation.   Mimi was thoroughly enjoying her visit, and she couldn't wait to get back to Troy's room.

"You're still so good to me," she told him as they reached Harbin.

"Yeah, I am," he acknowledged proudly.

"Where is everybody?" Mimi asked.

"Randy and Ill are somewhere around here. Everyone else must already be gone."

"So I have you all to myself again."

"Looks that way."

Troy put in his customized slow jam tape, turned the lights down, and found Mimi in the dark. The tranquillity of the evening lasted until dawn.

*   *   *   *

Troy wanted to give Mimi a chance to get dressed the next morning before Randy and Ill Will came in, but this time he was the one reluctant to move from the bed.

"Troy, wake up."

"Uh, I will, I will. Go and get in the shower, I'll be up by the time you get back."

"Yeah, right. You're going to stay here and sleep."

"Baby, just go. Randy and them will be knocking on the door any minute."

"All right, but you're getting up when I come back."

Mimi collected her clothes and headed out, just as she had the morning before. She left wearing Troy's bathrobe. Randy entered as Mimi made her way to the ladies' room.

"Good morning."

"Hi, Randy."

Randy was making his morning pit-stop before class. "Rise and shine, brother! Aren't you going to Philosophy?"

"Mmm, yeah," Troy grunted. "I just need sleep."

"I wonder why. She looked all happy. Look at you!"

"It's the Anita Baker show."

"That got you over, huh?"

"Most definitely. Where's Ill?"

"He was upstairs with Yvonne."

Troy heard Randy's reply vaguely before dozing off. A loud knock woke him back up.

"Come in!" Randy shouted.

The door opened to reveal Angel and Cyndi. Randy grimaced, looking over at Troy. He saw who it was, but tried to force the image out of his mind. He was frozen with fear, but all he could do was try to act natural

"Hey ladies," he offered.

"Hi!"

Angel ran over to Troy and hugged him. Now, with his old sweetheart down the hall, Angel was the bastion of affection. All he could manage was a weak, blank smile. It wouldn't have been as awkward if Troy had been wearing anything other than his underwear.

"Hi Angel."

"Baby, you don't seem too glad to see me."

"No, of course I am. I'm just sleepy. Cyndi, where have you been?"

"Oh, I've been around."

Troy could only look to the heavens in desperation. He had counted on Cyndi to run interference for him until Mimi left. When Angel turned to acknowledge Randy, Troy gave Angel's roommate an exaggerated look of horror, but she just shrugged her shoulders.

"I couldn't keep her away," she whispered. She turned back to Randy and Angel. "We just wanted to see you guys before we left for home. When are you leaving?"

"Me and Tee are out of here tomorrow."

"Cyndi's going now, and she's dropping me off. I couldn't leave without seeing my honey," she said, looking at Troy. She had made herself comfortable on Troy's bed now, and was rubbing his back. Where was all of this coming from?

When the door opened again, everyone turned to see who it was. Troy and Randy already knew. Mimi was still wearing Troy's bathrobe.

"Morning."

Ten

Randy and Cyndi stood still by Randy's desk. Then Angel, smiling, got up from Troy's bed to greet the guest.

"My name is Angel. Who are you?"

"I'm Mimi."

The two girls shook hands. Angel stood in font of Troy so he couldn't see Mimi's reaction.

"Pardon me, Angel."

"Oh, I'm sorry, I'm blocking the door."

"That's okay."

Mimi walked past her to get to Troy's desk, where her open suitcase waited. Troy checked Angel's expression. The smile was one meant to mask her discomfort. Troy felt his stomach turning.

"Mimi, that's Cyndi, Angel's roommate. They live down the hall."

Cyndi was also all smiles and walked over to greet her. "It's so nice to meet you. Troy's told us about you."

"No, really he hasn't," Angel interrupted. Randy rubbed his hand over his face.

"Yes he has. You'll have to excuse my roommate. She's not used to— "

"Strangers," Troy jumped in. "Mimi and I were, uh, in high school together."

"Yes, we were."

"You must have had a great time," Angel told her. "It's wonderful to have him here with us."

"I'm sure it is. Excuse me."

Mimi picked up her clothes and returned to the ladies' room. Cyndi broke into laughter as soon as Mimi left and Randy soon joined her. Troy felt Angel's hot glare. Randy could see the desperation on his roommate's face.

"You all looking forward to seeing the family?"

"No, Randy. We don't want to see them at all. That's why we're going home to see them."

"Angel, come on," Troy pleaded. "Why the attitude?"

"You shut up," she barked.

Troy wanted to avoid their meeting, but as he watched Angel's reaction, he didn't know if her jealousy worried him or excited him. Mimi returned from the ladies room fully dressed. Angel's disposition instantly became pleasant again.

"Where do you go to school, Mimi?"

"Cornell."

"What's your major?"

"Pre-law."

"I'm pre-med," Angel offered.

"You live in Maryland, Mimi?"

"Mm-hm."

"Me too! I went to Largo High."

"Oh. Well, you must be looking forward to going home."

"Actually she goes every weekend." The words left Troy's mouth before he could catch them. Angel shot him a nasty look.

"No, I don't. I just don't stay on campus that often."

"We're not the social butterflies that these two are," Cyndi interjected. "They're very popular."

"Apparently," Mimi observed.

"No more than anyone else," Randy told her. "We do have fun, though."

"I can tell," Mimi continued. "Troy's taking me to see Anita Baker tonight."

"Really?" Angel asked. "That's wonderful, I love Anita Baker!"

"I do, too. And I've never seen her before."

Troy felt a headache coming on. He could have sworn he saw steam coming from Angel's nostrils.

Cyndi broke the brief silence first.

"We'd better get going. Come on, Angel. Mimi, it's been so nice meeting you."

"Nice meeting you, too. Nice to meet you, Angel."

"Oh, you too, you too! We'll have to get together sometime."

"Yes. Sounds good."

Angel strolled over to Troy, grabbed him by the chin and kissed him on the mouth.

"Bye, *papi*," she said, looking right at Mimi. "Have fun at the concert."

"They will," Cyndi told her. "Bye."

Troy thought he'd be relieved to see Angel and Cyndi gone, but he wasn't. Sooner or later Angel, and her resentment, would be back. He wanted to talk to Randy about it, but he would be busy with his last classes before vacation.

"Peace black, I'll see you later. Mimi, lovely to see you again."

"Thank you, Randy. See you later."

Troy also had a final class to attend, Philosophy. McBride's class was a perfect place to think when Troy had something on his mind. Although more than half the students were gone for the holiday, the auditorium was still big enough for Troy to be unnoticed somewhere in the back row. McBride repeated the previous unit on Aristotle, and indicated that the material would be covered on the final exam. Once Troy had this information in his notes, he was free to concentrate on his ever-evolving girl problems. What the hell had happened with Cyndi? Was it a good sign that Angel was jealous of Mimi, or was she simply upset that she wasn't going to the concert? What if she really had been coming around, and now having Mimi over had blown his only chance? Angel had to think that he and Mimi were together, since when she met her, Mimi was wearing his bathrobe! And God forbid Mimi ask about Angel. The conversation at Spaghetti Den last night indicated that Mimi knew someone else was in Troy's sights. And he was sure that she was bright enough to recognize that it was Angel, which explained her amusement at the whole scene.

When he got back to his room, Mimi was reading her romance novel and waiting as patiently as before. She mentioned that Randy and Ill Will had stopped in. Mimi had called her family to let them know that she was on her way home, but only her older sister knew where she really was; her parents thought she was still at Cornell.

"Are you sure you shouldn't let them know?" Troy asked.

"I'll see them soon enough."

"All right, it's your world. You about ready to get out of this room?"

"Okay. It's not time to go to the show yet, is it?"

"No, we've got some time. We can get something to eat, then come back and change."

They had a light dinner at the American Café, another popular Georgetown restaurant. Troy could see Mimi's excitement about the concert. By the time they finished eating and headed back to Harbin Hall, Troy was ready for another memorable evening.

Mimi wore a turquoise dress with spaghetti straps, matching shawl and shoes. It was tasteful, yet tight enough to show off her figure beautifully. The color also accented her dark skin, which Troy loved. He couldn't match her style with his blue blazer and slacks, but Mimi still acted impressed with his outfit.

"Wow, look at you!"

"Please, this is nothing."

"Well, 'nothing' is looking good to me."

"Not as good as you look." Troy leaned in for a kiss. The moment his lips met hers, he wished for the same kind of exchange with Angel. They had shared a kiss once and he remembered how charged he was that day. Yet the effect that he got from Mimi's kiss was just as powerful. How could this still be happening? Troy refocused again, concentrating on Mimi and the concert.

Anita Baker was scheduled to perform at Constitution Hall. Their seats were enviably close to the stage since Troy had been swift in purchasing the tickets.

"Troy! The fifth row? You didn't tell me the seats were this good!"

"I wanted to surprise you."

"You're the best."

Elegantly dressed ticket holders slowly made their way to their seats in the concert hall which was festooned with colonial décor. Troy and Mimi silently admired what everyone else was wearing. None of the other outfits in the house struck Troy as Mimi's did. She seemed to have acquired an elegance beyond the girlish charm she had always possessed. Troy felt himself beaming.

The host for the evening was a disc jockey from a local radio station. He introduced the opening act, a local comedian and within the hour, Anita Baker was on stage, performing hits from her album, *Rapture.* Because they were so close, Troy and Mimi felt as though Anita Baker was singing exclusively to them. The singer's movements were often directed at the nice young couple in the fifth row. When she asked if there were any couples in the house, Troy was quick to raise his hand, bringing a smile to Mimi's face. At that moment, Troy wished he could have bottled the enchantment around him.

Walking along Pennsylvania Avenue after the concert, Troy and Mimi continued to enjoy the storybook flavor of the evening. The moment they got inside Harbin Hall, Troy could hardly keep his hands off Mimi and her dress. By the time they reached his room, Troy had practically taken it off. Mimi finished undressing on her own. Troy followed suit, acting as if he were in a race. Joining Mimi in bed, she stopped him from kissing her for a moment.

"I'm having a wonderful evening."

"I am, too."

"I love you, Troy. I hope you can handle that."

"I love you, too."

*   *   *   *

Ill Will knocked on the door of 228, intending to catch Troy and Randy before leaving for Philadelphia. Randy had been sleeping in his and Carl's room while Mimi was visiting, but most nights Ill Will had slept upstairs with Yvonne. Randy, Troy and Mimi were packing.

"*Vie Hisensie!*" Troy greeted him, mocking his German.

"You're getting better, homey! You guys packing up, huh?"

"Indeed," Randy told him. "What you gonna do in Philly?"

"Nothing big. See my sister, some of my boys from the neighborhood, you know. Maybe I'll come to New York!"

"You should," Troy told him.

"Yeah, maybe. Mimi, Troy show you a good time?"

"Wonderful."

"Oh, excuse us!" Ill Will and Randy laughed. Troy hoped the embarrassment wouldn't show on his face.

"I just wanted to say hey to you clowns before you took off."

"Yo, call me if you decide to come to New York," Troy told him.

"I got the number. Mimi, it's been a pleasure. You be sure to come back, all right?"

"Thank you Willard. And thank you for all your help."

"Oh, no problem. That's how we do things around here."

"You're not coming with us to the bus station?" Randy asked.

"Nah, my bus leaves in a half-hour. I gotta go."

"Okay, brother. Give us a call. 4-H."

"4-H. See you guys."

Mimi was getting a ride home from her sister Marianne, who had agreed to keep Mimi's Georgetown visit a secret from her parents. Troy and Randy would take a cab and ride the Greyhound bus together to New

York. Troy hadn't been to New York since last summer, and he was curious to see what was happening on his old block, where his mother had returned. No longer a Maryland resident, Troy couldn't wait to get back to the city. He would also be able to pick up rap records for his collection that weren't available in the D.C. area.

Troy walked Mimi downstairs to meet her sister who had directions to drive to the parking lot in back of Harbin Hall. Their goodbyes were as warm and loving as the night they'd spent together. He fondly greeted Marianne, whom he hadn't seen since his high school graduation. After a few more rounds of hugs and kisses, the sisters were gone. Troy returned to find Randy packed and eager to leave. He hadn't seen much of his roommate over the past few days, and he was looking forward to the trip.

"You ready, man?"

"Yeah, brother. Go ahead and call the cab."

"Nah, we can get one in front of Healy Circle. The bus leaves in an hour."

"Word. So how was the visit?"

"Dope, man, it was all of that. Didn't she look like she had a good time?"

"She was loving life, I could see that. I'm talking about you. You weren't just faking it?"

"Nah, man. Everything was cool. Even the drama with Angel."

"Yeah, I hear you, but..."

"But what?"

"I don't know. It's deep."

"What?"

"Mimi's a good sister, real sweet girl. She hasn't lost anything for you, and you obviously still have something for her. But you're on a mission for someone else. Hey, who am I to say anything?"

"So what would you do?"

"I don't know."

"Me neither. You got your bags? Let's go."

The magical warmth of the past few days was gone. A harsh November wind greeted Troy and Randy as they walked towards the bus station entrance. The Greyhound was a giant canister of travelers and luggage, filled to capacity. Troy could have taken a train to New York, charging the ticket to his father's MasterCard, but he was still uncomfortable with the impression it might give his friends. He also wanted to catch up with Randy, so he didn't mind the bus ride. While heading home on the "Sardine Special," the roommates discussed their last classes, how much work they would have to do for finals, and of course, the latest in rap music. Randy had some girls to look up when he got home to Queens.

"I'ma do like you and call my old girl."

"Just make sure you know what you're getting into."

Troy and Randy parted ways at Port Authority Bus Terminal in Manhattan. They agreed to speak on Thanksgiving Day to make plans for the weekend. New York City had not changed, and there was no better evidence of this than on the subway. Still, for Troy, the dirt, the crowd and the noise of the Number 2 was a welcoming committee. He was so happy to be back in the city, he didn't care about the rude passengers bumping him and stepping all over his bags. He was home!

West 110th Street looked the same, lined on both sides with apartment buildings, a short walk from Morningside Park. There were always a few kids in front of his apartment building; in this case, a few kids he didn't know. Both the C-Town across the street and the smaller *bodéga* on the corner were open, busy with shoppers young and old. He let himself into the lobby entrance with the keys he had kept for years. When his mother heard him unlocking the door upstairs, she came into the hallway.

"Hi!"

"Hi Mom!"

Troy and his mother embraced before he made his way inside the apartment. She still looked good, even younger than her forty years, but not as relaxed as she had been a couple of months before; Troy guessed that the stress of her new job, coupled with being back in New York City, had already begun to take a toll on her.

"Look at Moms, back in New York. You look so well adjusted."

"We do what we must. How was your trip?"

"It was cool. Took the bus."

"Troy! Why didn't you take the train?"

"I came up with Randy."

"Oh. How's he doing?"

"Fine."

"Come in, put your bags down."

Their apartment was spacious and nicely decorated with furniture from the old place in Maryland, including the couch, soft chairs and the piano he had grown up with.   Boxes that had not been unpacked indicated that the move-in wasn't yet complete.   He put his bags down and took a look around his bedroom and noticed that the furniture was slightly rearranged.   There was considerably more space since his records and DJ equipment were at school.

"Call your grandmother, she's been waiting for you."

"I will. How is she?"

"She's fine. We'll see her tomorrow. Call your father, too."

"What's to eat?"

"Sit down, I'll fix you a plate."

Troy returned to the living room, took a seat on the couch and put his feet up on the coffee table.   The TV now had a black box on top of it and the remote control was new.

Figures, he thought. *I go away to college and she gets cable.*

"Just so you know, Travis may be here."

"What?"

"You know, Travis Gordon, from your school?"

"You've been talking to Travis?"

"No," Troy's mother said, cracking a smile. "Not at first, anyway. He's called from time to time. He's coming to New York on a recruiting trip."

"Recruiting trip my ass," Troy muttered.

"You watch your mouth, before you get hurt. Anyway, he's coming to New York sometime soon. He's invited me out and…and I'm going to go."

"That's your business, isn't it?" Troy couldn't believe what he was hearing. His mother ignored Troy's last question.

"Would you like to eat now? I fixed your favorite."

"Save it, I lost my appetite." Just the possibility that his mother and Travis could get together was sickening to Troy. Having to face it when he came home was more than he could take. Troy stomped off to his room and slammed the door.

Later that night, after she was asleep, Troy found the dinner his mother had prepared. He made himself a plate of baked chicken, mashed potatoes and collard greens and devoured it while watching music videos on cable in his room. Although hearing about Travis from his mom infuriated him, Thanksgiving vacation would be just the break he needed.

Troy's bed was getting to be too small for him, but it still felt good. The TV was still on when he woke up in the morning. He hadn't planned on leaving his room until it was time to go to the Bronx, where his grandmother lived. All he needed was a phone and he'd be straight. The phone rang from his mother's room, but if it was for him, she would come and get him. He paused to listen for a few seconds. When she didn't call him, he found the remote control and began channel surfing.

"Troy!"

"Yeah?"

"Oh no, Troy!"

"What?" His mother sounded alarmed. Troy climbed out of bed just as his mother met him in the doorway. She looked horrified.

"Mom, what is it? What happened?"

"Troy, it, it's Mimi. She was killed yesterday in a car accident."

Troy fell back onto his bed. A numbness took over his entire body. He thought if he looked really well, maybe he could find some brandy in the kitchen.

Memories filled Troy's dreams. The dreams took him and Mimi back to their high school days, walking the halls together, going to movies with their friends, working on the homecoming float for the Senior Class Committee. One moment he was picking her up to go to the senior prom, the next he was listening as she explained the plot of the soap opera they watched together at his mother's apartment. Gradually, each episode became more physical, as the touch of her hand, the softness of her body tormented him. Lastly, he saw Mimi politely putting Angel in her place in Harbin. Would he be as grief-stricken if it were Angel who had been killed? He wanted to wake up and free himself of the nightmarish experience, but he could not.

In order to clear his mind and prepare for the funeral, Troy decided to return to Georgetown early Sunday morning. His mother was worried about him being alone and insisted that he take the train back. The campus was slowly coming back to life. Many underclassmen had returned to school early, creating a buzz around the school that Troy hadn't seen since midterms.

Winter was fast approaching, evidenced by the nip in the air that announced the season. Randy and Ill Will were still at home, and so was

Angel. Troy called Mimi's sister to offer his condolences and get information about the funeral service. He resented having to go to class the next morning, but he knew he would eventually have to get control of his shock and his grief to focus and study. If he could just get through the funeral. For God's sake, Mimi had just been in his arms, in his bed! So he stopped himself again from replaying their visit, fearful of being overwhelmed by the memories.

Troy returned from his last class the following Monday, dreading the wake he would attend in a few hours. Randy and Ill Will were shocked at the news, and neither of them knew what to say, other than to offer their sympathy. Room 228 soon took on the somberness of its occupants. Randy only came in if he needed something, just as he had done earlier. With her brief visit, Mimi had managed to win over his crew, and they were genuinely sorry for their friend's loss. Troy was changing his clothes when a knock on the door interrupted him.

"Come in!"

Angel swung the door open and marched right up to Troy's face, a storm of impatience.

"You weren't even going to come talk to me, were you?"

"Angel, this isn't a good time."

"Oh yes it is, goddammit. You have another girl in here, sleeping with you, and you take her to see Anita Baker? I'm supposed to take this lightly? No Troy, I think this is a real good time."

"No, it's not."

"And why the hell not?"

"Because Mimi was killed over Thanksgiving. I'm on my way to the wake now."

Angel fell silent, her mouth wide open. Angel's silence incensed Troy even more. He had heard enough.

"Could you excuse me? I'm trying to get dressed."

"Troy, oh Troy, I'm so sorry. I didn't know!"

"I know. I'll talk to you later."

"Is there anything I can do?"

"Yes. Leave."

Angel turned and walked back out the door., her angry storm of emotions temporarily subsided. Troy had no patience for Angel even if he was familiar with the hurt she was feeling; he had felt it because of her actions more than once.

*   *   *   *

The front room of the Landover Funeral Home was filled to capacity. There with Mimi's family were friends, former teachers and the parents of their classmates who Troy recognized. The gathering made for a strange, perverse version of a high school reunion. Mimi's funeral would be the first of the three students who were in the accident. Troy's mother had flown in from New York to join her son, but he still felt completely alone. His senior class from Landover High had only been apart for a few months, but it seemed to Troy as if years had passed since he had seen them. Some of Mimi's friends had even traveled from Cornell to pay their respects.

Since Troy had been Mimi's boyfriend, many of her friends were waiting to see him and wish him well. He was calm and polite to the guests, and he was far more composed than he thought he would be. Mimi's sister Marianne called to him from the other side of the parlor. Eventually, he made his way over. The two of them hugged.

"I'm so sorry."

"I know you are. Seems like just yesterday I was driving you guys to the movies."

"Yeah. I guess you never know."

"Guess not. Look Troy, I want you to know how happy Mimi was that she came to see you. I never told my Mom and Dad, they wouldn't have understood. Mimi's last days were happy because of you."

"I, I loved her." Grief was swelling inside of him now.

"I know. And she loved you. Come on, my mother wants to see you."

Marianne led Troy into the viewing room, where Mimi's mother was seated. She was surrounded by women who looked her age, no doubt sisters and girlfriends. When she looked up and saw Troy with her oldest daughter, she managed to smile through her tears.

"Troy. Come here, dear."

By the time he made his way over to Mimi's mother, Troy could no longer contain himself. On his knees, with his head in Mimi's mother's lap, he cried like he never had before.

"It's all right, boy. It's all right." His own mother looked on, in tears. Troy not only shared the grief of Mimi's family, but the guilt of his involvement in Mimi's visit, the secret of being in love with another girl. Now that Mimi was gone, he saw no possibility of redemption.

The next morning, he rode with Mimi's family in the limousine, and sat with her parents during the service. The service was a loving memorial filled with testimony about Mimi from Marianne and her close friends. Her favorite songs were played, and the church was filled with a special sadness unique to the death of a child.

*　　*　　*　　*

Shortly after he returned from the service, Troy was asked to DJ a party downtown at George Washington University that was being hosted by Alpha Phi Alpha, a black fraternity. Their usual disc jockey was unavailable, and one of the Alphas had remembered him as the freshman who ran his mouth about being a DJ. So they looked Troy up, knowing they could get him for a fraction of what they usually paid. Troy wasn't naïve to the situation, but he didn't care. All of the practice and all of the money he'd spent on records was finally going to pay off. Troy had been waiting for over a year to flex his skills, and it would soon come to pass. He would have been excited about the party anyway, but Mimi's passing gave the night a special purpose. His efforts would be dedicated to her memory.

Randy was in the room bopping his head to the music while Troy practiced.

"Brother, if you don't have your shit together by now, you ought to give it up."

Troy chuckled. "You crazy, boy! This'll be the best party you've ever been to!"

"I don't know, man. Some of these deejays can rock down here."

"What you talking about, boy, I'm from New York. These kids down here ain't got nothing for me!"

"Where's Ill?"

"I sent him to the store a half hour ago."

As if on cue, Ill Will came in, dancing frantically, armed with a bottle of malt liquor in each hand.

"4-H is in the house! *auf Wiedersein!*"

"You going somewhere, fool?"

"No Randy, why do you ask?"

"Because you just said goodbye to everybody."

"Don't you tell me about my German! *Vie Hisensie!*"

"You get my 40?" Troy asked.

"Yeah, but I'ma drink it if you don't come on!"

Troy turned around, still in front of his turntables.

"Yo, the party doesn't start until I get there, know what I'm saying?"

"Yeah, whatever. Randy, you want some brew?"

"You know I never touch the stuff."

"Right, right. Just checking."

"If you had any sense, you'd ease up on that yourself." Randy turned to Troy. "Come on roomie, it's time to jet."

"All right, I'm ready."

Troy put the records away, then began surveying his crates, organizing the meticulous inventory of his up-to-the-minute collection. He had also bought new mats and needles for his turntables. It was critical for him to be thoroughly prepared for the party; his reputation would be staked on this, his first college deejaying event. Randy was growing impatient with his ritual.

"Tee, would you come on?"

"Yeah, soon as you clowns come get these records."

"Come get these records," Ill Will laughed. "You can come get these nuts if you want to, you the DJ! Jam Master Flash wanna-be motherfucker!"

"Just come the fuck on please."

Ill Will managed to squeeze both 40-ounce bottles of malt liquor into one of the milk crates. The hosts of the party were waiting downstairs.

Black students from all over D.C. filled the university's ballroom. Many of them were from Georgetown, and the black contingent of the freshman class was there in full force. Troy recognized other faces from Howard as well. He didn't want to disappoint his classmates, many of whom were curious to see if their class really boasted a DJ. Troy was more concerned with what they wanted than with the Alphas who were paying for his services. Within a couple of hours, they had gotten what they paid for. Because he'd imagined such a party countless times while practicing in his dorm room, Troy knew exactly which songs would make the crowd respond. He was a natural, conducting an electronic orchestra of hip-hop and club hits, drawing almost everyone to the huge dance floor. Ill Will stayed close to the turntables, surveying the crowd with his friend.

"You the man!"

Troy suppressed a smile, his head down, his shoulder holding the headphones to his ear. When they heard Big Daddy Kane's "Ain't No Half Steppin," the crowd jumped up and cheered "Ho-oh!" He noticed that Angel was typically absent, but the success of the party, coupled with his thoughts of Mimi, eased the normal disappointment he felt when she wasn't around. Troy suspected that Mimi was watching him from somewhere, cheering him on. When he segued into "I Know You Got Soul" by Eric B. & Rakim, the crowd went berserk. Just as he had practiced, he mixed Rakim rapping "Pump up the volume," over and over, until the crowd began to shout the same line in unison. Right in the middle of the floor was Randy, doing his crazy dance with a couple of girls. The party was a smash, and the Alphas were more than happy to pay Troy his modest fee at the end of the night.

For the remainder of that weekend, Troy was greeted with compliments and congratulations from Georgetown students. Many of them wanted him to make tapes for them, and they were finally willing to pay for his services. Randy and Ill Will made fun of their friend's semi-celebrity status, but they were as proud of him as anyone. He would have loved for Angel to have been there, but the fact that she would hear about the party was enough for him. He was on Cloud Nine, but he didn't have time to enjoy his success, as final exams were on the horizon. And it would take all of his efforts just to give himself a chance in Accounting I, which held the biggest academic challenge for him.

Although Angel was still the girl of his dreams, Troy was held captive by painful memories of Mimi. The distractions of everyday life were enough, eventually, to ease the shock of Mimi's death. There were only a few weeks left in the semester. Troy, in particular, longed for his last exam because he also thought the end of the year would somehow provide him with a sense of closure. If he had his way, his future with Angel and his grades would blossom like his budding career as a DJ. His wish was at best ambitious; at worst unrealistic. Still, Troy couldn't help but be hopeful.

Eleven

Janice Harris sat in her living room, holding the phone, smiling from ear to ear.

"I wish you were here, you know," she said

"So do I," Travis replied. "I miss you already."

"And I miss you. As soon as I get some time off, we'll make plans."

"That sounds good. Maybe you can come down here. We can go to the Corcoran Museum."

"Only if I can stay with you."

"I always have room for an incredible, sexy lady."

"Sounds like you have my visit all planned out. But you know..." her voice trailed off.

"I know," Travis interrupted. "You'd have to see Troy."

"I'm sorry dear. I know I promised I wouldn't talk about him."

"That's all right, he's your son."

"So how is he?"

"His friend's death has been tough on him, but he seems to be holding up, at least as far as I can tell. You know he avoids me like the plague."

"I don't know why," Janice huffed. "He doesn't talk to his father, either."

"He knows you're there for him. That's what counts."

"I guess," Janice admitted. "But let's change the subject. I called to hear your voice."

"And I'm glad you did."

She beamed through the rest of the conversation and was still smiling after she and Travis ended their call. It had been a long time since she'd been so excited, so looking forward to seeing a man. She longed to tell Travis how she really felt, but she thought it might be too soon. Janice Harris had become conservative in her expectations of men over the years, so she was never more than mildly disappointed when things between them didn't work out. But it was hard not to have high hopes for her and Travis. Unlike other men she'd dated, he was her intellectual equal. Furthermore, she wouldn't have to support Travis the way she had supported Troy; one son was enough. In fact, his very job demanded that

he have her son's best interests at heart. Travis made her feel beautiful
and young. And did he ever look *good!* She wasn't usually attracted to
light-skinned men, but Travis Gordon had been too cute to resist.

"Mmm, mmph." She thought of Troy for a moment and she knew
seeing her with Travis might be uncomfortable for him. Still, her mind
was made up; she had sacrificed for Troy all through his childhood. It
was time she did something with herself in mind.

*   *   *   *

Given a choice between the French Revolution, the subject of his
current class, and the latest edition of *Street & Smith's College Basketball*,
Troy opted for the latter. The Hoyas had already won a couple of
exhibition games and Troy wanted to learn how they would fare during
the season. Troy appeared to take notes while he read about the team —
his magazine carefully concealed under a notebook. The trouble with
Euro Civ was Professor Shebel's robotic style of lecturing. Students
weren't required to discuss the material, but Shebel covered two or three
chapters in each class, which made for fifty minutes of intense notetaking.
Unless, of course, a student was reading something else.

Troy was convinced that Professor Shebel was cramming information
into these last classes to justify putting the material on the final. All that
mattered was what would — and wouldn't — be on the test and he
wished that Professor Shebel would just get to the damn exam review. If
the new stuff he was covering would be on it, Troy would make a note to
study it in the textbook. With this foolproof plan, Troy continued reading
his magazine. Meanwhile, Shebel was going a mile a minute and the
blackboard was quickly filling with his spidery but legible handwriting.

He knew all of his final exams would be tough, particularly
Accounting. Troy was barely keeping up even with his tutor Wendell's
help. Philosophy would be nearly as challenging, but the paper he'd
rewritten for McBride was enough for him to maintain a 'B' in the course.
If he did well on the final, he could still improve his grade. His
Novel/Short Story class had no final, only a final paper. This class would
probably yield an 'A,' but he had to stay on top of his class participation
to ensure it. This meant more reading, but he didn't mind. His remaining
allotted absences from class made for a perfect opportunity to study.

Preparing himself for the academic binge that was ahead of him weighed heavily on Troy, but he couldn't suppress the other matter of equal concern. Angel had begun to treat him like, of all things, an angel. Her calls were more frequent, as were her visits to his room. Their kisses were spontaneous and she never held back, particularly in public. He attributed her behavior to guilt over her remarks about Mimi, but her turnaround still struck him as ironic. At first his cynicism kept him from believing that Angel was being anything other than sympathetic. But after a week of her new attentiveness, Troy bought into it lock, stock and barrel. The only drawback was that whenever he tried to test the limits of her newfound affection, he was met with resistance and when he and Angel were alone, she would find some reason to leave, saying 'now isn't a good time.' Randy and Ill Will said they always heard her talking about how wonderful Troy was when he wasn't around, while face-to-face with him she was still vague about the status of their relationship.

*   *   *   *

Troy, Randy and Ill Will were now strictly academic. They had four 'study days' before exams, designed to allow students time to concentrate on preparing for finals. Troy had convinced Randy to study in Ill Will's room on designated days to keep him from drinking.

"Ill, how many exams you got?" Troy asked him.

"Three and a paper."

"That's what I got." Troy had finished his final paper for Novel/Short Story, but he wasn't going to let on.

"Yeah, but you don't have German."

"Nobody told you to take that shit," Randy interjected.

"If Carl can do it, fuck it."

"Carl isn't gonna fail, is he?" Randy asked.

"Neither am I."

"Yeah, okay." Randy was convinced Ill Will should have to pay for his decisions, especially now.

"Fuck you. What do you have, Tee?"

"Accounting, Euro Civ and Philosophy."

"You ready?"

"No," Troy confessed. "But I'll be all right."

"Yeah, as long as you can keep Angel out of here," Randy said without looking up.

"Whatever, nigga. What about that Econ, huh? What's up with that?"

Randy half-smiled, but he was silent.

"Yeah," Troy told him. "Thought so."

Ill Will chuckled.

"Fuck you laughing at, Ill?" Randy asked. "You think this shit is funny?"

"Sorry, man."

"Sorry my ass! I don't know why nobody said anything before."

"Here we go."

"Damn real! Motherfuckers almost got suspended! And your drunk ass wants to act like everything is cool? And you wonder why Yvonne has an attitude. What were you thinking about? Huh?"

Ill Will said nothing. He couldn't look Randy or Troy in the face.

"I know. I know I fucked up."

"Yeah, you know now, don't you?" Randy insisted. "I don't know what Troy was waiting on." Randy turned to Troy, who knew he was right. Ill Will got up and left without a word. Randy was still heated after Ill Will left. "What?" he asked.

"Nothing," Troy answered. "You're right."

The tension among the three of them was new to Troy, and he hated it. Troy was used to Randy's holier-than-thou routine when he was around other freshmen; few of them were as well-read as he was in history and politics. But even then, he never meant to come off so judgmentally. Now it felt as though he lacked respect for his friends, insistent on being the voice of reason. Troy resented this stance since Randy was still a freshman like them. Ill Will seemed to have taken the admonishment to heart. He really hadn't humbled himself much after the drinking incident a couple of months before, but Troy was certain that he regretted what had happened. Troy gambled that the animosity between them would pass with final exams.

Meanwhile, Troy hit the books whenever he had a free moment, as well as while at work in Copy Services. For once he was glad that Angel wasn't around; now that they were becoming closer, she was a distraction he couldn't possibly resist. Luckily, she had her own studying to do. He attempted to make the most of his study days by staying in the library, all day and late into the night after dinner. Students left their belongings at their desks, informally reserving the limited space in the building. Troy's confidence grew in his mastery of Philosophy ideals and Euro Civ dates and facts, but he still had to struggle just to maintain a basic understanding of Accounting. He could no longer deny the fact that he should have had this intensity with regard to classes months ago. No matter how disciplined he had become, a few days of concerted effort couldn't make up for a semester of loafing. He promised himself that next semester he would be more organized.

Philosophy was Troy's first exam. He felt well-prepared for it, attacking each essay question with careful, thorough answers. McBride's assistant, who had given him a C plus on his midterm, wouldn't punish him again. He felt some relief when it was over, but it was temporary. Troy wanted to maintain his newfound academic momentum, so he went directly to the library. At two in the afternoon, he had a fair shot at claiming a cubicle for the rest of the day. Accounting was last, but first he had to knock out Euro Civ. Armed with his notes and highlighted textbook, Troy began reviewing a semester's worth of material. He realized that it had taken the pressure of final exams for him to find a semblance of discipline.

He took a dinner break and returned to Room 228 to exchange books. When he was certain that he was ready for Euro Civ, Troy pushed himself through his notes again. When he could stay awake no longer, he headed back to the dorm. Randy was snoring loudly when he returned. It was 3:30 a.m.

Troy's clock radio blared at 11:00 a.m. He could have sworn he had just crawled into bed and he hardly felt rested, but from the way the sunlight pierced the room, he knew it was morning. There was enough time to shower, grab a snack and review before the 1:15 final.

When he faced the test questions in Shebel's classroom, Troy knew he had not studied long enough. The exam itself looked much like Shebel's study guide with the typical essay and multiple choice questions. But the study guide hadn't made a mockery of his memory as the questions before him did. To make matters worse, he suddenly thought of Mimi. It took all of his concentration just to write down his answers. The essay questions were manageable, but the short answer and multiple choice questions were tougher in reality than they had been in Troy's imagination. While struggling with a riddle about the French Revolution, again Mimi entered his mind. She didn't have a chance to finish her first semester. He could only think of how much she liked Cornell and her classes. The harder he tried to concentrate on the exam, the more distracted he became.

Leaving the Graveston building, Troy saw a few cheerful faces around him but he could not still his thoughts of Mimi. He walked more slowly in the cold, trying to shake her memory and plan his last few of days of test preparation. He returned to Harbin to find Randy gone. He was thankful to be alone. Before any of his Accounting strategy could be executed, Troy fell into a comatose sleep.

"Troy? Troy!"

Troy jumped up in a panic, certain that he was missing a final.

"Phone." Randy handed him the receiver.

"Oh. Thanks. Hello?"

"Hey Troy, how you doing!"

"Hey, Dad."

"Just waking up, huh?"

"Something like that."

"You taken any exams yet?"

"Yeah, two."

"You pass?"

"Of course! I did study, you know."

"Okay, okay! I just wanted to see how you were doing."

"I'm fine. Look, I need to get in the library," he said, trying to satisfy his father's questioning.

"I won't hold you. You'll be here for the holidays, right?"

"Yeah, I'm coming home Sunday."

"Call me when you get here."

"I will. See you."

"Take care."

"Bye." Troy wished Randy hadn't answered the phone. The last thing he thought he needed was his father's annoying intrusion.

"Your pops?"

"Yeah. He knows it's finals so he's checking up and shit."

Randy chuckled. "He *is* your father."

"Whatever. How many exams you got left?"

"Just one, political theory. What about you?"

"Accounting. How did you do so far?"

"I think I did all right. We'll see when the grades come out."

"Word. You breaking out?"

"Uh huh. Study group."

"All right. Good luck if I don't see you."

"You too, brother. Just a few more days."

Troy slapped hands with his roommate before he left. He was tempted to study in the room and although the second floor was quiet, he knew he wouldn't get anything accomplished there. As if to drive the point home, Angel slid through the open door.

"Hi sweetie."

"Hi. Is something wrong?"

"Does something have to be wrong for me to see you?"

"No, I just—"

Before he could answer, Angel closed in and kissed him. Troy forgot what he had begun to say.

"I missed you. I know you're studying, I am too. I'm taking a little break."

Troy tried to hide his paralysis.

"How's it going?"

"Terrible. I'm probably going to have to take organic chemistry again."

"You'll be fine," he assured her. "Listen, I have to go study. Will you walk me downstairs?"

"Sure. When are you leaving for New York?"

"Sunday."

"I will see you before then, won't I?"

"Of course." This time he interrupted her with a kiss before exiting Harbin.

"Later, baby."

"Bye."

He was still transfixed by Angel's scent, her lip gloss on his mouth. Preparing for this last exam would have been difficult enough without Angel injecting herself into his mind. Of all times, *now* she was acting like they would finally get together. Troy wiped the lip gloss off of his mouth, but he couldn't wipe her out of his mind.

By the time he arrived, the library was even more packed than it had been the day before. Reviewing the Accounting chapters and problems was the equivalent of a workout, like being in a gym with no air conditioning and having far too much weight on the bar. By breaking up the hours of studying with brisk walks outside, Troy developed some confidence with his rudimentary grasp of the subject. His comprehension grew, but his knowledge of some concepts wouldn't be enough. He reviewed the basics each hour, followed up with practice problems he'd worked on with Wendell, and then struggled with the most unfamiliar portions of the material. After battling with "Principles of Accounting" and his notes all day, Troy realized that whatever he didn't know by then, he certainly wouldn't know by test time.

A thin frost covered Georgetown's campus and turned walkways into darkly carved thoroughfares in the snow. Troy walked carefully along the path to Harbin Hall, which had been made passable by shovels and salt. He hadn't seen Ill Will since he and Randy had argued, so he stopped by his room. He found his friend sitting on the floor with Yvonne, playing gin rummy. A 40-ounce bottle of malt liquor sat by his hip. Troy couldn't take his eyes off the malt liquor.

"What, your exams are over?"

"Nah, one more. German."

"What's with the 40?"

"I knew you would say that. Listen, I feel like shit about what happened." He reached for Yvonne's hand. "So I'm chilling. No more hard stuff."

Troy grew tired at the very thought of addressing the matter.

"You *have* studied for German, right?"

"Yeah, but I either know it or I don't."

"And what about you, Yvonne? I know you have some more exams."

"You're right," Yvonne admitted. "I've been studying every day, though."

"Don't listen to this clown," Ill Will told her. "He's only getting academic now because he has to."

"You do, too, motherfucker!"

"I know, shit! Cut me some slack. I've been studying, believe me."

"Uh-huh, right."

"You still planning to go home Sunday?"

"Yeah."

"Good. I think I'll head up to New York with you. I even talked to Randy, he's cool with it."

"Now you're talking. Where's Carl?"

"I don't know, probably studying."

"Right. I'll see you before we leave."

"Peace."

Troy was happy to see FIFO vs. LIFO and other terms he recognized on the Accounting final that Thursday. And he found some reward on the exam in the form of a few easy questions. There was no doubt that it wouldn't be Troy's best performance, but at least he knew what he had to do to improve. When he finished nearly two hours later, he practically ran out of the classroom, overjoyed to have finished the first semester of his freshman year. He was overjoyed to know he'd be home for Christmas soon.

*   *   *   *

Randy was packing when Troy woke up the next day. With finals complete, the roommates let music replace the previous weeks' quiet rules. He bopped his head to a song by EPMD which blared from Troy's speakers.

"I guess I'm not getting any more sleep," Troy said, wiping his eyes.

"Pardon me brother, I'm just excited. Plus, this is the jam, 'It's My Thing.'"

"Now you got me ready for the city."

"We'll have a good time. That's if you make it up there. You might chase Angel around down here during break."

"I'll see her before I jet."

"You better hit that before you jet."

Troy smiled. He was certain that he would have Angel soon, but he chose not to jinx the event by speaking the words.

"How you getting home?" Randy asked.

"Amtrak."

"I hear that."

"Ill's coming up, right?"

"Most definitely. I invited him to stay with me.

"All right!"

"We talked, I told him I was just mad that day."

"I think he understands."

"I do, too. You were right, it could have been any of us. 4-H has to stick together."

"Word up."

"Listen, I'll call you when we get up there."

"Do that."

"Let me throw on some sweats, I'll walk you to the bus stop."

Twelve

Troy's mother was pulling lamb chops out of the oven while she spoke. Because of Mimi's death, this visit was really the first chance Troy and his mother had to catch up.

"The place was kept up well, don't you think?"

"Yeah, Moms. Subletting was a good idea. Did you miss New York?"

"Not at all. But you have to go where the money is. When NBC News calls, you have to answer."

"You'll get back to Landover one day."

"I hope so." Troy's mother brought the dish over to the kitchen table. It was another meal her son loved, lamb chops served with candied yams, collard greens, and macaroni and cheese. She hadn't always had the energy to cook when Troy was growing up, but when she did, it was usually a meal fit for royalty. Having Troy home was now a special occasion, so a home-cooked meal was in order. She also suspected that since he had been in college, he would appreciate her efforts more. As she watched her son inhale the meal, she knew she was right.

He and his mother made up for lost time over the first few days of Troy's vacation. She had been brought up to date on classes, she got to meet Randy and Ill Will, and they all spoke of Troy's new political aspirations. What he thought she wouldn't want to hear and what he didn't feel like explaining — Ill Will's drunken fiasco, the Howard parties with the girls, his combative conversations with his dad, and deejaying — he left out. When she asked how the girls were treating him, he only hinted that he may have been seeing someone. Telling her it was nothing serious quieted his mother's natural curiosity. He wanted to talk to her about Mimi's memory and Angel, too, but he wasn't convinced that his mother could offer him any constructive advice. She certainly couldn't if her own love life was any indication.

To Troy, none of her boyfriends had ever been worth her time and Travis Gordon would be no exception, given the chance. She had never been happy with any of them for long.

While he was having a good time with his friends, Troy found himself growing anxious to return to school. College had its ups and downs, but it seemed that his life didn't make sense anywhere else. When he went downstairs to visit with his friends from the block, he found that few of them were left. The brothers on the stoop filled Troy in on who was in jail, who had been shot, who had been videotaped selling drugs, who had just fathered another child.

"What the fuck?" he asked. "Didn't nobody finish school?"

"Not too many," Marlon offered, putting out his cigarette. Marlon was one of the few guys from the building Troy had kept up with after moving to Maryland.

"How about you, Marley? I know you have other things to do besides stay out here all night."

"Oh, uh, yeah!" he laughed. "I'm getting my GED in a minute. Besides, it's cold as shit out here anyway. I was just getting some air, you know."

"Yeah man, I hear you. Listen, I'm heading back upstairs."

"All right Tee, man. It's good to see you. Georgetown! That's cool man, I'm real proud of you."

"Thanks." They slapped hands and hugged. For some reason Troy found it hard to look Marlon in the face as he turned to go upstairs.

"Hey Troy!"

"Yeah man, what's up?"

"If you want to double up a little later, we'll be down here, you know? You might make some money."

"No thanks, man. Dice ain't my game. You take it easy."

*   *   *   *

Each time Angel called, Troy was closer to deciding to return to Georgetown. Randy and Ill Will, however, were looking to paint the town until it was time for registration. On New Year's Eve, the trio agreed to see Keith Sweat perform at the Red Parrot. Earlier that day they had met uptown at Harlem's Mart 125 to purchase tapes of Louis Farrakhan's speeches. Ill Will picked up some incense and some cards he thought Yvonne might like.

"Thank you brother, As-Salaam Alaikum," Randy told the bow-tied attendant.

"Wa-Alaikum Salaam."

"You come out here all the way from Queens to get Farrakhan tapes? Why don't you go to Brooklyn?"

"The stores aren't as good. Besides, when I come to the Mart, I can get my bean pies and vegetarian food. I can check out the bookstores and see what's up with the Nation. I go to the mosque up here, too."

Randy and Ill Will accompanied Troy home for another special lamb chop dinner. Troy couldn't resist the temptation to ask his mother about the minister.

"Moms, what do you make of Farrakhan?"

"What, you joining the Nation now? I bet your father would love that."

"No." Troy looked over at Randy apologetically, but his roommate was face down, eradicating his food.

"Just answer the question."

"I have some problems with him and the Nation, I think they're sexist."

"I agree, Miss Harris," Will added. "There seems to be a pattern of women in subservient roles in every respect."

"Please," Randy snapped. "What do you know about it?"

"No offense, *brother*, but you know how they do. They may talk that 'woman is your queen' stuff in them speeches, but as far as the day-to-day, they keep the ladies behind 'em, wrapped up in sheets, no less."

"Miss Harris, Ill has an active imagination," Randy insisted.

"Randy, there is some truth to Willard's point. There haven't been many apologies for some of the, ah, shortcomings of the Nation's leadership."

"Perhaps, but we haven't produced a better leader than the Honorable Elijah Muhammad, or Minister Farrakhan, for that matter."

"Didn't Elijah have six babies by five different women?" Ill Will asked. Troy nearly choked on his food.

"I guess none of us are without sin. I suppose anyone trying to do positive and empowering things for black people deserves to be heard, at least. Randy, you're the Muslim here, what do you think?"

"Yeah Randy, what do you think?" Ill Will asked.

"Miss Harris, there are sisters who have issues with the Nation and I can appreciate those issues. I don't subscribe totally to the Nation--"

"And just what do you subscribe to?" Troy's mother interrupted.

"Islam is my religion, Ms. Harris," Randy continued, "but the appeal of Minister Farrakhan isn't only that he's a Muslim. I, myself, believe whole-heartedly in the Nation's teachings about self-sufficiency and economic empowerment." Randy looked at Troy's mom, trying to read her expression.

"I see," she said, smiling. "I'm sure one day you'll be the Muslim you hope to be."

"Thank you, Ms. Harris," he said, relieved.

"Anytime."

*   *   *   *

Despite the bitter cold of that evening, a line snaked around the corner of 57th Street and 9th Avenue. Troy jumped at the opportunity to go to a real nightclub, since he and his friends had never been old enough to get into any in D.C. Back then they had settled for college parties. Now that he was a DJ, Troy saw club attendance as essential to his hobby. Furthermore, the Red Parrot was becoming popular as a hip-hop venue, often the performing home of DJ Red Alert, Boogie Down Productions and others. The Red Parrot didn't share the legendary hip-hop status of the Latin Quarter, but it was good enough for him.

"Shit, would you look at this line?"

"It's New Year's Eve," Randy said. "And this Keith Sweat guy is the man. That record is all over the radio."

"You ain't lying. Speaking of that, who's the DJ?"

"What are you going to do, battle him?" Ill asked, laughing.

"I bet I could."

"Don't get carried away. You're nice and all…"

"But not that nice, right? That's okay, I will be."

"Right, right."

Randy turned to a group of girls in line. "Excuse me ladies, but have you been in line long?"

Only one of them looked up. "Almost an hour."

"I see. Well, I guess it's worth it on a night like tonight."

"We'll see." The leader of this troop of females was petite, light-skinned, and draped in a fur coat. Troy wanted a look at her body, but he couldn't see any of it through the big animal hide she was flaunting.

In seconds, Troy, Randy and Ill Will were introduced to the rest of the group. The one wearing the fur coat was Wanda, behind her was Suzanne. Suzanne was closest, so Troy decided to focus on her. She was attractive, but, as with her friend, Troy couldn't see much through the coat.

At midnight the group found themselves still on line, but a club worker came out with champagne glasses and bottles of generic champagne for everyone. Eventually, Troy, Randy and Ill Will got in for a whopping $40 a head, while their acquaintances were admitted free of charge, due to the funny looking, laminated passes they showed at the door. Wanda, Suzanne and their cronies vanished as soon as they got inside. Troy was less disappointed than Randy, who had invested more time talking to them. Ill Will was surprisingly calm and nonchalant about the women. Troy's main interest was the music. By studying the DJ and the way Keith Sweat controlled the crowd, he was sure he could pick up some pointers. While observing the hundreds of people in the dark, on the dance floor and at the bar, Troy knew that neither he nor Ill Will had ever seen a party the likes of this. Randy was slightly more New York savvy and not as impressed. Even the faint, rotten smell of crack cocaine in the upstairs lounge couldn't affect his excitement. DJ Red Alert was conducting a hip-hop symphony with many of the songs that were hits back in Room 228. The three friends jumped along with everyone else to the bass-heavy music. Keith Sweat took the stage at around 2:30. Troy and Randy eyed each other in the crowd when they saw Wanda and Suzanne on stage dancing behind the singer. *Ah*, Troy thought. *Keith Sweat's dancers. That explains the furs.*

"Maybe we should start singing!" Randy yelled.

Several phone messages awaited Troy the next afternoon. People had been calling all morning, but his mother had let him sleep, something she would never have done a year ago. "Angel" was written three times on the notepad on his end table, along with the times she had called. Troy was letting go of the last bit of doubt that Angel was his and was encouraged by her desire to talk to him over the break. Mingling with the women in the club boosted his confidence, so he decided not to call Angel back.

On New Year's Day, Troy's mother had to work; such was the life of a television editor. He had been looking forward to hanging out with her more, but she didn't cancel her plans with Travis when he told her he was going back to Georgetown. Troy regretted the assurance he had given her that everything was fine at school. Maybe he had over-convinced her. The maternal signs of concern she showed in September were now non-existent. Troy told Ill Will he was welcome to stay at his place as long as he wanted, but he was heading back to D.C.

"I got it," Ill Will told him. "Angel."

Troy shrugged his shoulders, unable to deny the truth.

"No problem," Ill told him. "Randy's talking about hanging out again. We'll probably do something tomorrow, then I'll catch a bus to Philly, see my mom."

"Cool. I'll check y'all when you get back then."

*   *   *   *

On the train to Washington, Troy looked over Randy's notes. He had promised his roommate he would read his list of ideas for Black Student Union activities. Randy encouraged him to develop some ideas of his own, but it looked to him like everything was covered. With a VCR and audio-visual equipment, they could show films that were not only culturally, but also politically significant. "The Hate That Hate Produced" and "Eyes on the Prize" stood out in Troy's mind as good choices. Randy's list of guest speakers was particularly ambitious, including rapper Chuck D, Rev. Jesse Jackson, and Minister Farrakhan, who was clearly one of Randy's mentors. The list was light on social events and heavy on educational programs, but that would probably be a welcome change of pace. Black students did enough partying, and Troy thought the Black Student Union calendar, when it was finalized, would provide a good balance for the student body.

Troy returned to a mostly abandoned Georgetown campus, aside from an occasional security officer. As soon as he put his bags down, he called Angel's room, but had to settle for her answering machine. He left a message, and began unpacking. His father had bought him some nice new sweatsuits for Christmas, but Troy was more interested in the new vinyl releases he had acquired in New York. He imagined himself in the DJ booth back at the Manhattan nightclub, driving the crowd wild with his skills.

With one ear clutching his headphones and the stereo on, he still heard knocking. Troy dropped a record and the headphones and took two giant leaps over to the door. When he opened it, he was overjoyed to find Angel standing in the doorway smiling.

"Hi sweetie."

"Hi. Come in."

"I called you."

"Did you? I was out a lot, my mother must not have given me the message."

"Hmph." Angel took a seat on the bed.

"Hey. Don't be like that. I came back early to see you."

"And what made you so sure I would be here?"

"I don't know. I was just hoping."

Troy reached for her face, but she turned away.

"Come on now," he whispered, kissing her neck. "I couldn't wait to get back to you." Eventually, Angel's resistance faded.

Troy could not hold her tight enough, despite the fact that they were pressed together and locked at the mouth as he gently removed her dress. After unfastening her bra he was practically beside himself over the softness that welcomed him. Now that Troy was at her panties, Angel's moans were longer and louder, and he was letting out a few of his own. He had moved so quickly to get inside her, it was nearly impossible to slow himself down. He wanted to savor the feeling, but when Angel made the slightest gyration with her hips, he climaxed. It was the quickest, longest eruption he could remember, and like the kid that he still was, he continued pumping long after it was over. Angel was no longer vocal, but instead offered soft pats on Troy's back, as if to comfort him for his lack of experience. He was sorely disappointed with himself for not pleasing her; if only she hadn't made him wait so long.

"Hold on, baby," he told her. "This is just temporary. Just give me a minute."

"Okay, but hurry."

Angel reached below his waist and gently stroked him. Kissing his chest and his abdomen, she brought Troy's erection back in moments. He peeled back his sheet to see her in the nude, her thigh on top of his. Within moments he was scrambling for another condom. She obviously knew what to do and he would not disappoint her this time.

"Oooh," Angel moaned softly as they started again. It took everything he had to stay composed.

The shape and feel of Angel's body was still overwhelming to Troy, but he was determined to give her his best. This time their lovemaking began slowly and gently. He traced her shoulders and her hips with kisses before licking his way back up to her full breasts, which wiggled with his every move.

"Put it in," she said.

Troy moved in as slowly as he could, pushing himself as Angel pulled him forward. Gradually his strokes increased to a frenzied pace that he maintained until he brought a fierce, joyous shout from Angel. Neither of them moved an inch afterwards, keeping the same position until they both fell asleep.

To Troy, nothing was wrong with the world when spring registration began the following week. The lines were just as long as they had been in the fall. It was icy and freezing cold outside, and like other freshmen, most of the courses that Troy wanted to take were longshots at best. But since having sex with Angel, Troy's confidence had soared higher than the clock in Healy Tower. It was all quite inconsequential: his unknown grades, Travis and his mother together, his father's nagging, everything. Life was perfect.

"What's up, homey?" Troy turned to find Ill Will, who like him, had a handful of registration forms. The main registration line was crawling.

"What's up man? When you got back?"

"I just got off the bus. I didn't want to wear out my welcome with Randy, so I went home for a day. I wouldn't have had to come back until Wednesday, but I don't know what I'm taking."

Troy laughed. "What do you mean you don't know what you're taking?"

"I know what, but I don't know with who. Or with whom. But forget that. What happened?"

"With what?"

"Motherfucker, don't play dumb with me. You know."

"Oh, that. Yeah, yeah, it was good."

"My man! It's about time."

"I know. What you got up for later?"

"I don't know, probably the usual. Why?"

"Let's go up to the field house and play some ball or something."

"That'll work. Just let me know."

After two hours of lines, signatures and bills, Troy was enrolled for his second semester.

*   *   *   *

Troy sat in the back of the classroom while Professor Franklin, associate professor of Ethics, reviewed the syllabus. Whereas Philosophy had been a course that seemed simplistic on the surface, Ethics really was going to be simple. He had to be kidding, this guy. No exams? Two papers? Three books? What would he do to get them to show up, pay them? Troy smiled. At least there was one course he wouldn't have to worry about.

The next day Troy had Accounting II with Professor Newcomb, in the same classroom as last semester's Accounting I class. The professor insisted to his students, the same ones from Accounting I, that everyone had done well on the previous semester's exam. Troy knew a false assurance speech when he heard one. He must have really screwed up. Maybe if he got with Wendell earlier this time, he could ace this Accounting stuff. He realized this goal might require more studying and less mixing. It was a bitter pill to swallow, but as Newcomb began Chapter 13, where Accounting I left off, Troy knew he had to face this academic challenge with more discipline than he had applied previously. How could dating Angel and deejaying the parties take a back seat?

Second Semester

Thirteen

Randy unpacked his bags and put his clothes away in his usual neat and orderly manner.

"What up, man?" Troy greeted him. "As-Salaam Alaikum."

"Wa-Alaikum Salaam, brother. You got all your classes?"

"Yeah, I just came from one. You're kind of late, ain't you?"

"My mom didn't want me to leave. You know how that is."

"Of course."

"Why did you come back so early, anyway?"

"I had to." Troy's grin ended his roommate's line of questioning.

"Ha ha! You finally hit it!" Randy congratulated him with a back slap. "So you just the man now, huh?"

Troy changed the subject. "Yeah, but I want to get with you on this BSU stuff before you get deep into Macro and French."

"You mean you looked at the list?" Randy's eyes lit up.

"Most definitely. I'm trying to do this!"

"Now you're talking!"

The two sat at Randy's desk and began to draft an outline of their plans for the Black Student Union. The draft evolved into a calendar, each month a wealth of activities from which the students could choose. The BSU and NAACP elections would be held at the end of February, along with the rest of the student body elections. Officers would begin two weeks later, leaving them half of the spring semester and the bulk of next fall to implement their programming. Troy had heard white students arguing over budget allocations and the input of GUSA, the Georgetown University Student Association, regarding academic policy. Back in September it was nothing more than gibberish, an excuse to take up space on the walls with flyers. Now, Troy could appreciate the role of students in school politics, and how political activism was not just an activity, but often a necessary component of productive student life.

*   *   *   *

For the most part, Troy's mail was never particularly exciting. He only looked for something handwritten, meaning a letter from a friend or a 'David Harris Inc.' envelope, indicating money from his father. *Aw shit.* The return address of the envelope in his hand read 'Georgetown University, Office of the Registrar.' Except for one bright spot, an 'A' in Novel/Short Story, the rest were 'C' pluses.   He had expected this in Accounting and was actually surprised he had done that well.   The 'C' pluses in Philosophy and Euro Civ annoyed him, though; he had really tried to prepare for those finals.   Troy pulled out a calculator to figure the exact grade point average.   2.75 was the lowest GPA Troy had ever had in his life.   His mother would understand, but his father was going to shit when he saw the transcript.

Ill Will let himself in.

"What up, homey?"

"Hey."

"What's wrong with you?"

"My fucking grades."

"How'd you do?"

"2.75."

"What's wrong with that? You did better than me."

"What did you get?"

"2.5. Two "C" pluses, one "C." Got a "B" in German."

"All right! You should be proud of that."

"I am, but I got out what I put in. No big deal."

"Right."

"I would stay and chat wit'cha, but I see you want to drown your sorrows. Later."

"Yeah, later."   All the fun of last semester was suddenly not worth his current discomfort.   Troy told himself he wouldn't have changed the experience, for fear of losing the relationships he now enjoyed with Angel and his boys, but to fall short of the 3.0 mark was a serious problem.

                    *   *   *   *

Angel was smashing Troy against her door, her arms locking his head to her neck.   He was sliding both hands into her pantyhose when keys jangled in the door.

"Shit. Cyndi! Hold on!"   Angel led Troy to her bed, then rearranged her clothes.

"Okay!"

Angel's roommate came in giggling. "Sorry! I didn't know. Maybe we need a signal or something."

"Maybe you should get a life," Angel retorted.

"Well, excuse me! Don't worry, I'll be gone later."

"That's all right Cyndi," Troy interrupted. "I'm out."

"Troy, you don't have to go on my account."

"I know. Later." Troy kissed Angel, then turned to leave. Before the door closed completely he overheard Cyndi.

"You should be ashamed," Cyndi said harshly.

"Please."

"You're wrong. You're dead wrong."

                    *   *   *   *

He was done with class for the day, but it was only 4:00 and much too early for dinner. The big decision haunting him was whether to call his father directly with news of his grades, or wait until he demanded to know about them. By 4:15 he decided it would be better to get on with the sentencing. No time like the present.

"Good afternoon, David Harris's office."

"Hi, this is Troy Harris."

"Oh, hi Troy. Let me get your dad, okay?"

"Thanks." While on hold, he contemplated hanging up but realized that his dad's receptionist had his name. She would only have had him call back.

"Hello?"

"Dad, it's me."

"Hey, kid! How you doing?"

"I'm good, I'm good."

"What's going on?"

"I just wanted to tell you about my grades."

"So how'd you do?"

"Two seven-five."

"Not bad, not bad," he said quickly.

"I could have done better, but I did study. I only got one 'A'."

"In what?"

"English."

"At least you got one."

By keeping him talking, Troy mistakenly assumed that he had distracted his father from his sub-par performance. Instead, his dad took the opportunity to expound on adjusting to college-level work as a freshman.

"You better not join any of those clubs."

"Look Dad, that had nothing to do with it."

"What makes you think you're going to get your average up if you're in clubs? You've got about all you can handle now."

"I can handle it! Look, I just called to let you know. I wasn't asking!"

"Suit yourself. You want to blow your first year, you go ahead."

Troy slammed the phone down. Seconds later, it rang. Tears spilled over his face while the phone went unanswered.

When Randy returned from class, Troy was composed, but still stung by the fallout with his father. He was further annoyed when he noticed that nobody else seemed to have any hangups about their transcripts. Even Angel, who insisted she would fail organic chemistry, wasn't worried.

"Randy, how did you do last semester?"

"I got a three-one. I was hoping for more, but hey."

"Shit, you did better than me and Ill!"

"I studied."

"So what the fuck, we didn't study?"

"I didn't see Ill cracking any books. Only thing he cracked was a 40-ounce."

"I may have fucked around, but I studied."

"I know you did brother, I'm sorry. I'm actually surprised I didn't do worse."

"You the man."

"No, you the man."

Nearly all the residents of the second floor of Harbin gathered in the lounge a couple of days later to watch a close basketball game between the Hoyas and the Syracuse Orangemen, their sworn enemies.

"Hey you guys," Cyndi asked. "Where's Will?"

"He's at the game with Carl," Randy told her.

"They went to Syracuse?"

"Carl's dad had tickets. I think they took the train."

"Yeah," Troy added. "They claim they're both going to be on TV. Maybe they'll paint their faces blue or something."

Troy was draped around Angel in the back of the room, leaning against a built-in desk, oblivious to the game. As the game became more intense, students began cheering and yelling at the TV screen. During time-outs, the telecast showed Georgetown and Syracuse fans at the Carrier Dome enjoying themselves and mugging for the camera. Just before halftime, a student ran out on the court. When Troy took a closer look, he couldn't believe it.

"Oh, my God," Cyndi shouted. "Do you guys see who that is?"

"Nah," Randy replied, shocked. "It can't be."

"Oh, yes it can." Ill Will was racing around the basketball court nude. Officials and security guards were chasing him, but he was too fast for them and too busy getting his five minutes of fame. He was finally caught and escorted out, but not before giving a high-five to Georgetown coach John Thompson and receiving thunderous applause from the Carrier Dome audience. The students in the lounge cheered.

Andrea, the resident assistant, ran into the lounge.

"Did you guys see that?" she asked breathlessly. "Was that who I think it was?"

"Yeah, it was Willard," Cyndi told her.

"Jesus Christ, he's crazy! What could have gotten into him?"

Troy and Randy looked at each other, both of them well aware that the "spirit" that had probably influenced Ill Will had nothing to do with school spirit.

Eventually the game resumed but neither it nor Ill Will's streaking could distract Troy from Angel.

"Honey, what's with your boy?" she asked.

"Baby, we don't call him Ill for nothing."

"I guess not. He was butt naked! On national TV, no less!"

"Uh-huh. He just gave me a great idea. Let's go back to your room," he told her, nuzzling her neck.

"Troy, the game is still on."

"I'm on."

"When *I* was on before, you were all into your BSU stuff, you and little Malcolm X over there."

"That was different."

"Whatever. You know I have to study later, or I'll have to take Organic Chem for the third time. Let's just watch the game, okay?"

"Right."

Detecting his sulking, she turned and kissed him. Troy held her tighter, but kept quiet. The lounge erupted when Georgetown scored a basket to take the lead. Angel was screaming at the top of her lungs with the rest of their floormates. Randy was giving high-fives to everyone. Troy would not allow anything to compete for his attention when Angel was in the same room. The entire lounge rejoiced when the Hoyas held on to win the game. Troy was anxious to have a private celebration with Angel in her room.

"Baby, I've got something for you," Troy told her.

"I bet you do," Angel said, unlocking her door. "Come on in."

Troy closed the door behind them and snatched her in his arms. When his hands began to wander, Angel broke away from his kiss.

"Honey, please. You know I need to study."

"C'mon, it's Friday. You can study on Sunday."

"I'm working tomorrow. And I think I'm going home tonight."

"Tonight? For what?"

"I just need to do something with my mother."

"On a Friday night? Angel, you're always gone on the weekend. What the fuck am I supposed to think?"

"Don't be mad. I know it shouldn't be this way, but this is important."

"Whenever I call, she says you're not there."

"That's because she doesn't want me on the phone."

"What?"

"Sweetie, just give me a little more time."

"What kind of shit is this?" Troy fumed. "If you were going home, we could have watched the game by ourselves."

"I know, honey." Angel collected her belongings and headed for the door. Troy slowly followed. "I'll be back tomorrow. Soon as my shift is over I'll call you. I'll wear that nightie you like, even though I'm always coming out of it." Angel rubbed her hand under his crotch, closed the door and turned to Troy, who stood in front of her looking dejected.

"You really are very sweet," she told him before kissing him goodbye.

"Very sweet."

*   *   *   *

Whenever the Hoyas won, a party was always in the works, especially after a big win like the Syracuse game. Antoine, one of the freshmen on the team, had convinced the rest of the team to let Troy DJ for the victory celebration. Although Troy was no longer interested in the party after Angel's departure, Antoine's offer was able to lift his spirits. The team had returned that afternoon to an ecstatic campus. Troy had seen girls follow the team around during the summer. But now all kinds of women from law students to government workers had joined the groupie ranks, finding their way to the games, and later, to the players' apartments. Antoine, or 'Twan' as his friends called him, had the privilege of staying in an apartment with the rest of the team despite his freshman status. Troy wouldn't have traded living in Harbin Hall for anything, but twinges of envy pricked him when he visited Antoine. His two partners may not have cared, but Troy could not accept average status, and his consolation was that none of the ballplayers could mix; none of them could rock a party like he could. Nor could they give a speech or debate like Randy. And, of course, nobody was as flat-out crazy as Ill Will, on or off-campus. By the beginning of February, the Hellified Homeboys had each earned their own small slice of celebrity.

Troy was holed up in the back of one of the team apartments, headphone wires tangled around him. With his crates of records and equipment clogging the tiny hallway, it was almost impossible to get past the top of the stairs. Troy would have a limited view of the action below him, but the makeshift booth on the top floor gave the effect of a nightclub.

"Twan!" he called. "Yo, Twan!"

The lanky freshman climbed the partition of chairs to reach the bottom of the steps.

"What, nigga?"

"Make sure you save me some brew!"

"Do you know how hard it is to run out of brew in this house? Don't worry, I got you."

"And my boy, too," he said, pointing to Ill Will in the crowd.

Antoine laughed and pointed when he saw Ill Will.

"That's that fool that was naked at the Syracuse game! Hey everybody, it's him!"

Ill Will saluted his friend with a fistful of malt liquor. Troy returned the salute with his own fist, and waved to Yvonne, who was clearly impressed by her surroundings.

Ill Will was recognized by everyone in the party and received even more congratulations for his outrageous stunt.

Randy was also downstairs, deep in conversation with a girl Troy recognized, but whose name he couldn't remember. He wondered if his roommate would score with her, since he seemed to have forgotten about girls lately. His focus had shifted to the Black Student Union election and campaign strategy, so much so that when girls flirted with him, he only wanted to discuss his plans for the upcoming year. Troy didn't know whether to admire or pity him.

When the apartment swelled to capacity, Troy kicked the party into high gear with Big Daddy Kane, Public Enemy and Heavy D. Whenever he changed a record, the crowd shouted "Ho!" in excited response. When he performed his turntable tricks, now honed to perfection, the crowd screamed even louder. Still more cheers erupted when Troy began his reggae set with J.C. Lodge's "Telephone Love."

"Yo Troy, you the man!" It was Jason Jackson, starting forward for the Hoyas, who had climbed over the partition to personally congratulate Troy. Troy rubbed his eyes.

"Huh?"

"You the man, nigga! I think we're all getting extra pussy tonight because of you!"

The party went on until the morning. Troy and Ill Will were among the human remnants who had slept in the living room. Judging from the NBA game on TV, it looked to Troy like it was early afternoon.

"Y'all come through whenever you want," Jason told them. "Troy, you gonna make me that tape, right?"

"Of course, but don't forget my money."

"All right, all right. Hey, why don't y'all stay and watch the game?"

"Now you're talking," said Ill Will.

Jason treated his guests to beer and Cap'n Crunch while they watched the Lakers battle the Pistons. After the game, Troy and Ill Will carried Troy's records back to Harbin, with the help of a small luggage cart.

"Ill, did you see Randy?"

"Nah, but it's not like I was looking for him."

"Think he got some?"

"Who knows? He definitely wasn't hungover like us, he might have just left."

With Ill Will's help, Troy put away his records, using the crates as shelves. After Ill Will left to study, Troy decided he'd better do the same. The dorm was typically quiet for a Sunday. Troy sat at his desk with "Principles of Accounting," and stuck with it for several hours, catching up on the latest chapter and identifying what Wendell would help him with that week. Around the time Angel was due back from work, Troy was filled with concern instead of his usual lust. He needed to see her, despite his earlier private pledge.

Angel had an uphill battle with an "F" in Organic Chem from last semester. He didn't know what her study strategy was, and most students had trouble with the class, but Cyndi had managed a "C" plus. What was his girl doing wrong? He had been so caught up in the sex that other aspects of Angel's life had temporarily escaped him. He didn't want her to think that the BSU and his budding popularity on campus were more important to him than her. Maybe now that they were together, he could finally find out why she always went home on weekends. Whatever the problem was, he'd come too far with her not to see it through.

Fourteen

"Troy, the anniversary of Malcolm X's assassination is February 25th. We have to do something on or around that date!"

"That's right after the election. How are we going to do programming that soon? We haven't won yet."

"Oh, we'll win. It just seems like there's not enough time to get everything done."

"What are you talking about? We have all year!"

Ill Will bounded into the room without knocking, interrupting the argument. "S'up, homies? What's all the beef about?"

"The BSU, something we take seriously," Randy said over his shoulder.

"I take it serious. I didn't think you clowns did until recently. Maybe I'll run my damn self."

Randy turned around quickly. "Run for what?"

"For office. Don't worry, I don't want to be President. I know Member-at-Large is open."

Randy looked at him sternly. "You're a drunk. You don't want to run."

"And why not? 'Cause you're running? Who the fuck are you, you fake Muslim, Black Panther wannabe motherfucker?"

"At least I'm not a drunk, Ill! You're a goddamned disgrace!"

Ill Will chuckled and went on the offensive, playing it cool, opting not to continue exchanging insults.

"Look, you motherfuckers ain't perfect, either. You need someone who can talk to regular members. Let them know what you want to do and why you want to do it. You may not see me at the front gates with a picket sign, but I'll do the work. Besides, you guys are getting to be big shots."

"You're the big shot, the infamous Ill Will," Randy fumed. "Everybody from campus security to the alumni office has got to know who you are by now, especially after that stunt you pulled at the game."

Will shrugged Randy off with confidence and continued campaigning.

"Isolated incidents. Listen, you're the president, right? You run the show, set the program. Tee, you're VP, so you help him and run an occasional meeting or whatever yourself. You need a treasurer for the budget, a secretary for the paperwork, and me, for Member-at-Large. I'll let you know what people *really* want."

Randy was silenced by Ill Will's argument. When he couldn't answer any of Ill's points, he turned to Troy. "What do you think?"

"It's not like I need your approval to run. But that's all right. Tee, you my man. What you think?"

His eyes reverted from one friend to the other. He hated this position, having to choose one opinion over the other. No matter what he said, someone would be disappointed. Still, Ill Will had made sense to him, and he was all for Ill and Randy working together, even if they were forced by the circumstances.

"Ill should run. We need people who'll come at it from a different angle."

Randy sighed. "Fine. You want to run, run."

Ill shook his head and laughed. "Like I need your permission. Do you believe this guy?"

"No, you don't need my permission. But since you'll probably run uncontested, maybe you want to start helping us with the planning. Take a look at what we've drafted up so far."

"See, now you're talking." Ill Will pulled up a chair next to Randy's and the three of them began reviewing the tentative calendar for the next year.

"Y'all know Darnell and Layla are running, right?"

"We know."

Despite Ill Will's information, Troy could barely keep from smiling. 4-H was coming back together. Since he was already well versed in what Randy and Ill Will were reviewing, he fired up the turntables for a celebratory mixing session. By the end of that week, Troy, Randy and Ill Will had their election campaign in full swing.

Although he was running against them, Darnell Washington was required to give the freshmen publicity flyers to promote their campaign. The boys noticed that the printing on their flyers was of an inferior quality, with ink that rubbed off easily. To supplement Darnell's flyers, they made their own, embellishing them with their names, the offices they sought and drawings of Snoopy and Calvin and Hobbes, all of whom had brown faces in 4-H's representation of them.

Darnell's flyers simply read 'No Freshmen' and 'Get Some Credits First,' along with his name. Where Randy spoke to everyone, Darnell reserved his politicking for upperclassmen and was unusually reserved when several black freshmen were around. Both Troy and Randy suspected that he had a trick up his sleeve, they just hadn't yet discovered it. Still, Randy continued being the natural politician he was, discussing the need for strong black leadership at dinner, at basketball games, and whatever informal gatherings he could attend.

"Randy, what do expect to get done with a VP who has problems?" one student asked outside the cafeteria. Several students were gathered around.

"What kind of problems, brother?"

"You know he doesn't get along with Travis. Nothing moves in the BSU without Minority Affairs behind it. I'm just curious how you're going to get around that."

"Who told you Travis and Troy didn't get along?"

"That's just what I heard, partner."

Randy smiled, keeping a neutral expression on his face. "Whatever problems Troy and Travis may have had in the past are history. That won't be an issue. Distinguishing which candidate wants to get something done on this campus, now that's an issue. Y'all be good."

Randy couldn't wait to get back to the room and tell Troy.

"Do you believe that?" His roommate was clearly annoyed.

"Probably Darnell trying to be slick."

"Probably? Ain't no probably, that snake was behind that! Spreading rumors about you and Travis?"

"It's true, I hate him," Troy acknowledged matter-of-factly.

"So what? What's that got to do with the BSU? Travis is only an advisor. That fool questioning me had people thinking he controlled everything. It ain't right."

"Don't sweat it. We'll just do a little damage control tomorrow."

"I'm not going out like a punk. We're not losing this election on no bullshit."

*   *   *   *

A second floor classroom in Graveston Hall was standing room only the night of the election. Randy's aggressive campaigning had accomplished its goal: to pack the house. He also wanted to eliminate anyone who may have considered running against him. Their innovative flyers had made the crowd curious enough to show up. Now the black students at Georgetown would see if the two freshmen were serious. Troy, Randy, Ill Will and Jay, candidate for treasurer, sat in the second row behind Darnell and the current executive board. Yvonne was right behind them. Troy couldn't convince Angel to sit up front; she had claimed shyness, but Troy was still happy just to have her in the room.

"Okay everybody, quiet down. Can I have your attention please?" Darnell had been ignored all year as BSU president, and tonight was no different. "Please, y'all. Will you please! Your attention please!" The crowd settled down gradually, at its own pace.

"Thank you. Tonight we will hold our elections for the Black Student Union officers. All of the executive board offices are open, as you know and I'm running for re-election."

"So what, fool?" Bizzy Hendricks heckled from the back of the room. Rumblings of laughter followed.

Darnell fought to suppress a smile. "Anyway, tonight you'll hear from all the candidates, they will ask for your vote, and if you like, we'll have the results by the end of the evening. Some of the candidates are running uncontested, and many are freshmen. So let's give them all a hand."

Troy and Ill Will nodded at the applause, and acknowledged the crowd. Troy was sure he and Ill were thinking the same thing; they appreciated being recognized, but at the same time they felt certain that they deserved it. Randy, seated opposite Ill Will, was edgy, impatient.

"Now for our first candidate. Running for President, give it up for Randy Lambert."

A stoic Randy approached the podium, unaffected by the applause.

"Thank you. You all have seen the Black Student Union function this year and some of you have seen its effectiveness for a few years now. Darnell and the BSU have accomplished some good things, and I'm here to express my intention to improve upon those efforts. Now as a freshman coming into Georgetown, I didn't know what to expect, from my classes or from my environment. Fortunately, we have Mr. Gordon and Minority Affairs to help with that transition. I know Minority Affairs provides important support—scholarships, tutors, counseling, you know, just guidance. But to me, Minority Affairs can't do everything for us. We have to be prepared to do some things for ourselves while we're here. And since I always heard the expression 'put up or shut up,' I'm running." More applause erupted and Randy paused. He still looked serious, though somewhat more relaxed after his introduction.

"If elected, it will be my goal and the goal of my administration to offset the imbalance that we as a people have here at Georgetown." Administration? Troy and Ill Will looked at each other. "We shouldn't have to go to Howard to learn about our history, or to some consortium class. Granted this *is* Georgetown, but the Black Student Union is also a part of this school, just as we are individually. It's up to this organization to request what we aren't getting politically, culturally or academically. We shouldn't limit our experiences to just partying. The BSU is essentially a social organization, but we don't need a club to socialize! We do that on our own!"

A few people were clapping now, and shouts of 'That's right!' and 'Amen!' came from the back. Darnell, seated up front, did not appear to be impressed, but even he couldn't deny Randy's command of the audience.

"Now, I don't want you to think that we're going to have a revolution around here as soon as we take office. I'd like to, but that probably won't happen. But there's nothing to stop us from showing some black films and documentaries on a regular basis, though. Not just during Black History Month. Every month should be Black History Month! Last month we heard about Dr. King all month long, like we do every January. What about Malcolm X's birthday? What about his contributions to our history? You don't hear about that in your history classes. And there are so few African history classes or Afro-American Lit classes here, they fill up like that! We can't all take them! And speaking of that, why isn't there more of an eastern and Afrocentric curriculum? Why don't we have more black professors? These are the questions we have to ask as an organization. Just because we chose this school doesn't mean we have to give up all those things that affirm our blackness. Instead of just accepting that what is, is, I think we should do for ourselves and start filling in those gaps, those things we're missing. That's what the true function of the BSU should be."

The crowd erupted again. This time, Randy looked right at Darnell.

"Troy, Will and I have worked on what we think is a very balanced schedule of events. With your vote, we can implement these programs and make the Black Student Union all that it should be as a viable support system. Thank you and As-Salaam Alaikum."

If the students' cheers were any indication, Randy had struck a chord with many of them. The black students at Georgetown were apparently excited about the prospect of new blood in the BSU. When Darnell returned to the podium, the crowd calmed down.

"That's a tough act to follow, but I think my experience will get me through." Now Darnell shot a glare back at Randy. A couple of 'oohs' came from the crowd.

"I'm not even going to keep y'all here longer than you need to be. Y'all know me, and you know what we've been doing. So really, the choice is yours. Now me, I don't think I'm Jesse Jackson or anyone like that." Darnell paused for the laughter and smiled while looking at Randy.

"No, really. But I, or we, do what we can when you all need us. I've been there for many of you personally." He paused to let his reminder sink in.

"That's because I know if one of you is in trouble, we're all in trouble. Just so happens that many of us are doing well this year. We are doing well, aren't we?"

"Yeah!" Bizzy shouted. Troy saw other students nodding in agreement.

"Exactly. Now, I admire these gentlemen here for running. Especially for their courage. Most of y'all saw, or heard, how they came into Travis' meeting last semester, didn't you?"

Everyone in the audience laughed. Randy tried to remain calm, but he was visibly upset.

"Hold on. Calm down, we've all been there. But I think we all had to go through that kind of thing, you know, falling flat on our faces, before we were ready to assume responsibilities like carrying the mantle of the BSU. This isn't a perfect organization, but its effectiveness, if you will, has been based on true leadership. And experience. Think about it. Thank you."

The crowd reacted with thunderous applause. Everyone applauded except for the freshmen candidates and Travis Gordon.

"Thank you. Next up, running for Vice-President, Troy Harris." Troy and Ill Will slapped hands before he approached the podium. Randy raised his fist in support.

"4-H," Ill Will whispered to him.

"4-H," Troy repeated. He was greeted warmly, but not with the furious applause brought on by Randy and Darnell. He could hear Wendell and the other Kappas shouting 'Troy! Troy!' from the back of the room. Angel was cheering as loudly as she could.

"Thank you. I'm running for Vice-President, because it's obvious that Randy is the man for the job of President."

Applause.

"It's true that we put together a calendar of events for next year. We think it's real fly. A Malcolm X film series, 'Eyes on the Prize,' all kinds of films and videos. There's a lot of stuff out there that we need to see, a lot of it here in our own library. Like Randy said, you don't have to go to Howard to get black culture or black history. We're at G-Town, but we're still black, aren't we?" Troy paused, but only a few people clapped.

"We just want to provide some balance with the other student groups. If other student groups don't have any speakers we want to hear, we should try to bring them in. If we want more of our culture and interests represented in the curriculum, we have to try to bring attention to these issues. By really coming together, we can do some things, and we can educate and enlighten ourselves in the process. Don't get me wrong, we're still gonna party." Troy laughed along with the audience. "But we'll party with a purpose. Thank you. I'm out."

Troy cut his speech short, having surprised himself by sounding halfway decent. Like his roommate, his words were received positively. There was laughter from the crowd as well, but he sensed it was laughter of approval. His sense of humor could usually diffuse a potentially stressful situation, and tonight had been no different.

Darnell was back up front. "And now for Vice-President, Layla Johnson."

Layla took the podium to calm applause. Bizzy's laughter traveled all around the room.

"Do some sit-ups, bitch!"

The audience erupted with laughter. Troy and Ill Will doubled over in hysterics. Randy couldn't contain himself, either. Travis Gordon quickly met Bizzy at his seat and threw him out. "All right! All right, Travis! Chill!" Bizzy shouted as he was escorted out.

Travis marched toward the podium, but Layla signaled him to stay back.

"That's okay Travis, thank you. See, that's how they act when I don't give 'em none."

The ladies in the crowd roared. The classroom had become a hand-clapping, foot stomping party.

"Anyway, you all know about my work with the NAACP. I think this year it makes sense to work with Darnell in the same organization. I'm not going to make a long speech, but I will say this. Experience. No personal problems, with adjudication and the like. No radical talk, no opportunistic people trying to get in on the party scene for their own benefit. The only thing we sell is experience. If it ain't broke, don't fix it. Thank you."

Layla received overwhelming applause from the female students in the audience. Darnell returned to the podium, looking unaffected by the last few moments.

"Now running for Treasurer, Jay Morton."

Jay was also a freshman, but he had been fairly quiet all year. Aside from brief conversations, neither Troy nor Randy really knew him. Still, they all agreed that it would be a challenge to get the new BSU budget approved, and to collect more money in dues from the folks in the room. In his brief speech, he discussed these issues, and Troy wasn't surprised to hear weak applause when Jay was finished.

"Thank you Jay!" Darnell was suddenly more enthused. "Now for Secretary, Phyllis Meadows."

Randy elbowed Troy's side. "Is that who I think it is?"

"Word up. Wyoming." Phyllis was the same girl who had told them that America would be a better place without black folks. Darnell came to the second row while Phyllis began.

"She just decided to run today," he whispered. "There's no rule to stop her."

Randy's light-skinned face was turning red. Ill Will was fighting to keep from laughing, and his snickering was making it difficult for Troy to contain his own laughter. If he won, Randy was going to have one hell of an 'administration.'

"I don't agree with everything the president, I mean Randy, says, but I do think it's good to be doing something. And that's why I'm running for Secretary. Thank you."

The applause was just loud enough to muffle Troy and Ill Will's laughter. Phyllis gave them a glare as she walked out of the room. She wasn't staying for the results. Troy realized once again that when either Randy or Ill Will were involved — much less together, he should expect the unexpected. When Darnell returned to the podium, Ill Will became somber. Troy didn't understand why, but he could tell Ill was nervous about addressing the students.

"You got it," Troy told him.

"Oh yeah, yeah." Darnell introduced him to mild applause and chants of "Ill Will!" Ill Will wasn't the social butterfly that Troy or Randy were, but the hospital incident had made his name known by every black student at Georgetown.

"Thanks. I'm running for Member-at-Large, so I won't have the responsibilities of Randy, Troy, Jay, or Phyllis, heh heh. I'll be responsible for making sure the executive board is dealing with matters that you think are important. When you don't come to a meeting or a function, you can come to me to find out what went down."

"Great, he's telling people not to come out," Randy whispered.

"Shut up," Troy shushed him. "Let him finish."

"If you see something you like or you don't like, let me know, I'll be the one to take it to them. You'll be able to come to any of us, of course, but it'll be my job to be here so you can come."

Pause.

"You know, to me." The audience howled with laughter, and Ill Will started to lose his composure. "Thank you."

Ill Will's last remark left some students with bewildered expressions, others were more amused. Everyone had become generally giddy and impatient. The evening was winding down; people were now talking amongst themselves and most weren't staying for the results. Travis escorted Darnell and the other candidates outside the classroom before the vote. Jay decided not to wait around.

"Someone'll let me know if I don't win," he told Randy as they shook hands.

"Peace Jay, I'll talk to you tomorrow." After also exchanging handshakes with Troy and Ill Will, Jay was gone. Randy was clearly offended.

"What do you make of that?"

"He's the treasurer. He doesn't have to be here," Ill Will offered. "Hell, I'd be out too if y'all weren't my homies!"

"You clowns don't have to be here either, for real," Darnell added as he approached them.

"We'll see," Randy retorted. They stared at each other like boxers at the start of a prize fight.

The classroom door cracked open from the inside. Travis signaled the boys to come back in. They returned to an awkward silence. Travis stood at the podium.

"Ladies and gentlemen, we have a unique turn of events here. For the office of Vice-President, the winner is, by a close margin, Troy Harris."

The freshmen in the audience, who were roughly half the attendees, applauded. Troy and his partners were still hanging on Travis' every word.

"I also want to announce our other new board members, Jay Morton for Treasurer, Phyllis Meadows for Secretary, and Willard Dorsey for Member-at-Large."

More applause.

"Now, for the office of President. For the office of President of the Black Student Union, believe it or not, we have a tie."

"What? Come on, man!" Darnell shouted.

"Calm down, Darnell, you hear me? I will not have this election become more of a mockery than it already is! The two of you will report to my office Thursday afternoon. By then we will have had a full recount and an investigation."

"Investigation? For what?" Darnell asked.

"If I say an investigation is warranted, there will be an investigation. Anyone who doesn't want to cooperate will forfeit their office." Travis turned to face Randy, Ill Will and Troy.

"Am I clear?"

"Yes, sir," Randy conceded. "Whatever you need."

Congratulations and high-fives were offered to the freshmen. Despite the tie, Randy was determined to answer students' questions about programming for next year, as if he'd already won. Troy was expecting the most affectionate congratulations from Angel, but she was gone and he couldn't help feeling disappointed. *At least she was here for my speech*, he thought. He decided to return to Harbin, to see if anything was wrong with her.

"Troy?" He couldn't tell who was calling him. He was so wrapped up in thought, he almost forgot where he was.

"Troy?" He turned to find Travis Gordon.

"What do you want?"

"I want to talk to you in private. In my office tomorrow. "

"What the fuck for?"

Before Troy could react, Travis grabbed him by the arm and pulled him into the staircase.

"Let me go!"

"Shut up!"

"Look," Travis began while holding Troy against the wall. "I know you don't like me. Hell, I don't even blame you. But you will never disrespect me, least of all on this campus."

Troy struggled to break free, but Travis had used too much force for him.

"It is my job to check on all of our freshmen, and you are no exception, no matter how much static you give me. You don't want to come to me, fine, I'll come to you. I know what's bothering you. That's why I don't throw it in your face. But you want to test me," he paused to regain his composure.

"No, I don't."

"You shut your mouth!" he growled. "Understand who it is you're dealing with. I get students in and out of this institution every day with one phone call. Anytime you want to test me, boy, just say the word. I'll beat the black off your ass. Then I'll call your mom and we'll have a big laugh about it."

Troy kept trying to wiggle free. "You threatening me?"

"No, I'm telling you. What the hell do I need to threaten you for, I can have you gone in a heartbeat."

Finally he let loose Troy's arm, but he stood in front of him, blocking his exit.

"I work for every brother on this campus, including you. Make sure you come by my office tomorrow. Disrespect me again and you'll be an ex-Georgetown student. Understand?"

Troy was silent.

"Understand?"

"Yeah." Troy held back his tears, determined not to appear weak in front of Travis.

"Good. See you tomorrow."

"Wait up, Troy. I'm coming!" Randy ran after his roommate who had made a hasty exit. Lots of students wanted to talk to Randy after the election, but after a few minutes, Randy finally pulled himself away.

"What was that with you and Travis?"

"Nothing."

"Brother, are you all right?"

"I'm chilling. Good job tonight."

"You, too. Where's Ill?"

"He must have left, I thought he was back there with you."

"You're right, he probably jetted with Yvonne. What happened to Angel?"

"She broke out, too. Tired, I guess."

"Brother, we did it. You ready?"

"Ready as I'll ever be."

As it turned out, there were four more votes in the ballot box than there were students in audience. Travis' only recourse was a run-off election between Randy and Darnell. When Darnell didn't bother to show up for the run-off, Randy was elected by default. Rumor had it that since Layla, his lover and provider, had lost, he wasn't interested in the BSU anymore. Regardless of the reason, Randy was quite relieved to win office and begin his work within the organization. His enthusiasm carried over to Troy, Ill Will and the rest of the officers.

Fifteen

By the third go round in the library, Troy was starting to catch on to how Wendell was approaching the Accounting problem. "Now that makes sense. See, that's what I'm talking about."

"You can do it," Wendell told him. "Just keep working at it. By the way, congratulations on the BSU."

"Thanks."

"Y'all look like you're really going to do something. That's good, we need that around here."

"That's why we ran. We're gonna get busy."

"I don't doubt it. All right then, we're straight for now."

"Yeah, I'm cool," Troy told him. "You know I'm going to come see you before the test, though."

"No problem." The senior and the freshman slapped hands. "Hey Troy, you ever think about pledging? You know you'd make a hell of a Nupe."

"A what?"

"A Nupe. You know, a Kappa."

"Oh. Nah, man. Not now, anyway."

"All right, don't say I ain't tell you."

Wendell left Troy alone to review the rest of his Accounting problems. He was improving, but only the exam would really tell the tale. When he applied himself, Troy found he could rise to the challenges of Euro Civ Part II, Sociology, and even Accounting. The courses that were easy for him were guaranteed 'A's if he could just maintain his concentration.

$$* \qquad * \qquad * \qquad *$$

The enthusiasm Randy created on election night carried over into March, when he, Troy and Ill Will took office. Jay and Phyllis were less in the forefront, but both of them had a genuine team spirit that was contagious. Black women from every class were suddenly going out of their way to speak to Randy between classes. He addressed each one, got them excited about BSU events, and before long, some of them began to visit Room 228. Ill Will blew off executive board meetings on occasion, but Randy continued with his agenda. Troy was more interested in why he didn't show, but it was hard to catch Ill Will in his room, especially during the week.

Troy found himself in Angel's room early one Sunday afternoon. Since Angel was alone, they took the opportunity to make love. Afterwards, when Troy tried to get up from the bed, Angel held on to him.

"Honey, let me go."

"No."

"C'mon. I gotta get out of here. Otherwise I'll never leave."

"That sounds perfect. Let's spend the day in bed."

"That would be wonderful, but I can't do it today. Can we do it some other time?"

"Cyndi will be here some other time!" He leaned over to kiss her but she turned her head. Troy laughed. "Oh, it's like that? Look, we can do this next week. We'll go to--"

"I want to be with you today! The one time Cyndi's gone and you have to go. What's up with that?"

Her indignance grew as their argument escalated. Troy decided to head her off at the pass. He stopped her verbal assault while putting his shirt on. "What? You have the nerve to talk shit after all the weekends you've been gone? Now you want to spend the day together. Give me some of what you had, 'cause you're buggin'."

"Don't talk to me like that, *pendejo*." The playful tone of Angel's voice was gone.

"What is your problem?"

"No problem. You have things to do, go and do them."

"I'll be back."

"Whatever."

Surprised by her coldness, Troy returned to the bed. When he leaned closer, he was met by Angel's palm held in his face. This attitude of hers wasn't funny anymore.

"So what, I'm supposed to just give up my whole life now?"

"Not so long ago you would have."

Troy took that comment as his cue to leave. Later, while in the shower, he struggled to figure out what had just happened. Angel knew that Troy was trying to discipline himself, and that Sunday was the day he caught up on coursework and organized for the coming week. In order to do that, he'd have to be in the library. He was too comfortable in his room or in the lounge watching basketball and most certainly in bed with Angel. Troy noticed that she was becoming more and more upset at the fact that he had other things to do.

On his way back from the shower, Troy could hear music blasting. He recognized it as Billy Joel's "Back in the USSR." *Carl must be up,* he thought. Ill Will's door was open, and sitting in their usual post on the floor were Carl and Ill Will, playing cards, spitting tobacco, and drinking beer. Carl waved to Troy.

"S'up, Carl!" Troy had to shout over the music. Ill Will, his back to the door, waved, but did not turn around. Troy recognized the drunken movements of his friend.

"You two been going at it all night?"

"Hell yeah!" shouted Ill Will. "I got him fifteen games to ten in gin rummy!"

Unable to tolerate Billy Joel, Troy came in to turn the stereo down. Before he could reach the volume button, Carl grabbed his arm.

"Hey," he told him. "When you're across the hall rocking the mike, or uh, uh, mixing, on the uh, er ah…"

"Turntables," Ill Will assisted.

"Thank you. On the turntables, you don't see me in there trying to turn it down."

Troy had to fight off an urge to punch Carl in the face. That comment about 'rocking the mike' had gotten to him. His ego couldn't tolerate any kind of disrespect for what he did. Troy and his neighbor were eye to eye.

"I didn't hear you, that's all," he said calmly.

"Right." The heat of Carl's breath lingered on Troy's face. He grimaced at the smell of it. God only knew what and how much they had been drinking.

"Ill, let me talk to you outside!"

"What we got to outside for? We're homies, right?" Ill Will and Carl slapped hands, laughing wickedly. Ill Will interrupted his own laughter with a loud belch, which made Carl laugh more. A thin stream of saliva ran out of the corner of his mouth onto his chin. His white undershirt had brown tobacco stains. Troy recalled seeing his friend in the same terrible shape a few months back.

"Look, you need to think about laying off this shit. Carl can do what he wants to do, but you got a file in adjudication that's thick as shit."

Ill Will stood up stumbling. "Leave the caads right 'dere," he mumbled to Carl. "I'll be right back."

"Tell him to put some clothes on," Carl shouted.

Troy rushed toward Carl with his fists clenched, but Ill Will grabbed him by the arm, and after a brief struggle, pulled him out of the room. Just as before, when Ill Will drank, he was energized to superhuman levels.

"You just saved your boy from the worst ass-kicking of his life! What the fuck you doin'? He tryin' to dis me and you defending him?"

Ill Will had Troy's arms pinned, his back against the door of his own dorm room. In between blinks he saw Ill Will's bloodshot eyes, trying to focus on him but looking past him instead.

"First of all, it's his room, too. Second, he'll fuck you up."

"Nigga, please!"

"It's true. You think he's soft 'cause he white? He'll fuck you up, Troy. Besides, even if you kick his ass, then *I* got problems, you know?"

"So? So what? What the fuck, man! This all you about, drinking and chewing tobacco?"

"Calm down. Lemme ax you sump'n. Is today Sunday?"

"Yeah, so what?"

"Do we have a BSU meetin' today?"

"No."

"That's right, we don't. And you're not in charge of my schedule. Ain't nobody fuckin' with you when you in there mixin'. Carl is right. Don't get mad at him for tellin' the truth."

"This isn't about Carl, you idiot! Adjudication doesn't know him! He gets kicked out of school, his parents can send him somewhere else. Don't you understand?"

"Nah, homey, you're the one who don't understand. I, see, I take my chances. I know you want to look out, but worry about your damn self, not me. I'ma *be* all right. Whatever happens, happens. Now I'm goin' back in there to finish da game. I'll see ya, all right?"

Troy was fuming. He could not bring himself to speak.

"All right?" Ill asked again.

"Yeah, man." Ill Will relaxed his grip. When he turned around, Randy was in front of him, looking disappointed. Ill Will returned

Randy's glare as he stumbled back to his room. Troy entered Room 228 and began to get dressed.

"What was that all about?" Randy asked.

"Nothing."

"Yeah, right. He's drunk, isn't he?"

"Yes Randy, he's drunk."

"Don't get mad at me! This is what I'm talking about. It's gonna catch up to him, man."

"Not now, all right?"

"I'm just saying that —"

"I said not now, man! Shit! I know it's going to catch up to him! I know that, all right? Damn!"

Randy put up both hands to indicate he was backing off. Billy Joel's singing was just as loud, but Troy could hardly hear it now over the ringing in his ears. Never in his brief college career had he so looked forward to hitting the books.

*   *   *   *

All week long Troy concentrated on his courses, in class and in his dorm. The work was a welcome distraction from Angel, who was still angry at him, and Ill Will, with whom he was still upset. They saw each other at a BSU executive board meeting, but between Randy's plans and reports from Jay and Phyllis, Troy lost himself and settled into a somber, reflective mood. Ill Will was his normal, almost hyperactive self at the meeting. Watching him move around made Troy reminisce about the previous summer when they were both so full of energy and anticipation. Troy longed for some of that energy now, when he really needed it. Randy was adjourning the meeting.

"I'll talk to y'all later, I know everybody has work to do."

"That's right," Jay agreed, heading for the door. "Later." Phyllis waved goodbye and followed behind him. Randy headed out without a word to Troy or to Ill Will. Ill picked up his books, following the rest of the group. Troy walked behind him for a few seconds before speaking.

"Ill."

"S'up, man?"

"Look, I didn't have no beef with you on Sunday."

"Me neither. Matter of fact, I didn't even see you on Sunday."

"Sunday afternoon, man. You remember, in your room?"

"You were there? Really? I was there almost all night and I didn't see you."

"Sunday afternoon, Ill! Carl had the fucking Billy Joel blasting? I had just come out the shower?"

Ill Will was perplexed. "Only thing I remember was playing cards with Carl Saturday night. We were in there for a while, and the next thing I knew I was in my room in bed Sunday night."

"You don't remember?"

"Troy, what the hell are you talking about?"

"You, don't you...forget it. Fuck it man, it's okay."

"If you say so, partner."

Troy came out of the library to find Angel talking to a couple of girls, including Layla and Jasmine, who were both members of Alpha Kappa Alpha sorority. Angel was her usual sexy self in her Guess jeans and white blouse. She smiled when she saw him coming towards her.

"My aunt is an AKA," Angel was saying to the girls, "so that's kind of where it started. Oh yeah, and Troy seems to think it's a good idea, too."

"Who?"

"Troy," she said, wrapping her arm in his. "My man." Troy looked to his shoes, embarrassed. Layla and Jasmine, with their eyebrows raised, looked at each other.

"I hear that," said Jasmine. "I'll be talking to you all later. We'll hook up."

"Okay," Angel beamed. "Hi sweetie," she told him before kissing him.

"Hey, hey. How are you all doing?" he said, turning to the other ladies.

"Fine," Layla answered. "Bye."

"I guess you're not mad anymore."

"No Troy, in fact I wasn't really mad after you left. Where have you been, why haven't you called?" Angel asked.

"Just been trying to do some work. Besides, if you weren't mad, you could have called. C'mon, let's walk."

"I came by, you were never there."

"You didn't leave a note on the message board."

"Yeah, but — "

"Yeah, but nothing. Forget it, it's over."

"Oooh, my baby is forceful. *Ai, papi!*"

Angel clung to Troy's arm as they walked across campus to Harbin Hall. The frigid weather had finally given way to spring. The relatively warm weather brought everybody out, and on this day it was a pleasant 65 degrees. Troy and Angel hadn't spoken since last Sunday, yet today she had decided to let everyone know about their relationship by carrying on in front of a group of girls. Troy looked at her and rolled his eyes as they walked. To him it was just like being in high school, linking arms, to make a statement that they were together. He was still unsure of what Angel's motive was for this kind of display. If any of the black students hadn't known they were a couple, they would know soon. If he had any chance with another sister at Georgetown, Angel had just killed it. She didn't like the way he had spoken to her last Sunday, but now she acted like his being 'forceful' turned her on? Troy found that the more he witnessed Angel's actions, the more he realized how little he really knew about the opposite sex.

Later that day, Randy and Phyllis were looking at a newspaper on Randy's desk when Troy came in. Phyllis looked startled.

"Hey, Troy. You're just in time. Did you see the new edition of the Hoya?"

"Nah, what about it?"

"We're in it, man!"

Troy put his books down and began watering the plants. "Yeah?"

"Yes," Phyllis told him. "The article talks about how we're breathing new life into the organization, and they even quoted Randy! Oh, it's wonderful." Phyllis' enthusiasm seemed strange to Troy. He could not forget her comment the night they first met. Did she still think America was a better place without black people? He couldn't tell.

"I didn't know they were going to hook us up like this," Randy confessed. "Otherwise I would have talked to them a while ago."

"Take a look." Troy surveyed the article. Randy was quoted several times, but none of the other BSU officers were asked about anything.

"I didn't mean to do it without consulting you," Randy continued. "I was just outside talking to some brothers and one of these Hoya types came up to me. He was cool, so I answered some of his questions."

"Does Ill know?" Troy asked.

"If he's seen the paper, he does. But I haven't seen him."

Phyllis prepared to leave. "I'll see you boys later. Snookums, we're studying tonight, right?"

"Yes, sister. Take care."

"Okay." After Phyllis left, Troy turned to his roommate as if expecting an explanation.

"What?"

"Snookums?" Troy cracked up laughing. "Snookums? Damn, man."

"What, brother?"

"You and her? What, you hit that?"

"Come on now, please. We have most of the same classes, so we study together. And of course, we're in the BSU, so we talk about that. She's come a long way, you know. I've been wanting to refine the sister since that night during our first weekend here."

"Refine her, huh? Okay Randy, sure."

"You know brother, that's Five Percent terminology. If the sister thought America was better off without black folk, without her own self, she had to be in need of some refinement."

"Yeah, you've got me there. And you're just the one to do it. Ha ha, got all the sisters looking up to you!"

"It's not like that, brother."

"Sure it's not. You telling me you ain't gonna step to Phyllis, snookums?"

"Brother, it's not like that." Randy paused, apparently deep in thought. "She does have a fat ass, though."

*   *   *   *

Troy called his mother that night. She was, as always, happy to hear from him.

"So everything's going okay?"

"Yeah Mom, fine. Randy and I are revamping the BSU! It's going well."

Troy's mother had heard about the election, but she chose not to mention this fact. "What does your father have to say about that?"

"I haven't talked to him since the election."

"You need to call him. And don't try to screen your calls, it may be somebody important. You know your grandma doesn't like answering machines. Have you talked to her lately?"

"No, but I will. Hey, thanks for that care package!"

"You're welcome. Listen, make sure you call your grandma. And your father. I don't want him calling the house asking me about you. Whatever trouble you have with him is your problem, not mine."

"Yes, ma'am. How's everything up there? Work all right?"

"Work is work, Troy. But everything is fine. I may even go back to school."

"School? Mom, that's great! I know you can do it."

"We'll see. Anyway, I have to go, I'll talk to you soon. You're okay, right?"

"Sure Mom, fine."

"I love you."

"I love you, too. Bye."

Troy had contemplated telling her about the incident with Travis, but if she went back and told him, he'd look like a punk. She seemed to be content with their conversation and he saw no sense in disturbing the pleasant tone it had taken. She had probably heard about Travis' little chat with him after the election, or Travis' version, and she'd never believe that her new boyfriend was such an asshole.

He looked around at the room, at the comfort he and Randy had created. Randy's prayer rug was neatly across his desk and Troy's turntables were neatly on top of his record crates. The room looked the same as it did in September, but his circumstances were so different! Talking to his mother always caused Troy to reflect. The days seemed to move faster. 4-H was still a crew, but their relationship had changed. Randy and Ill Will seldom behaved as friends now, even though they were both BSU officers. Troy thought they all had so much in common in September, but now he wasn't so sure. He was deriving just as much satisfaction from improving his grades as he was from any other activity, including mixing. Did his dismal 2.75 GPA cause this newfound maturity, or was it simply remorse? Almost everything he had wished for months before was his, which made him uncertain of what else the future held.

Sixteen

Troy and Phyllis waited for Randy in back of the auditorium. They were at a rally for Calvin Witherspoon, who was running for re-election to the City Council in Washington D.C. Witherspoon had worked with Martin Luther King in the 1960s, and had since acquired many influential allies in Washington. His gift for public speaking and his influence with young voters was moving him into more mainstream political circles. Randy was in a spirited discussion with the Councilman while Troy and Phyllis looked on from a distance.

"They'll never be able to get rid of him," Troy observed.

"I know, but that's okay."

Troy could hear the admiration in her voice. Turning away from her, he rolled his eyes. Randy was signaling for them to come down to meet Witherspoon, who was one of his role models. Phyllis anxiously made her way down the aisle. She motioned for Troy to join her, but he shook his head.

"Troy, come on. You are the Vice-President."

"That's all right, you go ahead. I'll just chill back here."

Like his companions, Troy had been excited at the prospect of hearing Councilman Witherspoon. As student leaders, Troy, Randy and Phyllis had felt a natural obligation to be at the rally for a political figure who included in his platform many of the same causes they supported. Now, however, Troy's mind was wandering. What was Angel doing? Were they going to spend any time together soon? He had an Accounting exam coming up; should he cancel the party he was scheduled to DJ? Freshman year had proven to be far more hectic and challenging than he first imagined.

Randy and Phyllis came up the aisle together. "You ready, brother?" Randy asked.

"Yeah. Let's be out."

"Troy, why didn't you come over?" Phyllis asked. "You may not get another chance to meet the Councilman."

"Maybe I'll get to talk to him in the White House." All three of them laughed, but Troy's smile quickly faded and Randy took notice.

"Something on your mind, roommate?"

"No, no more than usual."

"You ready for your exam?"

"We'll know in a few days, won't we?"

"Troy, I know what you mean," Phyllis interjected. "Now that I'm in the BSU, I don't know how I can keep up with classes. Good thing Randy and I have a lot of the same professors."

"Yeah," Troy rolled his eyes again. It was clear that Randy and Phyllis weren't just classmates anymore. Phyllis was like a child around Randy. Troy didn't have anything against her, but he was growing tired of her constant enthusiasm.

The trio caught a bus back to Georgetown and talked about the rally and what they could bring back to other black students on campus. It was Sunday afternoon, but there was still time to get some studying in before dinner. The sun was setting later in the day, and students had again been tantalized with pleasant weather. They were scattered across the front lawns with frisbees, footballs and small picnics. Radios played rock music, and many students sat quietly with books, appreciating the 70-degree day. Randy and Phyllis headed off to her dorm, and Troy agreed to meet with them later. Thankful that he had his books with him, he turned toward the library. He wasn't in any real mood to study, but he hadn't cracked a book all weekend. Studying also provided another opportunity to avoid his father, who by now was calling every day.

Troy stopped by Copy Services to leave a request with Adelaide to change his schedule for the week. He needed extra time to prepare for his accounting exam. He was surprised to find Angel behind the counter. Her face lit up as soon as she saw him.

"Hi!"

"Hey girl."

He met her at the front of the counter, where she threw her arms around him. She wore a violet silk blouse with matching mini-skirt and shoes, which for once weren't high heels. As always, Troy was impressed. "What are you doing here?"

"I changed shifts with somebody. It's quiet today, too, so I've been getting a little bit done."

"Organic chemistry?"

"Yes, you know it. I'm still doing terrible, but I'm not failing anymore."

"You'll get through it," he encouraged her. "Everything will be fine."

"I wish I could believe that."

"What's the matter now?"

"Nothing, it's no big deal," she murmured, turning away.

"It must be. A second ago you were all excited." Troy came around the counter and sat down. There were students behind him waiting for service. He helped Angel with the customers so they could get back to their conversation. When the students left with their copies, he sat her down in front of him. "Now what is it?"

"I don't know, it's just that everything is so hard now. I study as well and as much as I can, and I'm just barely passing. Even Cyndi is doing okay now. I *thought* I was starting to make friends, but it seems like the AKAs have a problem with me. Troy, I don't even know if I'm going to make line. They have to let me pledge!" Tears welled up in her eyes.

"Baby, I feel the same way," Troy told her. "My classes are hard, too! And to tell you the truth, I'm still not really sure about this BSU stuff. I mean now I really have to work to stay on top of things."

"Oh please, Troy," she snapped. "Stop it. You have everything. The BSU is doing great, you're deejaying now, and you'll be fine. I know...I know you're going to get tired of me."

"Tired of you?" Troy had to laugh. "Angel, a lot of things may happen, but that will never happen. I'll never get tired of you."

"Well, you would *want* to act like it. I see these other girls around you. I see — "

"Hush," Troy told her, placing his index finger on her lips. He then replaced his finger with his own lips. Angel smiled through her tears. Troy held his head down, his hands in her lap. Involuntarily, as if his digits had a mind of their own, they began rubbing her thighs, reaching inside of her violet mini-skirt. A student rang the bell at the counter.

"Excuse me, but can I get some help here?"

"Sorry!" Angel jumped from her seat and smoothed her skirt. Troy came from behind the counter to leave her to her work.

"I'll see you later."

"Bye, sweetie."

When Troy sat down at a cubicle on the second floor of the library, he found himself too distracted to concentrate. Instead, he sat with a hard-on, staring at the wooden desk. Instead of seeing the desk, he fantasized that his hands were in between Angel's thighs again. He imagined the previous moment with all of his senses, her *Bijan* perfume and her shapely, caramel colored legs. He couldn't wait until later that night when he could continue what they'd started at Copy Services.

There was no use in trying to study, so he returned to Harbin Hall. Troy recalled that his roommate was with Phyllis when they parted ways, and he was assured that they weren't in the room. When he got to Room 228 he found an Opus magnet on the door, the signal they used when one of them had a girl in the room. *Damn!* he thought. *They said they were going to Phyllis' dorm?* It was only 7:00. Ill Will's door was closed, meaning neither he nor Carl was there. *What the hell,* Troy thought, walking through the men's room exit to Ill Will's cluster. When he knocked, the door slowly swung open. Ill Will was seated at his desk, reading a textbook. It was as calm as Troy had ever seen him.

"I know you're not in here trying to crack a book," Troy announced. "Oh, shit!"

"Oh, pipe down," Ill retorted. "You jokers think you're the only ones who study?"

"Where's Carl?"

"I don't know, probably jacking off somewhere. It's good that he's gone though, I have an exam."

"You want to come to dinner with me?"

"Told you homey, I gotta study. *auf Wiedersehen!*"

"Yeah, peace out."

Troy was happy to see his friend studying, but at the same time he had hoped Ill Will would join him in the cafeteria. They still saw each other often, but it was rare that the two of them just hung out; their friendship was stuck between the Black Student Union and Ill Will's drunken episodes.

As usual, the black students in the cafeteria were easy to find. When Troy came over with his tray, he noticed that the upperclassmen were in a heated snapping session. Troy really wasn't in the mood, but there was never a dull moment when the upperclassmen played "the dozens."

"Shut up fool," Curt shouted. "Your moms is so old, her titties squirt powdered milk!" People at the table laughed while waiting for the response.

"Mothers?" Bizzy asked. "You have to nerve to talk about people's mothers? Nigga, your mother still has a jheri curl! I can smell the activator from here!"

Troy had to laugh out loud at that one.

"And she been had a curl," Bizzy continued. "How you gonna talk about mothers when your moms got a curl. You know the back of her neck spongy than a motherfucker. The bitch scrub the floors on her back!" Bizzy had the entire table howling, dropping silverware and unable to eat for laughing so hard. When it came to "the dozens," he had the respect of every black student on campus.

"New York is in the house, y'all. What up, mister DJ?"

"S'up, Biz!" Troy feigned enthusiasm. Now that Bizzy Hendricks had seen Troy develop a friendship with Wendell and his other Kappa brothers, Bizzy always had something to say to him.

"You the man! Rocking all the parties, macking all the honies. I seen that little mama you been with."

"Her name is Angel," a girl added from across the table.

"Mind your business," Troy answered sternly. The boisterous group at the table fell silent. It was clear to everyone that the subject of Troy's girl was a sore spot. Since becoming Vice-President of the Black Student Union, his personal life had become very public.

"Just askin' dude, just askin'," Bizzy answered. "So what's with the BSU?"

"You know. Or you would, if you came out once in a while."

"Come on, man. You niggas ain't slick. Every time I see Randy he talking to some girl. Got 'em all thinking he's Malcolm X Junior or some shit. Your meetings are like Black Dance Expressions meetings. Nothing but hoes. The BSU ain't really about nothing but getting some ass!"

A few of the seniors laughed, but most of the table was quiet, waiting for Troy's reply.

"Michelyn is at every meeting."

"Uh-huh, and she's in my room after every meeting."

"Brian, you're smoking dust," Troy told him, half-smiling. "Everybody here knows we're trying to do something. Everybody but you!"

"Yeah, so you're telling me your boy ain't clocking more honies now? Like he's not gonna get with that secretary y'all got?" Troy was silenced.

"Uh huh," Bizzy said, answering his own question. "Now."

"You're on crack," Troy retorted, trying to divert attention away from Bizzy. "Now I know y'all are coming to our showing of 'Eyes On The Prize', right?"

"I tell you what, Troy," a junior girl replied. "I'll see you at the party." The group broke into laughter once again.

"See, now that's what I'm saying!" Bizzy added. "I'll be there, too. Ain't that right, DJ Troy?" Troy quietly fumed at Bizzy's sarcasm. He wanted to get up and leave, but he wasn't about to give the older student the satisfaction. Instead, he sat in silence, eventually cracking a smile so that his irritation wouldn't be noticed.

"What y'all laughing at?" Bizzy asked loudly. "That's my nigga. Troy know he my nigga."

Troy let out a sigh, wishing he were somewhere else.

*   *   *   *

Janice Harris got up to answer the doorbell.

"Who is it?"

"It's me."

She opened the door and let her guest in. Travis Gordon stepped into the doorway with a gym bag in his hand.

"I been waiting for this all week," he said as they embraced. He stood back to look at her. "My word. You look exquisite," he said, admiring her knee-length black dress, the snug fit accenting her curves.

"Thank you."

"No, thank *you*."

Janice let Travis inside, then put his bag down and wrapped her arms around his waist. They shared a long, deep kiss that expressed how they missed each other.

*   *   *   *

"Baby, let's just talk," Angel whispered to Troy. "Come on."

Cyndi was gone, so after dinner Troy had come over immediately, intent on making love. Once they were in bed, she had let him undress her almost completely before deciding that she wanted conversation instead. Normally he would have persisted, but he didn't want to have another fight. Troy and his passion-inflamed loins were in for an evening of frustration.

"Okay, what do you want to talk about?"

"Troy, do you love me?"

Troy was dumbfounded at the question. "Of course."

"You don't tell me, though."

"Yes I do. Maybe you just don't listen. Besides, what about you? I could ask you the same thing!"

"You know I love you."

"Yeah, right."

"If I weighed 250 pounds, would you still want me?"

"Actually, I would." Troy fought vigorously to keep a straight face as he lied. He threw in the 'actually' in an attempt to sound convincing.

"You're full of shit," Angel laughed. "What am I, an idiot?"

"Nah girl, you'd still be my girl. 250 pounds of good loving."

Angel smiled. "What a darling. That's why I love talking to you. You know, you're the only good thing I really have going for me."

"Oh, come on. Now you're being silly."

"No, I'm not. My grades are horrendous, and the AKAs, oh lord. Those girls just do not like me and I don't know why. My sisters always want me to come home and take them shopping, Troy, it's just too much!"

"Maria and Lindsay just want to be like you."

"Shit," she mumbled, sucking her teeth. Angel's words faded as Troy stared at her in her bra and panties.

"Troy, you're not listening to me!"

"Yes I am. You've got Cyndi, you've got your family. Just keep your head up. Oh, and you've got me." Troy put his index finger on her chin, to punctuate his point.

"I know I've got you," she said, "or at least I used to think so. Now it's all about the BSU, or all these parties you're doing now. Next year you'll be deejaying even more!"

"No I won't, baby."

"Yes, you will. If you barely have any time for me now as it is, next year will be even worse."

"It's just a busy time of year. Nobody has lots of free time."

"But you find some time when you want to get some. Men are a trip."

Troy knew better than to respond to that remark. "Let's do something special this week," he proposed, changing the subject.

"Okay, when?"

"I just have to see, because we're meeting with the Student Government."

"Uh hunh, figures."

"Don't worry, it'll be this week. We'll do something fun, I promise."

"Yeah, all right. Sounds good."

Troy could tell from the tone of her voice that he would have to leave soon. It was clear that they weren't going to make love, and he wasn't sure if he had consoled her at all. Staying, therefore, would only make matters worse.

"Listen, maybe I should get back to my room, huh?" he asked, feeling awkward.

"Yeah. I'm a little tired."

Tired my ass, he thought. "Okay. I'll see you tomorrow."

"Bye, honey." Before he could get up, Angel grabbed him by the back of his head and gave him a long kiss, punctuating his arousal. A hypnotized Troy headed for the door.

"Troy?"

"Hmm?"

"I'm sorry. There's so much I need to deal with, I get a little overworked sometimes."

"S'alright," he answered, closing the door.

That night, Troy tossed and turned in his bed. With sex still on his mind, he ended up sleeping on his back. Randy had left the room to study, and Troy had attempted to get some rest—since he was too distracted to do anything else. His father had called earlier, leaving yet another frantic message on the answering machine. He knew he'd have to face him sooner or later, he just wanted to delay the drama for as long as he could.

*   *   *   *

Students and faculty moved quickly through the halls of the New North building, which housed the School of Business. Troy was waiting outside of Professor Newcomb's office, in one last-ditch attempt to get help before the next day's accounting test, which was worth 30 percent of his grade. Wendell had advised him to talk to his professor last semester, but he hadn't seen the value in it; if he couldn't follow the work in class, what could a one-on-one in the professor's office offer him? Since then

Troy had developed some knowledge of the material, but he was far from where he needed to be. He felt like he wouldn't know any more of the material than he did already, but he was desperate to improve, so he decided to see the professor privately.

"Troy, come on in," Professor Newcomb called. His office was small and rectangular; with huge piles of papers and books covering the walls and his desk. Troy wondered how he got anything done in there.

"What can I do for you?"

"Professor, you know the exam is tomorrow and I'm just trying to make sure I'm as ready as possible."

"Son, if you're not ready by now, heaven help you!" The instructor chuckled, trying to lighten up the exchange. Troy already regretted the visit. "I'm sorry," he said. "Is there something specific you'd like to review?"

"Yeah, there is, but I wanted to tell you something first. This is my hardest class, and I really study hard and concentrate, but I'm barely keeping up."

"Have you considered getting a tutor?"

"I have one."

"I see. Well, maybe you've needed more help."

Of course I do, fool! Troy thought. *That's why I'm here.* "Maybe, but I've been practicing all of the problems until I can do them myself."

The professor pushed some papers aside on his desk. "Troy, what do you want to major in?"

"Finance, maybe marketing."

"I see. Do you have the same trouble in other classes as you do in mine?"

"Hardly."

"Have you ever thought about transferring schools? It's not too late for Arts and Sciences."

"Look professor, I don't want to--"

"Just think about it," Newcomb interrupted. Troy had never heard him speak so firmly. "Maybe we should go over some of these problems now, I'm afraid I don't have a lot of time. And next time, after the exam, come and see me so we can go over where you went wrong, together. If you were having trouble, you should have come to me before now."

Troy spent forty-five minutes reviewing with Professor Newcomb, and he left his office with a newfound respect for the man. After considering what the professor had told him, Troy knew he was right; he should have come to see him earlier. But he couldn't very well tell Newcomb about the BSU and Angel and being a DJ. He'd think it was no wonder Troy was fighting to keep a "C" plus in the class.

*   *   *   *

"I just don't understand what the problem is. I mean, we have as much right to be here as anyone else," a white student declared. He was one of two white males at the BSU general meeting and the only two whites in the auditorium. They stood out for the flannel shirts they wore as much as anything else.

"The problem is you're not black," Randy told them, inciting applause from the rest of the audience. "The Black Student Union has programs geared toward black students, but all students are welcome. To our films, our lectures, our parties, even the activities coming up next year, you two and anybody else are welcome. Next year we're going to re-establish the call for South African divestment, and we're going to talk about restructuring the encumbered and overly Eurocentric curriculum. Will you guys be around for that?"

"Yeah," said the other white student, "but only if we can join." He and his friend stood up.

"I'm sorry," Randy responded, "but that's not going to happen." Again, the crowd roared with furious applause. The two white students were unaffected.

"But why not?"

Randy was ready for them. "The reason why your membership is not acceptable is because the membership of the BSU has to be protected. Members are able to vote, members can run for office. And if whites or other students are able to infiltrate the ranks, even those with the best of intentions, then there's nothing to stop them from nullifying, or diluting, if you will, the organization. The membership rule mandates that we have to keep that from happening. Now when it comes to participating and organizing, we welcome everyone. But only black students can be members. If you really want to be down with us, I know you'll respect that."

The two white guys had no response after that explanation, and felt compelled to take their seats, inspiring more cheers from the crowd.

Randy signaled for the audience to quiet down. Troy's roommate was making him proud. His leadership and his confidence were as tangible as the wooden chairs they sat in on stage.

"Can you guys hang around after the meeting?" Randy asked. "I'd like to talk with you some more."

"Sure."

"No Bobby, screw that," said the other one. "It's clear they don't want us here."

"It's not like that," Randy offered.

"Seems that way to us," Bobby said, taking sides with his offended friend. When they got up and walked away, the other students watched them leave without a word.

The rest of the meeting proceeded with Jay and Phyllis giving their reports, and Ill Will briefly listing what students had told him they wanted to discuss. Troy and Randy had already detailed the events for the remainder of the semester. When the meeting ended, many of the students were still excited. Randy was in back of the auditorium, addressing a small group of students, as he always did after a meeting.

"Your boy ain't no joke, is he?" Ill Will whispered from the stage. Even he was impressed with Randy.

"Nah, he ain't," Troy affirmed. "I see you doing your thing too, now."

"You the man," Ill Will answered, embarrassed by the acknowledgment. Troy had been busy during the past week, but something told him that Ill had not been drinking lately. He probably didn't have time, now that he was trying to 'get academic.' The new Black Student Union officers had left a definite impression on the students at Georgetown, and tonight's meeting had cemented Randy's status as a leader. Randy had again invited a reporter from the *Hoya,* the school newspaper, which meant that by next week, his declaration to the two white students would be known all over campus. Troy hoped the BSU wouldn't be labeled as separatist because of it, but he suspected it might happen anyway.

Although many of the brothers came to meetings and expressed interest in what Randy was doing, it was the black women on campus who were most drawn to the organization. As a result, Troy and Randy found themselves talking with many co-eds whom they hadn't noticed earlier in the year. Phyllis became angry when she saw Randy with these other girls at BSU events, while the guys who wanted to talk to her were met with quick, cold rejection. Jay and Ill Will seldom hung around after BSU events, so Troy was often left with what he termed Randy's 'leftovers.' It didn't really matter since most of them knew that he was dating Angel, who was in the science library that night, like most nights when the BSU met. But when the conversation turned social, Troy never once heard any of the girls gathered ask about his girlfriend. He and his roommate walked home that night feeling ten feet tall.

"Brother, you really gave it to them tonight," Troy told him.

"Thank you. And don't think I didn't see you with the young ladies, either."

"You got some nerve! All them girls you be scooping. Phyllis is gonna flip!"

"I can take care of that. Besides, it's not like--"

"Come on now," Troy stopped him. "You know you hit it. That wasn't her the other night?"

"Yeah, it was," Randy admitted. "But I really didn't mean for it to happen." Troy laughed. Who was he trying to kid?

"Seriously," Randy continued. "We had just been spending a lot of time together. Next thing I knew we was boning."

"What are you going to do about the rest of them?"

"I don't know," Randy said. "It's kind of hard to say 'no' to the booty when it comes so easily. You're going to have the same problem."

"I don't think so, " Troy replied. In his mind, his situation was slightly different.

"Yes you are," Randy kept on him. "One of these days Angel is going to come through and get her feelings hurt!" They both laughed. Troy fought desperately to come up with some form of denial, but he found no words.

They walked along in the cool breeze, laughing and joking. The carefree attitude that they both shared was a welcome change for Troy. He felt like he needed it to deal with the subject that had indirectly come into the conversation—Angel. Why couldn't he deny Randy's argument? Despite the contradiction raised by his roommate, in his heart and mind he still wouldn't have chosen any other girl over Angel. Lately it took more effort from him to put her in a good mood since for the moment the AKAs ruled her every thought. Troy didn't see what the big deal was about the sorority. Last semester that kind of thing had been the furthest thing from her mind! He understood that changes were a part of freshman year, but he wasn't ready to give up on the girl he'd pursued for so long. She was still one of the finest girls he'd ever seen; he still wanted her and wanted to *be* hers. When he went to bed that night, Troy decided that he and Angel would work out whatever problems they may be having, whatever the sacrifice.

On the following Friday night, Cyndi loaned Troy her car to take Angel to a party at Howard. His mother also had a Nissan Sentra, so he felt comfortable driving it. Going to the Howard party was the special event he had promised her the week before. By providing two things she wanted, time with him and a way to get off campus, Troy was certain that Angel would be pleased.

They parked on a side street and walked up Georgia Avenue. It was raining, but the street was still active with students, running up and down, double-parking in front of stores. The incense dealers and T-shirt vendors were still on the crowded sidewalk, their tables covered with makeshift plastic tents. Rap music pumped from car stereos. Georgia Avenue was a popular shopping area for young blacks all over D.C.; the McDonald's, the record stores and clothing stores, combined with the front end of Howard's campus, made it a natural hangout.

Angel held his arm under the umbrella in silence.

"Why are you so quiet?"

"I'm okay. I'm just glad this week is over. I'm sick of studying all the time."

"I hear you. Well, you don't have to worry about that tonight. Let's just have a good time."

The party was in Blackburn Hall, one of the larger buildings on Howard's campus, a short walk from Georgia Avenue. Troy could hear the music from the front entrance which was wall-to-wall students, many of whom simply sought shelter from the rain. Troy found the sight of so many black people refreshing. It was something he knew he'd never see at Georgetown. He led Angel to the coat check area, where they both put away their jackets and the umbrella. Angel wore a short brown dress with matching brown suede pumps and a thick gold herringbone chain. He wore a blue and gray Georgetown jogging suit and a navy blue Yankee cap.

"Goddamn girl, you tight!" a boy said from behind the coat check area.

That's it, Troy thought, *I'ma have to fight.* The dress was hugging Angel's ample backside. It showed too much shoulder, too much back and definitely too much cleavage.

"Oh, stop that," she insisted, though she was clearly flattered. Troy was shocked. Why is she answering him?

"Come on 'round here and give me some love."

Angel walked around the partition and hugged the guy who had complimented her and enraged Troy. He fought to keep his composure. He thought those hugs were reserved for him.

"Troy, this is Mark. Mark, this is my boyfriend Troy."

"How you doing, Troy?"

"Hey." Troy could hardly speak. Angel returned to Troy's side.

"So this is why we haven't seen you for a while, huh?"

"Yes, but I've been trying to study, too."

"Whatever," Mark answered. Who is this kid? Troy thought. And who the fuck is 'we'? Why did she add the part about studying? Wasn't it enough that he was her man?

"Come on Troy," Angel called, sensing his anger. "Mark, it was nice to see you."

"You too, baby. Nice meeting you, Troy. Hey, when y'all get to the door, tell them you're with me, you'll get in free."

"Thanks," Angel told him. They worked their way through the crowd until they reached the entrance to the party.

"Five dollars," demanded a black girl seated at a table.

"We're here with Mark Parsons," Angel announced.

"Oh, you know Mark? Okay, go right in." The girl signaled for the couple to move on, but Troy stopped and turned around.

"We're not here with Mark," he announced, placing ten dollars on the table.

"I see," the girl said, taking the money. She turned to her friend at the table, who shrugged her shoulders.

"What did you do that for?" Angel asked, annoyed.

"He doesn't need to be hooking us up. You're with me."

"I know, but ten bucks is ten bucks. You could have used that money for gas or something."

"Don't worry about it, let's just go." He took Angel's hand behind him, leading her into the huge room which was dense with partying students. Angel was able to take Troy's mind off Mark by taking him out on the dance floor. The DJ had just put on Public Enemy's "Don't Believe The Hype," and everyone was cheering.

Troy and Angel had never danced together at a party. Before long, the two of them were laughing and smiling, enjoying each other as they danced. Troy was relieved not to have to contend with Mark, and Angel was pleased to have Troy on the dance floor with her rather than sulking. She didn't enjoy the one party she had attended at Georgetown, because Troy was providing the music and he hadn't paid her any attention. Troy watched his sexy companion as she twirled her hips to the music, pulling him closer, allowing his body to press against hers with uncensored abandon. Even at Howard, well-known as the Mecca of fine black women, Angel was turning heads.

When she wasn't dancing, Angel was being called over by one Howard guy or another. She knew four of them on a first name basis, and she seemed to know others by sight. She introduced Troy as her boyfriend, but there was no interest on their side, so his title held little meaning. He had noticed that Angel attracted dirty looks from many of the girls at the party. Troy made a feeble attempt to talk to some of the Howard girls when Angel really got wrapped up in another conversation. He did get some looks of his own and a few 'hellos', but not much more attention from the Howard girls. It soon became obvious to him that many of them had seen him come in with Angel, and the intimate way they had been dancing made it obvious that they were together. To make matters worse, he seemed to stand out in his Georgetown jogging suit.

On the ride back to the Georgetown campus, Troy was silent. He couldn't hide the fact that he was upset, but he figured if he kept quiet, at least he could say he had tried to avoid a fight. Angel rode along, bopping her head to the music from the radio. She looked as if a laugh was about to escape her lips.

"So what's all the attitude about?" she asked, smiling.

"Where do you know all those niggas from?" Troy asked, unable to contain himself.

"I met them at Howard. And some of them I went to high school with. I was going to go to Howard, you know."

"You never told me that."

"Yes I did," she insisted. "You just weren't listening."

"No, fuck all that. You knew every guy in that motherfucker!"

"So what, are you jealous?"

"I ain't jealous of shit, I'm just saying." Troy stopped short at a red light.

"Watch it!" Angel shouted. "You're saying what, Troy?"

"You had to have spent a lot of time at Howard to know all those guys. You sure some of those weekend trips weren't over there?"

"Are you calling me a liar?" Angel asked. She had a surprised expression, but Troy wasn't buying it.

"I don't know," he told her. "You tell me."

"Oh my God!" she shouted. "You are such a trip! Like you never went to any Howard parties! That's all you did first semester. I was only there once or twice."

"Once or twice?" Troy fumed. "Get the fuck out of here! You think I'm stupid?"

"Troy, listen to me! I just got to be cool with some people over there when I was visiting. Some of those guys I knew from before I got to Howard. I do live in Maryland, you know."

"Jesus Christ," Troy muttered. Suddenly he was feeling queasy. He pulled into the university parking lot. He wanted to vomit, but he couldn't do it in front of Angel. It was bad enough she had seen him so angry and jealous. She wasn't finished arguing.

"Look, didn't I stay with you the whole night? I didn't dance with any of them, I told them all who you were. Why are you so upset?"

"You could've danced with them if you wanted," he spat. "Don't do me no favors."

"Oh, it's like that now, huh Troy?"

Troy got out of the car and slammed the door. He took a deep breath, hoping the cool air would calm his nausea.

"Angel forget it, all right? Forget I said anything."

Angel came out on the passenger side where Troy was waiting.

"You know what I think your problem is?" she asked. *Lord*, he thought. *Why can't she just shut the fuck up?*

"You're not used to being in a different environment. You're getting to be the man around here, so when you go to another school where you're just another brother, it gets to you."

"No, that's not it."

"No? Then what is it?"

"I don't know," he answered, hoping she would drop the issue.

"Yeah, the hell you don't."

They walked the rest of the way in silence. When they got off the elevator, each went their separate ways without saying goodbye. Angel was only half-right. Troy was not hurt by not being 'the man' at Howard among Mark and her countless male friends, but it did seem to him that being 'the man' at Georgetown was evidently not enough for her. When he reached Room 228, he heard one of his slow jam tapes. Someone was breathing hard and a voice that sounded like Phyllis' was squealing. He had told Randy not to worry, because he'd be sleeping with Angel tonight. Now he had nowhere to go.

Troy heard shouts coming from down the hall. He traced the noise back to Angel's room. He didn't want Angel to see him, but he couldn't resist listening to what was happening.

"Bitch!" Cyndi shouted from inside. "You filthy bitch! How could you?"

"You see a bitch you smack a bitch!" Angel shouted.

"This had nothing to do with him! You had to get him involved? And me? Why?"

Who the hell is she talking about? Troy wondered.

"Look, shit happens. I didn't plan it. Your car was available at the time. He chose to come."

"Goddamn you!"

"Calm your country ass down. I took care of you and I will continue to."

"That's not the point and you know it."

"Oh, so he's your man now, huh?"

"You're just the biggest bitch!"

"I told you about that."

There was a brief silence before something shattered against the door. Troy heard Cyndi's voice escalating, so he bolted around the corner. Seconds later, he heard a door slam. An angry Cyndi came around the corner in tears.

"What's the matter?" he asked. She just stared at him and kept walking until she reached the staircase.

Troy wondered if Angel would tell him what had just happened. Angel's fight with Cyndi sounded worse than her fight with him. *Fuck it*, he thought, his pride kicking in. *That's between them.* Still, he would certainly speak to Cyndi about it later. Tired and not wanting to bother with anyone, Troy headed for the lounge, where he had only the couch and a TV for company. He turned the channel until he found a music video show to watch. A thick shadow appeared in the doorway, blocking the light of the TV.

"S'up, homey?" Ill Will came in carrying a 32-ounce bottle of scotch. He was dressed only in his underwear.

"What up, man," Troy answered, making no effort to hide his gloom.

"You hear that fight?"

"Yeah. I don't know what the hell's happening. But we just had a fight our damn selves."

"Hmm. Randy fucking again?"

"Most definitely."

"So is Carl."

"Where's Yvonne?"

"She's sleep. Wouldn't let me come with her. It's 3:30 dude! Everyone's asleep, really."

"Except us. Let me have some of that." Troy reached out for the liquor.

"Oh, you're going hard now, huh homey? All right, you're a big boy."

Troy took a long swig of scotch. It burned the back of his throat, but he liked it. By dawn, Troy and Ill Will had finished the bottle.

*   *   *   *

RING! It was the loudest, shrillest tone Troy had ever heard. He could hear himself turning over. He was back in his own bed, but he had no recollection of returning to his room. Everything sounded louder than it did normally. RING! *What time is it?* RING! "Shit," he said aloud. His head was pounding, and he had to stop the maddening telephone ring.

"Huh?" he said into the phone.

"Troy?"

"Yeah, yeah, what?"

"Troy, what the hell is going on down there?" The tone of his father's voice told Troy he was not in a playful mood.

"Oh shit, Dad."

"You're goddamned right it's your Dad! Why haven't you returned my calls? We were worried about you! What the hell is wrong with you?

You can't call? Huh?" Anger and disappointment echoed in his father's voice.

"Dad, can I call you back?"

"No, you cannot fucking call me back! You never answer the phone as it is! You must be hungover or something."

"No, I'm not," he lied.

"Troy, I don't know who you think you're dealing with. Now either you start talking or I come down to that campus today."

"All right, all right," Troy said. "Just stop yelling, please. I ran, I ran for BSU office."

"You did what? After I specifically told you not to? What the hell is the matter with you?"

"Come on now, Dad, it's not that bad," Troy insisted. Tears streamed down his face and his ears were ringing. He was in pain and overly sensitive to the slightest noise.

"You couldn't wait, huh? You just couldn't wait. Now how the hell are you going to bring your grades up and do that, too? That 'black power' shit won't do anything for you. Fuck around and you might get kicked out!"

"You don't know that, Dad," Troy whimpered.

"Don't you tell me what I don't know! The Black Student Union is the reason your mother was able to go to school! There were protests, demonstrations. People risked everything. I had to pull back because I had you, I had responsibilities."

Sure, Troy thought. *Responsibilities you ran out on.* Suddenly his father sounded like a victim rather than the victimizer he had become.

"I know what you're thinking," his father fumed. "Maybe I wasn't always there, but I took care of business! Your bills are paid, aren't they? You don't have to work, do you? Now I'm telling you, all you need to worry about is your grades. The Black Student Union won't do shit for you when you get out in the real world! You don't know about that yet, you're just a snot-nosed kid! But go ahead and blow your chance if you want to!" Troy could hear his bellowing even while holding the phone a half-foot from his ear.

"Dad," he cried, "I don't need this now, all right? That's why I didn't call you."

"You don't know what the hell you need, but I know one thing, you had better get your head on straight, Troy. I want to see some of your last exams. Get them up here this week. I'm calling your mother, too, so don't try to get slick. I'll be down there knocking on your goddamned door!"

"Yes, Dad," he replied, sniffling.

"Don't cry. You brought this on yourself. Now I want some exams this week, understand?"

"Yes, Dad."

"All right. Go back to sleep." Troy's father hung up loudly.

Still tearful, Troy searched for the aspirin. He almost fell over when he stood up, and his head was still pounding with the force of a hammer. There was no aspirin in his cabinet, so he searched through Randy's cabinet, finding Tylenol. In Randy's mirror he could see Randy's bed, which was lumpy. Troy turned to see his roommate in the bed, wrapped around Phyllis. He was sure they had probably heard the whole thing. *Jesus*, Troy thought. He found some orange juice in the mini-fridge and took four Tylenol. Afterwards, he changed into his robe, found some towels and headed for a long, hot shower.

Seventeen

Troy, Randy and Phyllis sat in Travis Gordon's office. Troy hadn't been in the Office of Minority Affairs office for months.

"So what you're telling me is you want to bring Louis Farrakhan to this campus?" Travis confirmed.

"Yes," Randy replied.

"Do you really think that can happen?" Travis inquired neutrally.

"I don't see why not," Randy offered. "We just wanted you to know."

"Actually Mr. Gordon, we know it will be hard to accomplish," Phyllis frantically interjected. "That's why we're here, to try to get a head start."

"Phyllis, call me Travis. Now what makes you all think we can help you in this matter?"

Troy could tell that Travis didn't want to deal with any controversy, which would surely be caused by a Farrakhan speech.

"Travis," Randy continued. "We know we're going to have to get approval from Student Affairs. We believe that we can generate enough of a demand for the Minister to speak. There will be an honorarium to deal with as well."

"Randy, you're going to have to deal with more than just an honorarium." Travis advised. "This is Georgetown University! Student Affairs isn't just going to roll over and let Farrakhan in here. They don't like to make waves up in the Jesuits' offices."

"They're going to have to get used to it. They can't deny us our right to hear the man speak, can they?"

Travis smiled. "Son, no one is trying to deny you anything. Now listen. Darnell already submitted the budget for next year, and you still don't know how much you're going to get. Student Affairs and the Jesuits control this school. Or have you forgotten that? And they're not going to want *him* here on campus. So, you'll have a fight on your hands."

"That's what we're here for," Randy insisted. "If enough students here want to see him so that they have to allow him to lecture, can we count on your support?" Randy was determined to take the issue right to Travis.

"It won't happen, but if you get that far, I'll see what I can do."

"You'll see what you can do?" Randy mimicked. "What does that mean, sir?"

"Don't get bent out of shape," Travis retorted. "There are consequences for everything we do here, good and bad. You have to learn to play the game, Randy. It's politics! If we go against Student Affairs on something like this, our very existence could be at risk. We have scholarships to provide, tutors to support! Is one Farrakhan speech worth jeopardizing the support system we've established here? You think about it."

"Yes sir, I'll do just that," a disgruntled Randy answered.

"I think that's about all for now," Travis said, standing up. Troy and Phyllis also stood, as if on cue.

"Come by next week, we'll talk." Travis offered. "We still have you guys for our recruiting weekend, don't we?"

"Of course," Randy returned, heading for the door. Travis could sense his anger. "Randy, you're doing good things, better than I've seen the BSU do in a long time. But you can't do everything all at once."

"You're right. Thanks."

Darnell was in the reception area typing on a computer keyboard as the freshmen were leaving.

"There's the new BSU," he called. "You guys working on something?"

"No concern of yours," Randy answered.

"You said it, not me."

"Darnell, let the lady and the gentlemen leave," Travis interrupted.

"Sure, sir. Y'all take care." Darnell tapped Troy on the shoulder before he could exit.

"Hey, DJ."

"What?"

"Give me a call sometime," he whispered. "We should talk."

"About what?"

"Travis, nigga! Don't you know-- "

"Darnell!" Travis barked. "Let the boy go and get back to work!"

"Yes, Travis." Travis looked over at Troy, just in time to catch the disgust on his face. He still couldn't understand what his mother saw in him. What could Darnell possibly have to say about Travis? He had to admit his curiosity was peaked.

Troy followed Randy out and looked on as Phyllis tried to console him. The threesome walked out of the Healy building to the front of the campus. Travis had said what they all thought he would say, so Troy wasn't surprised. He was discouraged, but the meeting just made Randy more determined to bring the leader to Georgetown.

"Honey, what did you expect?" Phyllis asked Randy. "Minority Affairs is part of the establishment."

"I know, but I didn't think Travis was a sellout."

"Wait a minute," Troy interrupted. As much as he hated Travis, he couldn't go along with Randy on this one. "He's a sellout because of what he said? He probably just told us the truth, brother."

"That doesn't make it right, Troy."

"I know, but at least he's being realistic. Student Affairs isn't trying to see Farrakhan up in here. It's going to take a lot of work. Protests, petitions, the whole nine yards."

"If Travis really wanted to make it happen, he could." Randy insisted.

Troy didn't feel like arguing, so he let the comment go. "Listen, I'll see you guys later, I'm going to the record store."

"All right roomie, peace." Troy turned in the opposite direction, leaving the couple to themselves. He found a pay phone by the front gates and made a call.

"Minority Affairs, can I help you?"

"Darnell?"

"Yes?"

"It's Troy. When you want to hook up?"

"Tomorrow night. Come by the house at eight, we'll rap."

"I'll be there."

*   *   *   *

Troy and Ill Will were headed towards the Black Student House.

"So you have no idea what it's about?" Ill Will asked.

"Nah, he's probably just got some shit on Travis." Troy knocked on the Black Student House door. Seconds later, a girl opened the door.

"And you are?"

"Troy Harris. Is Darnell here?"

"Yes. Is he expecting you?"

"He's the one who invited me."

"I see. Regarding what?"

"Bitch, would you just go get him?" Ill Will shouted. "Shit! Darnell, bring your bourgie ass down here!"

"I know he isn't talking to me," said the girl calmly.

"The hell I ain't! Where the fuck is Darnell?"

"Right here, right here," yelled Darnell, practically falling down the steps to the front door. "Come on in. It's all right, baby, I told him to come."

"You're not going to stand here and let this fool call me a bitch!"

Darnell jumped in front of the girl to separate her and Ill Will. "Troy, Ill Will, have a seat. I'll be right back."

Troy and his friend headed into the living room.

"What's wrong with you?" Troy asked.

"Nothing," Ill Will spat. "I just don't have time to waste. 4-H ain't no joke and I'm through with the bullshit."

Troy nodded. *Great*, he thought. *This nigga's drunk.*

Darnell's guest was taken into the kitchen against her will. Troy and Ill Will overheard a heated exchange which ended with Darnell sternly ordering her to go upstairs.

"Fuck you, motherfucker!" she yelled, pointing at Ill Will on her way up. "Fuck you!"

"Bye!" he retorted. "See ya!"

Darnell joined the boys and took a seat in a corner opposite the couch.

"Sorry about that, fellas. So Troy, you were just stopping by? When you trying to do this?"

"Now."

"Dude, you were supposed to be alone. This is between me and you."

"Nah. If you can tell me, you can tell Ill. This is a crew."

"Hmph."

Darnell stood, then moved closer to Ill Will until he stood directly over him. He stared at Ill Will for a moment, as if he were sizing him up.

"All right, but this conversation stays in this room. Understood?"

"I ain't no snitch," a defensive Ill Will replied.

"What's this all about, Darnell?"

"Listen. I'm real and I been real ever since I got here. I know what really goes down and you seem like the type that would appreciate that knowledge. Not like your hot-headed President."

"Get to the point."

"You don't like Travis, do you?"

"So what?"

"So he's fucking your mom, isn't he?"

Troy stood up and marched over to Darnell.

"No disrespect," Darnell said, putting out his palms. "But isn't he?"

Silence.

"If your mom is Janice Harris, he's on the phone with her every day. Believe me, he's been up in there." Ill Will's eyes lit up. He had no idea this had been going on.

"That's right. Now if I were you Troy, I'd be pretty pissed off. In fact, I'd be looking for a way to get back at Travis."

"And I suppose you have the way."

"Damn real! I've been working in Minority Affairs for almost two years. I know the system! Getting what you want ain't shit as long as you have some association with the office."

"Like the BSU," Ill Will said. "I get it."

"And I was getting it too, until you clowns came along." Darnell lamented. "Whatever niggas needed, they were getting. Food, money, campus vehicles, the whole nine. Except now that I'm just an office manager, I don't have the same privileges."

"So you need us to help you keep stealing," Troy deduced.

"Oh no, I don't need shit. I'ma get mine regardless. And we don't steal. We just use the system to our advantage when necessary. You can't do anything major behind Travis' back, but little things slip through the cracks. Purchase orders. Petty cash. I done signed his name on shit he don't even know about. So I don't need any of y'all, but I'm giving you a chance to get at him."

Troy considered the idea. He sure would love to stick it to Travis, but to do it at the expense of the BSU, and Randy, was a high price.

"Look, let me get back to you."

"Sure, man, but remember, the show must go on, with or without you."

*   *   *   *

Troy walked out of the front gates and on to the cobblestone sidewalk. April had just begun, and it was becoming harder to concentrate on academics, much less the BSU, Angel and the uncomfortable reality of Travis dating his mother. He had scored a "B" on his Accounting exam, and he had sent it to his father as he requested. This week he would receive his European Civilization and Sociology exams back and he was confident that he had done well. His father had been satisfied with the one grade and had since become friendlier with Troy over the phone, but Troy was still stung by that previous Saturday morning call. He had instructed Randy never to turn off the answering machine, and to make sure the tape was always rewound. If Troy could help it, his father wouldn't have an opportunity to talk to him for the rest of the semester.

Troy and Angel had eventually made up after their fight the night of the Howard party, though he was still disturbed by her fight with Cyndi. To smooth things over and to stay in her good graces, Troy told his girlfriend that she had been right about the whole thing. Since then, both of them pledged to stay together and spent as much time as they could talking, hugging, and frantically making love. After learning that she didn't make the AKA line, Angel was inconsolable. Troy sympathized with her and wished he could transfer some of his social status to her. Angel also seemed to be doing badly in her classes, receiving 'D's and 'C' minuses on her exams. Troy didn't know how to help, although he sensed she needed his support and understanding. However, when he tried to console her, she turned away. When the trips off campus became frequent again, Troy refused to sit by and watch. Finding himself in front of the library, he decided to look in on Ill Will while he was working.

"What up, homey?"

"What up, man. Listen, I need to talk to you."

"Sure, what about?"

"Come in the hall for a minute."

"All right, hold on."

Ill Will came from around the counter.

"Good thing it's slow today. So what's up?"

"Listen, can you get a car?"

"Absolutely. It's been a while, but —"

"Ill, I mean legally."

"Oh. Well, I can do that, too. You trying to get a ride somewhere?"

"No, no. I need you to follow Angel the next time she goes off campus."

"I see."

"She'll be back to go to class or to come here. Next time she leaves you gotta be on her."

"All right. I'll get Cyndi's car or one of Carl's boys' cars. They'll give up the keys."

"Doesn't matter, just get it. She takes the bus, but she's gotta be getting rides back. The G2 stops running by the time she gets back to the dorm."

"I got you. Don't worry, I'll see what the deal is."

"Thanks. And Ill?"

"Yeah?"

"Keep this between us."

Days later, it was Ill Will who came in to find Troy working at Copy Services. Angel shared his shift and Ill Will could see that they were acting very lovey-dovey. He rang the bell.

"Oh, what up, man?" Troy jumped up and came over.

"You tell me. Hey, Angel."

"Hi Will! How are you?"

"Not as good as you."

"What?"

"I'm just playing. Troy, come out to the lobby for a minute."

"Now?"

Ill Will rolled his eyes.

"Yes, Romeo, now."

Troy came around the counter and almost tripped while looking at Angel as he walked away. Ill Will was exasperated. Troy followed Ill Will all the way outside the library.

"Shit man, is her shit that good?"

"I just didn't want her to suspect anything. So, did you see something or what?"

"Yeah." Ill Will's face turned serious. "We'd better sit over here."

Ill Will led his friend to a nearby bench. Troy was now braced for the worst.

"What, man?"

"She takes the bus all the way to Howard. Then she meets some guy over there."

"That would be Mark."

"Don't know. But then they go over to the football field and do something under the bleachers."

"The bleachers? Shit."

"At first I think they're fucking, but this guy looks like he has a place to go, you know? So I get out and follow them, but all I could see was a bag."

Troy looked down at his shoes.

"So then they get back in the car," Ill Will continued. "They drive out to this apartment in Maryland."

"Landover? Do you remember?"

"Nah, I think it was Silver Spring. Actually it's a townhouse."

"How long were they there?"

Ill Will paused. "All night."

"Are you sure? What, you stayed in front of the house?"

"Troy, listen. I parked real close and took a nap. I figured if dude's car started, I'd hear it. Anyway, they were still there when I woke up. But get this. Cyndi shows up in the morning."

"Cyndi?"

"Yeah. She's got a cop with her. She tells the cop that the dude is a dealer and left coke in her car. Angel says Cyndi's lying and that she's only mad because Angel stole her man."

"Stole her man." Troy couldn't hide his despair.

"I'm sorry, dude."

"It's all right. So then what?"

"Angel and the guy come out arm in arm. They all drive to the police station in Maryland, but they're out in an hour. Angel gets a ride back here from the guy, she gets her books and goes to class. A little late, of course."

"And this was last Thursday, huh?"

"Yeah. Look, I'm sorry."

"It's okay."

"No, for real. If you need anything, let me know."

"Thanks."

The boys slapped hands and Ill Will gave Troy a hug before heading the other way. Troy gathered himself and headed back into Copy

Services, a contrived smile plastered on his face.   Angel was now overwhelmed with customers.

"Troy, what took you so long? I'm swamped."

"Sorry, Ill had a situation."

"Is everything all right?"

"Yeah. Fine."

After work, Troy was so disillusioned, he could hardly think straight. There was nothing in Ill Will's story for him to question, to pick apart. He couldn't have followed the wrong girl, he knew Angel as well as anyone. Ill Will had done just what he asked, and his worst fears were apparently true. But what was with the football field? And what did Cyndi have to do with it? After walking around Georgetown for a couple of hours, Troy returned to Harbin Hall. Thankfully, Randy was out somewhere. Troy's turntables weren't enough to pull him from his depression. Before it was 8:00, he was undressed and in bed.

*   *   *   *

The following afternoon, Troy saw Cyndi seated on a bench in front of Healy with a white guy he had never seen. Seeing her reminded him of Ill's news about Angel.

"Hey girl!" he called, trying to sound cheerful.

"Hey Troy!" Cyndi rose to hug her friend. The white guy looked on, perplexed.

"Troy, I'd like for you to meet Billy. Billy, this is Angel's boyfriend, Troy." Troy and Billy shook hands. Troy knew she identified him as Angel's boyfriend to put Billy's mind at ease.

"So how's it going, lady?"

"Good. Busy, but good." Troy sat down with the couple.

"I know what you mean."

"I'm trying to get ready for Organic Chem, but I'm loving these nice days too much."

"I hear you."

Billy stood up. "Cyn, I've got to go. See you later?"

"Sure." Cyndi stood up to give him a kiss. He waved goodbye to Troy, who returned the wave.

"So that's your new man, huh, 'Cyn'?"

"Yep. It's been a couple of months now. Of course, you wouldn't know that because you haven't been around as much lately."

"That's not my fault," Troy insisted. "Angel can't get that sorority thing off her mind."

"I know," Cyndi agreed. Then her face turned serious. "Troy, let's talk for a minute."

"Sure! Anything, 'Cyn.'"

"Look, I don't really know how to say this, so I'm just going to tell you. She's no good, Troy."

"Who, Angel?" Troy smiled and shook his head. "I know."

"I'm serious, Troy. She doesn't deserve somebody like you."

"And how do you figure that?"

"Troy, she's had other guys. I mean more than a few."

"I know that," Troy snapped, trying not to sound surprised.

"Troy, listen. She cheated on you. That bitch, she *is* cheating on you. She isn't home all those weekends, Troy, believe me. She acts real innocent around you, but that's not really her."

"I see."

"Troy, I'm sure deep down you've always suspected it. And I really don't know what's going on with you two now, but I don't want to see you hurt. You're such a sweet guy."

"Cyndi, why are you telling me this?"

"Look, just be aware. Angel can be a real bitch when she wants to, believe me."

"That's not what I asked you, all right? I know more about her than you think."

"No, you don't."

"Yes, I do! I, I been following her, okay?"

Troy could see that Cyndi was surprised.

"Oh."

"Now you and me are cool, right?"

"Of course."

"So, tell me, then. What's your part in all this?"

"One of the guys she, she's seeing is my ex-boyfriend."

"Oh. Damn, I see." Troy maintained his surprise but he was secretly relieved that her story and Ill's were the same.

"It's not just a girl stealing my guy. It's more than that. See, I'm not like these rich kids, either. And me and Angel got along quickly. We actually come from similar backgrounds."

"Where you from, Cyndi?"

"Lansing. Anyway, we were tight. And I confided in her about this guy. I was, I was pregnant by him."

Troy shook his head. He wasn't sure if he wanted to hear any more.

"Now this bastard, this bastard wanted me to have an abortion, and, and..."

Cyndi started sobbing before she could finish the sentence. Troy held on to her. He wouldn't have minded crying himself.

"I'm sorry," she cried.

"It's okay, Cyndi. Believe me, I understand."

"But wait, that's not even the point," she continued. "I had the abortion for him, when it turns out that that asshole was with her the whole time. They're in cahoots."

"I know, I know."

"They're not just screwing, Troy. He's a dealer. She works for him."

"Jesus Christ. How do you know?"

"The shit was in my car, all right? This isn't a fucking joke, Troy."

"All right, I'm sorry."

"I thought you deserved to know."

"Thanks. It's going to be okay, Cyndi. I'll do something."

Cyndi wiped her face and calmed down.

"I know this is tough to take, but Troy, I swear it's true. You just don't need this. I see you and Randy. White students know about the BSU, too! Truth is, everyone on our floor is really proud of you guys. You could probably have a lot of girls now, you had 'em before Angel! I know you love her, but look out for yourself. Please."

Troy nodded in silence. Nausea was building up in his stomach. Again, he could find no words. Cyndi could see he was upset.

"Troy, are you going to be okay?"

"Yeah. Are you?"

"I think so."

They both stood and hugged. Sensing his discomfort, Cyndi made a hasty exit, leaving Troy to sit back down on the bench in a painful trance, surrounded by students frolicking in the sun.

He didn't know what time it was when he finally stood up, but the Healy Tower bell had sounded on two occasions. Still crushed by Cyndi's revelation, he slowly walked along the path to Harbin Hall. In his room he felt stifled, so he opened one of the large panel windows which allowed a welcome breeze to drift in. Troy put on one of his new records, "My Philosophy" by Boogie Down Productions. Within minutes he was furiously mixing hip-hop, back and forth from one turntable to the next, just as if he were playing at a party. He felt compelled to lift up one of his huge speakers and place it directly in front of the open window. He then turned up the volume up on the stereo as high as it could go. With the headphones between his left ear and his shoulder, he was playing "Top Billin'" by the Audio Two, a party favorite.

'Emcee M-I, people call me Milk,
when I'm bustin' up a party I feel no guilt, bustin' up a party I feel no guilt,
...bustin' up a party, bustin' up a party, bustin' up a party I feel no guilt...'

A small crowd gathered outside the window, which included some black students who had begun to dance. Troy lost himself in the music; playing and mixing record after record. He was oblivious to the crowd that had formed downstairs, the party to which his DJ skills had given birth. Black and white students were captivated by the music booming from the window, one flight up. A couple of the black students began chanting 'Troy's trying to start a party,' while other black freshmen were gathering under the window, dancing and cheering. The weather had put everyone in a festive mood to begin with, and Troy's music was feeding it. Losing himself in the music was the best way he knew to forget about everything he had heard today. The faint sound of his name was invading the loud music.

"Troy! Troy!" the stern voice shouted. "Turn it down! Turn it down now!" Leslie, the Resident Director of Harbin Hall, was enraged. Casually, Troy pushed the stop button on both of his turntables.

"You're coming down to my office right now!" piped Leslie. Troy shrugged. His indifference further incensed the resident director, who then walked over to him from the hallway outside the door. A crowd of at least thirty students were looking up, wondering what had happened to the music. "The party's over!" Leslie shouted. "Go back to what you were doing, it's over!"

When Troy reached the first floor with Leslie, he could see the group of students outside, still congregating beneath his second floor window.

When they saw Leslie lead him into her ground floor office, they cheered for him. Troy appreciated it, but he could barely crack a smile. His impromptu jam session had been a violation of the quiet rules of the dorm, and it would earn him a trip to the adjudication office. Ironically, he welcomed it.

When Troy returned later, Randy was in the room with a female guest Troy barely recognized.

"Hey brother," he greeted Troy. "I heard you had everybody partying today!"

"Something like that," he replied dryly.

"I was there, Troy," the girl added. "I told Randy about it. It was fly!"

"Troy, this is Kim. You remember her, don't you?"

"Oh yeah, yeah. How are you?"

Kim was one of the older sisters who had become attached to Randy. She had a slim, elegant frame and like many girls who were his potential lovers, she also had a few inches of height on Randy. Troy knew it wouldn't matter in bed.

"We were just thinking about ordering some pizza," Randy announced. "You down?"

"Hell yeah, I haven't eaten all day."

"Where did you go after adjudication, brother?"

"I was just walking around."

"Angel was looking for you."

"Sheeit."

Randy raised his eyebrows at the remark. "I'll kick it to you later," Troy added, calming his friend's curiosity. Kim had also been listening intently. The roommates looked at her sternly, a silent warning that what was discussed in their room was to stay there.

Troy didn't want to delay the inevitable confrontation with Angel, so at ten minute intervals he checked around the corner for her return. When he went to the door to leave a note on her message board, he heard soft rock music and moaning, he knew it had to be Cyndi and that guy Billy. That meant Angel was bound to be in the hallway waiting to get in her room, increasing his chances of seeing her. During his fourth trip around the corner, Troy found his girlfriend. Angel was outside her door, but she knew she couldn't go in. She was close enough to the door to hear what was going on.

"Hey, girl."

"Oh, hi sweetie."

"Listen, why don't we take a walk? You know Cyndi's kind of busy."

"So I hear. All right, let's go."

They walked out of Harbin Hall hand in hand, with Troy carrying Angel's Jansport knapsack on his shoulder. They walked by the bench in front of the dorm where Troy had first seen her. As though it had just happened, he could recall staring out the dorm window, seeing Angel for the first time.

"So, what have you been into?" she asked.

"Nothing, same old stuff."

"You ready for the big weekend?"

"Yeah, I guess so."

"I think I'm going to be home this weekend. Gotta study." Troy knew, in honesty, Angel couldn't bear to see the AKA line from which she had been rejected. After the line was formed, Angel was quick to speak negatively about the whole sorority as well as the other girls who had made it. As a result, she had quickly alienated many of the black women on campus.

"Why did you want to take a walk?" Angel asked.

"I don't know, just felt like walking."

"Something on your mind?"

"Only you, darling."

"My goodness! You didn't talk so slick when I first met you."

Troy smirked. "Maybe you just weren't listening."

"I guess I'd better pay attention."

"C'mon, it's nice out."

They walked along the back end of the campus, past the main parking lot and the baseball field. Troy wanted time to think about what Cyndi had told him, and he knew the walk would help to clear his head. While waiting for Angel to return, he had tried to come up with ways to rationalize what Cyndi had said. He couldn't come up with one counterattack; the attention she had received at Howard and those endless weekends away from school were enough to validate what he had been told. Ill Will had provided him with solid evidence and Cyndi had no reason to lie. Further, he had seen enough of Angel's behavior on his own to see the truth. It had taken time to convince Angel to sleep with him, but since then she had been able to control Troy with sex. Still,

Troy's ascension to the status of big man on campus had boosted his confidence. Next year held nothing but bigger and better things for Troy and the rest of his crew. But damn it! He still loved her, and he wanted what they had to work.

Troy questioned himself repeatedly as they walked along, toward the north side of the campus. He wanted to share what was on his mind, but he couldn't forget the longing he felt, not having her around on weekends. And the intimidation of having all those Howard guys acknowledge her and act as if they had known her forever. His feelings of hurt and resentment resurfaced.

"Troy, this is really sweet," Angel insisted, stopping to give him a kiss. "I needed this. Classes are horrible, I'm not on line, all these bitches here hate me, it's ridiculous. I just, I just don't know what I'd do without you."

Troy half-smiled and felt both incredulous and clear-minded.

"Well, you're about to find out."

"Excuse me?"

"I said you're about to find out,"

"What are you talking about?"

"It's over."

"What?"

"You heard me, it's over. We're through."

Whack! The hard slap caught Troy totally off-guard.

"You bastard!" she cried. "You took me out *for a walk* to break up with me? You took me all the way out here to tell me this? You son of a bitch. You son of a bitch!" Angel was crying hysterically. Troy immediately wondered if he had done the right thing.

"Call me what you want, but we're done," he told her, trying to sound rational.

"Fuck you, you asshole!" she screamed. "Do you know what I gave up for you? Do you know the kind of guys I could have been with?"

"Bitch, you didn't give up shit!"

"Fuck you! I had real men, fool, with rides, with real money! I wouldn't have even had to work! You know you can't afford me. I gave that all up for you! And because you get jealous of some of my friends, you want to break up? You son of a bitch!"

"Save the drama, you fucking slut," Troy barked. "You had your chance!"

"Fuck you!" Angel pounded on his chest. Troy shielded the blows with her bag.

"I want a little time to myself, and you can't handle it!" she shouted. "You, dumping *me*! You're nobody, you're just a little punk! You just made a big mistake," she squealed, wiping her tears. "This was the best pussy you ever had!" Troy was shocked by her choice of words. "That's right, I'm the best! You know it, too. You blew it! Fuck you Troy, fuck you! You son of a bitch, fuck you!" she screamed, snatching her bag from him and running back toward Harbin Hall.

Troy stood in front of Georgetown University Hospital, attempting to sort out what had just happened. He had been rough on her, but she had played him for a fool all these months. What choice did he have? In his heart he still loved Angel, but he felt he had done what was necessary.

His heart was heavy, but not remorseful as it had been with Mimi. If Mimi hadn't been killed, he would have always known he could reach out to her. Angel had carried on as if Troy had beat up on her, as if he had been the one who had been so deceitful.

Randy and Ill Will were back in the room when Troy returned. Ill Will was putting a record on, trying his best to imitate his friend. Troy had too much on his mind to protest.

"What's going on, Troy?" Randy asked.

"I just broke it off with Angel."

"Whoa," Ill Will shouted. The record he was playing made a loud scratching noise.

"Oh shit, my fault. You say you broke up?"

"Yeah," Troy answered, flopping down on his bed.

"That would explain all the door slamming we heard a few minutes ago," Randy said.

"Word," Ill Will added. "Sounded like she was tearing shit up around the corner."

"Oh well," Troy lamented. He tried to match his friends' casual attitude.

"I think it's good," Ill Will said. "I mean, you know. Should have happened a while ago."

"That's true, brother." Randy added. It was rare to witness Randy and Ill Will in total agreement.

"I saw her a couple of times last semester with some other kid. Didn't you see him, Ill?"

"Yeah," affirmed Ill. "Looked like a drug dealer, right?"

Troy was becoming irritated at all of the after-the-fact information.

"Why you motherfuckers ain't say nothin' before?" he huffed.

"Easy now homey," Ill Will said. "No one was sure, we just saw different niggas going in there. 'Coulda been her cousins for all we knew."

"That's right brother," Randy added. "Besides, it wouldn't have made much difference what me or Ill said. Your nose was open. You wanted to get with her so bad."

"It would have fucked with you even more to hear us telling you about those other guys. Don't worry about it. It's not like you weren't getting yours!"

"That's true," Troy admitted.

The truth in their comments gnawed at him; his love had made him vulnerable and in a way he still was, so he could understand Randy and Ill Will's reluctance. They described these 'different niggas' as if there had been a parade of them and Angel's room had a revolving door. Had he really been that blind? He had always had his suspicions about Angel, but his love had overtaken his intuition. Neither Cyndi's nor his boys' judgment was clouded by love, they simply saw what they saw. He was certain they wouldn't lie, certainly not his 4-H cronies. Troy tried to take some comfort in their eyewitness accounts, but he couldn't. There was also some relief in seeing Randy and Ill Will getting along, but not enough to diminish the impact of his nasty exchange with the girl who had captured his heart.

Eighteen

Troy and Randy were in their room relaxing.

"So Randy, everything is straight?"

"True, indeed. Travis likes our additions to the schedule, and we finally got enough volunteers to provide housing for the recruits. Unfortunately, we're going to have to put one up ourselves."

"Yeah, that's a guaranteed 'cock block.' Oh well. You know, I think Travis is slipping."

"Come on, man. You're just mad because your mom likes him."

"Nah, man, I'm serious. He hasn't been taking care of things. I know tutors who haven't been paid, people who don't have housing for next year, a lot of stuff."

"Really?" Randy asked. "That's news to me."

"I'm telling you. He talks a lot of shit to the freshman class, but think about it. What does he do besides collect a check? He's not helping us get Farrakhan here, is he?"

Randy paused to consider the point.

"Nope," Troy continued. "He's not everything you think he is. You're just seeing him as the man who can take you under his wing."

"And you're seeing him as your mother's man!"

"He is not her man!" Troy shouted. "Listen. He's slipping. Dealing with him will just make it harder for us next year, unless he gets his act together."

"Yeah, okay."

"Just don't say I didn't tell you. It ain't got shit to do with him and moms."

"All right, man, I hear you. I didn't know you felt so strongly about it."

"Hey, I care about the brothers on campus, too."

Ill Will burst into the room in his usual dramatic fashion.

"What up, homies?" he called.

"S'up, man," Troy answered, exchanging hand slaps with him. Randy got in a hand slap as well.

"What are you two clowns doing?"

"Just getting ready for the weekend," Randy answered.

"Nobody told me. What's left to be done?"

"Nothing really," Troy told him.

"There's gotta be something." Ill Will came over to Randy's desk, anxious to look at his notes. He smiled when he saw the schedule of events.

"'Shaft' and 'Uptown Saturday Night,' huh? Not bad! Tee spinning at the talent show, looks like you've got the whole thing sewn up."

"We appreciate your enthusiasm, brother," Randy said matter-of-factly.

"Hey, I'm Member-at-Large! Weren't you having trouble getting volunteers to house the students? I'll volunteer." Ill Will was determined to make some kind of contribution.

"Cool, you can have our guy." Troy said. "His name's Charlie — "

"No, Troy," Randy interrupted. "No."

Ill Will looked at both of them, confused. "Why not? I'll take him, what's the problem?"

Troy and Randy sat in silence.

"What?" Ill Will continued.

"I don't want any recruits in your room, Ill," Randy said.

"Why not?"

"Because I'm afraid something might happen, that's why not."

"Hold up, wait a minute, you think I'd get fucked up with a recruit in the room?"

"You get drunk every weekend, and sometimes during the week." Randy answered. "Why should this weekend be any different? You're liable to wind up in the hospital again."

"Oh, would you give me a fucking break?" Ill shouted. "You just won't let me live it down, will you? I'm still paying for that night, all right? I'm the one who had to go to adjudication, I've got the record now, not you!"

"You were the one who was fucked up," Randy replied calmly.

"Fuck you! Like you never made a mistake! Just because I drink I can't be responsible for anything? Who the fuck do you think you are? You're a freshman just like me. You're Mr. BSU now, and you're judge *and* jury, huh?"

"Ill, it's not like that." Troy said, trying to intervene.

"No, it's okay Tee, I'm a big boy. Y'all don't trust me to handle anything, fine. But you better not flip the script if you need something.

And you, Mister President, you really need to check yourself. Thought you were in my corner, but you just wanna be somebody's father."

"Brother, I am in your corner," Randy insisted.

"Yeah, right."

Before either of them could respond, Ill Will stormed out, slamming the door behind him. Randy could tell from the look on Troy's face that he was disappointed in his two friends' heated exchange.

"Troy, am I wrong for not wanting a recruit in the room with him? I mean, am I wrong?"

"I don't know dude," Troy answered, noncommittal. "I don't know."

*   *   *   *

All the lights were out in the Office of Minority Affairs. Troy felt himself knocking something over.

"Damn it, stay still!" Darnell whispered.

"Shine the fucking light over here, then!"

"If you don't want to get caught, shut the fuck up."

Troy could hear Darnell shuffling through some files. He didn't see the need to come with Darnell to tamper with the files, but Darnell wouldn't agree to do it unless he 'shared the risk.' They were in Travis' office.

"All right. Now take these and get rid of them."

"What are they?"

"No fucking questions. Just destroy them."

Troy now held a thin pile of file folders and a couple of computer disks.

"He's going to know it's you. Who else would have access to this?"

"Only he has access, or so he thinks. And we're leaving no evidence. Come on."

Troy heard Darnell closing and re-locking the file cabinet. Quietly they slid out of the front door of the office, pressed against the wall to avoid being seen.

"Hurry up," Troy whispered.

"Shhh!"

The door slammed closed, prompting Darnell to take off with Troy right behind him. They both knew a security guard would be there in seconds. Darnell slid from the Coplin Hall exit and crawled behind an adjacent bush, with Troy right behind him on the ground. Troy was thankful now that they had dressed like burgulars. After what felt to him like hours, Troy thought the coast was clear and started to get up.

"Fuck you going?" Darnell asked, pulling him down.

"To my room. He's gone, what's the matter?"

"Just a few more minutes. He could still be looking."

"All right, shit."

"Shhh! I want you to take those files and drop them in the river."

"The Potomac?"

"You know any other rivers around here? Yes, lamebrain, the Potomac."

"Why there?"

"You want somebody to find them?"

Troy sulked in silence. Darnell was right and he was experienced. It was about 4:00 in the morning and the campus was quiet. Eventually, Darnell made his way back to the Black Student House while Troy took a roundabout path off campus to the Key Bridge. Troy tossed the files and disks before he could think about what he was doing, his hatred for Travis as strong as his guilt for what he'd started. Clearly, other people would be affected by the break-in. Troy had only wanted to hurt Travis.

*   *   *   *

It was Thursday night, and final preparations were being made for the black recruits who would arrive on campus the next day. Travis Gordon had allowed the input of the BSU officers for the weekend's activities. Both Travis and Randy were looking to attract more black students, and they worked together to plan an exciting two days of programming. Minority Affairs would provide a formal welcome when the high school seniors arrived as well as meetings with professors on Friday. The high point of the weekend would be the Star Search talent competition. Star Search was a showcase for would-be entertainers and wannabe models who wanted to strut their stuff. There were plenty of talented black students at Georgetown and Star Search was their chance to shine, in front of their peers and the visiting high school students. The show was held just once a year, and Troy had heard upperclassmen talking about it for months. Naturally, Troy wanted to provide the music for the event, and Travis Gordon had agreed to let him, more out of convenience than anything else. His subterfuge to remove Travis from his post would have to wait for now.

The recruits arrived on campus early the next afternoon. The sun smiled down on Georgetown and all of Washington, D.C. Travis Gordon, his staff and Randy had set up shifts for the welcoming committee and allowed student volunteers to assist high school students between classes. Most of the black students involved with the weekend were freshmen and sophomores who could still remember when had they visited Georgetown. Troy's shift began after his Ethics course. He quickly made his way to the bench by the Healy Building. Travis Gordon was busy meeting and greeting, handing out carefully prepared folders as he went along. Among the other volunteers was Ill Will, carrying bags and giving directions. At first Troy was surprised to see him, but then he remembered his friend's desire to prove Randy wrong. The carefree days when the three of them went all over the city seemed light years away.

"Who needs help?" Troy asked, hoping to avoid contact with Ill Will.

"Over there," Travis pointed to the front gates. "Two more are coming."

Troy carried the bags of two very cute teenaged female visitors. In just twenty steps, he knew their names and where they would be staying. It was important information. While continuing to check in the recruits, he and Ill Will occasionally made eye contact. Neither of them spoke, and Troy thought he saw his own feelings in the facial expression of his friend— one that was filled with regret over last night's words. The grim knowledge that things might not ever be the same settled over their brief exchange. Randy was also quiet besides some lighthearted chatter with Travis.

Troy returned to his a room a few hours later, after a quick stop at Hoya Vittles for Pop Tarts and juice. Randy was in the room with their weekend guest, who was big enough to be a football player.

"Oh, here he is. Charlie, this is my roommate Troy. Tee, this is Charlie."

"Nice to meet you," Troy offered, shaking hands with the heavyset recruit.

"Likewise, Ah'm sherr." Charlie's southern drawl hit Troy like a slap. He looked over at Randy, who laughed.

"Charlie's from Rocky Mount, North Carolina."

"Oh," Troy nodded, trying not to laugh. *North Carolina?* he thought. To Troy he sounded like a cross between Gomer Pyle and Parker, the cop on TV's *In The Heat Of The Night.* With an intense southern dialect and a goofy grin, Charlie had single-handedly moved Harbin Hall Room 228 to Sparta, Mississippi.

Troy put on one of his rap tapes while Randy went over the weekend's agenda with Charlie. Troy thought the recruit would have been more comfortable with Johnny Cash or Loretta Lynn, but his collection didn't include country music. He and Randy found themselves doing as much listening as talking. Charlie was animated, and his belly moved whenever he said something emphatically. He had played football that year, and Georgetown had offered him a scholarship. Charlie would be the first in his family to attend a private college and he was looking forward to getting a taste of city living. He was lighter in complexion than Troy and Randy, with dark, curly hair. Despite his girth, he was neatly dressed in an oxford, corduroy pants and a pair of bucks. When he went out to use the men's room, Troy and Randy had time for a brief assessment.

Laughing, Troy observed, "He might do okay with the girls with that country accent of his. Some of 'em like them big boys!"

Randy nodded in agreement. "Speaking of which, how are we going to feed that big motherfucker?" The roommates roared with laughter, barely calming themselves before Charlie's return. There was a party later that night at one of the basketball player's apartments, an unofficial welcome for the recruits. Troy and Randy were stunned to find that Charlie wasn't interested.

"That's okay, fellas. Ah'll jest stay here and read this here brochure," he told them.

"But Charlie," Troy pleaded, "don't you want to see the campus? You know, meet some of the other students?"

"Ah thank ah've done enough of that today. There'll be time for that tomorrow. And don't worry fellas. If you have some girls over, ah'll jes' disappear, heh heh!"

Troy stood in front of him, dumbfounded. *How is your big ass gonna disappear?* he thought. Randy pulled his roommate along. "All right Charlie, we'll see you later."

"Okey dokey."

The roommates laughed on their way to the party, joking about their Southern-bred friend. They also agreed that there were more than a few fine young ladies among the high school visitors.

"I helped two come in today," Troy shook his head. "Mmmph, mmph mmph. Thick as they wanna be! Honies looked good, I'm tellin' you. Didn't even make sense."

Randy laughed at his friend's excitement. "So now you all ready for some new ass, huh? Brother wouldn't even look at another girl before, now look at you!"

"It wasn't like that," Troy reflected. "I just couldn't do nothing before. Things are different now."

"Word. Did Ant pay you for the mix tapes?"

"Most definitely."

"Then I know it'll be fly. 4-H, baby!"

The courtyard of the Village A apartment complex was jammed with black students. The upstairs apartment was filled all the way back to the open window. Almost as many black students were crammed in on the third floor rooftop. Village A was designed for summer enjoyment; the complex provided a picturesque view of the city as well as the Potomac River and northern Virginia. The basketball team got three Village A apartments every year, and their celebrity status combined with the layout of the apartments made their parties legendary. Troy's performance at their last party had added to that appeal.

Troy heard his recorded selections blasting from upstairs —
Heavy D., Salt 'N' Pepa and others, all rapping over singsong melodies with thunderous rhythms. Troy and Randy were greeted warmly as they strolled through the courtyard, receiving hugs from the ladies, handslaps from the men. "Randy! Big Ran! Big Tee!" "Mister DJ!" "Yo Troy, this tape is the shit!" Troy and his roommate took it all in, focusing on the crowd, picking out the ladies. Lots of students happily stayed outside in the courtyard area and partied. *This is the shit*, Troy thought. Music, gorgeous weather, girls all over the place. He wished every weekend could be like this.

The girls were smiling at him and Randy. Troy sifted through the herd of people toward the girls, motioning for Randy to follow him. They had seen everyone else greet him and his man, so he knew it was the perfect time to strike.

"Hey ladies," Troy greeted them.

"Hi Troy," the first one answered. "Who is this?"

"This is my roommate Randy. Randy is President of the BSU. Randy, this is Daphne." Randy took the sister's right hand and placed it between his.

"It's a pleasure to meet you, sister." Randy's friendly tone, reserved for the ladies, no longer startled Troy. He chuckled to himself, familiar with the deadly combination of Afrocentrism and smooth talk that was to come. "And who might this be?"

"This is my friend Sabrina," Daphne told him. Both Daphne and Sabrina were fair-skinned, shapely high school cuties, wearing acid-washed jeans. Randy looked over to Sabrina and took her hand. She suppressed a laugh.

"How long have you been involved with the BSU?" asked Sabrina.

"Long enough to know what needs to be done," Randy told her, leading her away from her friend toward the back of the courtyard. From the curious look on Sabrina's face, Troy could see that she was doomed. Daphne remained by his side, her eyes never leaving his face.

"Let's go upstairs and dance."

On the way upstairs he noticed Ill Will across the courtyard who smiled at Troy and his date. Troy pointed back at his friend. Even Ill couldn't resist the party. Troy was sure his friend was in his normal drunken state, but he also noticed Yvonne's absence.

Troy had never been in an earthquake, but he was sure that one must have felt similar to the ballplayers' apartment that night. The whole place was bouncing; it seemed like two hundred people were inside, filling every space in the room. As he squeezed himself and Daphne inside, the party jumped again, taking on a life of its own. Troy's tape had reached the 'old school' segment, and Frankie Beverly and Maze's "Before I Let Go" was playing. Everyone on the floor threw their hands in the air, bodies bumping, girls from each class and recruits alike held tightly by their male partners. The very walls were perspiring, and the pictures and posters they held had peeled off. By then some of the white students had joined in, apparently in the 'if you can't beat 'em, join 'em' spirit. Troy pulled Daphne close to him with one hand, and put the other hand in the air. Someone put a beer in his hand. He turned to find Antoine, dancing with two girls. "For the tapes!" he yelled, but Troy couldn't hear him. Daphne knew the words to "Before I Let Go," and she was singing seductively in Troy's ear. Troy looked forward to leaving the party with his guest.

When Troy's dance party tape ended, it was replaced with love songs, the understood precursor for a sexual conclusion to the evening. Troy had managed to grab wine coolers for himself and Daphne, stored away in one of the rooms where he and Daphne talked in private. She spoke of her home in Houston, and how she couldn't wait to come to Georgetown. Troy kept his conversation to a minimum, listening to her but staring at her breasts, which were stretching out an Arlington High T-shirt. When he thought the timing was right, he invited Daphne back to Room 228, and as he expected, she obliged.

People in the courtyard were yelling upstairs for more beats. Some appealed to Troy for this, but he apologized as he headed back to Harbin Hall with Daphne. She was still talking, but Troy's mind was now on beating Randy back to the room. He didn't see him when he scanned the crowd, so he walked faster, hurrying the young girl along. He slowed down when he heard a shouting match among four girls, one of them being Angel, who seemed to be at odds with the other three. For a moment he felt sympathy and considered going to her side, certain that he could use his popularity to intervene. Then he remembered the hell he'd been through because of her. Observing the other girls' verbal war, Daphne turned Troy around by his chin.

"Are you ignoring me?"

"Oh, nah baby, nah. Let's go." *Shit*, Troy thought, *she's ready*. If he could only get to the room before Randy!

Troy signed Daphne in at the Harbin security desk, then he led her up the steps to the second floor. On the walk back he had managed to tell her about how much fun he and Randy had had in the dorm. She appeared to be as receptive now as she had been at the party. When Troy came around the corridor and saw no sign on the door, his heart raced. Yes! He unlocked the door, but he was frozen still by an odd noise before he could open it. It was Charlie, snoring as loud as he'd ever heard anyone snore. Damn it! He'd forgotten. To add insult to injury, Charlie slept on Troy's bed, his snoring creating the effect of a jackhammer in use. The shadow of his gut rising and falling made it look as if a light switch was going on and off in the hallway.

"What's the matter Troy?" Daphne asked sarcastically.

"Nothing. It's just that uh…"

"Someone's in there, hm?"

"Yeah, yeah. He's a recruit, just like you." Troy looked at his new companion. If they hurried, he could still return to the ballplayers' apartment and luck up on an empty bedroom.

"You're not ready to go back to your room, are you?" he asked, pulling Daphne over to him. It was now or never. She got on her tiptoes, put her arms around his neck, and kissed him on the mouth.

"Are you?"

Damn! Troy thought. Did Mimi kiss like that when they were in high school?

"Come on," he told her, taking her back down the steps. He'd kick somebody out of their room in Village A if he had to. When he exited Harbin's front doors with Daphne, to his right he saw an ambulance truck in the parking lot below Harbin's overpass. For some reason, ambulances were more a more common sight in front of Harbin than they were at any other dorm. Troy walked with Daphne toward the edge of the overpass so he could see, if briefly, what was going on. Her grown-up kiss was still warm on his lips, and he didn't want to give her a chance to cool off. When the horn sounded from the ambulance, Troy was sorry he had walked so close.

"Hey!"

"Hey, Tee! Troy!"

"Who's that?" Daphne asked as the couple went closer to the truck. Troy was shocked to find Ill Will in the driver's seat, laughing and waving.

"Do you know him?" Daphne asked again.

"Yeah, that's just my man Ill," he told her. "Come on." Troy's casual attitude masked his true bewilderment. Ill Will Dorsey really did live up to his name.

From the driver's side, Ill Will pointed them to the back doors of the truck. In the passenger seat was a real ambulance worker, a white girl whose nametag read Amy. Holding hands, the two of them walked around to the back of the Georgetown Emergency Medical Service vehicle. He smiled at her, his uncertainty now showing. She shrugged her shoulders to show approval. *Homegirl is definitely going to have some stories to take home*, he thought.

Troy helped her into the ambulance before climbing in himself. He sat her down on a stretcher and gave her a long kiss. The ambulance was moving.

"I'll be right back." Slowly he made his way to the front, bumping into the medical equipment on the walls.

"Ill, what the fuck are you doing?"

"Driving an ambulance, what does it look like?"

"You're not drunk, are you?"

"Come on, will you give me a break with that shit?"

"Are you?"

"No! Dude, I think Randy is starting to get to you."

"How did you get in here?"

"Relax homey, this one's out of the rotation."

"Out of the rotation? What are you, an ambulance worker now? Jesus Christ. Yo, let us out, fuck this."

"Okay, if that's what you want."

Ill Will pulled over at the north entrance of the campus.

"Where you gonna go with your little cutie, though? I saw Randy going in with his. And Carl's in my room. What you gonna do?"

Troy turned around and looked back at a beckoning Daphne, bulging in her Arlington High T-shirt.

"All right, all right," he complied. "Just be careful."

"I will," Ill Will assured him. "Amy, this is my man Troy. Troy, this is Amy."

"Hello."

Troy gave the white girl a silent nod. *Amy?* he thought. *What about Yvonne?* Amy was attractive, but Ill Will's girl would be crushed if she knew.

"Amy used to work for Georgetown EMS."

"Oh," Troy said, relieved. "So you knew where to get the keys?"

"No," Ill Will answered, "of course not. I hot-wired the truck."

They drove all around the D.C. metro area A couple of times Ill Will even put the sirens on, enabling him to weave through traffic and run red lights at will.

"That's my boy, but he's full of shit," Ill Will told Amy. "Looking at me like I'm wrong, and he's right here with us!"

"Maybe he wanted to look out for you," Amy mused.

"Yeah, well what do you think he's looking out for now, huh?"

Amy was silent, listening to the passionate moaning and groaning coming from the back of the truck.

"Yeah. See what I'm saying?"

Daphne's legs were wrapped around Troy's back. He held her behind in one hand and a bar on the ambulance wall in the other, thrusting in a quick, circular motion. He tried to be quiet, but he knew Ill Will and his date could hear his and Daphne's panting. He wanted to remove her T-shirt, but getting her jeans off had taken long enough. Troy had to hold one of the handles inside the ambulance to keep from rolling around. With Daphne's buttocks in his other hand, Troy pressed inside of her. Seeing her legs in the air only made him more excited. Still, he knew that if Ill Will kept hitting bumps in the road, he was going to lose control.

Thankfully, Ill Will put the sirens on again to cover Troy and Daphne's collective grunts. Daphne dug her nails into Troy's back and her grunting grew louder. Troy was close to climaxing and he felt the ambulance slowing down. The equipment on the walls was shaking and the slower the ambulance went, the more frantic and vocal Daphne became.

"Oh! Ooooh, shit! Oh!"

Just as he heard the back door swing open, Troy erupted furiously to Daphne's screams and shuddering. He felt a breeze on his naked behind and prayed that what he thought was happening was not. He turned to see Amy in front of them, but the doors were still open!

"Troy?" Daphne called while pulling her pants on. "What's your friend doing?"

"Hold on," he answered. Troy quickly pulled on his pants and came out from the front of the ambulance to find a small crowd on the street. Amy was now examining a middle-aged white man on the sidewalk.

"Okay folks, he'll be fine," Ill Will told the crowd. "We're going to need some room, please."

Troy pulled his friend to the side.

"What the hell are you doing?" Troy whispered.

"Making a pickup. What's it look like?"

"A pickup? You're no doctor! Ill, that guy is fucked up for real! What if his neck is broken or something?"

"Relax, Amy's got it." Amy checked the man's vital signs.

"There was no call, we just saw the guy."

"No call? No call? For the love of God, you hotwired the ambulance!"

"Yep."

"What if somebody finds out?"

"They won't if you stay cool. Now come on."

Amy was calling the boys over.

"Will, we're going to need the stretcher."

"All right."

Ill Will and a shocked Troy proceeded to pull out the stretcher, whose sheets were wrinkled. A friend of the man on the ground was concerned.

"He just passed out," she told Amy. "What do think it is?"

"He's breathing, that's the important thing. We'll get him taken care of."

Amy and Ill Will helped the man onto the stretcher. Troy helped load him inside. Daphne watched in silence. The patient's friend attempted to get in, but Troy stopped her.

"Riding inside won't be necessary, ma'am."

"I want to stay with him."

"Please ma'am, just follow behind us. We'll be treating him inside."

"Who's that girl in there?"

"She's an intern. Please, just follow us."

Ill Will drove the ambulance back to Georgetown University Hospital. Troy and Ill Will provided assistance getting the patient inside before waiting for Amy to return. Two hours after their departure, Ill Will parked the ambulance in back of Georgetown's parking lot by McDonough Gym, which was now flanked with other unoccupied ambulances. Troy was now adjusted to the evening's insanity and ready to stay in the truck; given the chance, he could make love much better with the stretcher not rolling around.

"All right dude, this was cool," he told Ill Will. Troy and Daphne sat in silence, waiting.

"What are you looking at?" Ill Will asked. "What, you think I'm leaving? I'm not leaving, you two are! You want privacy, get your own ambulance!"

"All right, you got it," Troy said, upset. "Later."

"Yeah, *auf Wiedersehen*." Ill Will turned to Amy. "You believe that shit, baby? "

Troy and Daphne walked back through the parking lot in silence, eventually finding the room of her freshman host in New South Hall. After a goodbye kiss, she left Troy in front of the dorm alone, still aroused by the feel of her half-naked body under his in the ambulance.

The same festive spirit of the first day of Minority Student Weekend carried into the next. Troy and Randy got up early to prepare for the BSU movie presentations. But first Charlie, their live-in recruit, needed to be fed breakfast. For both Troy and Randy, the breakfast had an implicit understanding; feed Charlie to keep him quiet about the exploits of the two BSU officers.

"You coming to the movie today, Charlie?" Randy asked.

"Ah sherr am," he said between gulps. Charlie was devouring a double order of scrambled eggs with cheese, home fries, grits, sausage and toast. Troy watched this wide load consume, amazed by his appetite.

"Don't forget there's Star Search tonight," Troy added.

"Ah won't. Gonna meet me some of these professors, too."

Troy decided not to try to engage Charlie in any further conversation. The way he was shoveling it in, a piece of food was liable to come flying out of his mouth.

The three of them walked back up N Street to the campus. Randy gave Charlie his dorm key so he could return to Harbin, freeing himself and Troy to set up the movie. They were alone for the first time since last night.

"Stop lying," Randy told his roommate.

"Word is bond. In the ambulance. And the boy had the nerve to pick some fool up downtown!"

"Y'all are crazy."

"Yeah, it was nuts. So what's up with Sabrina?"

"You know what time it is, brother."

"You hit that?"

"Had to." The two slapped hands in the congratulatory male ritual.

"Where did you take her?"

"The BSU office."

"You mean in the administration building?"

"Yeah."

Troy was stunned. *He* might have done the same, but it wasn't what he expected from Randy. Especially now, with many of the girls on campus turning their sights on to him, Troy was unsure about that kind of behavior from Georgetown's Black Student Union President. Was there any credence to what Ill Will and Bizzy had been saying about him? Where was the passion and the sincerity Troy had heard in Randy? Had the passion and sincerity simply transferred to the energy he used to get the panties?

"You mean to tell me that you, you fucked in the BSU office?" Troy was incredulous.

"I didn't want to go there Troy, but Charlie was in the room." Randy confessed. "I know what you're thinking, and maybe it was wrong. But no one was hurt by it, and who's Sabrina going to tell? She can't say anything without people knowing she was in there. Besides, the sister may not even come here next year."

"You just better hope Phyllis doesn't find out."

"She won't."

Troy nodded as his roommate spoke, but he wasn't sure if he totally agreed. Randy still seemed as impassioned as ever about uplifting black people, but it looked as if his one vice may have been getting the better of him.

By early evening, there were still students relaxing outside on the front lawn. Many of the white students had relinquished their lawn chairs after getting their quotient of sun for the day, while black students who had been outside were now returning to their dorms and apartments to get dressed for the student talent show. Troy tried to savor the casual feeling of the weekend, knowing that his books patiently awaited him. Tomorrow he'd have to get back to work. Randy had joined Travis to prepare for the show at Healy Hall. Troy didn't need to be there for another hour or so to test the sound system. He remembered that he hadn't seen Ill Will since last night's crazy ride. Although it was normal not to see him for a few days at a time, in this instance Troy was worried. He first checked in his room, where Carl was reading a book.

"Where's Ill?"

"I don't know," Carl told him blankly. "I haven't seen him."

Troy walked out, dissatisfied with Carl's answer. He checked the second floor lounge and listened in the hallway for Ill Will's antics in someone else's room. He could only hear the normal buzz of freshmen energy on Saturday night. Troy went outside and sat in front of Harbin for a few moments, thinking, when a memory flashed before him. Dreading his worst fear, Troy jumped up, ran down the corridor stairs and sprinted through the parking lot toward the ambulance. God, anything could have happened if he was still in there. And if he was drunk, shit! Ill Will could get kicked out of school!

An out-of-breath Troy found the spot where he thought Ill Will had parked the ambulance. There were several of them, all identical. He peeked through the back windows of each until he found his friend asleep with Amy in his arms. Banging on the back door with all his might, he managed to get Ill Will's attention. When Troy saw him stirring from a drunken stupor, he opened the back door and climbed in.

"Ill! Ill, come on! We've got to get the fuck out of here!"

Ill Will was tossing and turning, still in another world. Amy rolled along with him, unconscious. An empty bottle of Scotch lay next to her head.

"Shit!" Troy shouted. "Ill! Wake up!" he insisted, slapping Ill Will's face now.

"Huh? What, what is it?"

"Come on, we've got to go."

"Huh? Oh." Slowly Ill Will rose, grabbing the side of the ambulance wall for balance. Some of the items hanging on the wall fell down and broke.

"Shit, Ill! Just come on!"

"Coming, I'm coming. Hey, what about Amy?"

"Fuck her! She isn't waking up anyway. Can't you see we're in an ambulance?"

"Really?"

"Jesus Christ." Troy picked up the bottle of scotch, and eventually helped Ill Will out of the truck, his arm slumped around Troy's shoulders. Ill Will steadily called for Amy, but she wouldn't move.

"Damn it," Troy called. "Will you just come *on?*"

"I can't leave Amy here."

"You want to fuck around and get expelled, that's your business," said Troy, exasperated. "Go ahead then, stay in the goddamn ambulance."

"Okay, okay," Ill Will conceded. "I'm coming. She's gonna be pissed, though."

Troy steadied his friend while looking around for a place to put the bottle. He found a metal trash can by the gym and pitched it in.

"All right," he announced to Ill Will. "You ready to walk?"

"Yessir." As quickly as he could, Troy walked Ill Will back to Harbin Hall. He hoped his holding him would appear as though Ill Will had hurt himself on the basketball court instead of him being drunk. But with Ill

Will's head bowing and resting on his shoulder, Troy knew better. Carl was still in the room when they finally made it upstairs. He rushed over to help Troy.

"What happened?" he asked.

"You don't want to know."

"Is he drunk?"

"What do you think, you idiot? Of course he's drunk."

"Hey!" Carl poked his finger into Troy's chest. "He's my roommate. You don't have to tell me. I know you're his buddy and all, but I'm the one who has to live with him when he's like this. I can't go back to my room and forget it. You think about that the next time you talk to me." Carl was looking Troy right in the eyes.

"Yeah," Troy answered. "Let's get him into bed."

The two boys undressed their friend and got him settled. All the while Troy thought of what Carl had said. So what if Carl had to live with him! He did, too! Had he encouraged him this time? The ambulance ride surely hadn't helped. But Carl was just as guilty, taking him around to see these white girls, and running away when security came when Ill Will got really drunk. Then again, neither of them had been around when Ill Will had acquired that bottle of scotch, or the bottle of vodka he had gone through that time last semester.

*   *   *   *

Healy Hall auditorium was packed that night with recruits and students from Georgetown and other schools, almost all of whom were black. Many administrators, faculty and parents were in attendance as well. Like the outside of Healy Hall, its regal, colonial style was evident in its interior, with gargoyles and Latin phrases lining the stage wall, replete with fine oak floors, stain glass arched windows, and thick burgundy carpeting in the aisles. Georgetown's Star Search was not to be missed, and Troy was excited to be part of it. He had been late getting there because of Ill Will, but the sound system appeared to be in order. Aside from the music, he would also control the microphones, making him a genuine sound engineer. Troy was looking forward to seeing his upperclassmen friends on stage. Darnell, Wendell and Bizzy were modeling, as were Michelyn, Latanya, Jasmine and some other girls. Like many of the brothers, Troy couldn't wait for the swimsuit segment of the show.

When the lights went down Troy played the opening segment music, a tape of dance songs. Troy didn't care for house music, but he couldn't deny its popularity. He had even had some success with it deejaying parties. The audience cheered as the models, all black Georgetown students, sauntered out in the latest fashions. In addition to modeling, Michelyn performed a special dance segment courtesy of Black Expressions Dance Group. The crowd went wild afterwards; Michelyn wasn't just beautiful, she was talented, too. From stage right Troy could see the huge crowd. During intermission he tried to make out the folks he knew. People in the audience had also dressed for the occasion. Travis Gordon was there alone. *Moms probably had to work*, Troy thought. He knew she wouldn't refuse a chance to visit him. The Kappas were up top in the balcony along with Omegas and Alphas from neighboring schools. The basketball team was in attendance and members of the freshmen class were scattered among the crowd. Randy was sitting with Phyllis, but she didn't seem to be paying him any attention. The recruits had a special section on the floor near the front, and sure enough, Daphne and Sabrina were there. Angel was in the audience as well, making sure not to even look in the direction of the stage. Troy thought it was a shame she wasn't in the show, she would have made a sexy model and if she hadn't been so caught up in becoming an AKA, she could have auditioned.

After the show, the backstage area was busy with hangers-on and student contestants changing clothes. The basketball team was having another monster party at Village A. Troy hurried out to catch up with Daphne. They agreed to meet outside New South Hall, where she was staying.

What had been a gorgeous evening weatherwise ended when it started to rain. Troy was halfway between Harbin and the Village A courtyard when he felt raindrops. He had no umbrella, but he'd make it to the ballplayers' apartment a few feet away without getting totally soaked. Picking up speed to avoid the downpour, he neared Village A and could see the crowd scattering, taking shelter. Phyllis was running toward him with a jacket over her head.

"Phyllis, where are you going?"

"Over to your room. Is Randy there?"

"Oh no, he's not there."

"He isn't here, either."

"He isn't? Are you sure?" Troy tried to buy his roommate as much time as possible.

"I've been here for two hours, Troy. You probably just missed him. I'm sure he's home now. Go inside, it's pouring out here!"

Troy continued toward Village A. Had he said anything more, she would have known he was lying. He could call before Phyllis got there, but he couldn't warn Randy without Sabrina finding out somehow.

Because of the rain everyone was now crowded into the staircases at Village A. Like the night before, Troy's tape was blasting and the apartment was packed beyond fire safety standards. Although they had agreed to meet at New South Hall, Troy suspected that Daphne may still be inside Village A because of the rain. Troy battled his way up the staircase, past drunken students and groping couples to the third floor. He slapped hands and nodded to some people, but his main objective was to get through the bulging crowd. He found a phone in the hallway and called his room. He heard himself on the answering machine. Shaking his head, he left a message for Randy to come to the second floor elevator. If he heeded the message, he could intercept Phyllis.

Troy pushed his way through the party, surrounded by dancers and drinkers, black students celebrating their Star Search performance and just plain partying. Eventually he got to the staircase in back of the apartment and clawed his way up. The bedroom doors were all slightly open, so a peek would tell him in Daphne was in any of them.

"Daphne?" he shouted. She probably couldn't hear over the music, but he tried anyway.

"Daphne?"

The first two rooms were empty. Damn! She wasn't around. Maybe in the last room. Maybe she remembered. When Troy reached the third room, he was immediately sorry he had come that far. Through the cracked door he could see the tall frame of a ballplayer sitting up in a bunk bed. Daphne, buck naked, straddled him close to her body, his head buried in her breasts. It was Antoine. Troy was disappointed, but he still was somewhat happy for his fellow freshman. He guessed she really was the adventurous type.

The downpour had become a full-fledged thunderstorm and forced Troy to run all the way back to Harbin Hall. He could have stayed at the party and let his roommate try to score, but seeing Daphne with Antoine had taken him out of the party mood. He checked his pockets to discover that he had forgotten his ID. *Shit*, he thought, *of all times*. Troy stared through the front doors at the empty lobby. He was soaking wet, his only shelter the small partition in the building above the entrance. Troy banged on the door for what felt like hours. A figure came from the ladies room, and got all the way to the front door before stopping. Seeing Angel through the doors, Troy's head bowed. Her stare was colder than the rain that was soaking his clothes. She turned around and sat at the security desk, maintaining the most vicious glare she could muster. *Fucking bitch*, Troy thought. Did she take that much pleasure in seeing him drenched? Would a little push on the door hurt that much? Damn!

Troy banged and banged on the door, desperate for someone to hear him. Angel maintained her position, staring at him the whole time. *Where's the fucking security guard?* he thought. He went outside and called Randy from under their window, but got no answer. His voice was barely audible over the thunder and the pellets of rain hitting the windows. After a while Troy ignored her, but he couldn't ignore the anger rising in him. She was trying to pay him back for hurting her, but she had hurt him just as much, and she had a lot of damn nerve being this bitter and petty. He would have done anything for her had she just been there for him, instead of only being around when it was convenient for her. Somehow his love had not been enough, and now she was mad at him? Fuck her! Troy's simmering rage grew as he relentlessly beat upon the doors. Usually someone would have come out or gone in by now, he thought. Just then, a white girl descended the staircase and came towards the door. Troy rushed in after she pushed it open.

"Thank you," he said, staring at Angel. Angel turned away, but not before Troy saw the smirk on her face.

"You're welcome," said the girl. Troy headed for the staircase, leaving puddles on the ground with each step. He longed to give Angel a good slap, but he didn't want her to think she'd gotten the best of him. Instead, he slowly walked away, wiping his face.

Nineteen

Troy hung up before his father could say goodbye. Since referring to him as a snot-nosed kid, Troy made sure his conversations with his dad were as brief and infrequent as possible. What little motivation Troy had previously to see him or talk to him was nonexistent. He was even thinking of refusing his father's monthly check. But after a verbal thrashing from his mother, he thought better of the idea.

"What up, roomie?" Randy called as he came in. Phyllis was with him.

"What up. Hey, Phyllis."

"Hi, Troy. What's wrong?"

"Nothing."

"Oh, you must have seen Angel. Or talked to your pops."

Troy nodded at his roommate's guesswork.

"Yeah, but I got off the phone. I just can't fuck with him."

"That's too bad," Phyllis interjected. Troy gave her a strange look.

"No, really. Far too many black women are raising children on their own, on *our* own, and it's impossible to turn a boy into a man with no positive role models in his life."

"You been reading those sociology books again?"

"No, Troy. Well, I have been doing some reading. But really, many of us don't have fathers."

"Do you have a father?"

"Why, yes."

"That's what I thought."

"Brother, Phyllis is just trying to empathize with your situation," Randy interrupted.

Troy rolled his eyes. Since when was Randy defending Phyllis' honor? "You're right," he conceded. "Sorry, Phyllis."

"Oh, that's okay." Phyllis beamed.

"We just came to drop off our books," Randy told him. "We're going to see what this mess with Travis is about."

"What mess?"

"There's a petition to get him out of Minority Affairs," Phyllis told him matter-of-factly.

"Is that right?"

"Yes. I don't know why, but a lot of people just aren't happy with him anymore. A few of my girlfriends are having some problems with summer housing, but I didn't think it was Mr. Gordon's fault."

"Maybe Mr. Gordon's a screw-up," Troy declared sarcastically.

"That's what we're going to find out," Randy added. "We'll be outside Minority Affairs. There's a rally going on now."

"I'll be down there later."

"All right, sounds like a plan."

"See you, Troy," said Phyllis.

"Bye."

Troy waited a few seconds for the couple to leave, then picked up the phone.

"Hello?"

"Darnell?"

"Yeah."

"It's Troy."

"What up, man. So far, so good."

In addition to his new covert association with Darnell, Troy had again attempted to launch a full-out attack on his studies. His average had improved, if only slightly, in Euro Civ Part II and Accounting II, and he didn't want to screw up when final exams came around. Just when he thought he had a handle on the BSU and other social distractions, the weather had gotten warm and challenged his discipline to study.

Ill Will burst into Room 228, disturbing Troy's already feeble attempts to hit the books.

"S'up, partner?"

"What up, duke," Troy replied, slapping hands with his friend. It always felt like a long time had passed since seeing Ill Will.

"Where you been, Ill?"

"Same place I've always been."

"Carl hasn't been around lately."

"I know. I've been out too, though. Like today, I started looking for a new place to buy brew."

"What's wrong with Westmiller's?"

"Nothing. I'm just not fucking with them anymore."

"Why not?"

"They won't sell to me anymore. Say I'm too young and my ID is fake. You believe that shit? After all this time?"

"Yeah, somebody must have told them. Oh well."

"Anyway, I just came by to say hey. I'll let you go back to your Euro Civ."

"I'm done. Something's going down at Travis' office. Darnell is doing his thing."

"Yeah? Well, good luck."

"Yeah, later."

There was a small crowd outside of Travis Gordon's office. Darnell was trying to keep everyone calm.

"Y'all need to get a hold of yourselves. I work at Minority Affairs and I can assure you, all of this will be resolved."

"Nigga, please!" Jasmine shouted. "You should have warned us about this! I may lose my scholarship because of this office!"

"Hold on," Darnell continued. "Those of you who have been here know Travis won't let that happen."

"We have to support him," Randy interrupted. "Mr. Gordon and I may not agree on some things, but he does put in work for us." It was peculiar to see Darnell and Randy standing together, but Troy tried to look unaffected.

"Where is he, Randy?" Phyllis asked. "How come he hasn't answered these questions?"

"I'm sure he'll be here," he answered, trying to appear as calm and confident as possible.

"Excuse me darling, but he needs to be here now."

"That's right!" Jasmine shouted, inciting applause from the women outside the office. Troy couldn't help but notice that Phyllis no longer stood next to him; instead, she stayed close to the crowd. Randy, Troy and Darnell faced the group with nothing to say.

"How did you manage that?" Troy asked, later on in Darnell's living room.

"Simple. Travis had an appointment with Student Affairs. I just timed it so that he wouldn't be there. Most of those girls were told he'd be gone today."

"What about the rest of the staff?"

"They were busy. A couple of them didn't even know the front door was locked. See, the office wasn't really closed."

"Jesus." Either Darnell was a slick young man, or a lot of people just weren't paying attention. "I know you have some help with this."

"Yeah, your mama's got him open."

"I told you about that, motherfucker."

"Sorry. Yeah, I have help, but don't worry about that."

"So what do you want?"

"Nothing! Why do you keep asking me that? I'm just having fun."

Yeah, right, Troy thought.

"Farrakhan isn't coming next year anyway, so fuck it."

Darnell laughed. "It's too bad, though. You guys had some support, I know that petition had a lot of signatures."

Troy stood silent, considering Darnell's tactics. Now that students were looking for the BSU to look into the problems with Minority Affairs, Troy had second thoughts about accepting Darnell's assistance. Those second thoughts faded quickly, however, when he thought of Travis and his mother together.

"Hey, you're not still messing with that chick, are you?"

"You mean Angel?"

"Yeah."

"Nah, I'm done with that."

"Be careful if you are, that bitch is shady."

"You have the nerve to be calling somebody shady?"

"The girl is a runner."

"A what?"

"A runner! You know, for drug-dealer niggas. I know a couple of dudes who used her. They all hit it too, said that pussy was the shit."

Troy took deep breaths in the hopes of controlling his temper.

"I'll give her that," he offered, hoping to keep Darnell from informing him further.

"For a while I thought you were working with her, maybe even smoking that shit. But you didn't even know, did you?"

"I knew."

"No you didn't," Darnell laughed. "Mister New York, mister DJ."

"Who the fuck you think you talking to?"

"You, nigga!" Darnell walked up and stood in front of Troy. "I'm talking to you. What's up?"

Troy considered taking a swing at him, but he knew Darnell would make him pay dearly if he tried anything.

"I'll talk to you later, I'm out." He was angry but he didn't want to do anything to further reveal his emotions.

"All right! You still my man, right?"

Troy headed for the door to let himself out. He found Bizzy at the door.

"What up, DJ Troy?"

"What's up, Biz."

"Damn, what's wrong with you?"

"Nothing. Later."

Bizzy entered the house to find his friend waiting. "What's with him?" he asked Darnell.

"He's just in some shit he can't handle, that's all."

Bizzy chuckled. "You ought to be ashamed, fucking with them like that. They're still just freshmen."

"Hey, the nigga came to me. Besides, they think they run the school. Or at least they used to think so."

"Come on, they're gung ho just like you were. But they do things."

"I did things! Still do, I just do it differently."

"Sure, whatever you say. You got any brew?"

"In the fridge."

*   *   *   *

Troy definitely had to get some studying done. Classes were now little more than preliminary review sessions for finals. His Sociology and Ethics professors held classes outside, which Troy equated as license to look at all the skirts that paraded past the lawn. After class, Troy met Randy in their room. It was the first time they had spoken about Travis since the rally.

"Brother, he's the director," Randy said.

"I know, but he can't do anything on his own," Troy answered.

"Maybe not literally, but he has unspoken influence. Don't you see? People respect him. Except now that these protests are going on, his credibility is being tarnished."

"Yeah, well not with my moms. She works him into every conversation."

"So what, man? Do you deny that he cares about black students? Be reasonable."

"It's easy for you to say. He can say anything he wants to me and I can't do shit!"

"So?"

"So it's fucked up, Randy! How would you like it if he was dating your moms? What the fuck would you do? Huh?"

"I hear you. I do. But this thing is bigger than you."

"It's going to take a lot more than him to get the Minister here."

"Maybe, but we're on the road. Our trip to see him at UDC was a good idea, don't you think?"

"Yeah, but it was more like Phyllis' trip. The sisters all but ignored us. Seemed like Phyllis read up on Farrakhan just so she could talk to them."

Troy and Randy remained part of an informal gathering of black students who met on the lawns outside. Randy's words still commanded attention, but only when attempting to answer questions about Travis Gordon and Minority Affairs. The loudest voice of the BSU now belonged to Phyllis; she was encouraging the sisters on campus to take charge of their own lives on and off campus. She regularly took Randy to task in public, which Troy believed was taking the wind out of his roommate's sails. Male and female students alike were concerned with their housing and financial aid, much of which was in question because of the confusion at Minority Affairs. Travis pledged to find out why so many students had been denied scholarships and how the budget discrepancies arose, but he had to get more information. Until then, many black and Hispanic students were left in a quandary, making for lots of angry discussion.

Troy found himself at work in Copy Services when he was most desperate for a quiet place to study. Plenty of students and professors were coming in with work, but at least there he could retain what he read, since he wouldn't have the distraction of lovely weather and women. He was grateful that Angel wasn't in. He might actually be able to read in peace, instead of having to serve the customers she refused to help just to spite him.

Relieved, Troy settled down at a desk with a book. Adelaide Barnes, his supervisor, was working that day, and she agreed to let him study when it wasn't busy.

"That's okay dear," she insisted. "You go ahead."

"Thanks Mrs. Barnes." he told her. "You think I could pick up a shift tonight? It might be the only way I can get a seat in the library."

"No, I don't think anyone's giving up their night shifts."

"Oh."

"Troy, have you talked to Willard lately?"

"No, why?"

"The boy came in here drunk the other day. I had to have him thrown out."

Troy couldn't believe what he was hearing. "No way," he insisted.

"I'm afraid so. Now I'd heard about Willard having some problems, but I never wanted to believe it."

It was awful news, but Troy was still compelled to defend his friend.

"Mrs. Barnes, you couldn't have talked to him or something?" He knew she was usually lenient and considerate of students who had worked for her.

"Troy, now you *know* better. What do you think would have happened if he had stayed in here? I got rules to follow. Someone in here drunk puts me in a bad situation. He knows he can come back whenever he gets himself together, but until then I can't have him in here."

"Yeah, I guess so," Troy admitted.

An uneasy feeling rose from the pit of his stomach. Troy couldn't be around to pick him up or cover up for him every time he was drunk. No one could. What would be next? Where was Yvonne when all of this was happening? He made a mental reminder to talk to her.

He couldn't get much studying done after hearing about Ill Will, so Troy was more ready than usual to leave after his shift was over. Instead of heading for the cafeteria, he returned to Harbin. Harbin's fifth floor looked much like his own second floor, but it had a different vibe. The halls of the all-female floor were, not coincidentally, painted pink and white instead of the co-ed yellow and white. Troy found his way to Yvonne's room, where the door was open. Yvonne was quietly reading in bed. Her roommate was at her desk doing the same. Troy knocked.

"Oh, hi Troy," Yvonne said, looking up. "Come on in. Julie, you remember Willard's friend Troy, don't you?"

"Yes I do," said the white girl. "Hello."

"Hey. Uh, Yvonne, do you have a second?"

"Sure Troy, what's up?"

"It's about Ill."

Julie suddenly stood up and collected her books. "I think I'm going to the library."

"You don't have to leave," Troy insisted.

"No, it's okay. Yvonne, I'll see you later."

"Bye, Jul." Yvonne smiled politely at her roommate as she left. "So Troy, what is it?"

"You know Ill got thrown out of Copy Services, right?"

"Yes, that was a few days ago."

"Did he tell you why?"

"Mm-hm, him and Mrs. Barnes got into a fight." Yvonne's tone radiated absolute loyalty to her man.

"Yeah, well Mrs. Barnes told me he was drunk and I believe her." Yvonne's face sank. She sat in bed for a long time, analyzing what she had just heard.

"Why wouldn't he tell me the truth, Troy?"

"Probably too embarrassed. He didn't tell me, either. Look, do you think maybe he has a problem?"

"I don't know, Troy. Willard drinks, but I don't see him drinking any more than other people here." Troy struggled not to roll his eyes. Yvonne would instinctively come to Ill Will's defense, regardless of the situation.

"No more than other people? Come on, Yvonne. You've seen those big ass bottles."

"Yes, and groups of people have gotten drunk from them with him."

Not that one he had in the ambulance, Troy thought, but he couldn't tell her that. He didn't know what to say.

"Is this what you came here to tell me, Troy?" she asked impatiently. "That Willard drinks?"

"No, no. I want to help him. You see him more than I do though, I just thought you could tell me something. I mean, don't you remember last fall?"

"Of course! I was there too, Troy! It wasn't any more fun for me. But I love him, faults or no faults. If he does have a problem, I'll be there to help him deal with it."

If he has a problem, Troy thought in exasperation.

"Don't you think maybe you could talk to him? I mean, I've tried, but he could stand to hear it from you."

"Oh I bet you've tried," Yvonne retorted. "You talk to him like he's a child. I see you guys at the BSU meetings. You and Randy don't take him seriously. And yet he looks up to you guys."

"This don't have shit to do with Randy, all right?" Troy could feel his temper rising. "Yvonne, just talk to him if you can. I'll do the same. And try to look out for him."

"I always do." Just as Troy turned to leave, Phyllis and Layla were at the door. He was surprised to see Layla hanging with the younger girls. Troy stepped aside to let them in.

"Hi Troy," Phyllis said, smiling. "Looking for Ill Will?"

"No, no. Just passing through."

Layla was waving at Troy behind Phyllis.

"Yvonne, why don't you come shopping with us? Layla got out of work early so she can drive us."

"Great! I'll get my purse."

Yvonne got up and grabbed her purse, while Troy stood in silence.

"I'm ready," Yvonne told the girls. "Let's go."

"Don't look so shocked," she told him. "I have a life, too."

*   *   *   *

Troy returned to the second floor to find the familiar atmosphere that came about when finals were imminent: less chatter in the halls and more students with books open. And, perhaps the truest sign of all, increased pizza deliveries to the dorm. His roommate was gone, so Troy decided to use the time to map out his strategy for his upcoming exams. There was Sociology, Ethics, Euro Civ, and the always menacing Accounting II. Poetry, his favorite course, had no final; his last assignment would be to act in a theatrical poem selected by the professor during the last class. He hadn't heard of the play before Professor Lima's course, but he had managed to read it, a piece about East Germans trying to live like Americans. Troy would play a young man attempting to defect. He chuckled at the thought, picking up his Accounting book. Too bad all of his classes didn't require acting out scenes from a play.

Twenty

Randy returned to Room 228 as if something tragic had happened to him.

"What's the matter?" Troy asked from his desk.

Randy looked at his roommate in disgust.

"What?"

"Everything's going wrong."

"What are you talking about?"

"You know what I'm talking about. I just had a meeting with the Student Government. They're not supporting Farrakhan on campus."

"What did you expect?"

"I figured we had some defense with the basic right to freedom of speech, but they weren't hearing of it."

"And you're surprised?"

"No, but Travis could have helped."

"Save it for next year."

"Fuck that! It's going to take a year! Minority Affairs is under the gun and I can't get anything done because I'm trying to cover for Travis. He says he doesn't know what's going on! Somebody played with the files. He's handling the applications and stuff himself now, but a lot of the damage is already done."

"So that's it?"

"No, that's not it. Phyllis is trying to have me impeached."

"What?"

"She is. She's outside talking all the time. Half the girls want her for President. They don't trust me anymore."

"I see."

"That's not all. I didn't get Senegal. I got France for the summer instead."

"Shit, I've never even been outside the country."

Randy paused to catch his breath.

"I hear you brother. I guess this is almost as good."

"Why didn't you tell me?"

"I didn't know if I was going to be able to go, between the cost of the trip, my recommendations and everything. When the application was in, I figured I'd wait until I heard the results. It almost got screwed up because of Travis."

Troy guessed that Darnell had somehow spared Randy to avoid suspicion. He had covered his bases.

"Travis is on his job, though, I don't care what nobody says. I need to talk to Darnell."

Troy chuckled.

"Something funny?"

"No, I just don't know what makes you think Darnell's going to talk to you."

"Oh, so y'all are boys now, huh?"

"I didn't say that."

"What did you say? Huh?"

Troy paused to choose his words carefully.

"You're right, okay? Darnell knows something. But he's no friend of yours or mine."

"Maybe you should talk to him."

Troy considered it for a moment.

"I'll try to talk to him."

"You'll try?"

"Randy, he knows we're boys! I mean, what do you want?"

"I want things to be right, that's what the fuck I want! I've worked too hard, we've come too far to go out like this. If Travis has problems, we have problems. Sooner or later you'll see that." Before Troy could respond, Randy stormed out of the room, slamming the door.

Troy's finals started on the following day. The classroom in Graveston Hall took on the antiseptic feel of a final exam. Troy was happy that Sociology was first. It was an easy test; he had prepared for it well. When he rechecked his answers and was sure they were right, he left smiling. Rarely had he ever finished an exam before most of the other students. Ethics had been no different, and by the time he got to the play for Poetry, Troy thought he might really have improved his grade point average!

"How was Macro?" Troy asked Randy, hours later.

"Oh, it was rough, brother," Randy said, "but I think I did okay. At least I hope so."

Randy stared at the carpet in their room. He and Troy hadn't seen each other in a couple of days, except in passing on the way to study or to a final.

"What's wrong now?" Troy inquired.

Silence.

"What is it?"

"Darnell is behind this shit with Travis," Randy said quietly. "I know it."

"Maybe."

"Maybe my ass. Nobody else could do it."

"No, probably not."

"You knew about this, didn't you?"

"I had my suspicions."

"You knew! Brother, you knew all along? How could you not say anything? Because of Travis? So much was in jeopardy and you didn't say anything?"

"Look, I still don't know for sure," Troy lied. "It seemed funny to me when the shit first went down. You know he works there. What was I going to do, point at him?"

"Help me!" Randy barked. "Show some support! People were outside the office protesting and you weren't saying shit!"

"Oh, for Christ's sake! It's all talk, Randy! All this shit will blow over next year."

"He's still seeing your moms, isn't he?"

"Fuck you!"

Troy prepared to square off with his roommate.

"Hold it now, I don't think so," came a stern but excited voice from the door. A sober Ill Will came in. "What's happening here?"

"Nothing," said the both of them in unison.

"Phyllis is upstairs having a little meeting. Yvonne's there, too. Of course, she's from North Dakota and Phyllis is from Wyoming," Ill Will observed. "So you know they're gonna agree. Plus those girls just stick together. Like we used to." Both Troy and Randy were still solemn. Ill Will walked over to Randy.

"Now if I was like you, Mr. President, I'd tell you straight up, you shouldn't have been fucking her in the first place. Because this is what happens. But I'm not like that. I'll let you figure it out for yourself," Ill Will admonished sarcastically.

Randy looked up at him harshly. Ill Will's eyes met his with just as much intensity.

"I still have a German exam, so I really should get out of here. I'll check on you homies later. *auf Wiedersehen!*"

Troy knew that Randy was disappointed in him, but he didn't have to throw Travis's relationship with his mother in his face. Randy must have also felt vulnerable with Ill Will's news. Phyllis may not have had his title, but she had surely affected Randy's influence. Troy wondered what he would have done if it were he and Angel in that position and decided that she'd have a fight on her hands.

Although Troy was concerned about his roommate's morale, he couldn't allow it or anything else to overshadow his preparation for his last two finals. He was satisfied with his understanding of Western European history, but at the same time he became more offended at the utter lack of mention of African or Eastern contributions to world history. His class was a required European history course, but the material implied that there was no Eastern influence of any kind on Western civilization, and Troy had since learned that this was far from the truth. Nonetheless, he attacked Shebel's exam, regurgitating the bland information into palatable, thorough essays Accounting II, for all of Troy's attempts to prepare, was every bit as challenging as he had expected. He was able to draw on his understanding of basic concepts, applying them to the test questions in front of him. Miraculously, he also had time to rework some of the most troublesome problems. Math had never been easy for him, but he was determined to improve on the previous semester's 'C' plus. Once he finished the exam, Troy left it in God's hands and on the proxy's desk.

For the first time in a while, Troy found a new note on the message board of his door The latest note read,

"Troy and Randy, please report to MA office in Healy Hall as soon as possible. Travis Gordon wants to see you."

Randy wasn't in the room, so Troy assumed he must have already seen the note. He took his time walking toward the front of campus, unsure of what awaited him.

A mob of students had spilled into the hallway outside of the offices. It looked as if almost every black student on campus was inside the office's wide reception area. People sat on desks and stood on chairs to get a glimpse of Travis addressing the room. He was backed up against his office door. Bizzy, Wendell and a couple of Kappas were standing on coffee tables. Troy pushed his way forward; he could hear Travis talking, but he wasn't close enough to make out what he was saying. Phyllis and her girlfriends were up front. Randy and Darnell stood next to Travis along with a couple of staff members he didn't recognize.

"I completely understand your concerns. I wanted to see you all here because for the first time I finally have some answers. Our problems began as the result of someone infiltrating this office. That person had access, somehow, to critical documents both on file and on our computer system. There was tampering involved."

Troy briefly caught his roommate's eye, but Randy turned away.

"I didn't believe it possible at first, but it's true. In all my years at Georgetown, I never would have imagined tampering from within this office."

Travis turned to Darnell. *Shit*, Troy thought.

"Now I've had my suspicions, but nothing to date has been substantiated. I have met with both Student Affairs and campus security over the past several weeks. And although we still don't know exactly how, how all of this happened, I have to take full responsibility for all of the problems caused by this office."

"It's about time!" shouted Phyllis. Cheers erupted from the women in the crowd.

"You'll pardon the interruption," Travis continued. "Now it may take a little longer than we wish, but everyone's applications and accounts will be restored and corrected. That goes for housing, summer courses, everything. The office will be closing next Thursday. We'll be seeing students by appointment only until then."

The crowd groaned with disapproval.

"I apologize again. I know this is inconvenient for everyone." Travis turned and opened his office door. "Darnell, clear these folks out of here. I want to see Randy and Troy in here, too."

"Yes, sir."

Randy followed Travis into his office.

"Folks, we need you to clear out of here!" Darnell called. "Talk to Sarah, the receptionist if you want an appointment."

Armed with a clipboard, the young woman exited the office, leading the crowd into the hallway. Darnell waved Troy over to Travis' office.

"What the fuck happened?" Troy asked.

"It was fucked up," Darnell said.   "He fired one of his administrators."

"But not you, huh? You motherfucker."

"Hey, let the chips fall where they may.   Remember that next time you make a wish."

The door of Travis' office opened to let Randy out.   Troy didn't know what to say, standing there with Darnell.   Randy looked them both up and down and kept walking.

"Troy, get in here," Travis called.   Troy walked in behind Darnell.

"Have a seat, Mr. Harris.   Darnell, out."

The upperclassman turned to leave.

"Later, Troy."

"Yeah."

Travis waited for Darnell to leave.

"So how was your last exam?"

"Fine."

"Really?"

"Yeah, really!   I mean, I studied and I think I was ready for it."

"I'm sure you were."

"What am I doing here?"

Travis chuckled.   "Don't worry.   I just wanted to tell you a few things before you went home.   I'll probably see you in New York, but I won't be on duty."

"Hip hip, hooray."

Travis cracked a smile again, but he was clearly agitated.   Troy's face had no expression.

"That's real cute.   Believe it or not, I've been watching you two."

"Oh, you have?"

"You and Randy, that is.   I've seen how you've grown and what you're doing with the BSU.   I think it's positive.   Even the attempt to bring Farrakhan here, although I knew it wouldn't happen."

"It still might.   There's always next year."

"Let me finish.   You're probably aware that there's an uprising, if you will, within your organization that could hurt you and Randy next year.   I might add there's a very competent young lady behind it, one you may have underestimated."

"Why are you telling me?"

Travis hammered his desk with his fist, uprooting books and photos.

"Because you're the Vice-President, goddammit! Now I just told Randy the same thing, but you're Janice's son! Don't make this harder than it already is."

"I didn't ask to come in here."

Travis stood up and pointed at the boy. He started to speak, but stopped himself and sat down first.

"Troy, I want you to make sure that you learn from everything that's happened recently. You understand me?"

"Yeah."

"Do you?"

"Yes! Yes, I understand."

"Just make sure you keep your head on straight. You and Randy are moving into areas where I won't be able to help you as much, certainly not now. You're not freshmen anymore, either. So remember that. And don't forget to listen to what your parents tell you."

Troy sat quietly, trying to muster some patience.

"Another thing. Women are not to be taken lightly, particularly black women. Sometimes we forget that."

Troy had to nod at that one.

"That's true."

"So we agree on something after all."

"Maybe."

"That's all. Good luck on the rest of your finals."

Troy walked out of Minority Affairs to find Sarah still taking appointments. Latanya had just made an appointment when she saw him.

"Hey!"

"Hi, Latanya." Troy came over for one of her sisterly hugs. The two of them left the Healy building to find bright sunshine outside.

"Must be nice being Mr. BSU," she observed. "You can see Travis whenever you want to."

"If only you knew."

"He's a good brother, Troy."

"I know. He just thinks he knows everything."

"Maybe not everything, but he knows a lot."

"Yeah, well how does he know, huh? How does he know so much?"

"People talk, Troy," Latanya said. "Especially sisters. Travis listens. It's his job."

Troy had no reply and he could only nod again.

"Latanya, when are you going home?"

"Day after tomorrow. I'll be back in a few weeks."

"I'll see you before you leave."

"Hope so." The two friends embraced again before Latanya was on her way. Troy was left to contemplate her words as well as his conversation with Travis. Troy was amazed that Travis even attempted to offer him some kind of guidance under the circumstances. He was still seeing his mother, but for the first time, Troy felt that Travis was sincere, that his mother had nothing to do with it. And that thing about black women. *Damn*, Troy thought. It had taken him this long to become committed to his studies. Troy's anger had made him so overzealous that he had done things that were now unthinkable to him. He remembered the uneasy feeling of talking to Darnell, the guilt of throwing precious information into the river. Now, the Black Student Union could be weakened, many students were in a worse position and this guy, whom his mother cared for very much, was in professional jeopardy. Troy sat on a bench outside of Coplin Hall and looked around; he felt like he'd just arrived at Georgetown. He could hardly believe that he was the person who was the catalyst for so much trouble. It dawned on him what this whole college experience was about. Learning. It was the first time he truly felt he had learned something, not just from textbooks, but about himself. Troy wasn't pleased with himself, but he was thankful for the awareness that was now coming to him. Everything was still not as comfortable as he would have liked, but Troy was encouraged; the worst was over and there would be plenty of opportunities for improvement.

*   *   *   *

Randy was at his desk reading when Troy returned to the room. His roommate didn't look up when he let himself in. *I'd be wrong if I started mixing, though*, he thought. Troy found his Accounting book and sat at his desk, opposite Randy. He tried to concentrate, but he could only think of what Travis had told him. Randy appeared to be consumed by whatever he was reading, but Troy wasn't convinced.

"Look, Randy," he started.

"Save it." Randy quickly got up, snatched his book, and left the room.

Twenty-One

The students who hadn't left the campus were partying, to celebrate both the end of the semester and the upcoming graduation. Troy was sorry to see Wendell leaving, and happy that Latanya, Michelyn, and his other upperclassmen friends would still be around. He looked forward to more parties and girls, but dreaded the summer semester's upcoming Calculus class. All because of a lousy six points on the diagnostic test; with a bit of effort during those first few days of school, he could have placed out of Calculus. He was in for several weeks of brain-wracking mathematical theory and problem solving. If there was enough money left over in the Minority Affairs budget, he would try to get his Economics courses out of the way, too, so that his sophomore year wouldn't be as tough.

Troy found Ill Will in his own room on the phone. The conversation sounded important, so Troy was silent until his friend hung up. When he was finished with the call, he smiled. It was all Ill Will could do not to laugh.

"What are you smiling at?" Troy asked.

"Oh, what's up, man. Got a job, baby."

"Word? Congratulations," Troy said. "So who hired you?"

"Upward Bound, here on campus. I'm gonna be a counselor."

"You're gonna what?"

"Don't sound so surprised. A counselor. They wanted someone who cares about the kids, and someone with experience in the program. I was in it a couple of years ago, and plus I'm a City Scholar. How could they turn me down?"

How could they not? Troy thought. "Yeah, well cool, congratulations."

Troy was hit with mixed feelings. He didn't want to have to watch over his friend all summer long, but back in Philly, Ill Will might get into even more trouble. At least at Georgetown there was some semblance of a controlled environment.

"Hell yeah," Ill Will continued, " 'cause I wasn't going home. Even if I'da had to sleep on the street."

"Right. What dorm are they putting you in?"

"Xavier, inside the square."

"They'll probably put me up on the north side. I'll be lucky if I end up back here."

"You'll be all right." Troy couldn't get over the irony. The student most in need of counseling was about to become a counselor. Someone knocked on the open door. The boys looked over to find Randy in the doorway.

"What do you want?" Ill Will barked.

"Just came to say peace before I break out."

"Peace."

"Relax Ill," Troy mediated. "How long you going be in New York again?"

"About two weeks. Then it's off to Europe."

"I'll call you when I get up the way."

"Of course."

Randy came into the room to exchange handshakes with Troy. He reached out to Ill Will also, but received only a suspicious look in return.

"Oh, it's like that now?" Randy asked.

"Nah, it's been like that," Ill Will shot back.

"Yeah, all right," Randy said with sarcasm, turning away.

"It's cool now, Mr. President, 'cause I'm gonna be a counselor this summer. Work with kids. Not try to brainwash 'em like you would."

Randy grimaced. "Brainwash them? As usual, you don't even know what you're saying. I worked with kids in welfare hotels back in New York! Homeless kids! And they let you work as a counselor? What was it, the one who drinks the most shots gets the job?"

"See, Troy?" Ill Will asked. "See how he starts? He was humble as hell when he came in here, though. Phyllis been taking it to that ass, right?"

Randy poised himself as if to throw a punch, but he calmed himself. Troy could see the discussion soon disintegrating to fisticuffs.

"Like I said, I just came to say peace. Ill, you have a good summer."

"Yeah, you too, sucker. As-Salaam Alakium."

Randy closed the door behind him. Troy and Ill Will looked at each other, both still wrapped up in the negative tone of the words that had been exchanged. Troy was sure that Randy hadn't planned such an exit, and regretted the exchange between his two friends. *But,* he thought, *things happen and you just have to take things as they come.*

"Ill, what you doing later?"

"I don't know, probably just chillin.' Everybody's gone! Carl's home, Yvonne's home. Ain't much to do. What about you?"

"Don't know. I need to go see Travis about my housing. Pre-session starts next week and shit."

"Oh, that's right, you're taking a class."

"Yep. Calculus."

Ill Will cringed. "Good luck. I'll be around the dorm if I'm not in here."

"All right. Peace."

Troy left his friend in the half-empty room. Ill Will went to turn his radio on, but when he hit the button, a tape automatically began to play. It was him and Randy, rapping over one of Troy's mixes. Ill Will smiled in spite of himself. Then he quickly stopped the tape and replaced it with an Eric Clapton cassette.

*   *   *   *

Far quicker than he had expected, Troy's first year of college was history. The emptiness of the dorm and campus reminded him of the previous summer when he'd first arrived with his mother. Now of course, he knew where he was supposed to go and what he had to do, but for the first time since becoming a college student, he wasn't as thrilled about it. Maybe it was adulthood in general, but there were too many issues to think about. More classes, ex-girlfriends, political battles, problems with his friends. He would much rather have had the deejaying and the socializing in and of itself.

Troy entered the Minority Affairs office with a new attitude. Sarah, the former receptionist and new MA administrator, was going to see what he was made of today.

"Hi Troy," Sarah said, smiling.

"Hey there. It's been a while!"

"Yes," she agreed, laughing at his sarcasm. *I'm the man*, he thought.

"You know who I'm here to see, don't you?"

"Yes, he's expecting you."

"Actually, I'm here to see you."

"Me? Why Troy, whatever for?"

"You know, I just--" Troy was cut off by the beep of Sarah's intercom. Still smiling, she pushed the button to answer.

"Yes?"

"Will you send him in here, please?" asked Travis, who apparently overheard the conversation.

"Sure." Sarah looked at Troy apologetically. *Damn*, he thought. *The man is everywhere.*

"I'll be back," he mouthed to her in silence. She waved him into the office.

Troy was surprised to find Darnell and Bizzy on the couch. Bizzy smiled at his young friend, and Troy pointed at him. Darnell nodded, trying to appear professional in front of Travis. The head of Minority Affairs pointed Troy to a chair opposite his desk.

"Now as I was saying, I don't want any foolishness going on in that apartment. I know you two, or you three, and I'm warning you. These Nevins apartments are for seniors only and we usually get two. MA only got one this summer because of our, ah, troubles."

"Excuse me," Troy interrupted. "Nevins? We got a Nevins apartment?"

"That's right," Travis told him. "Don't ask me why. Since each of you are taking classes in different summer sessions, you'll be able to stay there, free of charge. You'll probably have some other roommates, but I'm holding you all responsible for any trouble. Especially you two," he said, pointing at Darnell and Bizzy.

"Don't worry Travis," Bizzy insisted. "We'll take care of it."

"Just don't screw up, Brian," Travis retorted. "We can't afford it. I don't want to see any of you back in this office until the end of July."

"So everything is straight?" Darnell asked.

"Yes, you can move in next week, as soon as pre-session starts. Troy, technically you should have until the end of the month in Harbin, so don't rush."

"Oh, I won't," Troy said. He was doing cartwheels in his head. The duplex, brick-walled Nevins apartments were Georgetown's most exclusive, a block away from the main campus. They were big enough to shoot movies in, much less throw parties.

Travis stood up, indicating he was finished with the students.

"Brian, come back later so we can talk about your courses."

"Okay, Travis," Bizzy said casually. "Thanks."

"Yes, thank you for the apartment," Darnell added.

"Don't mention it. Quiet as it's kept, it's still my job to help you clowns. Now go."

Travis held the door open for the three of them, and he followed them to the reception area. Troy was going to hang around and finish flirting with Sarah, but Travis' stern look pushed him out the door with the other two students. After they got down the hall, Darnell and Bizzy began the dance reminiscent of football players in the end zone after a touchdown.

"Yes, baby!" Darnell cried. "Nevins! That's the way to start the summer right! Troy, what up?" Darnell gave the younger student a two-hand slap.

"What up, man."

"Come on nigga, don't be mad," advised Bizzy. "We done come up! Darnell, the kid's a DJ, remember?"

"Hell, yeah! Oh, it's over. They fucked around and gave us a Nevins. It's over!"

The two upperclassmen skipped down the hall, laughing as Troy stayed behind. Even when scheming against Travis Gordon, Troy had never seen Darnell so excited. He couldn't help but notice Darnell's chameleon-like ability to adjust his behavior to whoever was addressing him. In Travis' office and in public, he was as quiet and conservative as he could be. With him and Bizzy, he was one of the homeboys. Troy couldn't decide if Darnell was really phony or simply a slick manipulator with good intentions.

Darnell left Bizzy outside in front of Healy Hall. The sun was blazing, and he had donned a pair of shades faster than Troy could react. He had to squint just to see what was in front of him.

"So Troy," Bizzy said, his hand on Troy's shoulder. "You want to be roommates, or what?"

"Roommates?"

"Yeah. I know the rooms in Nevins are big, but Travis is gonna have some more guys in there, and I don't want to get stuck with no fools."

Troy's mind immediately recalled the previous incidents when he had been the butt of Bizzy's jokes and ready to fight Bizzy over the verbal attacks. It wasn't so long ago when Troy would have been one of those fools. Still, Bizzy would be more bearable than Darnell.

"All right man, you got it."

"Cool!" Bizzy slapped his hand and could not stop laughing. "We're gonna have fun, man, I can tell. I can tell you be trippin'."

"No more than you, nigga," Troy answered. "But hey, what do we do about females? I know you're gonna have Michelyn up in the joint."

"Don't worry about that, we'll work it out."

"All right."

"I'll see you next week. I have to take care of some things."

"Me too. Later."

Troy remembered Michelyn ranting about her boyfriend during the first semester, and how he had been repulsed when he realized that the person she was so excited about was Bizzy Hendricks. Although Michelyn was Troy and Ill Will's big sister, Troy couldn't help but be jealous at that time because he admired Michelyn and she was drop-dead gorgeous. He still was envious in a way, but mostly he was happy for Michelyn. She and Latanya had returned home, but they would be back sometime in June. Troy was looking forward to seeing more of them during the summer.

*   *   *   *

Harbin Hall's lobby was deserted except for the student guard. Because he had time to spare, Troy decided to take the elevator one flight up. He regretted that move when he saw Angel waiting to get on the elevator. She seemed to be smiling until she saw him. Aside from her usual nasty look, she avoided contact with him. Despite his mental efforts against it, Troy's curiosity made him wonder who she was visiting. He was tempted to follow her, but his ego wouldn't let him. Instead, he went to his room. His plants, posters and records were still there, but Randy's side of the room was bare; gone were the prayer rug, the incense, the photos of Malcolm X, Martin Luther King, Marcus Garvey and Louis Farrakhan. Remembering his freedom, Troy turned on his stereo and started mixing; maybe another party would start outside his window. After an hour of spinning records, Troy was bored, and his music had failed to attract any attention. His mind was made up; it was time to go home. Although he cringed at the thought of seeing Travis in his apartment, he was sure that his mother would be happy to see him.

Troy found little relief from the heat that evening. The night air in New York was a bit cooler, but the humidity was stifling. He would have felt like he was still in D.C. if not for the constant bustle of Manhattan. Like a true New Yorker, the noise, the trash and the crowds on the subway were welcome sights to Troy. Although he had lived in Maryland two years before he came to Georgetown, he still felt most comfortable when he returned to the city. He fumbled with his keys for a moment before finally opening the apartment door. His mother was sitting in the living room.

"Hey, Mom. What are you doing sitting in the dark?"

"You told me you weren't coming until Saturday."

"So what? I'm still your son, ain't I?"

"Aren't I," she corrected him. "Of course you are."

"What's the matter with you?"

"Listen to me. You know a man has never had a chance with me if he couldn't accept you. But when it comes to Travis, I'm not going to wait for your approval. You're not a child anymore, but you're still my son. My son," she added, pointing to herself. "You wanted to do your own thing, you're doing it. I am too, and you're going to have to deal with it."

Troy made a face, feeling more like a child than the man his mother described, wondering why she felt she needed to start their visit this way.

"There's some chicken in the oven."

"Thanks."

*   *   *   *

Randy was doing some last-minute packing. Troy had taken the train out to Queens to visit him. The former roommates agreed to talk prior to Randy's departure. Based on the past week, Troy was unsure what to expect, but he was more than willing to attempt to reconcile their friendship.

"So you ready for France or what?" Troy asked Randy the next day.

"I am now. Have to be."

"Kinda ill how the semester turned out, huh?"

"Yeah." Randy agreed. "You get your grades back yet?"

"Nah."

"Me neither." Randy continued to pack. Troy watched, surveying the modest room, listening to Public Enemy on the radio. He could hear Randy's mother in the kitchen washing dishes.

"Hey Randy, you know I'm sorry. About everything."

"No need for you to be sorry. You didn't have any say over what Darnell was doing."

"But still, just the whole way it went down. It didn't have to be that way."

"Nope."

"I'm not just saying that. I told Ill the same thing."

Randy stopped packing to turn around.

"Just like you told me?"

"Told you about what?"

"You know, Phyllis. I can tell you tried to warn me."

Troy forced a friendly look. Randy's fear of losing the BSU leadership was clear. His uncertainty, his vulnerability, was an unwelcome visitor in the room.

"I did try, but it ain't over yet. We'll be back on point next year."

"But what about this summer? She got to be real cool with the Student Government, and the BSU is almost all sisters."

Sisters you were boning, Troy thought. *That was the problem.*

"Don't worry about it. We'll just have to come better next time, that's all. Both of us."

"You're probably right. Ay, do me a favor? Try to tell Ill, I mean, I'm still in his corner, you know?"

"That's good," Troy admitted, "but you need to do that on your own, you know what I'm saying? We supposed to be crew, 4-H. And if you can't talk to him like a man, well..."

"I hear you, I hear you. Well, get me his number when he moves or whatever."

"Will do."

"Cool. Mmm, you smell that? Let's go, I think the food is ready."

"Now you're talking," Troy said. Randy led him through the hall. "What's up with those girlies from Long Island?"

"We'll know tonight."

Randy's mother sent him off with a feast of whiting fish, fried chicken, rice with black-eyed peas, string beans and corn on the cob; Troy was glad he hadn't eaten lunch. As it turned out, Randy's girls from Long Island didn't want to come to Queens, and Troy had been unable to get his mother's car, so they had to settle for a movie. He returned on the subway late that night. Troy was mentally alert, his mental guard the result of having been robbed on the train as a child. When he got close to the 110th street stop, he relaxed. He thought about Randy's words as he walked from the subway. He was pleased at his roomie's forgiving attitude, but not as much as he thought he would be; it just didn't seem to matter to him as much now. In fact, aside from his grades, not much else did and Troy was sure he'd done well on his finals.

Troy found an unwanted house guest when he returned home.

"There he is," Travis observed from the couch.

What the fuck! Troy thought. *I can't get away from him.* "Where's my mom?"

"In the bedroom. She worked overtime tonight."

"So what are you doing, waiting for her to wake up?"

"No. Actually, I was waiting for you."

"As if I don't talk to you enough," Troy muttered, rolling his eyes.

"Just calm down for a minute."

"No, you calm down. I'm going to bed." Troy stormed off toward his room.

"I know what went on in my office."

Troy stopped in his tracks, feeling Travis's stare behind him. Reluctantly, he turned around and came back into the living room.

"Have a seat," Travis offered. Troy sat down, not taking his eyes off Travis.

"You want a brew?" the man asked.

"Brew? You, of all people should know I'm not old enough."

"I'm not responsible for you in your own home. You want one or not?"

"It's in the fridge?"

"Yes."

"No, I don't want one."

"I won't tell your mother."

"No, thank you," he insisted. "Now what are you talking about?'"

Travis shook his head. "You know, I searched all over that office, trying to trace the discrepancies in Minority Affairs the past few weeks. I couldn't figure out why it was happening. Why would anyone want to make my job difficult, make it harder for black students than it already is? What could anyone possibly gain from causing such problems?"

"Yeah, yeah. Now what's that got to do with me?"

"Nothing, I hope. But it would be a shame if it did. That would mean I looked after your records and made sure I looked out for you for nothing. You'd be in that Nevins apartment for nothing."

Troy turned away, looking down at his shoes.

"What are you saying, Travis?"

"I'm saying that because of some foolishness in my office, many students that I care about now have very serious problems. Many of them I had to fight to keep enrolled. The only way all those records could have gotten changed around is through internal channels. And only a student who was familiar with the office could have caused such damage. Of course, I can't prove this."

"I thought you were the director! You're in charge of MA, not, not some student."

"That's right," Travis agreed. "Except I forgot that I'm director, trying to take care of someone special to me instead of doing my job, which is to take care of as many as I can."

"Are you through?"

"Sure, Troy, I'm through. Just think about what I'm telling you. To damage the Office of Minority Affairs is to damage black students. Black students, Troy, not just me. MA may not be able to help people the way we did."

"That ain't got shit to do with me!" Troy shouted.

"It very well may not. But I would hope that responsible folks would do the right thing."

"Travis?" Janice called from her room. "Is everything okay?"

"Sure," Travis called back. "We're just talking."

"Oh. Well, I'll see you in the morning."

Troy stood up. "I heard you," he whispered.

"That's all I wanted you to do."

"Yeah, well, I'm going to bed now."

"Good night."

Troy retreated to his bedroom and shut the door. He had gotten so worked up, he was sure he'd tipped his hand to Travis. He didn't know what to think. Could Travis have spared him and Randy the problems that other students had with Minority Affairs? Had he done this just to stay in Troy's mother's good graces? He clearly knew that Darnell had been behind the whole thing and he correctly suspected that Troy was also involved. It had all blown up in his face, but there was nothing he could do about it now. He laid in bed and stared at the ceiling, tired but too uncomfortable to sleep. Travis Gordon was in his living room and had probably been with his mother. Suddenly he longed to be anywhere but there. *I'm going back tomorrow*, he thought. *When me and Bizzy get into that Nevins crib, things'll be popping again.*

The following night, Janice Harris walked down the hallway, arm in arm with her beau.

"So you like the Blue Note, huh?"

"Yes, ma'am. Very nice."

"I'd forgotten how long it's been."

"Baby, it's only been a couple months."

"That's a long time, Travis."

"I know. Come here." He stopped her for a kiss.

"What's that for?"

"That's because I missed you. Everything's been crazy without you."

"Well, you're here now."

Troy's mother found her keys and opened the apartment door. Travis remained in the hallway.

"What's the matter?"

"Are you sure I shouldn't go?"

"Don't be silly."

"Maybe I should."

"Why?"

"Honey, you know why."

"Travis, he may have already left by now. Besides, we've talked about this. He's just got to handle it."

"Baby, it's not that easy."

"Travis, this is my house. Troy doesn't have a damn thing to say about who comes in here. Now the two of you have talked, haven't you?"

"We have."

"So what's the matter?"

He wanted to tell her the talk with Troy didn't go the way he planned, but thought better of it.

"You're right, I'm overreacting. He says he's a man, he should understand."

She could see that he was upset. "Don't worry about it," she told him.

"Oh, I just can't tell you nothing, can I?"

"No, you can't."

Travis pulled Janice Harris to him in the doorway, where they shared a long embrace.

*   *   *   *

Georgetown University was still desolate when Troy returned the next day. He couldn't move out of Harbin until Monday, and it was Saturday, so again, he had nothing to do. It was if everyone he knew had vanished; old girls, new girls, friends from high school, nobody was around. When the phone rang, he jumped to answer it, anxious to hear from anyone he'd left a message for since he'd gotten back to campus.

"Hello?"

"Troy." The voice of his father brought him a profound sense of hopelessness.

"Hi, Dad."

"Troy, you were here, and you didn't come visit? You couldn't even call? Why?"

"I don't know. Just didn't want to."

"Susan was so disappointed. She thinks it's her."

Give me a fucking break, Troy thought. "It's not her, it's not that."

"Then it must, it must be me. Why are you so angry with me? What did I do?"

"If you don't know, I'm not telling you."

"That's not fair. How am I supposed to--"

"We can talk about this some other time. Goodbye."

Troy hung up the phone gently. Even when he was the aggressor, Troy was emotionally drained whenever he spoke to his father. He sat in his room, listening to the occasional breeze from outside, the one or two birds chirping above the second floor. His father, the great David Harris, was profoundly hurt, Troy could hear it in his voice. From that hurt, he drew a perverse satisfaction. For a moment, he had been vindicated.

*   *   *   *

Hours later, Troy saw Bizzy ahead of him, in front of the Nevins building on 36th Street.

"Biz!" he yelled. "What up?"

Bizzy turned around and chuckled. "What up, roomie?"

"Chillin," he told him while slapping hands. "I just got my keys from Travis. You got yours?"

"Hell yeah. I'ma start moving in a couple hours. Darnell's moving in tomorrow."

"Hey, how about I help you move and you help me?"

"Aw shit, all them records?"

Troy looked surprised.

"I'm just fucking with you," Bizzy laughed. "Sure, no problem."

Bizzy unlocked the side door with his ID. He and Troy walked through the corridor to the outside elevator, which would take them upstairs to their new home. The elevator also required an ID for operation. Troy had the honor of opening the door. He and Bizzy were all smiles when they came into the apartment. There were some empty plastic cups and cardboard boxes, but the place was still relatively clean. The living room was a wide, rectangular hallway, leading to a spacious kitchen. Immediately Troy picked out a spot for his turntables. The staircase overlooked the rest of the apartment, and the furnished rooms upstairs were larger than any other bedroom Troy had seen on campus. He and Bizzy decided on the largest upstairs room, which was close to both the stairs and the bathroom. The brick walls extended to the upstairs hallway. Bizzy was, as usual, jubilant.

"I'm tellin' you man, we gonna have fun!" he said.

"Most definitely," Troy agreed. "Travis made a mistake with this shit."

Shortly afterwards, Troy met Bizzy at Village C to help him move into Nevins. He had very little to carry compared to Troy. Troy noticed his new friend didn't really own much of anything; not a lot of clothes or books. He would never have known this the way Bizzy carried on in the cafeteria, talking about other people's clothes or their haircuts. Bizzy held up his end of the deal and helped Troy move out of Harbin. Ill Will met them at Room 228.

"Hey homey! What's up, Brian?"

Bizzy and Ill Will slapped hands. "Not this nigga," Bizzy said. "What up, crazy ass?"

"Oh, why I got to be crazy? You don't hear me calling you 'Bizzy' do you? You know Michelyn doesn't like that."

"Never mind Michelyn."

"Come on you two," Troy interrupted. "Let's get this show on the road."

With extra assistance from Ill Will, Troy's move into Nevins was swift and painless. Once during the move, Ill Will let out a loud belch, one so strong that Troy had smelled it. Until then, he had enjoyed the thought that Ill Will had gone without a drink that day. When they finally finished moving Troy's stuff, the three of them ventured into Georgetown proper, in search of cheap food and a place to watch the NBA playoffs.

*   *   *   *

"Shit!" Troy shouted aloud. He was in the library, staring at the twenty calculus problems given to him by Professor Bradley. He had to finish all of them by the next morning, the second day of class.

"This way," the professor had said, "we'll be able to determine how much work needs to be done with all of you."

Troy had been hoping for some more instruction in class, but Professor Bradley had only gone over a few points before handing out the problems. Troy had just purchased the textbook, and he was additionally armed with his Pre-Calculus book from high school. He figured the books would help him through the first four or five questions, and he was right, but he was lost after that. He had been considering cutting his work schedule down to allow more time to study. Now he knew that would have to be the case. On his way back to Nevins, he ran into Ali, a former City Scholar and a one of his Calculus classmates.

"What up, Ali?"

"Hey, man. Getting a jump on those problems?"

"Trying to. I think I'm done for the day, though."

"I hear you. Hey, I hear we're gonna be housemates!"

"You moving into Nevins?"

"Nevins 16, that's right."

"Cool." Troy was happy to have another calculus student around to suffer with him. "They got all the brothers together this session."

"Yeah, they do that a lot. Then they wonder why we sit together at dinner."

Troy cracked up, slapping hands with his classmate. "Word up! I'll see you later."

"Later."

Nevins 16 was taking on character as more people moved in. Troy heard a television blasting before he opened the door. He came in to find Darnell in the process of unpacking, evidenced by the color TV, microwave oven, and cookware. Darnell would be in the room adjoining his and Bizzy's room.

"Troy!" Darnell shouted. "DJ Troy, what up, baby?"

Troy shook Darnell's hand without saying anything. He could tell from his housemate's clumsy stance that he was drunk.

"DJ Troy in the house! You know we gonna have some slammin' parties up in here!"

"Of course," Troy said.

Troy thought Ill Will was probably moving into his new room, so he figured he might as well finish his homework. Could it be that this math struggle would be even worse than Accounting? Silently, Troy prayed for a way to get through the course, and for a few more hours, battled against the army of calculus problems. He closed his door to reduce the noise, but he could still hear the TV, the stereo, and his new housemates laughing and having fun downstairs. Before long, a telephone rang. He didn't even know the phone lines were back on! Troy shook his head, listening as the new place came to life. In a way it was fitting that he, the self-styled King of the Party, be there, but at the moment, his attendance wasn't helping his increasing need for academic discipline. Whether Troy liked it or not, though, it was clear that Nevins 16 was going to be a popular spot.

Twenty-Two

Troy mon frere,

Bonjour from Nice. France is treating me very well so far. There are even a couple of sisters on the trip with me. I'm taking a French course and a history course as well. It's a lot of work, but I'm seeing the country, too. We're also going to London before the end of the summer. How is Ill? I sent him a postcard. Phyllis also. She'll never have me removed, no matter what. Got some new ideas for the BSU next year. Know any black barbers in France? I'm growing a bush! Gotta go, stay cool.

Peace,
Randy

Troy sat outside Graveston Hall with the postcard. He had just returned from Harbin Hall, where he was still receiving mail. After class, he would walk over to Harbin, get his mail, and return to a Graveston classroom to do his homework. Among his mail was his transcript. It was so beautiful outside, Troy had decided to take a break and read it out on the bench before returning inside. Just as he opened the transcript, Ali joined him.

"What up, Troy?"

"Hey, man."

"You got your grades there, huh?"

"Yep."

"I haven't opened mine yet."

"That's what I'm about to do." Troy ripped the envelope open, ignoring Ali. Taking the hint, Ali opened his own envelope.

"Okay, okay," Ali nodded, looking pleased. "I swept 'em. Every class."

"I guess that's good," Troy observed.

"Good enough. How about you?"

"I didn't sweep anything."

Troy felt nauseous. Ali could see he wanted to be alone, so he excused himself and left. Troy was horrified by his grades. They weren't terrible by most standards, but having put more effort in this semester, somehow he had expected to do better. He had gotten 'B's, in Poetry/Drama, Sociology and Euro Civ II, a 'B'+ in Ethics, and worst of all, a 'C' in Accounting II. He had made no progress in his toughest course. In fact, he'd gotten worse.

He found a calculator in his room in Nevins, and computed his grade point average. It was a 2.9, barely an improvement on the previous 2.75 from fall semester. A deep disappointment took hold of him. He couldn't be too remorseful about Accounting, because he had really tried to do well. Damn it! He had tried in all those classes! How could he not get an 'A' in Ethics? In Poetry/Drama? He had come up a little in Euro Civ, but what did it matter? He had blown it.

"Oh Troy, come on," his mother had tried to console him "It's not that bad."

"Yes it is," he insisted. "I mean Mom, it's not like I played around. I mean, I really studied!"

"You'll just have to 'really study' harder this time. That's all you can do. Those grades are already posted, you can only bring up your average in other courses."

"Mom, are you listening to me? I'm in Calculus now!"

"Troy, I know it sounds strange, but things are never as bad as they seem. God never gives you more than you can handle."

Troy's patience was exhausted.

"Well, God doesn't have to worry about his GPA, does He?"

Troy's mother laughed. "Have you told your father?"

"Hell no!" he shouted, exasperated.

"Troy!"

"Sorry. No, I haven't told him. But I will."

"Please do. And don't worry, it'll be okay. Listen, I need to go, that's your grandmother on the other line."

"Tell her I said 'Hi.'"

"I will. Take care."

"Bye Mom."

Troy thought he would feel better after talking to his mother, but he didn't. Still, she did make a good point: he couldn't change the grades, he could only do better in other courses. Since he had already worked on his calculus, he headed downstairs, where Darnell, Bizzy and Ali were watching the NBA finals. Ill Will was also in attendance, and Troy was thrilled to see his former Kappa tutor as well.

"Wendell! I thought you graduated."

"What, I can't come back and chill with my boys?" Wendell's eyes were glued to the TV. Troy turned to Ill Will.

"Shouldn't you be across the square?"

"Relax, I'm off duty tonight. Can't you see the game is on?"

"Yeah, okay."

"Detroit is gonna do it this time, I'm telling you," Bizzy announced.

"Nah, baby," Bizzy said. "The Lakers will do it again, just like Pat said."

"Whatever. Just be ready to pay me!"

Troy smiled, enjoying the banter that was going on. During the commercial, Darnell got up and went to the kitchen.

"Troy, what do you want?"

"What do I want for what?"

"To drink, fool!"

"Oh. What do we have?"

"We have everything."

"What are you having?"

"A Brandy Alexander."

"Give me one of those." Troy hated drinking in front of Ill Will. He felt like he was validating Ill Will's alcohol abuse when he did, although there was no comparison between them. Ill Will had caught him at a weak moment last spring in the lounge, and besides, that was before he had really accepted that his friend had a problem. In order to set the example in Nevins, he would have had to disturb the harmony of the entire household, and he couldn't do that. Not tonight, anyway.

"Hey Ali, you down to do that thang tonight?" Troy asked.

"Yeah, we can go right after the game."

"Cool."

'That thang' was Troy and Ali's agreement to study for their calculus class together. Troy always felt the need to make it sound cool in front of everyone, but they all knew what it meant. Ali had some command over the course, and he'd agreed to help Troy, who was recommitted to doing well. He couldn't shake the fear that doing well, in this case, might only mean a passing grade.

During the next week another session of summer courses started, bringing more students back to the campus. The population was still a fraction of what it normally was, but the campus became more active with exchange students, high school students from D.C. and other students in a variety of programs and courses. Fewer undergraduates meant fewer black students as well, and the smaller black community at Georgetown became closer as a social necessity. Latanya and other senior girls were back, working and getting courses out of the way. Yvonne returned to campus, joining Ill Will as a late addition to the Upward Bound staff. These students and more made Nevins 16, as Troy predicted, the official hangout for black folk. Because his housemates demanded it, he would put in a mix tape and sometimes even DJ for them, creating impromptu parties that went on all night, in spite of Troy's coursework. Troy saw that in spite of having the dazzling Michelyn, Bizzy Hendricks was a philanderer and aptly nicknamed. Troy had to take the couch downstairs when Bizzy had female guests, and it was there that his own hormones were revived. Until then, he had forgotten how long it had been since he'd had some action.

*   *   *   *

Troy found Ill Will's room in Xavier Hall and knocked on the door. "Come in!"

Troy opened the door and found Ill Will, Yvonne, and a white guy sitting on the floor, smoking pot. The customary liquor bottle was also on the floor. A videotape of "Three the Hard Way" was on TV.

"S'up, homey?"

"What up, dude."

"Hey, don't get all high and mighty on me. I'm off duty. And you didn't say nothing when the booze was flowing over in Nevins." Yvonne looked up at Troy, assuring him that she had caught what her boyfriend had just said.

"Nah, it's not even like that. It's Friday, I came to chill. What's up, Yvonne?"

"Hi."

"Troy, I want you to meet Bob. Bob, this is my ace homey Troy. Lives across the square."

"Nice to meet you Bob," Troy said, shaking his hand.

"Likewise, likewise."

Bob was a dirty blond with horn-rimmed glasses, a thick mustache and a goatee. He was extremely thin, and the goatee made him resemble Shaggy from Scooby-Doo. Troy wondered if it was the marijuana that made him so skinny.

"Have a seat, Tee. Stay a while. How do you like the room?" Ill Will asked.

"It's different," Troy said.

"Yeah, it's no Nevins, but it's home for now."

The walls were painted turquoise, giving the effect of being inside a cheap fish tank. They sat on a burgundy shag rug which clashed horribly with the walls. The bunk beds seemed to take up almost half of the tiny dwelling, and the desk was adorned with pictures of Yvonne and her friends. "You want some weed?"

"Yeah, why not."

"Bob, hook him up."

"No problem."

From his lap, Bob produced a Ziploc bag, which held a dry marijuana plant. Troy couldn't believe what he was seeing. He had a tree! He broke of a piece of the dried plant and ground it into a bong, which he handed to Troy. The last time he had had a pipe in his mouth was as a kid years ago, trying to smoke his grandfather's tobacco.

"Thanks. You got a match?"

"Of course," Bob said, lighting him up. Troy inhaled the bong and was almost overwhelmed. He didn't have much experience with pot, much less in a bong.

"Hey," he asked, "which one of you guys is working tonight?"

"Gwendolyn's on duty," Bob said. "but I'm kind of on call, since I'm the senior counselor. The kids are cool. As long as they're in before ten and nobody's hurt, we're okay. If we catch someone sneaking out, or in, then it's a problem."

"That's why we stay in here!" Ill Will added.

"Right, right," Troy said, marijuana smoke dancing around his eyes. The weed was good.

Troy walked across the square as if he were gliding. "Three the Hard Way" was still playing on the screen in his mind. The fresh air sharpened his mind for a few minutes, but when he reached the elevator, he returned to a happy, disoriented state, high as a Georgia pine tree. Music from one of his mix tapes was pulsating from inside the door. He knocked.

"Troy! There go that nigga Troy, what up baby!" Bizzy shouted.

"What up nigga. There's a party in here, or what?"

"You know it! Look y'all, it's Troy!"

There were over a dozen people in the apartment, and Troy saw all of them twice. Latanya came over for a hug. Because it was the start of the weekend, the party atmosphere of the apartment had kicked into high gear. Troy noticed a few girls that he hadn't seen before. He didn't want to make a fool of himself, so he sat down on the couch as slowly as he could. Ali walked past him, on his way to the kitchen.

"Ali!" Troy called.

Ali could see that Troy was high, and he was loving it. "Ha ha! You're lit! What's up man?"

"Never mind that, where's Bizzy?"

"Upstairs." If Bizzy was in the bedroom in the middle of a party, it could only mean one thing.

"Shit! All right, whatever."

"Later, man!"

Troy gave Ali the finger behind his back. There was nothing to do but stay on the couch until he recovered. A girl sat quietly on his right, observing. He couldn't see her face very well, but he could see a firm, curvaceous body.

"Excuse me," he said, tapping her shoulder. "My name is Troy. I live here. Who are you?"

"Hi Troy. I'm Cathy."

"Weren't you in Westmiller's today?"

"Yes, I was in front of you."

"I was going to squeeze your butt."

"Why didn't you?"

"Wasn't trying to get slapped."

"I'll only slap you if you ask."

Troy saw no more need to talk at that point. He leaned over the girl and stuck his tongue as far into her mouth as he could. She grabbed him with one arm, pulling him on top of her. Troy felt firm, heavy breasts pressing against him. His housemates were oblivious, caught up in the party, dancing and shouting.

"We've got to go to your room," he told her. "My roommate's upstairs."

"That's fine."

"Where do you live?"

"Xavier."

"Shit!"

"What did you say?"

"Nothing. Come on." Troy led the girl out of the apartment, and back the way he had come. He kissed her again in the elevator, and considered stopping the elevator with his ID so they could screw right there, but he thought better of it. He would get the full effect of Cathy's body in a bed. They exited through the side corridor and went around the building outside the square. Troy opened the back door of Xavier using the secret combination on the door lock Ill Will had taught him, in case he wanted to come to his room from outside the square. Troy hiked up the back staircase, holding Cathy's hand as he went along. They were on the first floor.

"What room?"

"301."

"All right. Go around and act like you came in the front. Then go upstairs and wait by the door. I'ma knock once, then twice."

"Got it." She kissed him again, and left. He felt her behind as she ran off. Troy felt his erection rise another notch. With all the calm he could muster, he waited two minutes for her to get up the stairs. He smiled to himself. 'Once, then twice,' he thought. He was still high, but because there was sex on the line, he thought with the clarity of a secret agent. Troy headed up the back stairs like a cat burglar. The second floor was quiet, and most of the doors were closed. Since Cathy was an Upward Bound student and Ill Will was one of her counselors, he couldn't risk being seen. Carefully, Troy leaped by each doorway, pressed against the wall like a TV cop. Finally, he reached 301, and knocked once, then twice. The door creaked as it opened.

Cathy had the kind of build that young black boys dreamt of, a teenage version of Jackeé, a popular television actress. Troy almost ripped her shirt trying to take it off. Her jeans were just as troublesome. He almost broke his neck following her onto the top bunk bed, but he managed. Seeing her nude drove Troy out of his mind with lust, and

Cathy welcomed all of his excitement. Afterwards, he slept in her arms, smiling like an infant who had just been fed.

His watch read 6:22 a.m. Troy looked around at the sparse room, his and Cathy's clothes scattered about, the condom wrappers on the floor. His young playmate was now sleeping soundly in his arms, and he would have to move her very gently in order to sneak out of the bed. They had made love twice, stopping only to allow Troy a moment to recover and replace his condom. The sight of her naked back and the smell of her perfume tempted Troy to stay for another romp, but he could do that later. Carefully, Troy wiggled out from under Cathy, who was snoring faintly. He caught a glimpse of her smiling in her sleep, and was mortified to find a light brown film on her teeth. Jesus! He dressed quietly but swiftly and tiptoed to the door. Just as he cracked the door to check the hallway, he heard students talking and the showers running. Who the hell was up at this hour? *Goddamn it*, he thought. He was going to have to do it the hard way.

Troy faced the window by Cathy's bed. They were two stories up, but trying to leave through the building unseen was too risky. He looked up again at Cathy, who was still out like a light. He had to be gone before she woke up; for all he knew she might claim rape or something else crazy to keep herself out of trouble. As softly as he could, Troy raised the small window and looked down. There were two options, the concrete or a thick shrubbery facing the wall. Although he was slim, he had little room to maneuver, and Troy soon found himself hanging outside the window. He could only hope the shrubbery would be kind. It was not. He wanted to scream with every fiber of his being when he landed, but he couldn't. Instead, he limped back across the square, picking thorns and pieces of bush out of his arms, legs, back, neck and buttocks. Troy's T-shirt and shorts were perfect for summer, but not ideal for jumping out of dormitory windows.

"Ha hah! There he is!" Bizzy shouted from the staircase, announcing Troy's presence. "How come you're the first one up?"

"I been up," Troy said. He was in the living room, watching *NBA Inside Stuff*.

"I bet you have. What'd you do last night?"

"Same thing you was doing. I was high as a motherfucker, though."

"Oh, all right, so you've been creeping."

"Something like that." Although he knew Bizzy wouldn't care, Troy hoped he didn't suspect that he had been 'creeping' with a high schooler from Upward Bound.

"This place is a mess, I'm gonna start cleaning up. Why don't you throw on some tunes, wake the rest of these fools up?"

"Will do."

Troy got up and switched on his stereo equipment, which was now a part of a makeshift turntable stand, supported by milkcrates that were filled with records. The apartment was ransacked, a furnished garbage dump filled with pizza boxes, magazines, and endless beer and liquor bottles. Troy saw that someone had even tried to play DJ in his absence; many of his meticulously kept records were pulled out, and empty record jackets leaned against the speakers. He put on a tape and began putting trash into a plastic bag. Bizzy was washing the mountain of dishes in the kitchen.

They could hear rumblings from the first floor bedroom, but only Troy and Bizzy were in the living room. Troy joined him on the couch, after Bizzy had taken a break from his kitchen detail.

"Hey Bizzy, let me ask you something."

"What, man?"

"You still go with Michelyn, right?"

"Yeah."

"You've been together for a while, haven't you?"

"Yeah."

"I'm not trying to be in your business, but--"

"Why do I cheat on her?"

"Yeah! I mean she's dope!"

"I know, I know. I love Michelyn, I'm gonna marry her. And I don't mean to disrespect her, that's why I keep my shit undercover."

"Undercover? Everybody in the house knows!"

"That's true, but they know I'd cover for them if they were in the same position. Look man, I'm not saying it's right. Most times, I just can't help myself. Like now, she's not around, you know what I'm saying? Next week it'll be a different story. But when she isn't here, there's certain girls I got to hit."

Troy nodded, but Bizzy could tell he wasn't really accepting his answer.

"Remember Troy, I love her. I know that's you and Ill's big sister and all, but that's my girl. I would never want to hurt her. Remember that."

"Yeah, right."

It wasn't hard for Troy to take Michelyn's side in the face of his budding friendship with Bizzy. She had meant so much to him and Ill Will as freshmen. Wasn't he obligated in some way to tell her? Did she already know? And what about her upperclassmen friends? Did they have the same dilemma, or did they have something against Michelyn? *Nah*, he thought. Everybody loved her. She was sweet, warm, funny, smart, and she had the body of a goddess. Bizzy was stupid for not seeing that and giving up the girls on the side.

Troy sat at a desk in Copy Services, reviewing his Calculus exam. His long hours of studying had earned him a "C"plus, yet he was encouraged because he'd only been one correct answer short of a 'B.' Angel sat across from him, but he had become accustomed to blocking her out of his mind. He wondered why she still worked there, but asking her was out of the question; he supposed it was a front of some kind. Since he didn't have that many shifts, he hardly saw her. On this day he would pretend she wasn't there, staying focused on the math problems that he'd gotten wrong. Still, he caught her staring at him, then looking away and rolling her eyes. A couple of guys who Troy didn't recognize rang the bell at the counter.

"Can I help you?" Troy asked, used to Angel's refusal to help when he was there.

"No, but she can." Angel turned and looked, and Troy saw her face light up the way it used to when she saw him.

"Oh, Shamel, Brett! Hi, honey!"

She got up quickly to greet her friends at the counter.

"Hold on, I can't talk in here," she said, looking at Troy. "Let's go into the lobby."

Without a word to her co-worker, she excused herself to join her friends. Troy sighed and watched her leave. It was moments like those that made it impossible to pretend he was totally over her. His popularity and his ability to win other girls was comforting, but still not enough to erase his feelings for her. He knew everybody had one person that they never fully got over, but he thought his had been Mimi, and she was dead.

Troy's daydreaming was disturbed by another ring of the bell. It was Ill Will was at the counter with two younger boys from Upward Bound.

"Hey, uh, Willard!" Troy was so happy for the distraction, he almost forgot to address Ill Will by his name in front of his charges.

"Hey, homey. I was just giving the boys here a tour of the library, someplace where they can do some work. Fellas, you know Troy?"

"S'up, fellas."

"What's up, Troy," said the first one. "You the DJ, right?"

"Yes, he's a DJ," Ill Will told them impatiently. "You two clowns wait for me outside, I'll be right there."

The two boys left with no resistance.

"Anyway, I see your girl's outside with a couple of her boytoys."

"That's her business."

"Of course. You know when Michelyn's coming back?"

"Bizzy says sometime next week."

"It might be sooner than that, according to Latanya."

"She's in the crib all the time, you should come through!"

"Nah. Too busy working. Besides, believe it or not, I'm trying to cut down on the drinking. Yvonne wants me to. She says hanging around Nevins won't help."

"She could be right," Troy admitted.

"Yeah, so you'll have to come back by Xavier."

"What?"

"You know, like last weekend. Bob's got something special planned."

"Yeah, I'll think about it. You heard from your other boy?"

"Who, Carl? Yeah, he's up in Boston, chilling."

Troy nodded. He longed for Ill Will to say something about Randy.

"All right dude, I'll be around. If you see Michelyn before me, tell her I said hey. 4-H."

"4-H, most definitely." The two friends slapped hands, and Ill Will left to join his two students. Damn! Why did he smoke with Ill Will and his friend? At first he figured it was okay because Ill Will wasn't drinking. But now, if Troy really wanted to encourage his friend to stop any of his vices, he wouldn't have a leg to stand on.

*   *   *   *

Today his mother was coming to visit, and she was bringing his grandmother with her. Troy figured as long as all the liquor bottles were cleared out, he'd be okay. He had warned his housemates of the impending visit, but to no avail. It wasn't their problem. Troy found himself again cleaning up after his housemates. Most nights he was with Ali in the library, hammering away at his Calculus, while the rest of the Nevins 16 residents ran a nightclub out of the apartment. On one occasion Troy had convinced Shannon, a girl from Howard he'd met in April, to come by, and she had enjoyed herself, but it would take a few more visits to get her upstairs, and he didn't have the time. The intensive Calculus course would be over in a week. Afterwards he'd get to her and the other girls he'd met.

When he heard the knock on the door, Troy was still trying to get rid of the beer bottles. Now he would have to hide them in the kitchen and hope they wouldn't be seen. He could deal with his mother seeing them, but if his grandmother saw any, he would have grief until he graduated. He opened the door to greet them.

"Hi!"

"Hi, Mom. Hi, Grandma!"

Troy hugged them both. They came in, and immediately began a survey of Troy's summer home.

"Did you find the building okay?"

"Mm-hm, Travis gave me great directions."

Figures, he thought. "Grandma, it's so good to see you! How you doing?"

"Oh, fine and you? Boy, look at this place. Janice, do you see?"

Troy's grandmother was all smiles. All of 4'5", and in her seventies, she had more energy than the two of them.

"Yes, Ma," Troy's mother told her. "Troy, would you like to give us the tour?"

"Oh, sure, sure. Everybody's either at work or in class, but they'll be coming in soon." Troy led them upstairs, away from the kitchen. "Mom, you want something to drink or something? Grandma?"

"No, thank you dear," his grandmother said. "Just take us up to your room."

Both Troy's mother and his grandmother were impressed with the apartment. His mother was careful to respect the privacy of the other residents, but his grandmother poked around at everything she saw.

Bizzy's side of the room was messy, a marked contrast from Troy's side, where the bed was made and the books on the desk were in order. Troy's grandmother proceeded to make up Bizzy's bed.

"Grandma! Leave that! That's not mine!"

"Oh, don't worry. I'm sure he won't mind."

Troy moved to stop her, but his mother held his arm. "Troy, leave her be. It's just her way of making herself at home."

"What's the boy's name?" his grandmother asked.

"Bizzy, Bizzy Hendricks."

"Brian, huh? I see. What is he, a white boy?"

Troy's mother laughed. "Troy's friends have all kinds of names, Ma. He had another roommate named Ill Will."

"Oh, for heaven's sake. That's ridiculous."

Troy took a seat next to his mother, powerless to stop his grandmother from cleaning.

"So what's new in New York?"

"New York is New York. I still miss Maryland, but we do what we must."

"Hmph. How's Uncle Tom?"

"Travis is fine, Troy. And don't call him that."

"Whatever."

"When are you going to call your father?"

"What, has he been checking up on me again?"

"He says he doesn't even have your number."

"I was getting to that."

"Troy, he's your father. I know he's made some mistakes, but he wants what's best for you, just like I do."

"I know Mom, but he doesn't know me. I mean I try, I go out to Jersey, and it's cool, but, the things he says...it's like just because he's my dad, I have to take it? I'm just not about that, I'm sorry."

Troy's mother maintained her patience.

"Look, I don't know what happened, and how he deals with you is something the two of you are going to have to work out. But he's doing his best. It would be a lot tougher on you if not for him, you know that. I can't afford these summer classes."

"I got a scholarship."

"What about for the rest of the summer? Hm? You think about it the next time you come up to visit. You really hurt him when you didn't go and see him."

They both watched Troy's grandmother tidy up the rest of the room. Troy didn't respond, instead he let his mother's words sink in.

"Ma," she called, "that's enough. Let's go downstairs. We'll take Troy to lunch. Come on, Troy."

As Troy and his mother stood up, Bizzy appeared in the doorway. He was shocked to find his side of the room spotless.

"Grandma, this is Brian, my roommate. Brian, that's my grandmother."

"Nice to meet you, ma'am," he said, embarrassed. "You know, you didn't have to do that!"

"Oh, that's all right," Troy's grandmother said, smiling. "Everybody needs a little help sometimes. Troy?"

"Yes, Grandma?"

"Who's been drinking beer in here? I saw those bottles downstairs."

*   *   *   *

Tired of his mother's constant nagging, Troy finally broke down and called his father.

"David Harris's office."

"Hi, this is Troy."

"Hello, Troy. Hold on."

"If he's busy, I can call back."

"No, no, just hold on."

Troy immediately wished he hadn't called. He would wait a few more seconds, then hang up.

"Troy?"

"Hi Dad."

"Why if it isn't my son! To what do I owe this honor?"

"Okay. I got my grades back. Three 'B's, a 'B'+ and a 'C'."

"That's not bad. What did you get the 'C' in?"

"Accounting. I know you're disappointed."

"No, Troy, I'm not. You tried, and you're learning. I just want to make it easier for you. Remember, I've got some experience in that area. I want you to learn from my mistakes."

"Yeah, well, I'm not a snot-nosed kid."

"I know you're not. I'm sorry about that, okay?"

Silence.

"Okay? Troy?"

"I just called to see how you were doing. Tell Susan I said hi. My number is 944-4644. Bye."

Troy knew his father was trying, but he still wasn't completely comfortable talking to him. At least his mother couldn't nag him anymore. As he was about to go downstairs, he paused. He heard yelling and it sounded like Michelyn. Troy had never heard Michelyn raise her voice before. The front door slammed. Whatever was going on was serious.

Troy found Bizzy sitting alone on the couch. The TV was on but he stared blankly at the screen.

"What happened?"

"I don't know."

"Was that Michelyn?"

"Yeah, it was."

Troy left the apartment and caught up with Michelyn downstairs, running away in tears.

"Michelyn! Michelyn, wait! What's wrong?"

She kept running, until Troy got in front of her. She fought to get away from him.

"Troy, leave me alone! He probably sent you down here! Oh my God, I don't believe it!"

"What?"

"Oh, please! You know what!"

"Come sit over here for a second. Just for a second, okay?"

Troy sat with his big sister on the staircase leading up to Village B, another apartment complex outside the Healy Gates.

"I always suspected that Brian cheated," she said, whimpering. "But to do it while I'm here? It's so insulting. And everybody knew! Do you know a girl came over to see him?"

"Who?"

"Some heifer. Latanya might know her, I don't know. Brian said that you weren't here and that she should come back later. She went off and cussed everybody out. He couldn't deny it after that."

Troy empathized with her; it had to happen sometime. The black community was so small at Georgetown, particularly during the summer, that it was tough to keep one's business a secret. He held on to Michelyn, earnestly trying to comfort her.

"Troy, have you ever been in love? Do you know what it feels like to be humiliated like this?"

He knew all too well. "Remember when I used to talk to you about Angel?"

Michelyn wiped her tears. "I didn't know it was like this. The way she talked, I thought she really loved you."

"Maybe she did," Troy replied solemnly. "Didn't make any difference though."

Troy walked Michelyn to Latanya's dorm, then returned to Nevins. Bizzy was still on the couch. He looked up at his younger roommate, who was clearly disgusted. Troy climbed back up the staircase and shut the bedroom door without a word.

Twenty-Three

Dear Randy,

I'm glad things are going well for you over in France. Things are cool here — it's wild as ever. This Nevins crib is the shit! And it's like you get ass just because you live here. Remember that girl Shannon from Howard? I hit it…Bizzy Hendricks is my roommate. Michelyn came to visit him and caught him cheating. It's fucked up. Darnell lives here too, but he's not the same Darnell we knew last year. He's out there! Can't forget Ill (even though you may not want to hear it). He's doing okay as a counselor, and Yvonne's here, too. He still gets fucked up on the weekends, but during the week he doesn't drink as much. Being around those kids is good for him. My grades only went up a little, and Calculus is kicking my ass, but I'll come through. This is the last week of class. Taking Micro and Macro too, to get 'em out the way. Yvonne won't tell me shit about Phyllis. I know she's up to something, but we'll be ready for her. People are still asking about Farrakhan. It looks like we'll have a lot of support this fall. Anyway, I gotta jet. Stay up, and I hope you've found a barber by now.

As-Salaam Alaikum
Troy Harris (a.k.a. DJ Troy)

After reading the letter a final time, Troy sealed the envelope and mailed it. Relieved that he was done with class for the day and he didn't have to work, he headed back to Nevins. In the courtyard square, Ill Will, Yvonne and Bob were outside in the courtyard square with nearly a dozen of their students. He hoped Cathy wouldn't be among them, but there she was, so there would be no afternoon frolicking upstairs. He found no one in the apartment. He had a few people waiting for mix tapes and he still had some records to buy, so he decided to walk down to Wisconsin Avenue.

Thankful for the air conditioning in the record store, Troy browsed longer than usual. He recalled his excitement over winning the DJ gig at the University Café last year. Hopefully he wouldn't have to give it up, but he didn't know if he could spin records each week while trying to improve his grades.

Bizzy was waiting for Troy in the living room when he returned.

"I need to see you, man."

"What's going on?" Troy looked around. Darnell and Ali pretended to mind their own business.

"Why didn't you tell me Synette was coming over that day?"

"What, the day Michelyn was here? How the fuck was I supposed to know?"

"That's not what Synette said," Bizzy insisted, pointing his finger in Troy's face. "She said you were on the phone, and you knew she was here."

"That's bullshit!"

"You knew something, man! And you didn't come downstairs? I told Synette you weren't around, all you had to do was come downstairs and I would've had a chance."

"I was on the phone, nigga." Troy was fuming. "Who do think you're talking to?"

"Michelyn's little brother, that's who! I know you told her something." Bizzy was preparing to square off. Troy put his records down where they wouldn't be crushed. If Bizzy wanted a fight, he was going to get one.

"All I told her was that it would be all right, but the shit ain't my fault! That other bitch had no business coming over here! You gotta handle that, don't be jumping in my face."

"Why not," Bizzy asked. "What are you going to do?"

Before Troy could react, Darnell and Ali came between them, Darnell holding Troy, Ali holding Bizzy.

"Calm down, calm down," Darnell ordered. "It's over."

"Nah man," Bizzy persisted.

"Let him go!" Troy shouted. "I'll bust his ass! Let him go!"

"Come on!" Bizzy shot back.

"Relax Bizzy," Darnell barked. "The damage is done. I don't know what the fuck you're talking about. Michelyn was here, she saw Synette, you got caught. That's it. You need to think about how to get her back."

"That's right!" Troy shouted.

Darnell held up his hand, indicating that enough had been said.

"The rest of us have a party to plan. Let's do this, Ali."

"What party?" Troy guessed that as DJ for the party, he was the last to know. Apparently, this wouldn't be another one of their regular soirees.

"Lingerie party," Darnell said. "But fuck that. Bizzy, Troy, this shit is over. Won't be no beef in this house. I'll kick both your asses."

"Yeah, right," Bizzy said sarcastically.

"Whatever," Troy retorted. He wanted to go upstairs, but he stood his ground, staying in the living room with everyone else.

"What records you bought?" Darnell asked, changing the subject.

"Just-Ice, Teena Marie, some other shit. Put one on."

"That's a good idea." Normally, Troy would never have encouraged one of his housemates to DJ, but he made an exception and let Darnell play the record. Bizzy walked up the stairs full of attitude.

"Do you believe the nigga stepped to me like that?" Troy told Ill Will the next day. "I woulda fucked him up, yo. Niggas think they can step to you 'cause they older, but he was gonna get fucked up."

Ill Will laughed. "Sounds like it would have been a good one. If you ask me, he deserves it. What are you thinking if you fuck around on Michelyn? I mean, shit!"

"I know."

"She's really fucked up over this, you know."

"Yeah, I saw her after it happened. But she always goes back to him."

"I don't think she will this time. I mean, don't say anything, but she told Latanya she's through with him."

"I wouldn't be surprised."

Now Troy felt the same tension in Nevins 16 that he had with Angel at Copy Services. Since he and Bizzy weren't on friendly terms, Troy stayed out of the apartment most of the time. Most of his afternoons were spent with Ali doing Calculus. As was the case with Accounting, Troy had to work every day just to keep up, but he thought he was seeing some light at the end of the tunnel. Although the class was three hours long and a semester's worth of work was crammed into three weeks, Troy had somehow been able to keep up with the workload in the class. He didn't know if it was because he didn't have other classes to contend with, or if he was just motivated by his already dismal grades. Whatever the case, he certainly wasn't socializing any less than before. In fact, the upperclassmen in Nevins had shown him how to party on an entirely new level.

*   *   *   *

Angel was at the bus stop on N Street, a few blocks from Georgetown's front gates. Troy was on his way back to Nevins from Wisconsin Avenue and he saw her, as he invariably did whenever it was most inconvenient and uncomfortable for him. She looked away, as was her custom now. For some reason, this time Troy felt compelled to address her. He cornered her in the bus stop shelter before she could get away.

"Look, you can keep doing this all you want," he told her, "but you're still going to be seeing me. We can try to be civil, at least. I think this shit is stupid, regardless of what happened. Don't you?"

She didn't reply.

"Oh, it's like that? Forget it then." Troy walked off hastily. He deduced that this was what having an ex-girlfriend was all about.

"Troy!"

He turned around to answer her call. He was in the middle of the street, and a speeding car almost ran him over. Angel watched him jump when the car's horn sounded. It felt like an eternity since her smile been directed toward him.

"You're right. You were right."

He stood in front of her, unable to contain his own smile. Soon they were both grinning openly. Then Troy remembered how fine she was, dressed in a yellow tank top and white mini-skirt, both of which accented the curves he used to know. He moved closer, but she kept him at arm's length.

"Please. You're not all that."

He turned and walked away with what little was left of his ego. Still, after he got around the corner, he laughed to himself. She had gotten the best of him, but Troy knew she was only hiding how much he had hurt her. He had touched her heart, too.

Troy returned to find Darnell and Bizzy in the living room. Bizzy sat on the couch with a steno pad, Darnell stood behind the turntables. Troy was miffed to see Darnell playing his records, but he was even more curious about the serious looks on the brothers' faces.

"Let's go over the liquor again." Darnell said.

"Word," said Bizzy.

"We got the 151."

"Check."

"We got the Absolut."

"Check."

"We got the yak."

"What?" Troy asked.

"Cognac fool," Bizzy quipped.

"We got the Peach Schnapps," Darnell continued.

"Roger that," said Bizzy, checking the steno pad.

"Everclear?"

"Yup, for the punch."

"After that we have the usual."

"Frozen drinks, sangria and brew."

"That's going to cost some dough," Troy observed.

"Don't worry," Bizzy told him. "We all kick in a little somethin' and it's covered."

"Y'all ain't bullshittin," Troy noted.

"No sir," Darnell said. "But really, that's our only expense. The food and supplies'll be on Travis."

"Travis?" Troy asked. "How you figure that?"

"One of MA's expense accounts. One of the perks of the job."

Troy was silent, but his face gave away his concern.

"It's no problem, black," Darnell assured him. "Nothing's gonna happen. We've done it before, we'll do it again." The upperclassmen cracked up laughing. "Hey Bizzy, remember, the girls have to wear lingerie to get in. None of that bullshit. And don't be bringing them ugly hoes in here like you always do!"

"Nigga please," Bizzy retorted. "I'll leave your mother at home."

Troy laughed along with the upperclassmen, but he was in awe of what he was hearing. They were serious. He admired their vision of an apartment full of drunken, scantily clad girls, but what made them think they could pull it off? Then again, Troy found no reason why they couldn't. The apartment was already party central, and each resident was seeing his share of action with the ladies. Might as well make it official.

*   *   *   *

Hours of reworking problems with Ali, re-reading chapter after chapter, and several one-on-one meetings with Professor Bradley had come down to this moment. Troy meticulously worked through his final Calculus exam, treating it as the serious matter that it was. He re-checked each answer, and he was pleased to find that his answers made sense, at least to him. He practically sprinted out of the classroom he was so happy to be done. His Microeconomics course didn't start for another week. Troy smiled, seeing Ali ahead of him.

"My man! You going back to the crib?"

Ali turned around and nodded, stopping to wait for Troy. "I know you're glad that's over."

"Hell yeah! Ain't you?"

"Oh, for sure. And the party's tomorrow, too? Sheeeeit!"

Troy laughed. "It sure is. Them fools are probably in there now cleaning up."

"I know you're gonna be rocking the beats, right?"

"Yeah, man."

"I wish I could spin like you. I mean I used to fuck around a little, but you're nice!"

"Thanks, but I'd rather be good in math."

Ali looked perplexed, the remark having caught him off guard.

"At least a brother won't have to study for a minute."

"Word!"

The living room was empty except for Troy's huge speakers blasting his new Teena Marie album from the far corner of the room. *Why do they always leave my shit on?* he thought. Ali went to his room and Troy went upstairs, hoping to find the culprit who had left his stereo unattended. In his room he found Bizzy, sitting at the foot of his bed, his head in his hands. Maintaining their feud, Troy didn't speak. To his surprise, his roommate took the initiative.

"Troy."

Silence.

"Look, forget all those things I said. I was wrong."

Because Bizzy was hoarse and his voice was barely audible, Troy felt reluctant sympathy, but suppressed it.

"Don't worry about it."

"Nah man, for real. The truth is, I've lost her and it's nobody's fault," he sniffled, "nobody's fault but mine."

Troy sat down and took a long hard look at the upperclassman who, he noticed, could no longer keep from crying. Troy looked to Bizzy's side of the room in hopes of finding something to say, but the Kappa plaques and canes offered nothing.

"Bizzy...Brian, look. You're gonna have to deal with this thing somehow."

"I know, I know," he sniffled, "but the shit just hit me today. I mean, she's serious this time! What the fuck? I don't know what I'ma do man, damn!"

"Is she coming to the party?"

"Of course she is, everybody is."

"Then you'll have your chance tomorrow. Whatever you have to do to get back with her, do that shit."

"I don't even care about this party, man." Bizzy was calming down. "But she'll be up in here in her drawers, trying to get back at me and shit!"

"You just have to handle that," Troy said matter-of-factly.

"Troy?"

"Yeah, man?"

"Do you think she still loves me? Y'all are tight, you can tell me. You think I got a shot?"

"Yeah," Troy answered. "Yeah, you do." His patience was gone, but somehow he still couldn't lie to Bizzy. "I'm downstairs, dude."

"Alright man. You know it's like they say, sometimes you never know what you got until it's gone."

"Word up."

Bizzy had put him in a melancholy mood. He had almost forgotten that he had finished Calculus, and that he owed himself some relaxation. Teena Marie was still playing, and he replaced it with a more festive rap selection. Troy didn't leave the turntables for the rest of the day.

The next morning, Darnell and Troy were returning from the supermarket when they ran into Ill Will on M Street.

"Here, let me help you with these bags," he offered.

"Good looking out," Darnell said.

"This is a lot of shit! I know y'all ain't pay for all these groceries. Who's got the hookup?"

"My cousin works at Safeway," Darnell answered while looking at Troy sternly to keep him silent.

"I hear that. You know I didn't know about this lingerie thing for a minute."

"Troy didn't tell you?"

"Nah."

"'Cause you might come in there with one of those underage kids," Troy replied.

"Yeah, right. Some of 'em probably been in there already, knowing you clowns." Darnell laughed as Troy kept quiet, silenced by Ill Will's observation.

"I had to go out and get some new drawers just for the occasion!"

*   *   *   *

By 10:00, the apartment was ready. Each room was immaculate, accented with blue light bulbs in the lamps and an occasional purple balloon floating high above against the ceiling. Bizzy had his special "Eucalyptus Blossom" incense lit in the living room. The kitchen had enough liquor to stock a bar, and Darnell was preparing grain punch and storing it in a giant trash can lined with a Hefty bag. Troy had made a new slow jam tape, and each housemate had a copy for his respective bedroom. All the boys had on their best sleepwear — silk robes, pajamas and boxers. Troy had even snuck out to Victoria's Secret and purchased a pair of silver paisley print silk boxers. Darnell had bought condoms for everyone. Troy was uncomfortable about Darnell putting them on a Minority Affairs purchase order, but he Troy him it was fine — as Minority Affairs was supposed to support students in every facet of their lives. Troy's turntable console was backed into a corner and the couch, chairs, table and TV were all pulled back toward the kitchen. He had also made extra party tapes so he too could enjoy the party and not have to spin records all night. Troy had the music turned up so loud, only Bizzy, who was by the door, could hear the knocking.

"Aw, shit! Toni and Lisa," Bizzy was greeted with a hug from each of the guests. "Let me take those robes."

"Oh, Brian. Already?"

"See, y'all thought we was bullshittin'. Yes Toni, already." Toni and Lisa removed their robes to reveal themselves. Both of them were gorgeous and were now wearing only camisoles, panties and heels. Toni was practically coming out of hers.

"Jesus, Mary and Joseph! Y'all go on and make yourselves comfortable. I know y'all remember Darnell, right? And that's DJ Troy over there spinning."

The variety of undergarments worn by the ladies kept everyone talking and the brothers smiling. There were tie-dyed T-shirts with panties, modest robes with nothing underneath, tight shorts and silk pajamas. Troy recognized some of the girls from his visit to Victoria's Secret. Shannon from Howard hadn't shown up yet, but he recognized others from the Howard clique she ran with. Just as the residents had planned, there was nearly a three-to-one ratio of women to men, and outside of a few other guys from Georgetown, not many guys had been invited. Troy kept the party going with his latest blend of rap and R&B hits. Darnell handled the drinks, and made sure all the ladies had their glasses filled. Troy couldn't resist joining the party, and replaced himself on the turntables with recorded music. He greeted the women he knew as well as those he didn't know, hugging them and being as flirtatious as his older housemates.

"Troy! Lord, look at those silk boxers, and the bird legs sticking out of them," Latanya teased her young friend, no longer the wet-behind-the-ears freshman.

"What's up girl. I see you're looking tight yourself."

"Thank you. You guys got anything to drink besides this punch? It's too strong."

"That's probably the weakest thing in here. C'mon, I'll find you something." Troy quickly led Latanya through the crowd to the kitchen. He didn't want to spend too much time with her; she was keeping him from other girls with whom he could score.

"Michelyn here?"

"Yeah, she's in here somewhere."

Troy fixed a drink for Latanya and for himself. Moments later, Troy was back in the living room amid the almost deafening music, dancing with a sexy girl, Patrice, who was dressed in a T-shirt. He'd had his eye on her earlier. His tape included an old tunes remix; surefire club hits like Parliament's "Knee Deep" and Cheryl Lynn's "Encore." Each song energized the party, and Troy received handslaps and points of approval from Wendell, Bizzy, Darnell, and other guys in the crowd. For a few seconds, the floor shook from everyone jumping up and down. Across the room, Ill Will and Yvonne were dancing, along with Bob and one of the baddest looking white girls Troy had ever seen, Caucasian but with African hips and thighs.

Troy returned to the turntables for an hour or so, then played another extended tape so he could return to a girl he had his eye on, Patrice. The apartment was jam-packed, a combination of Victoria's Secret, Frederick's of Hollywood, a liquor store and a nightclub all rolled into one. Some of the ladies were now allowing Darnell to photograph them in their underwear; Troy was convinced that many of them would live to regret it. He was drinking hard liquor, but he tried to stay somewhat coherent; otherwise he couldn't watch out for Ill Will or his stereo equipment. Ill Will had been there for a while; when he could no longer find him in the crowd, he assumed he had gone off somewhere, probably with Yvonne and Bob. Michelyn was in the crowd dancing like a woman possessed. She had arrived to the howls of almost every guy by the door and rendered them all speechless with the peach silk teddy she wore; the contrast of her dark complexion with the peach silk was unforgettable. She was dancing with a guy Troy didn't recognize. Where the hell was Bizzy? He had to be stupid to mess that up. Someone squeezed Troy's hand.

"Hey, sexy," Patrice pursed her lips just inches from his ear. "We're going to talk later, right?"

"Oh, for sure," he answered with a smirk. What a party!

For a moment Troy was distracted by another rousing scream from the brothers at the door. Although he knew the screams were warranted, he wasn't as excited this time. Angel was the latest guest, dressed in high heels, a black bra, panties, stockings with garters, covered only with a see-through black housecoat. Troy felt slightly violated. What had once been his to enjoy privately was now on public display, and the guys around her were losing their minds. "Goddamn!" "You see her?" "P-H-A-T! Fatter than a Louisiana swamp possum!" He wanted to go over and say something, but if he did, she would know she'd been successful, showing up in his favorite underwear set just to get under his skin. Besides, Patrice was no slouch.

"Listen," he whispered to her. "Just let me check things out for a minute, then we'll go somewhere, okay?"

"I'll be waiting."

Troy sent Patrice to the turntable area to wait for him. *Shit!* he thought. *Bizzy better not be upstairs.* They had agreed that he would ask to stay with Michelyn that night, but that might not happen. He made his final walkthrough, seeing who was where and doing what. One by one, the brothers in the apartment had started to vanish, leaving for the bedrooms, or leaving the party altogether with women. Troy put on his slow tape. Bizzy were in their first floor bedroom playing strip spades with a couple of girls who could have been models. Troy stood at the door in awe.

"Close the door, fool!" Ali shouted.

Hmph, Troy thought. *Brother knows a little more than some math.* Ill Will was nowhere to be found, and Troy was finding it hard to concentrate, so he decided it was time to get back to Patrice. She had remained at the turntables, right where he had sent her.

"Let's go."

He took her up to his room, shut the door behind him, and pulled her toward him, kissing her as she pressed him against the door. Troy could hear Al B. Sure!'s "Nite and Day" on Darnell's slow tape in the next room. He was lightheaded, but Patrice's tongue at the back of his throat kept him alert. Both his hands rubbed the back of her panties. Troy was in heaven, and he ignored the knock on the door while leading Patrice to his bed. *Fuck it,* he thought. *It's locked.*

"Who is that?"

"I don't know," he whispered, lifting her T-shirt over her. He paused at the sight of Patrice's perfect, naked body. "Great day in the morning," he mumbled.

The knock persisted.

"Why don't you see who it is," Patrice said, stopping Troy's hands at her underwear.

"It don't matter, my roommate's gone."

"Brian!" It was Michelyn.

"See?" Troy told Patrice between kisses. "He ain't here."

Just then, a high-pitched scream came from the other side of the door.

The scream was enough to sober Troy a little. *What the fuck?* he thought. He was halfway out of his silk boxers, and his prize was literally right in front of him. But if Michelyn was that distressed, sexing Patrice would have to wait, at least temporarily.

"Sweetie, that's my man's girlfriend. She's also my big sister. Just let me see what's wrong, I'll be right back."

"Okay," she told him, licking his ear. "See what's wrong."

Troy got up and pulled his boxers back on. He was ready to punch Michelyn square in the face. Unlocking the door, he thought she had better have a good reason for 'cock-blocking' him.

"Michelyn, what the fuck is wrong?" he asked, outside in the hallway.

"Oh Troy, I'm sorry. I didn't know you had company."

"You didn't know? Nobody answered, the door was locked, fuck you mean you didn't know? What is it?" Troy was uncontrollably annoyed.

"I was just, I was just looking for Brian."

"Brian isn't here. I thought he was with you!"

"He was," she whimpered, "but he left. We were going back to my room after the party. He told me to wait for him downstairs by the elevator. When he came back, he saw a guy trying to talk to me outside, and he got mad."

"Were you talking to him?"

"No! I told him I was waiting for someone."

"Keep your voice down," he whispered.

"Sorry. I told him I was waiting for someone, but he had seen me in the party. I guess he thought he had a chance, but I'm not like that Troy. The only reason I'm out here half-naked is because Darnell and Latanya and all of them begged me to come. Anyway, Brian saw the whole thing and got mad. And I haven't seen him since!" Her eyes were bloodshot, but Michelyn wasn't a drinker. She had been crying for some time.

"Come on," Troy told her. "Let's just go and sit for a while."

Troy led her down the stairs, but Michelyn burst into tears after a couple of steps. "It's alright, it's alright," he consoled her. "We can stay right here." He sat his big sister down, and she proceeded to cry on his shoulder. Troy's mind raced back to voluptuous Patrice, who was still upstairs in his bed. He shook his head, thinking to himself, *this good guy shit sucks.*

Troy still found himself on the steps with Michelyn when the first rays of sun began to pierce the living room below. Darnell's bedroom tape had stopped, but he could hear his own slow jams playing downstairs on the auto reverse, continuous playing tape deck. He also heard faint snoring in the distance. Was it morning already? Had he been there that long? He turned to Michelyn, who was now resting quietly in his arms.

She let him know that she was still awake by gently touching his chest, her head wiggling under his neck. Troy was also taking in her pleasant, feminine scent, and he found himself almost as aroused as he had been a few hours ago. He had never seen his big sister in this light before, but he couldn't help but love it. He held her tighter, and she responded with soft pecks on his chest and neck. That clinched his decision to take her upstairs. Bizzy had not proven himself worthy of her, or his own defense of her boyfriend. And hell, she knew who she was with, so it wouldn't be like he was taking advantage. Patrice was no doubt sleeping by now.

Silently he led Michelyn back upstairs. Her eyes were closed and she was dazed, but she didn't put up a fight when Troy kissed her on Bizzy's bed. Patrice was over in his bed, fast asleep. When Troy laid his sexy big sister down on the bed, her eyes opened, and she looked at him warmly.

"Troy. What are you doing?"

"What does it look like?" he retorted, his head bowed. Michelyn's legs, inside a pair of sheer stockings, forbid him to even blink.

She put her hand on his face. "Troy, I'm glad you were here for me, but this isn't right."

She smiled as she said it, leaving Troy a glimmer of hope. He was desperate for the right words, words that would keep her from backing out.

"I don't know what Bizzy was thinking. He's my man, but he's out of his mind. Nobody here even compares to you."

"You're drunk."

"But I'm not stupid."

He stared at her for a long time, and eventually, inch by inch, he closed the distance between them. The feel of her skin, her leg rubbing against his, was overwhelming. But after a few minutes and several long kisses, an emotionally drained Michelyn fell asleep. Troy squirmed out of his roommate's bed, not caring if he were to come in right then, and rejoined Patrice in his own. He thought about a shower to wash Michelyn's scent off, but if Patrice noticed, he could easily make up a lie. Besides, they had just met. Patrice rolled over and snuggled up next to Troy, who was content that his evening had been full.

Troy knew it was the next afternoon, but still it seemed like morning. The silence told him everyone was still asleep. Patrice slept on, and he decided to let her rest, although if he continued to stare at her nearly nude body, he would end up waking her, so he climbed out of bed. He found a note on his end table that read:

> *Dear Troy,*
> *Thanks for everything. I hope I wasn't too rough on you.*
>
> *Love,*
> *Michelyn*

He wasn't surprised to find Michelyn gone, but another figure was in the room, unconscious at the foot of Bizzy's bed, by the door. It was Bizzy himself, and a small orange stain was under him on the carpet, its sour stench catching Troy off guard. He shook his head. Bizzy was sleeping in his own vomit.

"Come on Biz," he coached, helping him to stand. "Get up. Let's get you in the bathroom." Bizzy was a zombie, oblivious to Troy's commands. Troy got him to the bathroom, took his T-shirt off and slumped him over the bathtub.

"Biz, wake up!" he shouted, splashing water on his face. "Come on, now!"

Bizzy finally opened his eyes, and with Troy's assistance, began to clean himself. When his roommate began to come around, Troy stepped back and kept close watch from the bathroom doorway. He reread Michelyn's note, ignoring the running water. Within minutes, Bizzy was nearly back to his old self.

"Who's the note from?" he asked.

"Nobody. Come on, you've got some serious rug cleaning to do."

When Troy came downstairs he knew he was going to see a mess, but he still was shocked by its magnitude. Nevins 16 was a textbook example of the absolute destruction of an apartment; beer bottles and assorted trash was everywhere, many of the blinds on the windows were crushed, and strangers slept on makeshift beds from scattered couch parts all over the floor. When he looked down, Troy could hardly see the floor for all the clothes and drunk people that covered it. Some ladies had been separated from their lingerie. The windows were open and the air conditioning was on, but the funk of a room full of bodies remained. The kitchen had also been hit with a barrage of beer bottles, cans, and empty containers of food. The trash can that held the punch was toppled over, and a giant punch stain was dried up on the floor. Dishes were piled in the sink a foot above the counter, and a group of flies was circling above the faucet. Only the kitchen table, the TV and Troy's turntables were upright.

Troy made his way over to his turntables, clueless where to begin to clean up. Might as well change the slow tape. Troy put the radio on and went back to the kitchen. The table had a bunch of white residue all over it that looked like flour. Troy's eyes darted from the kitchen counter back to the table across the room. Who the hell was baking last night? He filled the sink with water and squeezed *Palmolive* over the monstrous load of dishes. He started to wash a few, but curiosity brought him back over to the table. He feared the worst for a second, then dismissed the thought. It couldn't be. Troy touched the table and saw the white residue on his finger. He touched the table again with his finger, and sniffed his finger as hard as he could. His nostrils flared, and he felt a sting inside his head. "Fuck," he said to himself. He remembered that the police had been downstairs last night, and now there was cocaine on the table. Anything could have happened. To make matters worse, by his foot under the table he saw Ill Will's Phillies cap. The cap showed no traces of coke, but since the two of them had been there for the summer, Ill Will had never been far from his cap, a gift to himself purchased with his first Upward Bound paycheck.

Bizzy and Darnell came downstairs. Darnell laughed at the mess. "Oh shit! Will you look at this?"

"Hey y'all, come over here."

"What's up?"

"Just come here!"

"Okay, shit! Don't get your drawers bunched up!" Bizzy laughed. When they made their way over and Troy showed them the table, the smiles faded from each of their faces.

"Yo, we got to get this shit out of here," Bizzy noted.

"No shit! Darnell, you know anybody who--"

"Hell no! Don't even. Let's start waking these motherfuckers up and getting them out of here."

"Yeah, maybe one of them knows something," Bizzy added. "Troy, why don't you go upstairs. I think your girl is getting ready to leave."

"Patrice! Shit, that's right." Troy quickly hopped over the bodies to get to the stairs. "Hey, call me if you find the niggas that had that shit."

"Will do," Bizzy assured him. Troy went upstairs and found Patrice, who was dressed in one of his T-shirts and a pair of his shorts.

"I hope you don't mind."

"Not at all."

They exchanged phone numbers. She agreed to get together with him next week. He got a kiss out of her before she left, but it wasn't nearly as strong as the ones he'd received last night.

The apartment was still a mess that night, though the brothers had begun to make a dent. Wendell and some of the other Kappas came by to help clean up. Troy couldn't get his mind off of the cocaine residue he'd seen and he was upset that they never found the idiot that had brought it in. Of the people they interrogated, none of them claimed to have any knowledge of it. Somebody rang the bell, and the brothers in the apartment, all on edge, looked up when it rang.

"I'll get it." Troy jumped up to get the door, praying it wasn't the police. He saw Ill Will through the peephole, looking as dejected as he had ever seen him.

"Ill! What's up?"

"Can I talk to you?"

"Yeah, come on in."

"Nah. Out here."

"Okay, hang on."

Troy closed the door behind him, and followed his friend down the hall. Ill Will stopped at the end of the corridor, a grave expression on his face.

"Ill, what is it? What's up?"

"They're kicking me out."

"Kicking you out? For what?"

"Simple Assualt and Sexual Misconduct."

Twenty-Four

Troy couldn't believe what he had just heard.

"What? Sexual Misconduct?"

"Sexual Misconduct and Simple Assault, those are the charges. Attempted rape is what it amounts to."

"Aw, no! Ill, you didn't!"

"No, but I can't say that."

"What the fuck are you talking about? You did or didn't!"

"They said I was in the bathroom with her, this counselor."

"Were you?"

"I don't remember. I was high."

Troy grimaced as if he'd been punched in the stomach. "Jesus Christ. Ill, there was cocaine in the party. Do you know anything about that?"

"I don't know."

"Your hat was under the table, Ill! That's where the shit was. Now I'm asking you for the last time. Do you know about it? Did you have something to do with that shit?"

Silence.

"I don't fucking believe you!"

Troy pushed him against the wall, smoldering with anger. He would do anything to get an answer out of him, but Ill Will said nothing.

"You motherfucker! We're fucked! Everybody in there is fucked now! Goddamn it!"

Ill Will took the punishment with a blank stare, tears running down his face. The two friends stayed in the hallway for fifteen minutes, one screaming, the other saying nothing. Troy finally pushed Ill Will away angrily and walked off in silence.

Epilogue

By Monday morning, the news of Ill Will's expulsion, and of the party, had spread all over campus. The Upward Bound student who accused Ill Will said he had attempted to rape her in the ladies room at Xavier. Her screams brought students and other counselors running in, where they found Ill Will in the stall with her. Having come from the lingerie party, he wore only a bathrobe with his lower extremities in plain view. The eyewitness accounts, coupled with his honest claim that he couldn't remember anything, gave Georgetown's adjudication board a strong case against him. Losing the counseling job and his dorm room was the least of his problems.

His prior offense all but insured Ill Will's expulsion. The adjudication board sought to set an example for incoming freshmen who tended to be reckless; many of them felt they could do no less with such serious charges before him. The incident hurt black students politically, because Travis Gordon had been one of Ill Will's references for the counseling job and his own credibility had already been called into question that spring semester. Travis could only answer questions posed by the adjudication board with Ill Will's file, which was like fighting fire with gasoline. Still, Travis Gordon went before the board, doing whatever he could to keep Ill Will out of jail. The questions led to an investigation of all related events, including, as Troy had feared, the party. It was soon discovered that Darnell had used a Minority Affairs expense account to purchase some of the refreshments for the party, which, of course cost him his job. Georgetown security was questioned about the incident, and after they affirmed that many non-Georgetown students had been in the apartment, police detectives were called in to inspect the apartment, where they found traces of cocaine on the table and marijuana elsewhere. Although Ill Will had not been on duty that night, the adjudication board felt he made the party accessible to the Upward Bound students, who were too young to drink. When the news of the alcohol and illegal substances got out, Travis had no choice but to take the keys to the apartment, leaving Bizzy, Darnell, Bizzy, Ali and Troy with no place to go.

Bizzy ended up staying with Wendell in a house not too far from campus. Ali, who had a spotless file, was in no way implicated and was placed in a dorm on the north side of campus. Bizzy replied "Darnell Washington" to almost every question he was asked, prompting a separate investigation that uncovered Darnell's previous actions at the Office of Minority Affairs. Very few of the MA mishaps with course registration and scholarship money could be linked directly to Darnell, but he was given a one semester suspension and academic probation for one year. Travis had fought for leniency for Darnell in exchange for Darnell's silence about him and his relationship with Troy's mother, knowledge of which would have raised ethical questions that would have placed his career at Georgetown in worse jeopardy. Darnell found an off-campus apartment with one Angel Davis. The two of them were soon brainstorming to come up with a new moneymaking scheme.

Troy's file had also been marred due to blasting his music after breaking up with Angel. It was also well-known that he was Ill Will's friend and he was an officer in the BSU. Since the adjudication board knew of his desire to be a DJ, they felt that he therefore had to have had a part in putting the party together. Troy hoped by telling Travis the truth about the party, he could help to spare Ill Will in some way. He couldn't, but he was allowed to stay in a Harbin dorm room, ironically, for his cooperation. Travis Gordon was assured by several Georgetown deans that Minority Affairs would never have access to another Nevins apartment, and any students associated with MA, especially City Scholars, would be carefully screened before being considered for any positions or programs that involved younger students. Eventually, the administrator was also advised to seek employment elsewhere. His plea for Darnell's silence about Janice Harris had been for nothing.

Troy had an opportunity to reflect on the whole incident after the first few days of mind-blowing repercussions. He wrote Randy a long letter about it. Sitting in his Harbin room, empty except for his stereo equipment and records, he wondered how Randy would react to the fiasco.

Two weeks later, Ill Will found Troy in his room.

"What's up, Troy?"

"Hey."

"Just passing through. How's that Microeconomics coming?"

"So far, so good. I got a 'B' in Calculus, too."

"Cool! Pops must have been happy about that."

"Yeah, we've been talking a lot lately. What's with you, you still holed up at Yvonne's?"

"Yup, but the program'll be over soon. Then I'm rolling. 'Course my court date is next month, too."

"What are you going to do?"

"I don't know. If I want to go to another school I gotta get in AA."

"That's good."

"Yeah, but I'm not staying at home, which means I'll have to get a job, and try to save some money for wherever I go. Not much chance of coming back here, that's for sure."

Troy wanted to be sympathetic, but he had been so hurt by everything that had happened that he hardly knew how to interact with his friend.

"Something good did happen, though."

"What's that?"

"Here, check it out." Ill Will pulled a letter out from his pocket and handed it to Troy. It read:

To The Members Of The Adjudication Board:

Thank you for allowing me the opportunity to write to you to address this matter. It is with great regret and sadness that I make this appeal to you, but it is also with the hope that you have some compassion, as well as a sense of what is right and just. I realize that I cannot defend the behavior of Willard Dorsey, but I can speak from the perspective of someone who has witnessed both his positive and negative sides. I concede that Willard has a drinking problem, and it would serve him well to check into a program that will rehabilitate him. As a person who has spent a substantial amount of time with Willard, I admit that this is no news to me. Myself and others encouraged Willard to seek help when we became concerned that he might have a problem. However, as his friends we also pledged to support him along the way, and perhaps we have not done that. Although I am not on campus right now, I take full responsibility for my failure in that regard and I'm sure his other friends will do the same. Since hearing about what happened, I have had extensive correspondence with Travis Gordon and other administrators in an effort to piece together what happened.

Again, I concede Willard has a problem. Still, I submit to you that charges of sexual misconduct are another matter. A person with Willard's problem is not fit to work as a counselor, and certainly his removal is just. A suspension is even in order as well, to give him a chance to straighten up and to relieve our school of the burden of a troubled student. But ladies and gentlemen, expulsion is in my opinion too harsh a punishment for Willard's indiscretions. Allow me to say now that if any hard evidence does turn up that shows sexual misconduct occurred, then please disregard this letter. I have been made to understand that there is no physical evidence of rape, and that Willard's accuser herself admitted that the whole thing may be the result of a misunderstanding. Willard had no business in the ladies' room, but if he heard screaming, he could very well have been reacting. Certainly if he was drunk or high, he shouldn't have been around his students, or otherwise, but I am told that there were no sobriety tests done to see if Willard had been drinking. Also, Willard wasn't on duty that night, which would explain his presence at a party in an apartment across the courtyard. I'm sure you will check your information against mine.

Finally, you must be aware also that Willard doesn't have the best home situation, hence his selection for the City Scholars program. This is not to evoke sympathy for Willard, only to show that keeping him out of school may do him more harm than good. One semester, in addition to the summer weeks he's already lost, is sufficient time for Willard to correct his problem while preparing to return to Georgetown with his mind where it should be, on his coursework. Willard is far from perfect, but he is a young man of character, which is why he was so honest with you. He has made serious mistakes, but he should not be judged solely on his mistakes. Indeed, none of us should. To conclude, I ask you, please supervise the treatment program. Monitor Willard, maintain your discipline of him, and do not spare him any challenges when he returns. But allow him to return after next semester. All parties involved would benefit most from this arrangement.

Thank You Very Much,
Randy Lambert

Ill Will could see that Troy was pleasantly surprised.

"Something, huh? Motherfucker might have to give up the BSU, but he still did this."

"Yeah. I wondered why I hadn't heard from him."

"The board didn't change their mind, but when they looked at everything, the girl's family said they may not press charges. Carl and Yvonne wrote, too, but I think that one may have done it."

"That's cool. Maybe you'll get to come back one day."

"I hope so. I'll do my part."

"You better. When are you and Yvonne breaking out again?"

"Friday."

Troy laughed.

"You know that's when the new City Scholars get here?"

"No shit! You think they'll let you work with 'em?"

"Probably not."

"Oh well! Hey, Latanya and Michelyn are still here. Let's go see if they want to get some ice cream or something."

"I'm with you, dude."

Troy hopped up from his bed, invigorated. Ill Will held the letter in his hand, beaming.

"Good ol' 4-H. Maybe the Hellified Homeboys will get back together!"

"Yeah, if we can all stay in this motherfucker!"

The two boys laughed on their way out. The 4-H Crew getting back together? Troy smiled. Anything was possible.

Acknowledgements

At the risk of sounding a bit cliché, I could not have completed this book without the support of lots of special human beings. I am blessed to have many associates, close friends and family (not all of whom are blood relatives) whose contributions have helped me to realize a dream. Like many novels, **Hellified** is a project that was several years in the making. And though the process has taken me on some bumpy roads, never once have I traveled alone. So please indulge me for a moment while I shout out my peoples.

To the Creator, for your guidance and strength. To my family: Lauren and Vernon Grant, Matthew Holmes, Stewart and Rosetta Holmes, Kevin Holmes, Robiln Howell-Jones, Sophia Green, Tangie and Hampton Holmes, Monica Holmes, Angela Holmes, little Kevin, Delva, Lisa Cox Witty (and Pam, Savannah, Leslie and Carlos), Tanya Blackwood, Yolanda Blackwood, Nikole Shirley, Tyrese, Dot, Jeanie and Bob, Erica and Bobby, Timothy and Sydney, Colin, Jennifer and Rashaun, Melvin and Alice Holmes, Melvin Holmes III and Family, Keith and Cheri, Keiron Holmes, Joshua Holmes. Grandma Sylvia, Granddaddy, Grayland, Tony and Valentino, rest well.

To my extended family: Betty and James Withers, Samara Withers, Dorothy and Terry Reid, Beverly Barnes, Aishah Pae, Gregory Taylor. To the Georgetown University classes of '89, '90, '91, '92 and '93. Tia, I will never forget you. To the Georgetown faculty who molded me in and out of class — Dr. Leona Fisher, Dr. Kim Hall, Dr. Diana Hayes, Dr. Paul Cardaci, Eric Cheyfitz, Rev. Gloria Jackson. To Jim Slevin and Michael Ragussis for letting me in (and teaching me once I got in), to George O'Brien for letting me out with a Master's. To Keith Fort, for teaching me the craft of fiction. To my friend Elizabeth Velez, who fought for me. To my former students, who continue to make me proud in all of their endeavors.

To Bill Reid for staying in my corner and to Gordon Chavis, wherever you are.

To my 'industry' crew: Kate Ferguson, you're the best. Jackie Bazan, the Blackspot, Lauren Coleman, Angelo Ellerbee, Juliette Fairley, Mikel Husband, Haqq Islam and University Music (those were the days!), Darryl James (good looking), Charles Rogers, Kane, Kurupt, Sean 'Shyboy' Davis. To the artists who showed love over the years — Big Pun, Busta Rhymes, Fat Joe and the Terror Squad, Funkmaster Flex, Gang Starr, Jay-Z, KRS-One, Queen Latifah, Gerald Levert, Lil' Kim, The Lox, Missy Elliott, The Sugarhill Gang, Whodini, Wu-Tang Clan and Zhané. DJ Mecca (and family), Rachel Noerdlinger, Jennifer Mitchum and Rhoda Lawrence, please know that y'all are not just industry folks to me. Yasmin, you're still the bomb. It's you and me, until these people recognize and even after that. Lesley, thanks for always taking care of me. I miss you.

To Darnice, for encouragement from Day One. To Kimberlee Snodgrass, Carmen Ambar, Althea Elliott, Teombé Pickett, David and Joy Twille, Rob and Cheryl Cantanio. Thanks to Pat Houser, Ron Kavanaugh, Andrea Mullins and to my group of critical readers for keeping me on point. Janée Trotman, you did a hell of a job. To my publicist Jill Goldsberry and my team at Visão Press, for tireless work and true friendship.

To my N***as for Life: Malcolm Alexander, Din Ambar, Lorne (Shabazz) Barry, Boss Brown, William Demps, Jr., David Jasper, Russell Jones, George Knight, Andrew Milisits, Shean Robinson, Hakim Taylor, Eddie Vasquez, Darius Withers. Until the end.

Special thanks to two people without whom I would be nowhere. To David Lamb, for years of time, support, advice and help. We're in this together. To my friend, my sister and the best editor in the country, Cynthia Ray. You continue to do wonders with my work and you put up with me when I'm not so pleasant to be around. I love you, with or without your incredible expertise.

Finally, to my most constant sources of inspiration: my Grandma Susie, my cousins Latoya and Sophia, my godchildren Robyn, Candace, Kenyatta and Ellis, and my sister Ashley. I hope to be all you expect.

TRACY GRANT, a New York native, is a freelance journalist and music producer. Although he's never home, he lives in New York City. *Hellified* is his first novel.

Contact Tracy Grant at:
Visão Press, Inc.
P.O. Box 20596
New York, NY 10025-1515
(800) 609-9745
VizPress@aol.com
www.visaopress.com